THE GIRL EMPRESS

The Chronicle of Maud - Volume I

Amy Mantravadi

TABLE OF CONTENTS

Dear Reader,

I hope you will enjoy this first book in the Chronicle of Maud series, which tells the story of Maud's early life. Two more books are to follow: *The Forgotten Monarch* and *The Eternal Queen*.

Empress Mathilda (1102–1167), commonly known by the name Maud, was a real person, the daughter of King Henry I of England and granddaughter of William the Conqueror. She is also my ancestor twenty-eight generations removed, through the Grey and Hungerford families. It is my sincere hope that her story will be told more fully in these novels than it has been before, and that the twelfth century will come alive for a new generation of readers.

Just a few logistical notes: You will find a variety of foreign words and phrases in this book, which are typically placed in italics. You will also find quotations from works both ancient and medieval. These are meant to help you get inside the head of the main character and truly experience her world, but if you find them confusing, not to worry! There are more than enough words written in modern English.

There are also a number of Scripture quotations, which are taken primarily from the 1599 Geneva Bible. Why Geneva? Because it is the oldest complete and readily available modern English version, and it is less familiar to the ear than the King James. In a few cases I edited the text, usually to change a *thee* or *thy* to a *you* or *your*. I did borrow from the King James Version on a few occasions.

The languages used in this book are the modern standard versions of English, German, French, and Italian. All were in different forms in the twelfth century and split into various dialects, but for the sake of simplicity, I did not attempt to restore them to their medieval roots. The sections in Latin are not particularly modern or standard, as it is famously a dead language. Nevertheless, it was used by the educated elite in Maud's day and long after that.

Perhaps you will find it interesting that nearly all the words in this novel have origins in the year 1500 AD/CE or earlier. I made this choice in order to help create a style of language that would sound authentic coming from a medieval person, while at the same time avoiding certain vernacular oddities of that period. (It also ensured that I, an American author, would not be using Americanisms!) There is nothing magical about the year 1500 from a linguistic standpoint, but the cutoff did minimize the words with origins further afield. This process required me to step out of my comfort zone and adopt a slightly different vocabulary—a very rewarding process.

I would be remiss if I did not thank the following people for their assistance with this project. Katja Böttcher reviewed the portions of the text that are in German. Julie Vaselopulos reviewed those that are in French. Shawnie Moore assisted me with the Italian phrases at the eleventh hour. Katrina Kittle helped me revise my initial chapters. Amanda Tiffany did some editing of my rough draft. I was blessed to have the University of Dayton's Roesch Library at my disposal free of charge. I received encouragement and support from people such as Dorothy May Mercer, Siri Mitchell, Andrew Wolgemuth, and Aimee Byrd. Carl Trueman did little to help and yet is somehow immortalized in these pages in the spirit of Graham Greene's "whisky priest." I would be remiss if I did not thank the many people who supported my Kindle Scout campaign and the whole team at Amazon.

Finally, thank you to my husband, who encouraged me to write this book and tolerated my constant chatter about things of little interest to anybody, and thank you to you who are about to embark on this journey with Maud. I wish you as much joy in reading as I had in writing.

Blessings,
Amy Mantravadi

PRIMARY CHARACTERS

The Norman Court

- Henry I, king of England, Duke of Normandy
- Mathilda of Scotland, queen of England
- Mathilda, oldest child of the king, also known as Maud
- William Ætheling, son and heir of the king
- "The king's lads":
  - Robert fitz Roy, King Henry's illegitimate eldest son
  - Brian fitz Count, illegitimate son of the Duke of Brittany
  - Stephen of Blois, nephew of the king
- Roger, bishop of Salisbury, chief justiciar of England
- Anselm of Bec, archbishop of Canterbury
- David, prince of Scotland, brother of the queen
- Lady Beatrice, caretaker of the royal children
- Godfrey of Bayeux, tutor of the royal children
- William d'Aubigny, butler in the king's household

The Imperial Court

- Henry V, king of Germany, Holy Roman emperor
- Frederick, Duke of Swabia, nephew of the emperor

- Conrad, Duke of Franconia, nephew of the emperor
- Adalbert von Saarbrücken, imperial chancellor, later archbishop of Mainz
- David, imperial chancellor after Adalbert
- Bruno, archbishop of Trier
- Friedrich, archbishop of Cologne
- Lothair of Supplinburg, Count of Nordheim, later Duke of Saxony
- Agnes, margravine of the Eastern March, sister of the emperor
- Welf II, Duke of Bavaria
- Altmann, the empress's chaplain
- Burchard, a clerk
- Drogo of Polwheile, a knight in the empress's service
- Gertrude, a lady-in-waiting
- Adelaide, a lady-in-waiting

Others

- Popes:
  - Paschal II
  - Gelasius II (Giovanni da Gaeta), formerly papal chancellor
  - Calixtus II (Guy of Burgundy), formerly bishop of Vienne
- Robert Curthose, brother of King Henry I, imprisoned
- William Clito, son of Robert Curthose, claimant to the dukedom of Normandy
- Mary of Scotland, Countess of Boulogne, sister of the queen of England
- Philip of Ravenna, imperial chancellor in Italy
- Mathilda of Tuscany, *contessa* of northern Italy, wife of Duke Welf of Bavaria

- Pontius, abbot of Cluny
- Maurice, bishop of Braga
- Ptolemy, Count of Tusculum

For Shelley and Emily,
daughters of Mathilda,
who read this book first

Civil dissension is a viperous worm
That gnaws the bowels of the commonwealth.

William Shakespeare, *Henry VI: Part One*

CHAPTER ONE

Many are the tales men tell about me. Many are the names I have been given.

"Tyrant" they called me. They hated and despised me. But they will never know me, not as you shall know me, for my blood flows in your veins.

When I first asked Lawrence to help me write my story, he became the latest man to question my judgment.

"My lady, if I may be so bold, what need is there for such an account? Have the scribes not sung your praises? Has Robert of Torigny not recorded it all, even as those before him?"

"Yes, Lawrence," I said, "but that is just the problem. The accounts of my deeds are both too many and too few, for they tell the world about me, but they omit my true self."

"And why does the world need to know you?" he asked.

"Not the whole world—only one."

Some tales are not meant for public show. There are things that must remain secret for a time, until the day when they may be revealed. What my own age lacks, I pray that yours might gain.

For though today I may be a tyrant, I have had other names as well—names that are worthy of remembrance.

My Christian name is Mathilda, the same that was borne by my beloved mother. It is taken from the ancient language of the Germans: *mahta*, meaning strength, and *hildr*, signifying battle. To the people of that land, I was *die Kaiserin*, "the empress." I have carried that name for so long that I can scarce remember any time before it. It is strange to consider that in the flower of youth I should have acquired that highest of titles. Stranger still is how one may strive unceasingly for something less than the bounty already provided by God. So I shall remain *die Kaiserin*.

They have also called me *regina*, noting my time as queen of the Romans. Truly a deceptive title, and one in which I take little solace. Where now are the Romans, descendants of the Caesars of old? Is there an empire so impregnable, so immune to the forces of nature and time? And still it fell. Thus always to queens . . .

To two men I have been a wife, and to three I have been a mother. Yet though they call me by name, my words fall upon their ears as into a void. I ask myself, what good is such a reference, which is not accompanied by reverence? But perhaps I am too harsh, for I still have hope for my offspring, and I pray that they may excel their aged mother in all her virtues.

Yes, many names men have called me, but none can soon compare to that which was spoken to me at the beginning, the world of love that was granted to me as my mother, in the language of her ancestors, proclaimed me to be Maud. That is my true self, the woman whom God created and not man, and the name by which he will summon me on Judgment Day to recite all that I have done in this temporal realm. Whether it be good or evil, you must decide.

Even as I write these words, the eternal bounds press in on me, and the veil that separates the quick from the dead shall soon be pulled back. The ship makes out to sea and plots its windward course, each new tempest threatening to draw it down. I look now for that safe harbor in which, returning, I may find my eternal peace. Yet it is peace that is denied me in these final days, much as it has been throughout my time on this earth.

Thus it seems proper to me that I should make known to you the things I have done, and beyond that the things I have seen. I pray that in these tales you will find something to rouse your spirit, some pearl of wisdom that may enable you not only to rise to the level of your ancestors, but to journey even further, rise even higher, and know things beyond the power of a single generation. Remember me, I say, not only for my mistakes, but for what I have endured. May it make you stronger—may you persevere longer.

Hear now my story, dear daughter, for you were born

> To know wisdom and instruction, to understand the words of knowledge,
> To receive instruction to do wisely, by justice and judgment and equity.

How shall I begin? As I have no memory of the day of my birth, I rely on the chroniclers for my account. My mother bore me on the seventh before the ides of February, in the second year of the reign of my father, King Henry. As was so often the case in those days, the king was traveling throughout England with the royal household, making his court at different fortresses. Heavy with child, my mother was no longer able to maintain the pace at which he traversed the land. So it was that for a time she resided in the village of Sutton, a quiet sort of place that sits upon the River Thames in the fair land of Oxfordshire. It is home to but one church of any consequence, a pair of inns beckoning travelers along the river, and one of the loveliest market squares you will find in that part of the world. My mother made her dwelling in a small manor house for the extent of her lying-in, with only her ladies, her faithful knights, her traveling clerks, and a few visiting officials for company.

Two others were there: Faritius, the abbot of Abingdon and longtime royal physician who, at the king's bidding, remained with the queen while she was in childbed, and Grimbald, a physician with whom my mother had become acquainted and who, having remained with her throughout the king's progress, now pledged to stay by her side until the long-awaited birth. It was Grimbald who advised that the queen's retinue must be small, in order to avoid undue stress to mother and child. Where better to spend those days than in his native village, so close to where the king continued his travels throughout the land? Of course, neither man could be allowed in the birth chamber unless there was some problem beyond the skills of the midwives. Such circumstances were few, but my mother surely felt better knowing that should things go ill, both Faritius and Grimbald, with their years of experience, would be close at hand.

The day of my birth was one of muted rejoicing, for it was the express wish of everyone involved that I be born a boy. Indeed, the court astrologer had promised as much when the queen visited him at Michaelmas. I never set much store by the stars, but my mother longed for hope from any source. Though I believe that for herself she would have been satisfied with a child of either sex, a queen's duty is well known to all.

My father's position was rather delicate given the quarrel with his brother, Duke Robert of Normandy, who was always intent on claiming the throne of England for himself. The duke was without a proper sense of fraternal devotion, nor did he pay any regard to the wishes of their father—William called "the Conqueror"—whose firm desire was that Robert should have no part of the English inheritance. My own father, Henry, was always the truest to his father William's desires, but Robert was a man without proper feelings.

A son would have ensured greater stability for my father's reign and established a mode of succession, but these hopes came to naught. When my father first set eyes on me, he is said to have told his queen, "A pretty girl, I'll grant you, with all the graces of her mother. Do not be too hard on yourself, my dear, for such things cannot be helped. When you are well again, we may yet find that our dearest wish is fulfilled within the year."

So it was that my brother William's birth took place in the third year of my father's reign. The whole kingdom greeted this news with great satisfaction, and I am sure that my mother's countenance was raised to think that her chief obligation had been so happily fulfilled. As with Rachel and Hannah of old, the Lord had heard the cries of his daughter and ensured that she not be put to shame.

This also took place beyond the bounds of my memory, for to me William Ætheling had always been. I can remember trying to play with him in the garden when he was little more than a year old, attempting to take him by the hand and run through the arbor without much success. Alas, he was rather poor company then, but he soon became a more able companion. Those were sunny days, or so they seemed, with little to vex us.

My first years were spent mostly in the old palace of Winchester, which is now exceeded in splendor by Bishop Henry's edifice on the banks of the River Itchen. In the shadow of the great cathedral I lived out those days, scarcely aware of the wider world. Two times only did I make my home in that castle: in my younger days, and at a far less happy juncture. But I must not trespass the historical order.

Having ensured the succession, though the clamoring masses ever hoped for her to increase her progeny, my mother the queen made her primary residence at Westminster, less than a mile from London town. I confess that I do not understand her decision, for she cannot have taken any great pleasure in such proximity to the realm of the merchants. So close was that palace to the city that the smells of the London fishmongers, butchers, tanners, and others would be caught up in the air, and when the wind was directed along a certain path, they would make their way even to our abode. How lucky we were that our home lay farther up the River Thames, before it became tainted with the waste of those thousands of residents!

The window of my nursery faced north, and I would often look toward the city with its imposing walls, built by the Romans and improved by further generations. Along the river, ships dispensed their wares, and upon the higher ground the road could be seen entering the city by the Ludgate, which lies quite close to the cathedral of Saint Paul. Sadly, the church has been under construction for the entirety of my natural life, owing to the great fire some fifteen years before my birth. The masons persevere with their work, and with each year there comes new hope that it might be finished.

Farthest away was the great tower first built by my grandfather William and then fortified by my uncle William—also called Rufus—at the expense of the taxpayer, as many have noted. It stood guard upon the eastern border of the city; its stone walls were so impregnable that some declared it would last until the end of time. Of course, men once spoke in the same manner of Rome.

Westminster itself was quieter, save when the royal presence drew persons of all kinds to court, hoping as they so often did to receive some favor from the royal hand. Queen Mathilda established herself there in the great hall, another project of my uncle, the second King William. It had at first met with controversy, as many feared it would empty his exchequer. When the king arrived to view his mighty creation, those present declared that it had been built too large, exceeding even the great cathedrals in its dimensions. The immense wood roof had no equal in the kingdom.

"Too big? Hardly!" the king proclaimed. "I declare it is not half as large as it ought to be!"

All who gathered there wondered at his words. Though this excess created many enemies for the king during his reign, they were soon filled with pride to receive such largesse.

As a girl I was not allowed to join in the queen's regular audiences or attend on special occasions in the great hall. This was harsh punishment indeed, since my mother was fond of bringing in the most eminent musicians of the day to entertain both herself and her guests. Lady Beatrice, who was charged with my care, would at times allow me to sit with her in the upper walk and listen to the melodious sounds issuing from within, provided that I had been on my best behavior, which I am loath to report was not often. On occasion, when none but the servants were present, my brother and I were given free rein to run throughout the hall. This was undoubtedly one of our choicest pastimes. There were few other children with whom we visited, and none with whom we shared a close acquaintance. Barefoot, we would dash across the straw-covered floor, running circles around the long wood tables and hiding beneath them.

My mother the queen was a constant presence in my life. At the time I did not comprehend that such a circumstance was rather odd for the child of a sovereign. Indeed, I scarcely saw my father in those early years. His visits became more frequent only when the time came for my brother's training. The king preferred to apply himself to other matters. In times of war, he was much occupied across the Channel, where his affairs might keep him for years at a time. In times of peace, he preferred the hunt, and such a pursuit is not fit for a young lady, nor did the queen find particular joy in such occasions.

My mother, Mathilda of Scotland, was descended from the kings of Wessex, a true daughter of Britannia. She delighted in telling us myths and legends that had been passed down for a thousand years. Provided she was in residence, she put me to bed herself rather than leaving it to Lady Beatrice. As she held me in her arms, she would read to me such lovely passages that still echo in my mind to the present day. Most dear was that great *Hymn* of Caedmon, which was set down for us by Bede:

Now we must honor the guardian of heaven
The might of the architect, and his purpose
The work of the father of glory
As he, the eternal Lord, established the beginning of wonders
He first created for the children of men
Heaven as a roof, the holy Creator
Then the guardian of mankind, the eternal Lord
Afterward appointed the middle earth, the lands for men
The Lord Almighty

Few women could equal Mathilda of Scotland in piety and devotion to our Lord Jesus Christ. Her own excellent mother and my grandmother was Saint Margaret, queen of the Scots, about whom Turgot wrote a satisfying account at my mother's express request. This heritage was passed down and further strengthened by the long years that my mother spent at Romsey and Wilton Abbeys. The abbess Cristina, her own aunt, impressed upon my mother the need for singular devotion to the Almighty.

Provided there was not some pressing matter to attend to, my mother would follow much the same schedule each day throughout my childhood. She would rise before dawn to say her first prayers, and usually to read a portion of Scripture or one of the lives of the saints, for my mother was entirely literate. She carried with her always a small book of hours, colored but sparely compared to the glorious volumes found in the monasteries, and a rosary of jasper beads that had once belonged to her mother. In between audiences, my mother could often be seen fingering through the beads. She would hear the Mass daily and three times on Sundays from the household priest, Maelgwyn, who hailed from a mountain village in the Welsh lands. Day after day, she would urge me, "Maud, you must not forsake the Almighty God, for in the word of the Lord you shall be made content."

At least once a week, my mother would appear outside the castle gate to grant alms to the beggars who came daily to await her beneficence. Some said she was too liberal with such offerings, but it was merely the product of her generosity of spirit. When the queen was away or unwell, this duty was passed on to her attendants. During the season of Lent, Queen Mathilda forbade the presence of meat in the castle, and she would even wear a hair shirt underneath her garments to better understand the Lord's sufferings.

It was not until I grew older that I understood why my mother spent so much time in solitude, why she often chose not to join the king's progress, and why she felt the need to commit herself almost solely to the raising of her children and works of righteousness. Where I had seen only piety and firmness of character, there was in fact a darker side to my mother's tale, of which I only became aware from conversations of less discreet members of the household.

My parents must have loved each other deeply when they married. Why else would my father have gone to such great lengths to induce His Grace Anselm of Canterbury to permit the marriage when so much of the world denounced the union, falsely claiming that my mother had taken the veil during her time with the sisters? Some claimed that he merely sought to increase his own standing among the men of England, but perchance such persons did not understand the depth of feeling that was evident to those who knew them well.

When my father's brother William made a visit to the nunnery to court my mother for his bride, young Edith—for so she was known in those days—placed a veil upon her head so as to ward off his attentions, knowing him to be a man of poor character. Her description of my father's visits was quite different. He was a Norman prince with black hair and dark eyes, who never neglected to bring her a gift of flowers or a ballad declaring his undying affection. She was a young maiden raised in the wilds of the North, with bright-red hair and the gentility and poise of a much older woman. She would allow him to join in her daily walk, prolonging his desire for as long as seemed necessary, until she finally consented to be his bride. As you can see, Daughter, the beginning was as happy as any two people could wish.

Even so, the marriage was also one of great convenience for both parties. My mother was, by that time, an orphan with little to recommend herself to the world, save for her family name. My father was a young Norman prince, the son of England's conqueror, who desired to increase his own authority as king of England by forming an alliance with one of the last living descendants of the great line of Wessex.

I have no doubt that their marriage was at first a great triumph. However, it was not long before Mathilda, as she had come to be known, was made aware that my father's great love of the female sex, which had already produced offspring before my parents married, could not be limited merely to herself. King Henry had several concubines, none of whom I shall condescend to name. These noble ladies would often travel with the king's court, and few were left to wonder with whom the king shared his bed. My mother was the best of royal consorts; she never drew attention to my father's transgressions nor sought to induce a change of behavior, choosing instead to live out her life in quiet submission, knowing that from God she would receive her reward and that there was little she could do to change the ways of the world.

I was well aware of my father's other children. The eldest, Robert, later Earl of Gloucester, exceeded me in age by more than a decade. He was old enough to take his place by my father's side and accompany him on his journeys while I was still a baby. I would see Robert more often as I advanced in years, and in time I came to regard him with affection, but from my mother he always received a cool, if completely courteous, reception. I was far along in life before I was able to understand what my mother must have endured.

Robert was but one member of the group that came to be known as "the king's lads," for there were several young men who benefited from my father's grace and favor. However, Robert was the eldest and also the most charming. He was well liked at court, a fine rider and even finer soldier from his early manhood, who first made a name for himself in the king's battles in Normandy. In truth, he was but a half brother to me, being the natural son of Constance, she of the Gay family line that has its roots in the north of Oxfordshire. Before he was four years old, my father the king summoned young Robert to court to be raised as his undoubted son, and I suspect Robert never saw Constance again. Perhaps this explains why in our lifetime together I never observed anything remotely feminine in Robert. He was all strength and resolve, a man not without mercy, but willing to stoop to no one.

Close to him in age was Brian fitz Count. His mother was also of somewhat obscure origin, but his father was said to be the Duke of Brittany, Alan Fergant, the last name meaning "iron glove" in the language of the French. In the years long before my birth, the Breton duke had been at war with my grandfather, the first King William. Seeking to prevent any further incursions into Norman territory, my grandfather offered his own daughter Constance in marriage, the blessed union taking place in the city of Bayeux.

However, as fate would have it, there was little wedded bliss in store for Alan and Constance, the lady having a rather harsh temperament that actively discouraged any kind of affection. So it was that some say the duke was driven to take a mistress, his own wife being barren in addition to her other faults. Brian was the child produced by this unlawful union.

Although the duke wished to acknowledge his son openly, Constance demanded that the child not be given any of the advantages afforded by such a position. Instead they sent young Brian to be raised in England by my own father. Constance died of consumption the following year, and Alan Fergant was forced to relinquish his title some time later.

My memory of Brian in those early days was that he was a great scholar of the written word, more so than his cousin Robert, devoting hours at a time to the study of the ancient philosophers and making visits to Malmesbury Abbey to view the monks' extensive collection of books. Despite this difference, the two young men became great friends, and they could often be seen sparring with each other in the inner ward ere they were called in to supper. Perhaps Brian had more of a gentleness of character, but he was also strong after his own manner and would later prove to be equally formidable.

The third of the king's lads was a cousin of mine, this one of legitimate parentage: Stephen of Blois. He was the son of Stephen-Henry, Count of Blois and Chartres, and my aunt Adela, a woman of great temperance. The count was a leader of the army that made its way to the Holy Land during the pilgrimage of 1096, but he gained a poor reputation as rumors of his ill conduct made their way back to Western Europe. He is said to have fled before the Turks at one point, and upon his return received just humiliation for such a misdeed.

The count once again sojourned to Palestine when Stephen was yet a boy, where he met his doom in the Battle of Ramleh.

Eager for her son to be raised at the feet of a truly great man, and perhaps never believing her husband to be up to the task, Lady Adela sent her middle son—for so he was, having two elder brothers and one younger—to benefit from her brother King Henry's care. Stephen was a few years younger than Robert fitz Roy and Brian fitz Count, and thus he naturally followed their lead. Though more reserved than the others, he was nevertheless resolute in all his dealings and became a firm challenger in all manner of sport. My cousin was all courtesy, and I seldom remember hearing a cross word from him one way or the other, except perhaps to express the general feeling that the weather was not fit for any proper endeavor, or that some ill food was not to be borne, or that it was too long since he had known a decent kill on one of the king's hunting expeditions.

This I will say of Stephen, that as the youngest of the three men, he always appeared the most eager to prove himself, and he did not possess that easy confidence that seemed to come naturally to the older boys. Whether this was on account of his inferior age, the rumors surrounding his father, or some other business unknown to us all, I was never able to fully ascertain.

My brother and I were of a different stock entirely, for we were the offspring of both King Henry and the rightful Queen Mathilda of England. Growing up side by side, close in age though we were, William Ætheling and I were bound to be treated differently, he being the future king of England. I never saw my father take such joy in anything as he did in young William, and he was determined from the beginning to make sure that his son received the full recognition he was due. I had my mother to provide the chief share of my comforts, and the king was not remiss in ensuring that all the rest was provided for.

When time for our schooling came, no ordinary scholar would do. My father employed Godfrey de Bayeux, a man of letters noted for his work as a tutor to many of Normandy's brightest young sons. He was to become my brother's and my second great teacher, the first being our mother. His was a more regimented form of study than that to which I had been accustomed. He believed that we must achieve mastery of Latin, a language of which I knew little in my early years. Most of my experience came from the daily Mass in the upper chapel, or on grander occasions in King Edward's abbey church.

Of course, we understood both the Norman and English languages through my mother. Each had its own kind of beauty. I also knew a few words in the language of the Scots, mostly gained from visits by my mother's kinsman to the English court. (Her brother David was always most favored and often among us.) Sadly, my own mother was not skilled in that tongue, for she had spent so much of her life in an English monastery, far away from the northern heights. Yes, all these I knew, but Latin was another matter entirely.

Master Godfrey had a great regard for Julius Caesar, having committed many hours of his life to the *Commentarii de bello Gallico* and the *Commentarii de bello civili*. "One day when you are old enough, you too will enjoy these pleasures," he would tell us. I could never make out whether or not he meant it as a threat.

He did make a point of reading to us from the works of our own people, especially Gildas. Perhaps he felt that because of my brother's destiny to rule over the people of England, he ought to be made aware of the vanities and weaknesses of character that had caused those before him to stumble. "An illiterate king is no more than a crowned ass," was one of his choice sayings, though I was fairly certain it did not originate with him.

On many a fair summer afternoon, when our thoughts were only of the endless adventures that awaited outside, Godfrey would continue his attempts to expand our minds.

"'This island, stiff necked and stubborn minded'—for so the Lord referred to the ancient Israelites, you will note—'from its first being inhabited, ungratefully rebels, sometimes against God, sometimes against its own citizens'—Heaven forbid! They take no heed of the words of Saint Paul!—'and frequently also, against foreign kings and their subjects.'"

Here he was forced to subdue any commentary about "foreign kings," for the Norman rule of England was yet young.

"Listen now, young master, young mistress: 'For what can there either be, or be committed, more disgraceful or more unrighteous in human affairs, than to refuse to show fear to God or affection to one's own countrymen, and without detriment to one's faith to refuse due honor to those of higher dignity, to cast off all regard to reason, human and divine, and, in contempt of heaven and earth, to be guided by one's own sensual inventions?' May all such men perish in the manner that God deems fit!"

I owed it to my mother that I was included in these lessons. While the training of royal children was considered necessary, it was often not as formal for girls as it was for boys. Indeed, I must have been Master Godfrey's first female pupil. Fortunately, despite his resistance—for I am sure he thought my time would have been better spent embroidering—the queen induced Godfrey to take me on, and my father did not stand in the way. Although I did not know it at the time, for I found many of those lectures quite dull, I possessed a privilege that had been granted to few women in the entirety of history, and this preparation was essential for what was to come. I would not say that my mind was opposed to learning, but I did find Master Godfrey's lessons exceedingly tedious, and he always seemed to take a keener interest in my brother than he did in me.

Despite any faults that he may have had, Godfrey did possess a firm devotion to the Holy Scriptures, particularly the works of

Saint Paul, which he seemed to quote unceasingly. One occasion stands at the fore of my memory.

It was during the early days of my seventh year, and Godfrey was reading to us from one of the works of Saint Augustine when I saw through the window a fox, bright red against a field of green, making a rare appearance. Forgetting the purpose of the lecture, I said to my brother, "Look, William—a fox!"

Now William's attention was also turned from the afternoon reading to the sight unfolding outside the window as the fox, perhaps aware of so many eyes upon his form, quickly darted away into the nearby brush. My brother let out a mournful sigh, but he was not the only one to offer a commentary.

"Lady Mathilda, you ought to take better care than to allow such exclamations to escape your mouth while we are in the midst of hearing from one of the most serene fathers of our holy Church!"

I pulled my eyes away from the window and turned my head to face Master Godfrey, who I was dismayed to see was now standing directly in front of me, close enough to strike me with his rod. His eyes were wide and his nostrils, to my great alarm, were flaring slightly as he took heavy breaths in and out, the very skin of his face now taut. I sensed that much depended on each word I chose.

"I am sorry, Master Godfrey, but we do not often see a fox so near to the town, and I knew that William would want to see it as well. I have no wish to dishonor you or Saint Augustine."

The tutor quickly turned and began to pace back and forth in front of our desks, his hands clasped behind his back and his mind apparently busy deciding his next move. So deliberate was his stride that the wood floor seemed to groan with each step. Having continued in this manner for what seemed an eternity, he finally spoke.

"Lady Mathilda, this is hardly the first time that you have interrupted our lessons. It is wrong for you to behave in such an unseemly manner. While I attempt to instruct you in the ways of God, I find you half the time either lost in some thought of your own or eager to pull your brother into your mischief. I am forced to conclude that you have no regard for the subject at hand, but allow yourself to be controlled by your feminine weakness."

"You are incorrect, sir," I replied, and then tempered my comment as I saw him cast another evil glance my way. "I only mean to say that I hold all the workings of our Lord in the highest regard. After all, do not the Scriptures teach us that God created all the creeping things that creep upon the earth? Surely the fox is such a good creation."

"That is beside the point," he answered. "My concern is that you show a lack of respect for authority, and particularly for the natural order of things. You seem to think that each moment in time is established not for you to learn obedience, but rather to amuse yourself by regaling us all with the latest workings of your overly active mind. This would be a serious enough vice in a male pupil, but in a female . . ."

Here he seemed to cringe for a moment, upset by the thought of such unfettered feminine speech. I turned to my brother for support, but could see by the look on his face that he was more afraid of the tutor's rod than he was of any torment he was likely to receive from me. Now Godfrey was speaking again.

"Perhaps you remember the words of Saint Paul in his first letter to Timothy, when he clearly forbade a woman 'to speak or to exercise authority over a man,' but rather to learn from him quietly and in complete submission. He then noted that it was Eve rather than Adam who first tasted the forbidden fruit and through her undue influence was able to draw her husband into sin. Surely even you are familiar with this tale?"

"Yes, Master Godfrey."

"As I said, we have the word from the apostle, which is now confirmed through observation. I have borne your presence here, young lady, because it was the express wish of your great mother, the queen, from whom you ought to be taking a better example. She is all goodness and restraint, and she never seeks to trespass the rights and responsibilities assigned by God. It pains me to see how her hopes for you have been frustrated by your own unwillingness to learn. Not only that, but you would seek to poison the instruction of your brother, on whom the future of this kingdom depends, for he is to follow in the footsteps of his renowned father."

"Sir, I would never do anything to hurt my brother . . ."

"Silence! Again you display your inability to sense the proper time for speech. Rightly did Tertullian say of your kind that you alone sought to pervert the glory and conscience of man, which even Beelzebub was too fearful to assault. 'You are the devil's gateway,' and through this gate you would seek to cast your brother into the fires of hell!"

Daughter, I do not know what made me do it. Prudence was attempting in that moment to hold my words in check, to help me weather the storm, accept the punishment being meted out, and recover another day. Sadly, I could not brook such abuse, so troubled was my spirit within me. My entire being compelled me to answer him in kind.

"Master Godfrey, if it be true that I am the devil's gateway, then I shall be glad to welcome you to your eternal home."

As fate would have it, those were the last words I ever spoke in my tutor's presence. As soon as they had left my mouth, he was too consumed with fury to reply and simply pointed in the direction of the door. My brother granted me a look of pity as I walked past and closed the door behind me, my eyes now free to let loose the tears I had been holding back. For of all the things Master Godfrey had said, I believe none cut so deep as his assertion that I had failed my mother.

CHAPTER TWO

It was Lady Beatrice who found me sitting just outside the entrance to the chamber where I ought to have been with my brother and Master Godfrey for lessons. Instead I was crouched against the wall, rocking back and forth. She had come to verify that all was well, only to find that it clearly was not.

"Lady Mathilda, what on earth are you doing? Your lesson is not due to finish for another hour, and you know it is not proper for you to wander the halls alone! But what is this? Are you weeping? Has your brother stolen one of your toys again?"

"No such thing, Lady Beatrice. Master Godfrey commanded me to leave the room."

"What madness is this? I have no idea why he would do such a thing, unless you were an undue nuisance."

"He said I was misbehaving because I pointed to something I saw out the window. He blamed me for drawing William into sin. He called me the devil's gateway!"

Now, Lady Beatrice was the kind of woman who depended on things being a certain way. Normally I suspect she would have ardently supported my tutor if there was a report that I had created disorder, and commanded me to return and beg forgiveness. However, those final words of Godfrey's seemed to change her mood. She appeared to set aside whatever stern lecture she had been preparing for me and instead grasped my hand and started pulling me down the hall.

"Where are we going?" I asked her, my short legs struggling to keep up with her own determined stride.

"To the queen's audience chamber."

This was a blow. I had assumed that I would not be able to prevent my mother from becoming aware of the day's circumstances for long, but I had hoped that I might have a moment or two longer to ready myself for what was sure to be a most painful business.

"Please, Lady Beatrice! Would you not prefer to lock me in my bedchamber for a while to ponder my heinous actions?"

"No."

I tried another ploy. "Would you not prefer to punish me yourself rather than taking up the queen's time?"

"No, Lady Mathilda. This matter must be taken to your mother directly."

My heart sank. We were now within a few paces of the door to the audience chamber.

"I promise I shall not misbehave again."

"Save your apologies. They are neither helpful nor timely."

It was too late. The door was opened, and Lady Beatrice dragged me before my mother, who sat in her regal chair working on some stitching while a few of her attendants at a table nearby did the same. My mother looked up and spoke.

"Lady Beatrice, is all well? I understood that Maud was still to be at her lessons."

"And so she was, Your Grace, but Master Godfrey has sent her away."

Lady Beatrice shoved me forward so that I was standing directly before my mother. By now all the ladies had set aside their embroidery and were viewing the unfolding spectacle with rapt attention.

"Tell your mother what Master Godfrey said to you."

"All of it, Lady Beatrice?"

"Yes, not a word left out."

For the first time, I looked up into my mother's eyes. I was somewhat relieved to see that rather than giving me the stern look I had received from my tutor, they seemed to welcome, as if beckoning me to share. My spirit was lifted by the smallest of degrees, and thus I began my tale.

"Master Godfrey was reading to us from the works of Saint Augustine when I saw a fox out in the yard. I told William to look because I knew how much he likes animals, but then Master Godfrey became upset. He said I was obstinate and always getting my brother and myself into trouble. Then he quoted from Saint Paul and another author whom I cannot remember, and he said that women were the ones who led men into sin and that now I was doing this to William. He told me, 'You are the devil's gateway.'"

Here I paused. I was too afraid to speak the words with which I had replied, but my mother sensed there was something more.

"What did you say to him? Maud, you must tell me if I am to know the truth."

I looked up, my eyes becoming moist once again. "I am sorry, Mother, but I told him that if what he said was true, I would look forward to seeing him in hell."

There was much laughter from my mother's attendants, and even the queen struggled to suppress a smile.

"And this is your full account, my daughter? All of it is true?"

"I swear by the Virgin Mary, these were all the words that were spoken between us, at least as far as my memory serves."

My mother nodded in the direction of her attendants, and they silently picked up their stitching and moved into the adjoining room.

"Lady Beatrice," Mother said, "I thank you for bringing this to my attention. I must now ask you to go and retrieve Master Godfrey and bring him here. Have one of the girls see that William is taken back to the nursery."

"Certainly, my lady. I will do so at once."

With a deep bow, she took her leave and shut the door behind her. With only my mother and me in the room, it suddenly seemed a great deal larger. I allowed my eyes to wander for just a moment to the wide hearth that remained unused throughout the summer, then to the fine tapestries on the other three walls, each of which my mother had sent to England from Cologne. The pelt of a brown bear lay on the floor: a goodwill gift from the leader of the Poles, Bolesław. The queen's chair was made of carved oak and an exquisite red fabric. Everything seemed to blend together in perfect harmony.

"Come here, Maud."

My attention was drawn back to the matter at hand. My mother had moved to a chair near the fire and was beckoning me to come join her. I moved toward her and she pulled me up to sit on her lap, her arms enclosing me.

"You must understand, Daughter, that what Master Godfrey said to you was very wrong."

"It was?" Such an idea had not entered my mind. Certainly my own sense of justice had been offended by his claims, but I'd doubted that any grown person, let alone my pious mother, would agree with me.

"Yes, of course! He is perhaps right that you ought to lend more attention to your lessons, and I would not be surprised if you caused a distraction from time to time, but he was completely wrong to have said those terrible things about you.

"Listen to me, Maud," she continued. "You are my beloved daughter and you have a bright future ahead of you. I know that your heart desires to do the will of God. You must set your mind on what is truly of consequence. One day you will be a queen as I am, and your husband and people will look to you to be strong. This training you now receive is essential for that. Do you understand?"

"Yes, Mother, but it is hard when he speaks of things that seem to belong to another world. I do so wish that we could have a new kind of lesson."

"Ah, thus goes the world, my daughter. We are not always granted that which we would prefer, yet we must make the best of it, for we only have one opportunity to make it right."

"I suppose so."

"Yes, quite right. Now, Maud, Lady Beatrice must be almost returned with Master Godfrey, and I cannot have you here when I speak to him. Go hide yourself behind one of the tapestries."

My eyes must have opened wide at this suggestion. I actually detected some mischief in my mother's command. Never one to disobey such an order, I ran across the room and hid behind the tapestry that showed a hunting party chasing after a giant stag. No sooner had I concealed myself than the door opened again.

"My lady, Master Godfrey is here to see you," I could hear Lady Beatrice say, and then there was the distinct sound of the scholar's footsteps. I gave a slight shudder.

"Yes, thank you, Lady Beatrice. That will be all for now," the queen replied.

There was a silence in which Master Godfrey must have approached the queen and made a deep bow before saying, "Your Grace, may God bless you and keep you! I declare you grow more lovely every time I see you! To what do I owe the honor of this audience?"

"Actually, Master Godfrey, it is in regard to my daughter, Maud. I understand that she was sent away from your lecture today after some words were exchanged."

There was a slight pause. Godfrey was likely trying to judge the situation and decide how he should proceed.

"Yes, my lady, what you say is correct."

"I do hope that your work has not been adversely affected by any actions of my children, sir."

This small dose of flattery seemed to produce a marked change in the scholar's tone.

"Well, my queen, all children do tend to err on occasion, as they have not yet reached maturity, but I have full confidence that I can continue in my post without any problems."

"That is a relief to hear, Master Godfrey. And your discussion with Maud today; of what nature was this exchange?"

He paused again. "I am afraid, Your Grace, that she spoke most impertinently. It is difficult to hold her attention during our lessons, and she does cause serious distractions. More to the point, I am certain that she does not care at all for Latin, as she puts little effort into her studies, while her brother seems to flourish."

"These are serious charges indeed," my mother replied. "Yet I am sure you cannot presume that all children would enjoy such a path of study."

Godfrey seemed a bit perplexed. "Surely, my lady, you must see that as it is the chief language of the learned, a knowledge of Latin is essential for your children, although I must admit that your daughter will have less use for it than your son."

"And why is that?"

"Because, Your Grace, it is not the place of a woman to take part in such things as a matter of course. I attempted to explain to you when I was first employed that it would be useless to place both your son and daughter under the same training regimen, and now the evidence is before us. I request that I be allowed to continue training the prince, and that the care of the princess be assigned to Lady Beatrice or one of the other ladies in the palace. There, I have said it. I await your judgment."

There was now a brief interlude in which neither party spoke, and for the first time I began to regret my position behind the tapestry, as I was trapped and unable to discern what actions might be taking place. Finally my mother broke the silence.

"Master Godfrey, I understand that you have grown accustomed to conducting your affairs in a certain manner, and that this manner does not involve training women. You were good enough to take my daughter on as a pupil, and I thank you, but I have now decided that, as you say, the situation cannot continue."

"Thank you, my queen. I knew that you would see reason."

"Not so fast, if you please. I was very troubled to hear from my daughter only a few moments ago that you have slandered her in a most wicked manner, referring to her as an ally of Satan, I believe."

"My lady, I was merely employing a device used by the great Tertullian, one of the fathers of our Church . . ."

"Please take care to hold your tongue, Master Godfrey, for I intend to make this brief. I fail to understand how you could ever suppose that I would be party to such an affront against my own sex, including my precious daughter. The problems you have described are due to a flaw in your system of instruction, not any fault on the part of Maud, who is perhaps unable to show you the same level of patience as her elders are forced to muster. If she is failing in her studies, it is because you believed from the first day that she was either unable or unworthy to learn, and you have continually shown your attentions to William instead. While I love my son and wish his instruction to be of the highest possible quality, this cannot result from abasing his sister. Your own words, sir, have betrayed you. You are not fit to set foot in the presence of my daughter, let alone teach her. I must ask you to go now."

The next sound was of the palace guards opening the door to see Master Godfrey out. The tutor made a few attempts at protest as the men came to collect him, saying things such as, "Your Highness, I beg you to see reason!" and then, "I am sure the king would not have mistreated me in such a manner!" But it was all for naught; Master Godfrey was gone, and I would never see him again.

Godfrey de Bayeux's departure from Westminster was soon spoken of not only throughout the royal court, but also on the streets of London. Few had been present during the actions in question, and the tales and rumors proved to be highly contradictory. Some said that he had proven a poor guardian of the royal children, while others went so far as to charge that he had devised ghastly punishments for them: secretly locking them in a chamber with naught to eat or drink, beating them until bloody with his rod, or depriving them of a fire during the winter, and all without the knowledge or consent of Queen Mathilda. Others were certain that he had verbally assaulted the queen herself or been caught in bed with one of her attendants. However, the wisest members of the royal household were able to surmise the true reasons for my tutor's departure, and to them I think it came as no great surprise.

About a week after this, my mother received a letter from the king informing her that he was soon to arrive in Westminster to prepare for his return to Normandy. It also contained something of his thoughts on the subject of Master Godfrey's expulsion. Apparently he believed that the queen had acted quite rashly, but he did not intend to overturn her decision. Instead he had found a position for the scholar in his native Normandy as tutor to the Earl of Leicester's twin sons, Waleran and Robert de Beaumont, who had some of the French royal blood through their mother. They will come into our story again at a later time, but suffice it to say that I pitied them upon hearing of their fate.

The court at Westminster was now bracing for the arrival of the king's party, with all the necessary preparations that accompany such a visit. Rooms were made ready for their noble guests, and more servants were brought in to attend those lords and ladies who would be spending the month in our company. An endless line of boats sailed up and down the Thames, bringing supplies for the king's kitchens. The king's hunting party sent fresh game for the great feasts that would ensue.

At such a time, the members of the queen's household were far too busy to concern themselves with my brother and me. Whereas we normally could depend on some of the queen's ladies to include us in their recreation, they now directed all their efforts to readying the queen's raiment. My mother would generally accompany us on an afternoon walk about the palace gardens, on which we always sought to name the different plants and insects, but we now had only Lady Beatrice for company— and a rather stern companion she was, bombarding us with commands not to touch, not to soil our garments, and not to stray beyond the bounds of the cloister.

After we had spent many days in this state, the great moment finally arrived. The king had resided at Windsor for several days, and now his party approached along the western road, a glittering display in the afternoon sun. The entire household made to welcome them, and William and I were pulled along with the rest, Lady Beatrice having taken great pains to ensure that we looked especially presentable.

We were all lined up in perfect order, with my mother at the head of the welcome party. I could hear the officials behind us commenting on how lovely the queen was, and it was certainly the truth. Her undergarment was of a pale hue, and her outer garment was made of silk the color of violets covered in an intricate pattern of gold thread. These were the lighter fabrics that the queen preferred for the summer heat, as opposed to the thick wool employed in the winter. Her auburn tresses were held up in a pair of interlaced braids, and she wore pearls from her native Scotland. Brighter than all of these things was the smile on her face, which seemed to lend a light of its own to her attire. She looked back at us and we smiled in return, content simply to bask in the glow of her personage.

In due course the main gate was pulled open, and a swarm of horsemen entered the grounds, each steed adorned with the heraldry of its master. First were several of the king's household knights, then a few of the nobles who had joined him on his progress throughout the country. Finally the king himself entered on his tall gray horse, which he had named Merlin after the magician of legend. By his side was Roger, who was both the bishop of Salisbury and the king's foremost justiciar. He rode a slightly smaller brown horse.

Following closely in their train, with many of their sworn companions riding alongside, were the king's lads: Robert fitz Roy, the king's son; Stephen of Blois, the king's nephew and my cousin; and Brian fitz Count. This was the first time I had ever laid eyes upon Cousin Stephen, for he had yet to permanently join the king's court. The journey did not appear to have sapped the lads' vigor, for they continued to jest as their horses kicked up enough dust to make us sneeze.

Last of all, the carts and carriages bearing the females of the party and the infinite array of trunks, tents, weapons, apparel, and the like could be seen pulling around the back entrance to the palace to deliver their burdens. Among them, undoubtedly, would be my father's latest mistress, whose name was not even spoken in my mother's household except in whispers, and who naturally could not be seen accompanying the king in the queen's presence. Rumor had it that she was to stay with a relative who owned a great house just south of the river. The king would be deprived of her company during his stay in Westminster, but there was talk that he might attempt to include her on his voyage across the Channel, a prospect that was sure to be a subject of discussion with my mother over the course of the next month. For the moment such thoughts were placed aside, and the queen stepped forward as the men alighted. She made a deep bow and welcomed them.

"My lord king, bishop of Salisbury, members of the king's council, it is my great honor to welcome you all back to Westminster. Too long we have suffered in the absence of your most regal presence, and now we understand that you are to leave us once again for quite some time. But let us not talk about such things, for we must embrace the joyful bliss that nature has offered us in this summer season! Come and have some refreshment, for you must be weary from your long travels."

"My lady, your beauty is surely the greatest healing a man could receive on such an occasion," the king said, stepping toward her and bestowing a brief kiss.

"Too long you have been away," I could hear my mother say, not loud enough for most of the company to hear.

"Yes, but a king's business is to be among his people, wherever that call may arise. I trust that you and the children have borne this separation most nobly," he said, then, loud enough for the whole assembly to hear, "Roger, I believe you have not seen my wife since we were all in Normandy more than a year ago?"

"Too true, Your Highness, I have not had that pleasure of late," he replied, stepping forward to greet her.

My mother offered her hand, and the bishop bent low to kiss it. I knew, as did most of the people there, that the two of them were not the dearest of friends. Bishop Roger of Salisbury was said to be the most powerful man in the kingdom, save for the king. During my father's absences, there had been some controversy regarding the maintenance of government in England, with both the queen and the bishop seeking to fulfill certain aspects of the role of regent. For the present it appeared that they were on good terms, but there was no way to tell how long that might last. The bishop was the king's chief counselor, and my mother was suspicious of his influence over the king. Perhaps she disapproved of the bishop's willingness to overlook any transgressions in the king's personal affairs in the interest of increasing his own ecclesiastical and secular power. Such enmity was beyond a child's ability to inquire into, so I received most of my information from less discreet members of the queen's household.

Her Royal Highness turned now to the three young men accompanying the king, each of whom appeared to stand taller upon catching her glance.

"My lords, welcome to my home and yours for the coming days. I see you have grown both in height and strength. I trust the king feeds you well."

"No man could wish for more," Robert replied. "We have been out stalking every day for the past week and sent our killings on to the palace, save for what we were able to feast on each night. As long as your cellars are well stocked, we shall want for nothing, and your ladyship's hospitality is highly praised throughout the land."

"Is that so?" my mother said. "I fear with the number of friends you have collected during your travels, even our cellars may be bare at the end of two fortnights."

"If that be so, my queen, then you may be sure that we will send you all the best from across the water once we have returned," Brian offered.

"Oh, there is no need for that! Indeed, there will be no need for sending anything, for I intend to accompany you all, and what a grand time we shall have!"

This was clearly a surprise to all the men standing there, including the king, whose attention had wandered until this comment was made.

"My dear, surely you would rather stay here with the children. Remember how you longed for home upon our last journey!"

"I assure you, my husband, that I am quite resolute in this matter. If I am to fulfill my duty as your consort, it is only proper that I should be with you wherever you are, and Normandy is no less your kingdom than England. In any case, the bishop of Salisbury will attend to matters while we are away."

I suspect this is precisely what the bishop longed to hear. He seemed to be working hard to suppress a smile even as he bowed and said, "Your Graces, I must assure you that I am ready to carry out the task that lies before me."

I knew my mother was unlikely to hand power to the bishop willingly, as she never trusted him completely, so her determination to join the progress to Normandy revealed her fear of an advance from some other corner. I suspect she must have been hoping to prevent any incursions into the king's bedchamber.

At last my brother William broke into the conversation. "Are we to travel with Father as well, or will you leave us?"

"Ah, fear not, my William," the queen said, stooping down to meet his eyes. "I will not leave you as orphans, nor shall you remain idle during my absence. I have spoken with the archbishop, and he is able to undertake your training for as long as necessary."

"Archbishop Anselm?" I asked. "But he is very old now, and surely his health is not good."

"He has strength to master both of you, I'll be bound." Here she stood back up and faced the king. "What say you to all of this?"

"I say that you seem to have arranged this all exceedingly well," my father answered with a knowing look on his face.

"'Tis the duty of a queen to make sure all things are in order, as you are no doubt aware."

"Yes, and were I not, you would surely let me know it. Come, let us have some supper. I am famished from our long ride. Herbert! See to the horses!"

The steeds were then transferred to Herbert, the king's chief groom, and the men under him, to be fed, watered, given a good washing, and installed in the stables. The king led his queen into the palace, with the bishop of Salisbury and the rest of the council following behind. I gathered from his disposition that the conversation with Mother was not yet complete, but that he had no wish to continue with so many witnesses present. Meanwhile, the king's lads tarried in the yard. Lady Beatrice attempted to lead my brother and me back to our chambers, but William was determined to welcome his heroes.

"Brother Robert, you came back!"

"Yes, my young master, I have indeed. And here with me are the others of your friends; you remember Brian?"

"Of course I do!"

"Then you must remember what I gave you last Christmastide," Brian said.

"Yes, you gave me a whelp, and I have been taking the greatest care of it ever since!"

"I suspect that one of the servants has been taking very good care of it," the older lad teased.

"No, sir! I feed him every day and fetch his water and take him outside to play!"

"Pay no heed to him," I finally said, adding myself to the conversation. "He does not feed him but half the days. Master Edmund is placed in charge of all the dogs, including the prince's bloodhound."

"You stand mightily accused by your sister," Robert said to him. "What have you to say to that?"

"I say what did you bring me this time?"

All three of the young men laughed at William's cheek.

"Bring you? Now, what made you think we would bring you something? Don't you know we are unfeeling knaves?" Stephen jested.

My brother looked much aggrieved, and I too was feeling sorely cheated. "Who are you?" William asked with suspicion.

"This is your cousin, Stephen of Blois. He is joining us for the length of the king's stay here so that he may learn the ways of the royal court," Robert explained.

"Also, I was keen to see this England that I have heard so much about," Stephen added.

The attempt at humor seemed to be lost on William. "I still want to know what you brought for me!"

I looked in the direction of one who might take pity on us. "Brian, surely you have brought back something for William and me?"

"Indeed I have, Princess Maud."

He reached into a small satchel he had on his person, and out of it he pulled a stone of amber, dark yellow in color. He placed it into my open palm and bid me examine it. As I turned it over and viewed it from each direction, I could see that there was something inside it: a moth that had been caught. Its wings were partially open, giving it the appearance of flight.

"I remember your love of all living things. When I saw this, I knew I had found something truly magnificent, and I must bestow it upon a young lady who was most worthy."

It was certainly a magnificent gift. Yet for some reason it troubled me deeply, so much so that I began to cry.

"Is she weeping?" Stephen scoffed.

"Perhaps it was not the perfect gift we were hoping for," Robert concluded, digging through his own pockets for a piece of cloth.

Brian placed his hand on my shoulder and knelt down to ask, "Lady Maud, what is the matter? Has my gift upset you in some way?"

"I am sorry for my tears. I just feel . . . it is a shame that the poor moth will always be trapped inside this stone. It looks as if it is struggling to break free, but I know that it never will. I do not know why it distresses me so."

"Here, let me take her," Robert said, picking me up in both arms. "By Jove, you are heavier than I remembered, Maud! You must have grown half a foot since I saw you last!"

"And yet I am still a little girl."

"You will not always be," was his reply.

Behind us, Brian and Stephen each took William by one of his hands and swung him back and forth as we walked toward the front entrance of the palace. Lady Beatrice was there to meet us with a look of displeasure on her face.

"Young masters, what have you done? I see that Lady Mathilda has been crying."

"It is not their fault, Lady Beatrice . . ."

"What she means to say," Brian interrupted, "is that I was merely a bit careless and upset the princess for a moment, but she is all better now."

"I hope for your sake that is the full truth. I should hate to hear that you have been misusing the king's children in any way," answered Lady Beatrice. She instructed Robert to place me on my feet and then took me by the hand. "I think you children have had enough excitement for one afternoon. We must start on your next lesson."

Still attempting to swing upon the arms of the taller men, William let out a sigh that seemed to say, "Why can I not just be a boy for once as God intended?"

It was not possible to sleep that evening. The sound of the feast might have woken an animal from its winter slumber, and I longed to join the festivity below, but the presence of Lady Beatrice in our darkened room, with several other ladies beyond the door, held me in check. So I aimed to rest my mind and enter the land of dreaming. Finally, having determined that there was no great likelihood of slumber in the near future, I slid out of my bed in all quietness, taking care not to wake my brother, who was sleeping soundly on the other side of the bedchamber. I now had a clear view of Lady Beatrice's chair, in which I saw the old lady sitting, her eyes apparently closed.

Even so, I was not completely satisfied that I could slip out in secret, for William and I had always observed that Lady Beatrice slept rather like a cat, with eyes closed but mind on guard, ready to spring at the slightest noise. Further investigation was necessary.

It was difficult to move across the floor without creating a loud creaking noise that might wake my watcher, but I did so to the best of my ability, advancing within one pace of the chair. I could make out her features clearly now. As I had suspected, her eyes were shut, a faint sound of wheezing came forth from her nose, and her mouth was partially ajar.

"Surely Lady Beatrice would never allow herself to be caught in such a state unless she was truly asleep," I thought.

Having witnessed Lady Beatrice's slumber, I started to turn around and make for the door, when I heard something that almost caused my heart to stop in fear.

"What are you doing?"

I spun back toward Lady Beatrice, but she was still asleep. I then turned and saw that William had been standing just behind me. I struggled mightily to contain a yelp, so great was my surprise.

"William!" I said in a hushed tone. "Why are you out of bed?"

"No, why are you out of bed?" he asked.

"I was unable to sleep, so I thought if I paced around the room a bit, it might help to relieve my mind."

"Liar! You were sneaking out! You know that is against the rules."

My brother had appealed to that immutable standard which had been placed upon us in our infancy, but I sensed there might be a way around it.

"Yes, I admit that I was hoping to see the feast. Why do you care?"

"Mother says we have to stay in our room till morning."

"William," I said, "would you like to come with me?"

The young boy was clearly uncertain of what he should say. Surely he ought to follow the commands of Mother and Lady Beatrice, and he may have even wished to spare me from trouble. However, I had now excited his curiosity and tempted him with an enticing prospect.

"I shouldn't. It would be bad."

"But no one will see us, and even if they did, you can say it was all my idea. We both know they will believe you."

William now paused to think for so long that I had begun to despair of his ever making a decision when suddenly he nodded, and we both moved in the direction of the door. With the greatest of care, I strained my small fingers to pull on the door that led to the small adjoining room. Here the women under Lady Beatrice were supposed to be keeping further watch. As I opened the door just a bit, I peeked through the crack to determine if an escape was possible.

In the center of the room, I could see a table, surrounded by four chairs, at which the ladies had apparently been playing some type of game and where they had left their hour candle burning. However, there was no sign of their presence.

"They must have slipped out too," I whispered to my brother.

Ever so carefully we wedged our small bodies through the opening, taking care not to let too much light into the bedchamber. We then moved quickly out the open door and into the main passage. I was afraid that we might encounter someone at that point, but our luck held, as there was not a soul in sight. I looked in both directions and saw naught but the torches that stood to guard our way. It was strange wandering through the palace without a guardian, and both William and I found ourselves uncertain of which way to take.

We started walking to the left, toward a place that I knew would give us a view of the festivities from above. The sound of manifold voices grew louder with each step we took. In time we came to the passage that led to the great hall's upper walk, where we hoped to enjoy the benefit of concealment. We rounded the corner toward our destination, and we both stopped in our tracks as we saw one of the palace guards at the other end of the passage. Fortune must have been smiling upon us, for he walked by without so much as a glance in our direction. My heart beat so powerfully that I believed my brother, now cowering beside me, must have heard it.

"Maud," William whispered, "I think we should go back."

"Rubbish, we're almost there. Follow me!"

A few more paces and we reached the entrance to the upper walk. I looked around, but there was only the guard we had seen—who had now staked out a position opposite our own—and one of his fellow watchers standing another ten paces away. We bent down and crawled up to the edge, peeking beneath the rail. Below we could see all the revelers. Seldom had I enjoyed such a feast for the eyes. The hall seemed to be filled with every color on earth. In the midst of the dancers, I was able to make out Brother Robert and Cousins Brian and Stephen with several ladies I did not recognize, but who seemed to be thoroughly enjoying themselves. The Bishop of Salisbury could be seen discussing something with a man I knew to be the Earl of Surrey. Rather, it would be more correct to say that he was listening to the earl complain about something, for I saw no words escaping the bishop's mouth. The queen sat at the high table on the dais and was speaking with the Earl of Warwick's wife, Margaret. However, I could see neither my father nor Warwick himself anywhere in the hall.

It was at this moment that two figures appeared on the upper walk from another entrance and made their way in our direction. Struck with fear, William began running back in the direction of the bedchamber.

"William!" I said as loudly as I dared. "We should stay together!"

It was too late, for my brother was beyond hearing and the steps were coming closer. I had little time left and flung myself toward a small nook in the dark passage behind me. None too soon was I out of sight, for the king and the Earl of Warwick were now rounding the corner and pausing near enough that I could hear their conversation.

"And you are sure he will abide by his word?" I could hear the earl say.

"Yes, both I and Ranulf are satisfied that this is the right course of action. The matter is yet in the early stages, but I foresee that discussions will begin in earnest once I am in Normandy."

"His position is certainly one to be favored. He rules over the most powerful empire in Christendom. Still, one cannot overlook his faults. His father, as you know, utterly defied the pope and died excommunicate."

"What you mean to say is that he was unwilling to give up that right which had been granted him by the Lord's anointing, and I must say I agree with the old man there," the king countered.

"Forgive me, Your Highness. I do not mean to say that there is no place for reform within the Church or that the emperor has not on occasion been treated most abominably by those who ought to be his faithful subjects, but we must also employ a little caution if the new Henry is to have a more prosperous reign than his predecessor. The absence of the Holy Father's favor, however unfair, would weaken him just as it did his father. Whether justified or not, he courts danger with this quarrel regarding the investiture."

"Warwick, no sovereign prince can bear to be impotent within his own kingdom. Even His Grace Anselm of Bec has come to see that, and I have been keen to prove it to him!"

I struggled to work out the full meaning of their words. I had gathered that they were speaking of Henry, the new emperor of the Romans, but I did not see what he had to do with England. Finally, Warwick spoke again, returning to the original issue.

"Is Roger of Salisbury in favor of this alliance?"

"Yes, he responded with support when we spoke to the emperor's ambassador."

"And what does the queen think?"

"She will think whatever I instruct her to think. It's not her decision."

"Yes, but it is her daughter."

For the first time, I understood that this whole conversation was about me, and my interest was now so great that I had to suppress the desire to move closer.

"It is the task of a mother to nurture a daughter, but a father must ensure her future stability. Through marriage, Maud will achieve for us all a most favorable alliance with the descendant of Charles the Great, the Holy Roman emperor. She will be raised higher even than her own mother, and her children will sit on a throne endowed by the pope, nay, by God himself! Who could possibly object to such a match?"

"It does present an opportunity to join forces against that errant knave, the king of France."

"Philip? They say he is finally dying. I take no solace in it, for I am sure the son will be just as irksome as the father. Always they attempt to steal the rightful inheritance passed down from my ancestors. The French must never have Normandy."

"Nor shall they, my king, for as long as you and your descendants sit on the throne."

"Yes, that is a happy thought. But what is this? The ladies are beckoning us to come down. Well, Warwick, I suppose we must go join them. Obligation is an onerous thing."

With that the men left the way they had come, and I was free to move away from my hiding place and return to the safety of my bed. I found no rest or satisfaction there for quite some time, as I continued to ponder what I had just heard. It seemed that the king had already decided to send me off to the land of the Germans, to wed a man far older than me and whom I had never met, and to prevent me from living in England ever again.

Did my mother know of his intent? Surely the idea of her child's departure would break her heart. Or was I mistaken? Perhaps William was all the offspring she and my father required. My brother would become the ruler of destiny, following my father's example, and I would be the lamb for slaughter, sent to achieve through marriage what it was less possible to gain on the field of battle. While I had known from early childhood that this fate was likely, the fact of such a match now hung over me as the sword of Damocles. I knew without a doubt that there was no possible remedy. I must go, and I would likely never return.

No matter how hard I tried, I could not escape those words nor forget that moment in which my future had been changed for all time. In my weariness I fell at last into troubled dreams, and found little relief in waking the following morning.

CHAPTER THREE

I must say a word regarding my father and Archbishop Anselm, two titans alike in strength, yet thoroughly opposed. Each had his role to play in the great tales of our age, yet far too often they were placed in opposition to each other. Father Anselm, as my mother was apt to name him, was perhaps the brightest of all the lights that shone in that era, the highest and most accomplished of scholars. He was from the town of Aosta in the realm of Savoy, and his family was linked in some manner with the rulers of that region. My mother the queen knew him on far more intimate terms than I, for she was among his most faithful children and exchanged letters with him throughout my childhood.

She told me that Anselm had desired in the days of his youth to enter the local abbey, but his own relations would have none of it. Thus began a period in which he wandered far and wide seeking peace for his soul, uncertain whither the path might lead. God only knows how long he might have continued in that state had he not arrived at the most blessed house of Notre-Dame du Bec, at which that servant of God Lanfranc was prior.

It was there, at the age of twenty-seven, that Anselm placed himself under the rule of Saint Benedict and found in Bec Abbey a home more dear than any he had ever known. Though he became one of the most respected scholars of our time, the Lord had reserved still greater things for him. Upon the death of Archbishop Lanfranc, my uncle King William appointed him to the See of Canterbury, a charge Anselm accepted with the most comely humility, though he swore he would rather live out his days in the solitude and austerity of the monastery than with the luxurious trappings of such an office.

It is said that this appointment was against the king's own will, for he was a man who had no great love for the Church, believing it to be a usurper of his own rightful place. Thus was the archbishop forced into exile from England almost as soon as he had arrived, and not for the last time. It was my own father who called him back to his post, and then only for a brief period, for controversy soon arose over who should invest the bishops with their staffs, the same argument that had fractured the Continent for some years. I was only a baby in those days and ignorant of all that was taking place, even as the archbishop was forced to flee yet again to Normandy and seek the protection of His Holiness Pope Paschal II.

As you will have noted, Daughter, it was my mother who set in motion the sequence of actions by which Archbishop Anselm became our tutor, for she desired that her children might benefit from the teaching of a man whom she believed to be superior to all other persons then alive, save perhaps the Holy Father himself. I fear that King Henry must have hated to draft that letter to Anselm, in which he bid him come and safeguard his two great prizes. With each stroke of the pen, his pride was surely dealt a bitter blow.

Nevertheless they reached an understanding: the archbishop would come to Westminster, there to serve as protector and teacher for my brother and me in the months of our father's absence. I suspect the condition by which the queen gained this agreement was that she would remain in England to serve as intercessor between king and archbishop, for as dear as she held every word that proceeded from Anselm's lips, she also maintained a proper respect for the decrees of her royal husband. I reached this conclusion upon hearing that the queen was not to travel to Normandy after all.

The days of that summer held no great joy for me, for I was well aware of what lay in wait. For the first time in my life, I found my mind continually troubled by restless thoughts. I was too afraid to mention what I knew regarding the proposed alliance with the emperor, for to do so would have forced me to reveal the circumstances under which I heard it. Instead I allowed my silent fears to torment me and consume the good cheer I ought to have enjoyed at a time when my family was finally together.

The week before the king's departure, I received the strange news that William and I were to join the king and queen for a private supper. Such an occasion is no doubt common for the peasant in the fields who comes home after dark to a wife, four children, a loaf of bread, and a pot of stew, but it is hardly a matter of course in royal households. William and I took most of our meals with Lady Beatrice and were not often summoned to dine with our mother. For the four of us to join together in private was quite rare indeed. While the royal departure may have been reason enough for such a request, I suspected upon hearing the news of the common meal that there must be another purpose behind the king's proposition beyond the desire to eat and drink collectively.

On the appointed evening, Lady Beatrice bid me set aside my customary tunic and instead placed upon me a new gown of brightest green silk. I had been forced to stand and be measured on four occasions, and each time I was charged not to wince when the needle went astray and poked me in the leg or shoulder. This gown was of a higher class than my usual attire. I suppose it was meant to provide an outward sign of my entry into a new phase of life: one in which I must start fulfilling the demands placed upon me since birth. This being the case, I both loved it for its beauty and loathed it for what it signified.

Lady Beatrice was unmerciful as she tied the laces, and I feared that my containment was becoming far too literal. After she finished this work, she began combing my hair, a rather dull gathering of brown curls. I couldn't help yelping as she tugged and pinned each strand. At last Lady Beatrice draped a great chain of beads over my head. She stepped back to survey her work.

"Oh, child, this gown is marvelous, but I fear no one will notice if you continue in that awkward manner. Stand up straight and wipe that scowl off your face! The king greatly favors you by summoning you to dine with him."

I was on the verge of saying something that wasn't as regal as Lady Beatrice preferred, when Eleanor, her chief assistant, entered the room. She was holding the hand of William, who enjoyed a great laugh upon seeing me in the strange garment.

"Master William, if you please, calm yourself! I will not have you behaving so in Her Royal Highness's presence!"

"You look strange," William said, paying no heed to Lady Beatrice's edict. "Why is your hair like that? You look even uglier than usual."

"You little imp!" I shouted and hurled myself at him. But I caught my foot on the hem of my gown and quickly found myself facedown on the floor, prompting a new shower of laughter from William.

"Truly, children, show some dignity! Be still this instant!" Lady Beatrice shouted with growing anger.

Gripping me beneath the arm, she pulled me to my feet and looked me in the eye, her mind clearly racing to devise an especially piercing rebuke. However, I was saved, as it were, by the large scrape that she noticed on my chin, the blood now flowing freely.

"Good Lord in heaven! Am I to suffer the torments of purgatory before my time?" she muttered to herself as she handed me a scrap of linen to hold against the wound. "Eleanor, take the prince to supper now. I will follow with Lady Mathilda when she is again presentable."

It was impossible for Lady Beatrice to bandage my face without making me look an absolute fool, so she settled for cleaning the cut with water and covering it with a substance she used to conceal the mole that grew upon the point of her nose. She reviewed her work and determined that the situation was unlikely to improve, and so led me to the chamber where the king took his meals, save for the feasts that were held in the great hall. My mother and William were already seated at the long oak table. An embroidered banner on the wall portrayed the great feast of Dionysus, and the windows looked out across the river toward the place that was called by the Anglo-Saxons Sudweca, "the southern fortification." Beyond, the lands of Surrey stretched as far as the eye could see.

One of the king's men pulled my chair back from the table and bade me sit down, which I did without delay. The queen had a smile on her face that showed she approved of my appearance far more than William, and that Lady Beatrice's trick had succeeded in hiding the wound on my face.

"How pretty you look, Maud! That color is a perfect match for your eyes. Is it to your liking?"

"Why yes, Mother, it is wonderful." Daughter, in such cases honesty cannot be pardoned, so you must forgive me if I sought to please rather than speak truth.

We sat there for what felt like an eternity, waiting upon the king. I did my best to maintain a proper demeanor as I had been commanded. My mother seemed content to stare off into the distance, no doubt contemplating some great matter of state or mystery of the spiritual realm. Servants stood at the edges of the room, ready for any crisis. For his part, William was Herculean in his attempt to remain still, and he was clearly distraught over our father's delay.

"When are we going to eat? I'm hungry!" he complained loudly.

"As soon as the king arrives, we will begin, but until then you must silence these complaints," the queen replied.

"But what is he doing?"

"He was conversing with the Bishop of Salisbury and should be joining us shortly."

"I hate waiting."

"As do we all, but waiting is part of life, William, and it is better that you learned that now than to be utterly surprised later. Do not make me call Lady Beatrice back."

An array of groans was all my brother could produce in return.

Finally the king's butler, William d'Aubigny, opened the door and proclaimed, "His Grace King Henry!"

My mother and I moved to our feet by instinct, but young William required some chiding in order to assume the proper position. The king strode through the door and moved directly to his chair at the head of the table, taking little notice of the three other persons present.

"Aubigny, bring me some wine! I am parched," he said to the butler as we all were seated.

One of the cupbearers produced the sought-after liquid and handed it to the butler, who in turn gave it to the king.

"Wait!" my father cried. "Taste it first."

With a swift nod of the head, the butler set about his task, tipping the goblet slowly until a few drops fell into his mouth. He gave the drink a moment to settle in his mouth, then swallowed.

"I feel no ill effects," Aubigny declared, setting the goblet in front of the king.

"Not so fast!" he replied. "I require one further test. Fetch the horn."

"The horn?"

"The unicorn horn, man! Fetch it at once!"

"Ah, of course . . . ," the butler said, then made haste to recover it, searching a nearby chest with one of the servant boys. I could just hear him mutter, "Where is the damned thing?" as he and the boy turned over every item. At last they retrieved an object wrapped in linens and uncovered a gray, pointed horn that was at least the length of a man's arm. I looked on in wonder as they lowered the tip first into the king's drink, then into the remainder of the wine.

"Very good. Now it is pure," the king said, finally satisfied that his drink was safe to consume. As we watched, my father drained the goblet and said, "I'll have another."

It was at this point that the king turned his head to look upon the rest of us at the table. If I did not know better, I would have said that he was surprised to see us.

"So, my queen, how are you this fine evening?"

"I am well to be sitting next to you."

"It was hotter than hell today," he said, oblivious to her reply. "Six hours of stalking and naught but a few grouse to show for it. The beasts seem to know when the weather is too unseasonable for going out. Would that we had been so wise. The whole lot of us plunged into the river to cool ourselves."

"Lady Beatrice says we are not allowed to swim," William complained.

Once again Father seemed to be taken by surprise that someone else was present. His thoughts clearly remained with the hunting party. Nevertheless he recovered.

"My son, when you are king as I am now, you will experience what a blessed relief it is to live your life in whatever form seems most desirable, rather than according to the demands of lesser persons."

The servants were now laying out the food before us and passing the water basin around. My father began devouring his meal with the same eagerness he had shown for the wine, dipping his meat directly into the salt dish, an action for which Lady Beatrice would have surely chided me. William attempted to imitate him, but he left most of the salt strewn across the table.

"William," the queen started to say, but her husband cut her off.

"You man, take care of that!" he ordered one of the servants, who immediately disposed of the excess salt.

"Perhaps you wish to inform us of the reason you have called this meeting," Mother offered, having clearly determined that a lesson in table manners was not going to be possible.

"Ah, yes! Children, I have been setting all my affairs in order before my departure to our lands across the Channel. The three of you will remain here, and your mother and I are intent that this time should not be idly spent. You have heard, of course, that the archbishop is due to join you here and take over as your guardian for the coming months. In addition, William, you are to begin your preparations for the knighthood. I have spoken with my chief groom, Herbert, and he is to conduct riding lessons for you starting next week. You will also be taught how to handle a sword, and with any luck spend some time on archery as well."

"Lord king, are you sure that the time is right? Our son is still quite young," Mother said.

"Woman, when I want your opinion, I will ask for it. Did you think I would not notice how you have slipped that miscreant Anselm into my own house when I was not aware?"

"I intended no such thing," she said calmly but deliberately, her face now as red with anger as her husband's was with heat.

"And yet you know that he has been a continual adversary of mine since first I came to the throne, seeking to strip me of my God-given authority at every turn!"

"Please, dear, the wine has made you agitated."

"Do I not have some excuse when my place is being usurped?" he shouted at her.

"My lord, the children . . ."

The king shot a look in our direction and saw that both William and I were upset. This seemed to affect him, and he made a clear effort to recover serenity.

"Children," he started again in a more friendly tone, "The archbishop is indeed a great teacher of literature and matters of Scripture, but you must exercise caution in this case and not accept everything you hear. Anselm of Bec may make great claims to piety, but in truth he loves most that which exalts himself, and he will pour honeyed words into your ears. He would undoubtedly paint me as the worst of sinners in your eyes, but I assure you that if there is any blame to be had, it lies in his corner, or better yet with his master in Rome."

He returned to the food in front of him and the rest of us followed his lead, my mother having apparently decided that as much as she loved and respected the archbishop, now was not the proper time to leap to his defense. Although I was well aware of my royal parents' disputes, they did not often display them so clearly before our young eyes and ears. I felt quite shaken, and I could tell from a sideways glance at William that he was likewise troubled.

"Now to the other matters at hand," the king finally said. "The Countess of Perche has written expressing her desire to stop over in Westminster on her way north to stay with Lady Warwick, and I am quite disposed to grant her request. Do you have any objections, my dear?"

"None whatsoever. We shall make ready for her visit," the queen replied.

I was certain that this answer showed only part of my mother's true feelings, for the Countess of Perche, Mathilda fitz Roy, was one of the king's many children by other women. As this particular dalliance happened before my parents' own marriage, the blade did not pierce so deep as it might have, but it nevertheless proved that the queen was not at that point, nor would she ever be, the sole mistress of her husband's affections.

"Also, I wanted to make known to you, William, as it will affect you most of all, that the French king's son, Louis, who will any day now take the throne, has declared that he will throw his support behind that usurper, William Clito, my brother Robert's son, to become Duke of Normandy. It seems that as I have already maintained the land of Normandy for myself and my descendants, the French now seek every opportunity to sow discord and rebellion in the hope of reclaiming that which was hard won by our ancient father, Rollo. Rest assured, my son, I have no intention of allowing them to succeed, but you must be made aware of these things, for some day you may very well find yourself in the middle of them."

"I am not worried, Father," William replied. "When you ride into battle, you will defeat the false William just like his father."

"Well spoken, my son. That is just what I intend to do. When you are old enough, I shall be proud to see you take your place by my side as we make war against the Franks and all their malicious allies."

I sensed that this was the moment at which I might broach the subject of the German king's offer of marriage without being forced to reveal the original source of my information.

"Father," I said with all the courage I could muster, "I have heard talk that you may seek to counter the French through a marriage alliance. Are these rumors true?"

"Who told you such a thing?" my mother asked. "Was it one of my ladies? I must command them not to spread such foolish gossip." She looked in the direction of the king. "You have no intention of arranging a marriage for Maud now, do you?"

My father declined to answer her directly, but after taking a moment to collect his thoughts, he instead turned to me.

"Maud, you are the firstborn child of the king of England and Normandy. With that comes a duty both to your sovereign and to your country. Marriage is the path by which opposing nations may be knit together in a bond of mutual protection. The fiercest threat to our territories comes from the king of France, and we must do whatever we can to counter him. I may as well tell you that I have indeed begun the process of seeking the most esteemed applicants for your hand, those who will play the role of husband to you in a proper manner and help to maintain our possessions for future generations. You must understand how essential this is."

"Yes, but surely Maud is a bit young to be formally betrothed. She is not yet in her eighth year," the queen protested.

"Marriages have been settled at far younger ages than that, and in any case he will not attempt to consummate the match until she is full grown."

"He? So you already have a suitor in mind?" The concern in my mother's voice was rising.

"Well, yes, if you must know, I have entertained some early offers, one of which seems quite acceptable."

"Why have you not told me of this before now?"

"Because—and do not hate me for this—I was quite certain that the man in question would not be to your liking, though I am sure he is as good a choice as we will be able to find."

"Who is it? Surely not an Italian!"

"Italian? Ha! I might as well give my daughter to one of the Saracens! In fact, it is Henry, king of the Germans. I have already spoken with one of his ambassadors, and intend to receive a larger party upon our arrival in Rouen."

My mother was clearly stunned by this latest revelation, and her manner became contentious.

"Am I to understand that you mean to betroth our daughter to a man whose father was the shame of Christendom and who now seems ready to follow in his footsteps?"

"The very same, though I do declare, you choose your words quite harshly. After all, it is only out of fear for his own level of influence in this realm that the pope has so far declined to excommunicate me."

"This is no laughing matter!" my mother protested. "If you are to strip away my daughter from my side before her time has come, at least allow me the consolation of knowing that she goes to a good house in which the will of the Lord is honored. You owe that to your daughter if not to me."

"My lady, you must think me no better than one of the heathen. I tell you, the will of the Lord will indeed be honored by such an alliance, assuming that it does take place, for it will ensure the future security of this kingdom. If ever the fat king in Paris decides to test his luck against us in battle, we shall have the strength of the empire on our side."

"From what I can tell, the strength of the empire is barely sufficient to keep out the Wends," she said to herself as much as to him.

"I think in time you will come to think better of him. Of course, this is all still conjecture until an agreement is signed," he added, providing small comfort for the queen's nerves. "Never fear, my daughter! I will find you a husband who will treat you properly and provide for this kingdom the alliance it requires. It is a matter of necessity."

"I will do as you say, Father." Even as I said them, the words seemed to stick in my throat.

"You have always been my good girl, and you always will be," he concluded. "Well, that's supper finished. William, come with me and I will show you something."

My father led him out of the room toward whatever new adventure awaited them, leaving Mother and me to consider all that had taken place. Neither of us spoke a word as the servants silently removed the articles from the table.

"Do you wish for me to call Lady Beatrice, my queen?" Aubigny inquired.

"No, thank you, I shall see to the princess myself."

"As you wish."

My mother rose and walked around the table to where I sat, then bent down and pulled me into a long embrace in which neither of us spoke for some time. Finally she pulled back and looked me in the eye.

"Maud, you must never be afraid. Nothing has been decided yet, but even if this is the path the king chooses for you, you will not be alone. Our beloved Savior and the Virgin Mary will watch over you with every step you take."

She kissed my brow and then led me by the hand back to the nursery. There was an odd firmness in her grip, an outward sign of her desire not to lose me. For my own part, I held on equally tight, wanting to believe that whatever future God decreed for me would be more agreeable than the one I now feared.

With only a few days remaining until their departure, my brother and I were eager to spend more time in the company of the king's lads, although, being much younger, I was somewhat nervous in their presence. Lady Beatrice arranged for William to join the young men in the inner ward for some sport, and I was permitted to go along, though I would not take part in their game.

We found the three of them on that afternoon kicking a ball back and forth while they waited for us. Stephen seemed to be the most skilled, despite his slightly inferior size. Those simply passing by darted this way and that to avoid any errant kicks. At length the lads became aware of our presence and briefly halted their sport.

"Hello there, William!" Brian greeted him. "Do you fancy trying your hand at this?"

"Best not let him get anywhere near Stephen. With that degree of force, he's likely to get walloped," said Robert.

"I'm not going to knock him over!" Stephen argued. "You are more likely to do that since you lack the ability to hit your target."

"I beg your pardon, I do not! You should see how I do when I get in a proper space. This is too restrictive."

"Now that's a fine excuse! This was your idea."

Brian took that opportunity to mention to the gentlemen that, "None of this is particularly helpful," and that "I am sure there is no great danger in young master William taking part."

"Have you ever kicked a ball before, William?" Robert asked.

"Not one like this."

"Well, then it is time that you learned. Come, stand over here."

I watched as William made his way to the assigned spot in the dirt. Our elder brother placed the ball on the ground and demonstrated the motion with which it was to be struck.

"You hit it like so, right with the front of your boot, or you will not get the necessary force and it will trail off to the right or left."

The three men then stepped back and let the boy have a try. He made contact and sent the ball in Brian's direction. It was not a superior kick, but it did show some strength.

"Good! Now try it again," Brian instructed him, pushing the ball back toward him.

William tried again, this time sending it toward Stephen. With each successive kick, he grew better. Soon the four of them were sending the ball back and forth. Even as my brother seemed to be thoroughly enjoying himself, I felt quite excluded, standing to the side in my dress, unable to do much but retrieve the ball when it flew in my direction.

"I don't know how long we should keep at this. Soon he'll have us all beat," Robert declared.

It was at that moment that William sent the ball toward Stephen. But Stephen was distracted and thus not ready when the ball arrived, and it rushed past him in my direction.

"Here, give it to me," Stephen said, walking toward me as the ball continued to hop and roll across the ground.

I chose to ignore him and instead run at the ball and kick it. I took a few strides toward the ball and hit it as hard as I could with my right foot. I still remember the look of surprise on Stephen's face, as he had to bend low to avoid it. The ball was flying through the air, but it was not going in the direction of the others. Instead to my dismay, it was moving to the right and about to come into contact with the chicken coop. All five of us watched as the ball landed in the middle of a flock of hens, all of them leaping in different directions, crashing into one another, and sending a momentary cloud of feathers into the air. A few of them actually took flight and made it over the short fence and into the yard, where several ladies of court, who had been taking in the afternoon delights of such a manly display, now let out great screams more fit for a savage wolf than a few startled chickens.

The three lads went into action and tried their best to herd the hens, though they found it a difficult task. I, on the other hand, was feeling quite foolish, so much so that before any of the men returned their attention to me, I slipped into the palace and made my way back to the nursery, where I intended to inform Lady Beatrice that I suddenly had a great desire to help with her afternoon duties. It would be many years before I again had the courage to kick a ball, and what became of the one I sent to join the chickens, I shall never know.

All was now ready for the king's departure. The ships were loaded with possessions to be brought over water to Normandy. So many objects were placed in the hull of each ship that it was hard to believe they would stay afloat. Next, Herbert and the rest of the king's grooms boarded the horses, always a tiresome endeavor. The animals seemed to rue the experience, uncertain of their footing and wishing very much to be back on shore.

For such an occasion, the entire royal court dressed in its grandest attire and took the path down to the river to bid the travelers farewell. Of course, half of them would be accompanying the king on his travels, but the remainder would depart for their own lands scattered throughout England. A small company of ambassadors, merchants, and simple travelers in need of passage to Normandy would also be joining the passage, the latter for a price. Bishop Roger of Salisbury invoked the blessing of God upon the royal voyage. The king seemed to grow weary as the supplications continued to pour forth, so eager was he to make for open sea. I could see the young men cast longing glances at the noble daughters who would now be placed once again under their fathers' lock and key.

At last the moment arrived. My father shook hands with the bishop and bid him keep all things in order during his absence. He said a few brief words to the members of the king's council. He embraced William and charged him to apply himself to his training, following this with the standard pat on the head. For me there was a tap on the cheek, but no words that I can remember. Finally he said farewell to the queen, kissing her hand and bidding her to serve as his advocate, to which she heartily consented.

After my father had made his way on board, with all the dogs following close behind him, the king's lads came by as well to offer their final words of friendship. I remembered all too easily the last time we had spoken, when I behaved in a most impetuous manner. I am certain that my cheeks turned red as I looked out toward the shimmering river, unable even to meet their glances.

"William, my lad, I shall miss our times together," Robert said. William's only response was to hold on to both his legs and command him not to go.

"Oh, but we must, Master William," Stephen told him, "for my mother cannot bear to be parted from me for long, and I must visit with my brothers, particularly young Henry. I shall tell him that you say hello and good day."

"I am sure I am better at sport than Henry," my brother replied, clearly outraged that any person could be considered a more worthy subject of attention, even for a moment, than himself.

"Yes, you are very good," Stephen agreed, "and certainly a bit more careful than your sister. I feel somewhat fortunate to still have a head on my shoulders."

I could tell from the look he gave me that this comment was made in jest, but I was still ashamed. I was searching for some apt words when Brian fitz Count spared me.

"It is not Maud's fault for kicking the ball, but rather your fault for getting in the way," he offered. "Had her view not been blocked, I am certain she would have had a clearer shot, and as it was, you must admit that it provided us with the chance to play rescuer to several of the most lovely maidens of the court."

"Come now, we all know that Stephen will be the last one to admit when he has made an error. It is not in his nature to accept such shame," Robert mocked. The look on Stephen's face seemed to imply that he did not take to that comment any better than I had to his own.

"We shall miss you too, Princess Maud," Brian said to me. "I think your father has great hopes for you."

"He speaks of marriage to the German emperor. My mother is hardly pleased."

"I should think not! As honorable as such an alliance may be, you are most dear to her, and I am sure she would be loath to part with you, even to please the king and the world beside."

I do not know why, but I felt in that moment that here was a person with whom I might share my most secret thoughts without fear of reprisal. William was distracting the others and it was only the two of us in conversation.

"Brian, may I tell you something?"

"Anything, Lady Maud. You know I will hold it in confidence."

I paused for courage, then said, "I am afraid. All I have ever known is this land and these people. It seems such a long way to go, and I am sad to think that I should never see those dearest to me again."

He did not respond immediately, but simply listened as I spoke. Even though I was merely a girl myself, I could sense that he must be quite advanced for his years. His thoughtfulness exceeded that of his companions, however amiable they may have been. At length he spoke.

"Such feelings are natural, but I do not think you have any reason to fear. This will not be the end for you, but the beginning. You are the daughter of the king, and your entire life lies before you. We all feel at times that we are the victims of fate, that God himself is playing a cruel game with our lives, but we must have faith. When the time is right, you too will know the thrill and the burden of deciding for yourself how to spend your time on this earth. In any case, you will not be separated from us eternally. I am certain that we shall all visit with one another whenever possible."

The idea that I might be able to travel to see my friends, or that any of them might visit me, served to strengthen my resolve.

"Thank you, Brian. I am sure you are right. I wish you a safe voyage."

The final farewells having been issued, the last passengers entered the boats and set sail for the land across the sea. Lady Beatrice led my brother and me back to a much quieter palace as the bells of King Edward's church rang out to signal the sovereign's departure. How much longer the queen stood there by the riverside watching the ships set out, I cannot say. All that remained now was for the archbishop to make his return to court.

CHAPTER FOUR

The heat of summer had died down and the leaves had begun to adopt their autumn hues by the time His Grace the archbishop of Canterbury arrived at Westminster. He had traveled down to Portsmouth to be near the king's party, but now came north to assume the care of my brother and me in accordance with the king's wishes—well, truly my mother's wishes. We received the news on a Wednesday evening that the party had advanced as far as Chertsey Abbey, where the archbishop wished to rest for the night before completing his journey. There were rumors that his health was failing, and he surely would not have undertaken such an expedition had it not been according to the express wishes of King Henry and his queen.

Although I had heard tales of Anselm of Bec all my life, I had seldom had the pleasure of his company. This was primarily due to his continual disputes with the king, on account of which the archbishop was twice exiled to Normandy. Even my mother, whom Anselm regarded as his faithful daughter in Christ, was often forced to converse with him through letters. Happily, she had a firm enough grasp of Latin to achieve this, helped by one or two royal clerks.

Friday morning we were all ready for him to arrive. However, we were informed that he would be stopping in town first so the newly consecrated bishop of London could pay his respects. Perhaps it would be more correct to say that this would give the archbishop a chance to further establish his ecclesiastical authority in the most powerful city within his jurisdiction; this was particularly important, as Londoners are apt to consider their metropolis a kingdom unto itself. I did hear that they received him favorably despite the controversy of former years.

By that afternoon Anselm had taken his leave of the bishop and boarded the craft that would carry him the short distance to the Palace of Westminster. As the lord chancellor had traveled with the king to Normandy and the bishop of Salisbury was reportedly too consumed with the affairs of his own see to make the journey, none of the chief officers of state were on hand to receive the archbishop. Accordingly, my mother arranged for a welcoming party that included William d'Aubigny, the chief butler then in the royal household; the constable of Westminster, Edmund fitz Hugh; and Gilbert Crispin, the respected abbot of Westminster Abbey and a former pupil of Anselm. All three men were on hand at the riverside, along with other members of the royal household and men of the cloth.

At the time of the archbishop's arrival, I was bent over a piece of needlework in one of the upper chambers, with my mother instructing me in the proper way to form the stitches. I had counted seven and twenty different colors of thread in the queen's collection, each having gone through a rigorous process with several dyes in order to achieve the desired hue. The pattern we sought to create that afternoon was a simple flower of the thistle plant, but I fear my own efforts were far surpassed by those of the other ladies in the queen's household, who each seemed to my less trained eyes to possess an unnatural skill for embroidery.

Upon hearing the sound of trumpets I sought permission to move to the window, which my mother granted me on condition that I return to my embroidery later in the day. I was not yet tall enough to see properly out of the windows in that room without climbing onto the stone ledge, so thick was the palace wall. Once there, I caught a glimpse of Archbishop Anselm making his descent from the boat in his long, flowing robes. Both his stole and his cope were clearly made from cloth of gold and embroidered with symbols in red thread. I had imagined he would be wearing the traditional miter of the archbishops, but on this occasion he wore only a simple red cap on his head, as he was not performing ecclesiastical duties.

The archbishop was now walking with the aid of a staff, and I could see that he felt the full weight of his age. Abbot Crispin stepped forward to help his old instructor onto shore, taking him by the arm. Father Anselm seemed to lean on the younger man for support, but he was clearly not defeated, for he could be seen greeting all in attendance with a great smile upon his face. After the exchange of greetings, the party moved to enter the palace, and my mother instructed me to make ready for the royal audience that was about to take place. The queen's chief lady, Eleanor, took my hand and led me along with the rest of the females, all of us following in the train of royalty as we might a mother duck.

Upon reaching the lower level, we were met by the butler William D'Aubigny, who bowed to the queen and informed her that the archbishop was waiting just outside the audience chamber.

"Thank you, Master Aubigny. I am much obliged to you in this matter."

"Not at all, my lady."

"Tell me, where was Prince William last seen?"

"Last I knew he was with Master Herbert," the butler answered, "most likely practicing his riding skills."

"I am not surprised," the queen replied with evident displeasure. "Tell me, Aubigny, do you think it seemly that the prince should take part in such pursuits at his young age?"

The butler was clearly taken aback by this line of inquiry, but he made the best of it. "The king declares it is necessary if the boy is to be properly trained for his future duties."

"And yet, if he were to take a tumble, the prince may well end up unable to perform future duties of any kind, which would hardly be beneficial for the kingdom, do you not agree?"

"Such a level of concern most befits Your Ladyship, and the prince is fortunate to have such a caring mother. Nevertheless, allow me to place your mind at ease, for I am certain that no harm shall befall your prized jewel."

"Are you?" she replied. "Well then, go and tell Master Herbert that my prized jewel must come to the audience chamber so that I might display him for the world to praise."

"I shall carry out this task with all haste," he said, bowing and taking his leave of us.

We began walking again, and Lady Eleanor attempted to quiet her royal patroness's fears.

"My lady, I understand your concern, but I am certain the king's men do not intend to place the prince in any serious danger. Many have gone before him and suffered no ill effects."

"Maybe so, but you cannot know my feelings, Eleanor. He is my son. Perhaps if you have children of your own someday, you will understand. Ah, here we are."

The side door was opened and we entered the room, each of us taking her assigned place. My mother sat on the intricately carved throne that was reserved for such occasions, and I stood at her right hand, with the other ladies forming a half circle around us. Lady Beatrice had apparently received her summons as well, for she soon appeared and took her place directly behind me, placing my shoulders in an almost iron grip with both hands. I wondered that she felt a need to do so, for I had no intention of moving from my position. Many lords and ladies of the court were on hand for the occasion, their gossip stilling as the tall wood doors opened and the cry went up: "His Grace the archbishop of Canterbury!"

The crowd parted to let the esteemed visitor through. He had apparently eschewed the support of Gilbert Crispin for this most vital moment and walked with the aid of his staff only. The abbot of Westminster followed close behind him, no doubt ready to leap into action should the archbishop experience any difficulties. Anselm was not to be defeated, however. He made his way, slowly but deliberately, toward the throne, calling out, "Good Queen Mathilda, I beg your pardon for my slow pace. These last few years have not been kind to my temporal form."

"Not at all, Archbishop. I bid you welcome to our royal court at Westminster. It seems criminal that we have not had the benefit of your presence before this time. We have set everything in order for your stay here. I hope that the lodgings will meet with your satisfaction."

"I am sure, Your Highness, that even the smallest such offering would be sufficient for me," he said, finally arriving at the front of the room and breathing rather heavily with the effort. "I find that the older I become, the less I esteem the things of this world. Even so, I shall be glad for a place to rest my head, and I am most beholden for your hospitality."

"I trust you had no trouble on your journey?" the queen inquired.

"Have no fear, my lady. I may be showing the effects of age, but I have some strength left in me. I see you have your lovely daughter with you."

A poke from Lady Beatrice let me know that I was to step forward and bow, which I did immediately.

"Another Mathilda! If she is but half as faithful a servant of Christ as her mother, England will be all the better for it. Tell me, Princess, how are you getting on with your studies?"

"Not very well, Excellency," I answered honestly, then sensed that this was the wrong choice of words, as I could hear a soft groan from Lady Beatrice behind me. "What I mean to say, Your Grace, is that we have been without a tutor for a few weeks, but my mother has been encouraging my studies in the meantime. Now that you are here, I am sure that I shall improve even further."

"You reply rather boldly for someone so young," he said. "Both your esteemed mother and her own mother before her have been great examples of feminine righteousness and scholarship in our modern age. I trust that, in time, you will follow in their footsteps."

"That is my greatest hope, sir," I replied, wishing very much that the conversation would be over quickly. As luck would have it, the archbishop changed the subject, addressing the queen once again.

"And where is your son?"

"William has been training with some of the king's men this past fortnight," the queen answered. "I have sent word for him to return now that you have arrived, but it seems he has not yet received the message."

"No matter! I shall see him when the time is right. The king has set me a great task to guide these two of his children. I assure you that my methods will be strictly in line with your desires, my lady, provided there is no conflict with his commands."

"I do not imagine that there would be such a conflict. He asked merely that the prince be allowed to continue his training regimen while you are here."

"As he wishes. With your leave, Queen Mathilda, I shall return to my chamber now. I find myself in need of rest."

"Of course. Please let us know if there is anything that you need."

The archbishop had started to make his departure when the side door opened and my brother entered the room, spurred on by William D'Aubigny.

"Wait, Your Grace, my son has finally arrived!" the queen called out.

The old man turned toward William, who had been brought forward to face him directly. He smiled and put a hand on the boy's shoulder.

"My lad, how like your father you are! I can see traces of him in all your features. Yet there is something of the old Saxon line there too, I think. I am sure you possess a great firmness of character."

William looked confused, and I could not imagine what the archbishop saw to justify such confidence, but nevertheless the two of them shook hands and agreed that they would meet again as soon as Anselm recovered from his journey. Once the archbishop had left the room, my mother pulled William aside.

"Why did you not come when I first called you earlier today? Is Herbert preventing you from fulfilling your duties?"

"No, Mother. Herbert is the best teacher. I like being with all the men. I would have come earlier, but we couldn't stop, because we were doing this . . ."

"Enough. Perhaps I should have a talk with your trainers. There is nothing more urgent than doing as your mother commands, and even more so on great occasions of state. I do not fault you, William, but we must try harder to ensure that your time is put to the best possible use."

"Why do I have to be here anyway?" he complained. "Why should I sit around all day waiting for someone else to show up? I am the prince! They should be waiting for me!"

Mother pulled him closer, clearly willing him to lower his voice so that no one else could hear.

"I will not allow this lack of respect, William! Anselm is a great man of God."

"But Father says he just wants power like the rest of them. He says we should not listen to everything Anselm says, because he speaks for Rome, not England."

"William, your father left you in the archbishop's care, and that shows his true intentions. He wants you to obey both him and me as long as the progress in Normandy continues. I will not accept this level of defiance from you. I fear you have been spending too much time among the older men. Lady Beatrice, please take the prince back to his chamber. His lessons are done for today."

"Certainly, my lady," she replied, half dragging a still-whining William out of the room.

After pausing, I asked, "Mother, what shall I do? Am I to go along with him?"

"No, you must come and finish your embroidery as you promised. Eleanor, please make sure that Maud makes her way back to my rooms. I need a brief walk in the garden, and then I shall rejoin you all."

"As you command, my lady."

Several of the courtiers were still standing in the outer passage as we walked by, and those who noticed our presence stopped to give a brief bow. I had always felt it a bit strange that people should bow to me, as in my own household I was constantly being commanded rather than giving commands. It was an odd kind of irony, this high placement of mine that still seemed low in my own eyes. I may have been a princess, but I felt no more powerful than a common peasant girl. Before long I was back in front of my poor attempt at a thistle bloom, needle in hand, mind still thoroughly absent.

The following morning, Lady Beatrice brought us to our former study chamber to meet with Father Anselm for our first lesson. Walking back into that room felt quite strange, as I had not set foot within its walls since Master Godfrey ordered me to leave. I was surprised to see that our former lecterns had been removed and a simple round table placed in the center of the room with three chairs set around it. We had always been made to wait for Godfrey's arrival, but I saw that the archbishop was already seated at the table and reading a worn volume, which he had apparently taken from one of the many shelves. When he became aware of our presence, he set the book down and stood up, motioning for the two of us to take the chairs opposite him. He clasped his hands and leaned forward, smiling at each of us in turn.

"Good morning, dear children. I am delighted to see you again. Whether you will be as delighted to see me is, I suppose, yet to be determined. Tell me, how did your lessons with Master Godfrey usually proceed?"

"Sir, he usually began by reading to us a portion of the Scriptures and calling us to recite the Lord's Prayer and the doxology, with prayers for our esteemed parents. He then proceeded with a lecture on one of the philosophical writings. He loved Cicero and all the church fathers," I said.

"Master Godfrey had good taste. Cicero is a true treasure, and you will seldom hear a cross word from me about any of our great predecessors in the Christian faith."

"Yes, but it never made sense," William replied. "Half the time we had no idea what he was saying."

"Is that so?" Archbishop Anselm asked. "Well, I trust we can now excite your minds more fully. I recommend that we start by following his usual pattern, but perhaps with a few changes along the way. Does this seem good to you?"

Both my brother and I nodded. We had no desire to challenge him.

"Right, let us begin with a reading from the Old Testament. Lady Mathilda, which book do you most prefer?"

Here was something that I had never considered. I offered the best reply I could muster.

"Master Godfrey liked to read to us from the Law of Moses. He said that all the laws of man are taken from it, at least those which are legitimate, and that we must learn them in order to abide by the divine statutes."

"And were you fond of these works?"

"Not so much, sir. That is to say, one can have too much of a good thing."

His laugh was merry. "Rightly spoken, but you still have not chosen a book."

I paused to reflect. Other than the stories of the creation, Flood, early patriarchs, and ten plagues of Egypt, I had to confess that I had minimal interest in the books of Moses. Of the rest of the first testament I had little knowledge, though there was one book that I greatly loved, one that my mother had read to me time and again since I was a babe.

"The Psalms, sir. I most prefer the Psalms."

"Then the Psalms it is."

I thought he would refer to a copy of the Scriptures, but instead he began reciting from memory. However, this was not the greatest surprise, for I did not hear the words of the Latin tongue pour forth from his mouth, but those of our Norman forebears. He was translating the words for us to understand.

"'Blessed is the man that does not walk in the counsel of the wicked, nor stand in the way of sinners, nor sit in the seat of the scornful. But his delight is in the law of the Lord, and in his law does he meditate day and night.'"

The archbishop had closed his eyes to recite these words, and he now opened them again and glanced at the two of us. He must have been pleased to catch the looks of rapt attention. He once again shut his eyes and continued.

"'For he shall be like a tree planted by the rivers of waters, that will bring forth her fruits in due season: whose leaf shall not fade, so whatsoever he shall do, shall prosper.'"

"Archbishop," William interrupted, "what are these words you are saying?"

"Surely you have heard the first psalm of David before?" Anselm replied.

"Not like that. We hear them in the language of the Church."

"Ah, yes, so it must be during the Mass, but for two such young persons who have not yet mastered the Latin tongue, surely some explanation must be provided. You will understand far more easily this way."

"I liked it," I offered. "Master Godfrey would often explain to us the meanings of the words, but he did not actually translate the text directly. I fear it is not an easy skill."

"No, I should think not, but once you have achieved it, Lady Mathilda, you will find that the world opens to you in a new way. In any case, the words of the Lord have appeared in the common tongue for generations. Your own ancestor, King Alfred the Great, may he rest in peace, oversaw a translation into the language of the Britons, though it was not completed. It seems right for one such as yourself to benefit from hearing the words of God in your own tongue, ere you are able to comprehend them in Latin."

I began to see why my mother was so fond of Anselm. He did not just recite facts, but made them plain and beloved to the learner.

"Shall we have something from the New Testament, then?" the old man asked. "William, I believe it is your turn to choose."

"I don't know," he answered. "You can pick something."

"Really? I shall endeavor to oblige you, then." He closed his eyes again and appeared to be giving the matter deep consideration, softly muttering, "That one? No, that won't do. Perhaps . . . No, too long . . ." Finally he appeared to come to a decision and opened his eyes again. "The Epistle of Saint James," he began.

"'My brethren, count it exceeding joy when you fall into diverse temptations, knowing that the trying of your faith brings forth patience; and let patience have her perfect work, that you may be perfect and entire, lacking nothing. If any of you lack wisdom, let him ask of God, which gives to all men liberally and reproaches no man, and it shall be given to him.'"

I knew myself to be devoid of both patience and wisdom, and thus I felt the cold embrace of conviction. He now turned his gaze from William to me as he recited the next portion.

"'But let him ask in faith and waver not: for he that wavers is like a wave of the sea, tossed of the wind and carried away. Neither let that man think that he shall receive anything of the Lord. A double-minded man is unstable in all his ways.'"

These words seemed serious, and I missed most of the next few lines while considering their meaning. Finally he finished thus:

"'Blessed is the man that endures temptation: for when he is tried, he shall receive the crown of life, which the Lord has promised to them that love him.'"

"Now, what do you think it means?" Anselm asked, glancing at each of us in turn.

"It means that we must be strong," I answered. "If we are not strong, we shall not receive anything from the Lord, but if we are strong, he will reward us."

"Strong in what way?"

"We must not give in to fear or temptation."

"And how does one achieve that?"

Here I was forced to admit my ignorance. Anselm looked to William.

"What do you think?"

"What does *double-minded* mean?" my brother asked. "Is that like two brains?"

"Ah, I see you are familiar with the writings of Galen!" The archbishop appeared impressed. "Did Master Godfrey share with you Galen's thoughts concerning the seat of thought?"

I could tell from the look on William's face that he had waded out of his depth, so I attempted to answer the question.

"My mother's physician, Grimbald, always had the latest writings on hand from the East and from Spain, believing them to be essential to the practice of medicine. He was able to speak the language of the Moors, as well as that of the Greeks. He passed on some of what he knew to the queen, and that is how we came to know it."

"Wonderful! I have always known your mother to be a great student. To answer your question, William, to be double minded means that you cannot make a proper decision, but are always pulled this way and that. This is why Saint James writes that one needs a strong foundation of faith in God."

"May I ask you something, sir?" I said meekly.

"Yes, of course."

"How are we to commune with God? They say the saints converse with him openly, but I cannot hear his voice. At times I feel that he takes no interest in our affairs. I am to be sent far away, and I fear that . . ." Here my small voice trailed off, and I knew not how to continue.

"Mathilda, do not think that this silence is evidence of God's displeasure. The greatest men and women of God have often found themselves wandering through the wilderness like the prophets of old, unable to sense the divine will. You must have faith, as Saint James tells us! We are not asked to possess this strength at the beginning of the journey, but to form it with each step we take, receiving from the Holy Spirit the gifts of patience and wisdom."

"Were you ever there, sir, in the wilderness?"

"Yes, I believe I was, when I was a young man. Perhaps your mother has told you how I traveled far and wide seeking the Lord's direction."

"She did. She told me you found it at the Abbey of Bec."

"I would not say I found it, Lady Mathilda, but rather that it found me. When the time is right, you too shall feel that call. For now, you must continue to trust and believe."

"Are we going to say the Lord's Prayer now?" William asked, apparently tired of the conversation.

"Yes, as that is your custom, I suppose we must proceed." He turned to give me one last word. "Never fear, young one. The Lord is with you."

Thus our discussion ended with those words so familiar to all:

"'Our Father, who art in heaven . . .'"

Several weeks passed in this manner, with my brother and me joining Anselm for our daily lessons each morning, then departing to our separate affairs in the afternoon: William to his training with Master Herbert, and I to the ladies' quarters to learn all the graces necessary for a woman of royal standing. Every day my mother, Lady Eleanor, and the rest of the ladies of the royal household took it upon themselves to teach me sewing, flower arranging, writing, drawing, dressing, and dancing, and about all matters relating to conversation and government.

I confess that I grew weary under this new regimen. You must imagine how my poor fingers were worked beyond what they could bear and how my feet ached with the continual repetition of each step of those dances, all of which seemed to go on interminably. Even so, I found myself improving despite my flaws. Lady Beatrice commented that my drawing of one of the palace cats was a fairly true likeness, if still the work of a beginner. The queen smiled with pleasure at my performance of a round dance with several of the other ladies.

News came of Emperor Henry's formal offer of marriage. Apparently only the final terms remained to be settled before the marriage agreement was completed. With the holiday season approaching, in which it was more proper to be joyful, I did everything in my power to push it from my mind, holding out hope that some shift in power within the empire might bring an end to the deliberations. I still maintained my usual lessons with the archbishop. On account of his teaching, I had gained a new admiration for the Holy Scriptures and the great works of philosophy. He was a keen adherent of the reforms of Pope Gregory, of whom my mother the queen was also a great supporter, and I found his vision of a renewed Church laudable. Such men were called sons of Gregory or Gregorians.

Nevertheless, when he attempted to share with me his famous argument for the existence of God, which was based on the powers of logic rather than a mere appeal to the Scriptures, I found myself rather confused. Though he sought to prove to me how his explanation demonstrated the necessity of the divine, I concluded that Father Anselm's reasoning was simply too high above my own.

Around this time my paternal sister, the Countess of Perche, finally made her visit to court and passed many hours with the queen. They worked on looms during the day and played at dice in the evening. At Mass they sat side by side, and in like manner at meals. Only a person intimately connected with my mother could have noticed the signs of weariness in her eyes as the countess explained yet again how superior was the Norman style of dress to that favored in England, that we lacked a pleasing diversity in our diet, and that the appearance of certain men in the royal household was most vulgar.

Having stayed with us a full fortnight, the countess departed with her retinue to the north, where she'd foretold she should find no company fit to be had. I believe the queen was by no means upset to see the countess go. After all, Queen Mathilda had not forgotten that her origins lay even farther to the north than where the countess intended to make her stay. "Just as frivolous as her mother," I heard the queen whisper to Lady Eleanor as the countess's carriage made off on the northern road.

On the next Lord's Day, William, who had to make me aware of the arrival of the year's first snow, roused me from my sleep. A rather pitiful offering it was, disappearing in the course of a single hour, but still it served to cheer us as we celebrated the beginning of the Advent season.

Throughout the palace grounds, the servants were hard at work assembling boughs of holly with bright-red berries, twisting ivy around every column, and spreading rosemary across the floors to fill the air with its rich scent. The queen ordered a thousand candles to be lit throughout the grounds every evening. They illuminated the cold night sky with their glow and created a magic world I shall never forget.

We hung the Nativity tapestries in the great hall, and I loved to cast my gaze upon every magnificent element. One by one, they told the story of the Annunciation, the birth of John the Baptist, the travel of the holy family to Bethlehem and the birth of the Christ child, the appearance of the heavenly host to the shepherds, and the coming of the Magi. Lady Beatrice had once told me that these tapestries were worth more than the royal orb and scepter.

The Nativity feast was always a blessed time of year, but my hopes rose even higher when I heard that my mother's brother David would be joining us at Westminster. Though she never declared it, I could tell that he was the queen's most beloved brother and the one with whom she shared the closest bond, despite the fact that their older brother, Alexander, sat upon the throne of Scotland. Uncle David had lately been granted lands in Cumbria upon Alexander's ascension. Thus his visits to the English court were less frequent, though he was always beloved of both King Henry and his queen.

No one was more eager for David to arrive than William, who had long idolized his older relative. "Uncle David will be impressed when he sees what I have learned," he assured me. "I will challenge him to a fight."

We were sitting at one of the tables in the great hall as he said this, each of us going over material from the day's lesson, while Lady Beatrice and the rest of the servants prepared the hall for the many feasts soon to commence. Upon hearing my brother's assertion, I looked up from the book I had been reading.

"You cannot be serious, William. A few weeks of lessons are not enough to make you the equal of a fully trained warrior of wide renown."

"You are just jealous because you cannot fight with a sword or even hold it!" he protested. "What would you do if a Saracen came here and threatened you with his crooked blade?"

"I suspect I should depart as quickly as possible and leave the matter to the royal guard. One heathen would be hard pressed to defeat all the men in this castle. Master Edmund would see to it."

"No, he already slit the throats of all the knights one by one!"

Although I had it on good authority that both William and I had been born of the same mother, I often wondered at the lack of affinity between us. "Oh, really! Tell me then, since you are so wise, how was he able to get them all on their own? That seems rather convenient."

My teasing was clearly pushing William toward the edge. "Don't be daft! He just did! Now tell me, Maud, what would you do?"

"Children!" Lady Beatrice bellowed from across the room. Our eyes were instantly drawn to her figure. In her right hand she held a golden angel, and in her left a bough of holly. Under normal circumstances these would be cheerful sights, but her glance was as cold as the ice that had formed around the windows, and the ornaments took on a newly fearful appearance. Fortunately, she seemed too occupied to walk over to where we were sitting, and instead returned to her work once we were quiet.

"That was close!" William whispered in my direction.

"Yes, I think I prefer an armed Saracen to a cross Lady Beatrice."

Days passed as we awaited our uncle, but we soon received word that he had been detained on business for his brother, the Scottish king. In the meantime the queen's court hosted mummers dressed in the most magnificent disguises. I cherished these performances, and how I adored the music!

On each Advent Sunday we made our way across the Old Palace Yard to Saint Edward's Church for Mass, which was led by the abbot, Gilbert Crispin. At that time of year, he was fond of invoking the prophet Isaiah in his sermons. Archbishop Anselm surely would have joined us, but his failing health prevented him from walking outdoors in the cold, for fear that he might be struck by some illness or infirmity. The queen would only consent for him to conduct services in the royal chapel of Saint Stephen. I remember that walk from the abbey back to the palace, across the grounds covered in a mixture of snow and ice. The poor and destitute lined up on either side, hoping that the queen or one of her ladies would favor them with her beneficence. They were a ghastly sight, their clothes worn and tattered, their feet bound in scraps of linen and well-nigh blue from the cold, and their skin covered with sores. Even in the chill of winter, their odor was most disagreeable.

Yet my mother stopped to greet as many as she could, touching the faces of their children and grasping the hands of the old and decrepit. She offered them a smile and her words of blessing, and they bestowed on her such smiles as they could in return, though what teeth they had were brown with age. "God bless you, Queen Mathilda!" they would call after her, declaring that the Virgin Mary had sent her angel for the Nativity season. Once the queen had passed, they would haste back to whatever fire they could find that might provide some warmth.

The day before the Angels' Mass, there was still no sign of the queen's brother. We had heard not a week earlier that he had been making his way south on the road from Durham, only to be halted by a terrible storm that left so much snow upon the highway that the horses were unable to pass through without great difficulty, and Prince David feared that some of their number might take such a chill that it would cause them to depart too soon from this world. Finally, on that day before Christmas, one of the royal messengers informed us of his arrival at Warwick Castle two days earlier.

"I sense the work of the devil in this delay," Mother declared.

"Patience, my daughter. As the nation of Israel was forced to await the coming of the Lord in long years of hardship, so we must endure these last moments before the consummation of our hopes," Anselm counseled her.

"As always, your logic is firm, but you have forgotten one thing, Archbishop: my brother is not the messiah."

"Yes, there I shall not attempt to argue with your reason, nor would anyone who has made his acquaintance, as faithful a follower of Christ as he may be," he said with a smile. "His long years at court were not quite enough to remove the Scot from him."

Shortly before the blessed hour was upon us, the castle gates opened and David, Prince of the Cumbrians, entered the grounds of the Palace of Westminster on a brown stallion, accompanied by several members of his household. So eager was his sister to behold his face that she entered the snowy yard draped in her best fur cloak in order to welcome him. He was taller and pulled her up into his arms, spinning her in a full circle before finally setting her back to earth. I thought this a most odd sight and observed that only Uncle David could do such a thing to the queen and still be welcome at court.

Once the guests were all inside, they abandoned their outer coats and warmed themselves by the hearth. William D'Aubigny and Edmund fitz Hugh bid the prince welcome to Westminster and made all the usual inquiries after the nature of his journey, the state of his health, the fortunes of his family, and his current level of hunger and thirst. My uncle paid them as much heed as was necessary to prevent their sense of honor from being offended, but little enough to ensure that the conversation reached a quick conclusion.

The servants were left to attend to the items from the prince's journey, and we made our way to the queen's audience chamber, there to enjoy a few moments of peace. William had been so weary from the day's pursuits that Lady Beatrice had demanded he take a few hours of sleep before Mass; thus I was the only person on hand to witness their conversation.

Prince David selected one of the chairs next to the fire and sank into it, letting out a great sigh that spoke to the onerous nature of his journey. He then bent forward, rubbing his hands over his bearded face, which was red from the cold. My mother sat in the chair opposite him, and I knelt at her feet.

"Brother, is there anything I can offer you for your comfort?"

This caused him to look up. "No, thank you, your men and ladies have been most efficient. I am sure I could want for nothing."

"You look as if a hot bath would do you some good."

"Do you offer such things after dark here? I must inform my servants that they have fallen off the pace." He placed his feet upon an available stool and leaned back with his arms folded across his chest.

"Well, it might not be common, but for a long-awaited brother on the eve of Christmas, I should think it could be arranged. We will surely all reap the benefits. I will have Eleanor tell the kitchen staff to boil some water. They were not intending to sleep this night, for they must arrange for the feast tomorrow."

"Yes, the feast! The thought of it alone was enough to propel me through many an icy ditch. My horse hurt its leg, poor thing. God only knows if it will be any good to me now. I was forced to borrow one, which left Bernard to stumble through on foot. I finally told him around Coventry that if he preferred to wait for our return at the inn, he was welcome to do so, but he would come the whole way. I am surprised none of my men lost a toe."

"This really is dreadful weather. I cannot remember seeing an Advent season like this since Mary and I were at Romsey."

Daughter, you will note that Mary was the queen's younger sister and the wife of the Count of Boulogne. They had been sent to live with their aunt Cristina at the abbey before both their dear parents departed from this world.

"Tell me, how did the sisters celebrate the birth of our Lord?" David asked with one of those mischievous glances worn by brothers seeking to tease their sisters.

"They embraced it with the same degree of austerity and devotion which they displayed every day of the year. I believe they may have resorted to the rod less frequently in the spirit of mercy that marked the season, but come the New Year it would always reappear with a vengeance."

"I still find it hard to believe that our dear mother, formidable as she was, sent you there when you were scarcely six years old, and Mary younger still! Most women make it through a marriage or two before they are forced into that particular misfortune."

"Perhaps it was for my good. I trust that I gained a certain degree of discipline and piety while I lived among the sisters, though I can hardly make a claim to perfect righteousness."

"And how are you, dear Maud?" David asked. "I trust that your brother has not been making life too miserable for you."

"I am tolerably well, sir," I answered, "though I confess myself to be ill at ease when it comes to the matter of my espousal."

"Ah, yes, Emperor Henry—I heard of it from King Alexander. Is it in fact confirmed that she is to marry him?" he asked with a look to my mother.

"My husband tells me as much," she replied. "He thinks it is for the best, given the situation with the new French king, Louis, who seems to have his eye on our lands in Normandy ever since his father Philip died and left him in charge. Robert Curthose may be locked away, but his son William Clito could be a danger to King Henry if the French king supports his claim to the throne. I am assured that this new alliance will help to contain Louis's ambitions as well as any future meddling regarding the dukedom. As for the German king, he is in need of capital to fund his ventures."

"It is a wise match, to be sure, though I am certain you must be loath to see your daughter go."

"As it is, the debate is at an end and the time for action is upon us," the queen told him with a sense of resignation. "What of yourself? How go your efforts in Cumbria?"

His mood changed considerably. "You know Brother Alexander as well as I do. He is not one to surrender lightly. He continues to deny me many of the lands and privileges laid out in the agreement with King Edgar. He would have me, the brother of one king by blood and another by your marriage, consigned to the life of a minor noble. Still, patience is my best policy. In time he will come to see that this game he plays will only hurt his cause, for I have gained the support of all the men not only in Cumbria and Strathclyde, but farther to the north as well. I have it on good authority that more than half the men in both Stirling and Edinburgh favor my cause."

"Oh, David, have we not seen enough conflict over these past years to last a lifetime? The throne of Scotland has become a die for men to throw in the hope that fortune might smile upon them."

He seemed taken aback. "Do you not think that I would make a better king than Alexander?"

"Yes, you know I favor your cause and I always will, but we must also consider the effects of this division upon the future of the kingdom. Were Father and Mother yet alive, they should shudder to see what has become of their inheritance."

"If Father and Mother were here, we should not have a dispute in the first place," he said with an air of conclusion. "How long now until the Angels' Mass?"

"The candle shows but half an hour," the queen replied, glancing at the wax pillar, which burned low. "Perhaps we should make our way down."

"One thing first, Sister. Tell me the truth: does the king still take other women to his bed?"

My eyes must have grown wide, for I could scarcely believe that he should say such a thing with me in the room. Nevertheless my mother answered him.

"You are aware of the ways of this world as well as any man, Brother."

"I am aware that some men are knaves, if that is what you mean."

"And I suppose you have never brought another to your bed on those many lonely nights, or will you now argue that, even at your age, you have not felt the touch of a woman?"

"What I do is immaterial to this discussion. I have not entered into wedlock as your husband the king has done. My concern is that he has not done right by my beloved sister."

"And if I say that he has done wrong, what do you intend to do about it?"

"Hang him up by the balls, I should think," he replied with a degree of audacity that caused me to let out a gasp. "My niece laughs, but I assure you I am not one to suffer betrayal."

"The offense is not against you, Brother, and I should thank you not to speak in such vulgar terms in front of Maud, nor in the context of our Lord's Nativity."

"As usual, you have hit close to the mark, Sister. I will save such talk for another time—perhaps a gathering of Scotsmen?"

At length the three of us made our way out of the chamber and down the passage to Saint Stephen's chapel, where Father Anselm, William, and the rest of the royal household were awaiting our presence. As we neared the entrance, I whispered to my uncle, "I am so glad that you are back. I was beginning to think you would never make it."

"As was I, but remember, Niece, Advent is the time for miracles."

CHAPTER FIVE

Is it not strange how the ardor of youth becomes, with the passing of time, a faint memory that seems so utterly separated from the present as to be almost a tale from the life of another, rather than one's own? So I have often felt when bringing to mind those years, for both past and future become the vellum on which we write our hopes and fears. Were we to be gifted the clarity we once possessed, then perhaps we might see clearly the confluence of these diverse streams of our existence, thus gaining a better understanding of who we are and who we may yet become. Even in the midst of all this forgetfulness, there are some things that remain, moments that time cannot drive away. Such a time was the last Advent season that I spent at Westminster, and such a day was the day that I must now describe.

I have already explained how David, Prince of the Cumbrians and brother to Queen Mathilda of England, made his way south under treacherous conditions, arriving on the eve of Christmas. The following day was the feast, an occasion of great magnificence. All who were able attended the queen's court that morning to receive her blessing for the New Year. They all expressed their undying fealty and bestowed upon Her Royal Highness the gifts due to her person.

After the midday meal, I enjoyed a private family celebration with William, Uncle David, and my mother. This was held in the queen's smaller chamber, which along with the rest of the castle had been decorated in accordance with the season. Prince David declared that he had not seen such a wealth of holly in all his years. As a special treat, the cooks had created an array of delicacies, with the tarts and pies being the main attraction.

"How many of those have you eaten?" the queen asked upon seeing William return from the table with both his hands and mouth stuffed with sweets. He was unable to provide an answer beyond a few grunts, which implied that this was not his first portion.

As usual, I was a bit more sparing in my selection, choosing only those morsels that were most appealing. Although I was still a child, Lady Beatrice had already warned me that the public would not suffer a woman to become too large in the same manner that they would a man. This double standard was fortunate for my father, who in addition to gaining a bald head had increased in mass over the past few years. No one at court dared to mention this corpulence, but I knew that my eyes did not deceive me.

Our uncle had brought New Year's gifts for my brother and me, which he presented to us in turn. First was William's: a young Talbot that was brown in color and, once introduced, began running around the room and putting its wet nose to anything it could find. William was lavish in his gratitude, embracing uncle David's legs and assuring him that he could not have bestowed the gift upon anyone more eager.

"It seemed right given the strides you have been making toward manhood," David replied. "I know that Herbert and Edmund have taken great pains to ensure that your training includes all that is required for a future king. I have no doubt that they will soon take you out hunting, and this new hound can be trained up with you. The two of you will make a fine pair—I am certain of it."

"William already has one dog that is under the care of Master Edmund. I see you intend to create more work for that man," the queen said to her brother. "Even so, I suppose I ought to laud you for making the prince so happy."

"From one prince to another!" David said to his nephew, releasing him to chase the whelp around the room.

"I name you Colin!" the young boy declared, catching the poor thing by the tail and pressing it to his chest. The hound let out a pitiful sound before succumbing to this childish fervor.

"Well, at least Colin is an apt name, for that is what the Scots call a young dog. Here, Maud, I have brought something for you as well."

He handed me a bound volume, which I opened to reveal illustrations of what appeared to be every beast known to man. I leafed through the pages, enamored by the rich colors and fine craftsmanship. Each page contained a description of a different animal.

"This is a *bestiarum*," my uncle said to me, confirming what I already knew. "It was compiled by the monks of the Holy Island of Lindisfarne and is a true treasure of learning. I hope you are pleased with it."

I did not know how to reply. That I was pleased was beyond any doubt, but it was written in Latin, and I was well aware that my knowledge of that language was lacking. My face dropped slightly and I was ashamed to admit my failing. Perhaps sensing whence the difficulty arose, Uncle David encouraged me to climb onto his lap so that we could read over one of the pages together. I did as I was commanded and turned to a page that was labeled "*Simia*."

"What do you make of this creature, Maud?"

I looked over the drawing, which showed a figure covered in dark-brown hair clinging to a tree branch with three of its legs. The other leg it used to carry one of its young, and another clung to its back. Its eyes gleamed with a fierce red light. I did not imagine that one would want to be caught alone with such an animal.

"It looks frightful," I said. "What is it? I do not think that it lives in England."

"Right you are. It says that this beast is only found in the lands to the south and east, where it is called *kurut*, but in Latin it is called *simia*."

"Why does it bear that name?"

"Because it is similar to men. See, this is a female shown in the picture with two of her young. The text states that the mother will always love one child and hate the other, and that is why she carries one in her arms and the other must ride on her back. It also says that the *simia* is a most cunning creature and not to be trusted."

"Like Jacob and Esau?"

"What do you mean?"

I looked to my mother and could see by the smile upon her face that she had guessed my meaning.

"'I loved Jacob, and I hated Esau.' That is from Scripture, Uncle."

"Ah, and who taught you that?"

"Father Anselm. He knows everything there is to know about the Scriptures."

"Child, no one may know the entirety of the Scriptures, not even Anselm," Mother said, "though I can see that you have learned a great deal these past few months."

"How is the great Anselm?" David asked, still holding me in his arms, my brother now playing with the dog on the floor.

"It is a matter of some concern to me, as you might have guessed. He is well on in years, and I am afraid that King Henry has not made things easy for him since he ascended to the throne," the queen answered.

"I hear he still writes works of meditation as he used to in the former days. Well, he is fortunate to remain in the See of Canterbury. I know what a faithful daughter you have been to him. He owes you a debt that he is likely never to comprehend."

"You flatter me, but I possess no great degree of influence. I fear that my words often fall on deaf ears."

For the first time all day, the queen seemed to drift into sadness. Prince David attempted to change the subject of conversation.

"I understand that the king has sent more of the Flemings off to live in Wales. Are they really so unbearable?"

"The English are not fond of aliens," Mother replied. "They feared that, should the number of foreigners continue to increase, there would be very little of the English left in England. I think it a bit incredible, particularly given the mixing of blood now taking place throughout the kingdom, but as usual I was denied. Still, I am certain that they shall thrive in their new situation, and as long as the cloth trade continues in London, the Flemish will seek our shores."

"Ow, he bit me!" William cried, his body curled up on the floor and his left hand holding one of the fingers of his right. Colin continued to run circles round him as if completely innocent.

"Let me see," Mother said, bending down to examine his finger. "It looks a bit red, but I see no sign of a cut. I daresay you shall survive this one."

"But it hurts!" William protested. He looked to each of us in turn, craving some form of pity to equal the pain he was apparently experiencing. When it was denied him, he retreated to a corner of the room, where he took up again with the same creature he had declared to be a menace.

"There is a lesson for you," the queen said to her brother. "When you have sons of your own, remember this day and the proper manner in which to handle such minor calamities."

"You always did love instructing me," he said with a smile. "Tell me, have you heard when the king will return?"

"Not yet, but if he keeps to his usual pattern, he will return when winter ends."

"Maud hopes he will never come back," William charged.

"William, you liar!" I shouted. "You know I never said such a thing."

"No, but you whine about having to marry the emperor, and how sad it will be when you can't see us again."

I shifted my glance to my mother, who had a look of concern upon her face.

"I swear, Mother, I am ready to carry out the duty laid upon me. I would not say such things."

"I listen to you at night, when you think I am asleep," William continued. "I heard you cry and whisper things that you don't want Lady Beatrice to know."

"That is enough, William," the queen declared, and then turned to face me. I could feel the tears forming in my eyes once again. "I understand the fears you are experiencing."

"I know, Mother, and I shall try my hardest to be good. I shall put such thoughts away."

"What I am trying to say is that what you are feeling is precisely what I felt when I was sent away to live at the nunnery, or when your uncle David was forced to come to the English court because the Kingdom of Scotland was thrown into chaos. We have spoken of this before, and I know you intend to be brave, but I pray that you will not trouble yourself to such a degree, for neither your father nor"—here she paused as if struggling to accept the words that escaped her lips—"neither your father nor I would place you in any situation unless we were sure it was for your own good. You shall be well looked after, believe me."

"What your mother says is true," my uncle offered, embracing me still more tightly. "There is no reason to fear your father's coming."

"I am not afraid," I said definitively. "You can tell anyone you like that I am not afraid."

Following the end of Advent, things began to change quickly. Prince David left again for the realm of Cumbria, with the queen's promise that she would continue to support his efforts to strengthen his position, provided that he did not resort to open warfare. Anselm was forced to take his leave of Westminster, as his health had begun its final decline. That parting was a sorrowful one, for there was little doubt on the part of either the archbishop or the queen that it would be the last time they met on this earth. What words were exchanged between them, I cannot say, but my mother had a look of mourning about her as she watched his boat travel down the River Thames and out of our lives. A few weeks later, we received word of his demise.

Scarcely had these noble gentlemen departed when we received word that the king's return was at hand. He had completed his affairs in Normandy and was ready to set foot once more in England. William and I were particularly glad to hear that both Robert fitz Roy and Brian fitz Count would be in the king's retinue. Cousin Stephen had remained in Blois to spend more time with his mother and two brothers, Theobald and Henry. The full truth was that Stephen had another brother, William, who was the eldest of all the sons of the Count of Blois and his wife, Adela. However, this William had been passed over for the throne on account of his poor character and erratic behavior.

It is said that he once threatened the bishop of Chartres with death over some petty dispute.

Furthermore, there was a claim oft repeated concerning Cousin William, that there was not a brothel this side of the Rhine that had not enjoyed his patronage. I never set much store by that rumor, believing it to be an utter impossibility, but it must have had some foundation in fact. Such a son not even a mother could find worthy of elevation, and thus he was forced to content himself with his wife's ancestral lands in Sully.

You must forgive me, Daughter, for I have strayed from the main purpose of this tale. With the king due back any day, the people of Westminster as well as those in London were eager to have their monarch with them once again. Indeed, I believe all but the queen and I were looking forward to his arrival with great joy. I could not wish for it, for I knew that it meant the final days of relative freedom were upon me.

When the king's fleet was sighted upon the river, the bells of London town rang out with great jubilation. Nobles and servants alike made their way to the water's edge to catch a glimpse of the king in all his glory gliding along the river as in the Roman processions of old. Truly he was *vir triumphalis*, for though he had made few gains on the field of battle, he had accomplished a great conquest in the form of the imperial espousal.

As was often the case on such occasions, Roger of Salisbury had found his way not only to Westminster, but also to the head of the welcome party. Many felt that the honor ought to have gone to Her Royal Highness Queen Mathilda, but as was her wont, she saw little need to demur over such a trifling matter, knowing that the truest exercise of power takes place beyond the prying eyes of the masses.

As the fleet made its way around the river's bend, the water before us filled with a great number of boats; William ceased counting at twenty. Some carried warriors, others officials, still others food and drink from the Continent. The few poor men who had to travel with the animals undoubtedly longed for more pleasant odors. Then there were boats packed high with other trade goods: fabrics, tools crafted by the blacksmiths in Normandy and points farther to the east, and some materials that the queen had purchased from a Milanese merchant.

The craft that carried the king was the first to pull up to the wharf. King Henry stood on the upper deck with the ship's captain, both taking in the view. He was quite the valiant figure dressed in his ceremonial armor, and how magnificent was his ship! The head of a great lion rose at its front, with its twin looking backward at the city. I recognized several of the men closest to the king on board, including the two I was most eager to see: Robert and Brian.

"Hail, King Henry, lord of all England and Normandy!" the bishop of Salisbury proclaimed as my father made his descent. He extended his hand to grasp that of the sovereign, but instead the king wrapped him in a full embrace.

"Dear Roger, it is good to see you again. Tell me, how go our affairs?"

"Quite well, my lord. There have been no rebellions during your absence, so great is the love of the people for their king. Every parish church from Canterbury to Carlisle continues to proclaim the word of God, and I hear that you have repulsed the efforts of the new French king. Surely the Lord has seen the justice of your cause." Then, in a more hushed tone, "I have been devising new methods to replenish your exchequer. I do not doubt that we shall be able to come up with the necessary monies to satisfy the emperor's dowry request."

"Excellent!" the king replied, striking the bishop's back in a manner that seemed to shake the smaller man's entire body. "We have a great many things to discuss, but no more of that now. We will talk on the morrow."

"As you wish, Your Highness. I shall be ready to give a full account."

Having left matters thus, King Henry moved down the line to where we were standing. The queen performed her usual bow.

"Welcome home, Your Grace," the queen said. "I trust you shall find that everything is in order."

"I have no reason to suspect otherwise, but my men tell me that I am not to meet with the archbishop of Canterbury, who has lately quit the town."

"That is correct," she answered. "He was forced to leave on account of his health, but he performed well in his assigned role, looking after the interests of your children throughout your absence."

"I would prefer to see him look to my interests, but I suppose my children will have to do. What a pity he was not here to greet me!" the king said with a laugh.

After a brief acknowledgment of William and me, along with the officials on hand, the king moved to enter the palace, where he would receive what I could only assume would be a meal fit for a king.

"Come, Lady Mathilda. You have been summoned."

"By whom, Lady Beatrice?"

"By the king, naturally. Your father wishes to speak with you."

"Is it about my espousal to the emperor?" I asked this with some difficulty, as Lady Beatrice was mounting a savage attack upon my hair with an ivory comb.

"The king's messenger did not specify, but I think it likely."

"Will my mother be there as well?"

"No, the king wishes to speak to you *in camera*."

Even as Lady Beatrice continued happily subjecting me to all manner of outward preparation, I became quite troubled. Why would the king wish to speak with me alone? I tried to think of a time when I had ever been in his presence absent any observers. Perhaps there had been an instance when I was young and rushed in unwittingly, but that would be all.

How ought one to behave? Should I wait for him to speak, or did I possess some kind of daughterly prerogative to raise an issue at will? No, that could not possibly be the way of things. I was nervous enough around the king when my mother and brother were there, not to mention visitors and other residents of the castle. The idea of facing him alone was enough to cause my heart to race.

"You are strangely quiet, Lady Mathilda. I cannot remember the last time I have placed a comb through your hair without a litany of complaints."

I was too lost in my fears to answer. "In truth, I should not dread the idea of facing my father," I thought. "Soon enough I will be married to another ruler, this one a complete stranger. No, I must be strong. I am setting out on a journey on which none can aid me. I must learn to overcome these feelings which seem to plague my soul."

Breaking into my mental dispute was a shrill voice. "Goodness, child, your hands are filthy! How can that possibly be? Girl, fetch the basin!"

One of Lady Beatrice's assistants immediately seized the bowl and pitcher sitting nearby. The older woman held first my right hand and then my left under the water, putting each through a stern regimen of scrubbing. By the time she had finished, the water had turned brown and my hands were beginning to take on a shade of pink.

"Please, Lady Mathilda, in the space between here and your father's chambers, do try your best not to touch anything."

It would have been impossible for me to disobey Lady Beatrice's instruction, for she kept a tight hold on me as we walked across the palace, taking care to steer me away from anything that presented the slightest danger to my appearance. On the outside I must have appeared every bit the lovely princess, but inside I was trembling. We had arrived at the entrance to the king's chambers. This was the moment of truth.

Lady Beatrice spoke to the guards at the door. "Here is the lady Mathilda. The king has summoned her."

"Wait here," said the taller of the two guards as he entered the room, closing the door behind him. The other guard continued to stand there, his face providing no sign of what awaited.

I had been making an intense study of my shoes when the guard returned and informed us that the king was busy with a matter of state and we must wait a moment longer. He then shut the door again, and we continued to stand before it in silence, the remaining guard acting as if we were not there. I returned to my downward glance until Lady Beatrice let me know with one of her usual comments that a lady does not allow her chin to dip in such a manner.

After another minute or two, I finally asked, "Lady Beatrice, should we return to the nursery? It seems that the king is quite busy at the moment."

"We shall remain here until you are called."

"Perhaps he has forgotten about us."

"Patience! He will receive you soon enough."

In truth, I was merely hoping to delay what I believed would be an awkward situation, but I was not surprised that Lady Beatrice would deny me this opportunity. Comfort had never been her highest priority.

Finally the door was pulled fully open, and the guard who had until that point overlooked our presence motioned for us to go into the chamber. As we entered, I could see my father studying a map of the Norman possessions across the Channel. He had evidently been speaking with some of his martial counselors.

"Your Highness, here is Lady Mathilda as you requested. I shall leave the two of you now."

A new wave of fear hit me as Lady Beatrice released my hand and departed from the room. I glanced back, unwilling that she should leave, but she motioned for me to look at my father. Turning again, I could see that he was still examining the map. Without looking up he motioned for me to come closer, which I did with the most halting of footsteps. I stopped a few paces away, afraid that any further progress might be deemed an invasion of his privacy. However, when he did not sense me right at his side, the king finally cast his gaze in my direction and said, "What are you doing all the way over there? Come closer!" He must have observed my nervous disposition, for he added, "There is no need to be afraid."

A few steps more, and I was within arm's length of him, but he once again repeated, "Closer! I need you to be able to see this." He directed me to a spot directly in front of him where I could see the whole Frankish kingdom spread out before me.

"Do you know what all of these places are, Maud?"

Upon concluding that there was no other option but to respond, I made my best attempt.

"This water over here is part of the great sea, and beyond it is England."

"Good."

"And here are our lands along the coast, the Duchy of Normandy."

"What is that to the west?"

This one escaped me and I was forced to try to read the faded inscription.

"Brittany. It is the Duchy of Brittany."

"Where is France?"

"To the east, my lord."

"And what would you get if you went even farther east?"

"Well, that depends. If you were to go directly east, you should hit the mountains that lie within the realm of the emperor. If you were to turn north, you would arrive in the land of the Danes. And if your course leads you south, you will reach Lombardy, and farther on Rome and the Middle Sea."

I looked up and was relieved to see a smile on my father's face. I must have performed well.

"Very good. Who taught you all that?"

"Father Anselm, sir."

"Ah, I see." His voice betrayed a slight degree of annoyance. "And did he also explain the situation we are facing in Normandy?"

"With all respect, Father, I do not need to hear about that from Anselm. It is the talk of all the court."

"Then I suppose you know that the fat boy ruling France, King Louis, has demanded that I pay homage to him?"

"And will you?"

"Certainly not! He also had the audacity to command that I turn over the fortresses in the border regions to alleged 'neutral castellans,' but that is the very last place where one wishes a man to be neutral. Remember this, Daughter: the man who stands on the front line of battle must be the most steadfast in the service of his king. That is the only way to prevent incursions from the outside. In any case, a man who refuses to set his foot firmly in one camp or the other is nothing but a flattering ingrate."

"What did King Louis do when you refused?"

"He gathered together his best men, which of course is not saying much, since they were Franks, after all. He attempted to force me into submission, but we were able to apply enough pressure to force an agreement. No king of England will be paying homage to a king of France, not if I have anything to say about it! Now, what do you see here?"

"Those are the lands of Maine and Anjou."

"Precisely. They lie directly to the south of our ancestral lands. Fulk of Anjou is about to come into possession of both of them. The king of France is already attempting to bring Fulk under his influence. Indeed, he seeks to place all the counties of France under his direct authority so that they must all act in complete obedience to his will."

"Do you think that this Fulk of Anjou will do so? Would that not place Normandy in greater peril?"

"Whether or not he will do so is yet to be seen, but it is concerning." He paused to allow me a moment of reflection and then continued. "Surely you must see now why an alliance with the emperor is so vital. He is the only other ruler with an army that can pose a substantial threat to Louis's ambitions."

"I understand, sir." We had now come to the possibility of marriage—the subject I had feared all along.

"Emperor Henry is sending his legates here to Westminster. They should arrive in a few months. At that time we will complete the marriage agreement."

"And when am I to leave for Germany, my lord?" Whether it was ladylike or not, my eyes had once again resorted to studying my shoes.

"It will most likely be early next year, after the weather improves. The coming months will be a time of final preparation for you, Maud. You have already made great strides from what your mother the queen tells me."

"But I do not feel ready, sir. I have never performed any official duties—never sat at a royal feast or attended the signing of a charter."

"This will be the year in which all of that changes. You will be placed before the eyes of the people more often. In time you will adjust and become comfortable with your new situation."

I was unsure that I could ever feel comfortable in such a situation, but nevertheless I forced myself to continue listening.

My father paused a moment. During our conversation he had been picking up the metal weights used to hold down the map and polishing each one with his shirtsleeve. Now he returned the last one to its appointed place and sat on the edge of the table with his arms crossed, looking me directly in the eye.

"Mathilda, this is a duty you must perform on behalf of the kingdom, one equally essential to anything our warriors accomplish in battle. I am counting on you to make both your mother and me proud. Such an alliance is the greatest height to which a woman can rise."

"I understand, sir."

"Very good. There is a person I wish you to meet, a knight trained in my household." He called for one of the guards, who appeared immediately. "You may let him in now."

The man who entered next was one of the largest I had ever seen. So great was his height that he towered over the king, and each of his hands looked as if they could crush a man's skull. A large scar ran down the side of his face, adding to the savage nature of his appearance. It looked as if the injury that caused it must have threatened his left eye. He stood at attention awaiting the king's instruction.

"Mathilda, I present to you Drogo. He entered my household several years ago and has since completed his training for knighthood. His father was in the great host that landed with King William at Hastings, and he played no small part in the victory that day, for which his family was awarded their lands in Cornwall. He has accepted my commission to accompany you to your new home and to remain in your service."

My eyes were still attempting to take in everything before me. Although Drogo was a large man, his bright eyes softened his otherwise harsh appearance. Sensing that it was the correct response at such a time, I made a short bow to him and said, "Master Drogo, I am pleased to make your acquaintance."

I wondered if this was the wrong thing to say, for the knight looked to the king for help as to what his next move should be. Was it possible that he knew even less about how to behave in this circumstance than I did, despite his extensive training?

"It would be proper for you to return the princess's greeting," the king finally instructed him.

"Apologies, my liege. Lady Mathilda, it is a great honor to serve you," he said, trying his best to bow low. I could see that bending down to my level was more difficult for him than it would have been for most men, so high was his head perched upon his shoulders.

He then took my hand and was about to kiss it, but another glance at the king seemed to prove to Drogo that this was incorrect as well. He settled for simply gripping it and nodding his head in an affirmative manner.

"Good. Now that's done. You may return to wherever you came from," father said to the knight, dismissing him with a wave of his right hand.

"Thank you, my lord," he replied, hastily departing.

"Do not worry, my daughter," the king said after the door was closed. "He is a far more effective soldier than he is a speaker."

In the few days since their arrival back at court, I desired to once again enjoy the company of the king's lads. However, it was not to be, for with each new day came the news that the king was once again taking Prince William out to continue his training, and it was only natural that the young men should come along. Meanwhile I learned about the proper method for couching, in addition to my daily lessons in Latin, which were administered by Lady Beatrice. The two soon became combined, as a stern *"Fac! Fac!"* met any pause when I ought to have been stitching.

Then, one day, the Lord smiled upon me. The clouds were rent asunder and water poured forth in unnatural abundance.

The roads were impassable, and the weather was simply not fit for a prince of the realm, let alone a king, to be out of doors. I was informed that the king's lads were spending the afternoon in the old study chamber, attempting to best one another at checks. Sensing my chance, I inquired of my mother if I might go visit my older brother. After some persuasion she permitted me to leave the day's lessons for the space of one half hour.

Excitedly I made my way to the study chamber, where I found Robert and Brian bent forward over the small table sitting between them, their eyes fixed upon the game board. I had no knowledge of checks, being yet a young girl who did not possess the patience necessary for mastering it. Nevertheless, I was determined to make an attempt.

"Brother Robert!" I called out to him.

He looked up from his pondering with a slight frown on his face, apparently displeased with the interruption. However, when he saw me his features softened.

"Hello, Maud. Have you come to join the game?"

I felt slightly embarrassed. "I have no experience with it."

"Then we must teach you!" he replied, beckoning for me to come and stand by his side, which I did with all haste.

Unlike his friend's, Brian's eyes had remained on the board the entire time, and he now reached out to move one of the pieces. I marveled at the carving of each of the ivory figures, some made to look like members of the clergy, others like knights mounted on horses, and still others having the fierce look of warriors set for battle.

"What do all of them do?" I asked Robert.

"This one is the king. It is the key," he told me. "As in life, if this piece is lost, the kingdom will fall and all will be lost."

"So this is like a real war?" I asked.

"Yes and no. There are rules that govern each of the different types of pieces. The ones with bishops' miters can move either this way . . . or . . . that way. These can only move forward and not back. Oh, you will like this one: it is the queen, the only lady on the board."

As he said these words, he picked up the piece, which indeed had the look of a queen seated on a throne, her veil held in place by a crown. The expression on her face was that of the Stoics.

"I do not think she looks very happy," I said as he set the queen back in her place.

"That is because I am about to take her out of play," Brian responded, reaching with both his hands to make the exchange for one of his own red pieces.

Robert was none too pleased, letting out a cry of, "Oh damn!" and following it with, "How did I miss that?"

"You were not thinking of the game," said his adversary. "Like so many who have come before, you allowed your mind to wander when encountering a female." He winked in my direction as he said this.

Robert refused to accept this explanation, and he spent the next few moments attempting to review each move, determined to discover the exact point at which he had misstepped. Finally he smiled and declared that he should not have moved his queen so far forward three moves earlier.

"You may delight yourself with whatever explanations you like," Brian countered, "but the fact remains that you are still down in the game. You have but one knight still in play, while I have both a bishop and a rook, as well as that pawn."

"This is not the end. Do not underestimate my knack for escape."

"How are you going to do that if you have so few pieces?" I asked him.

"In moving to take my queen, my foe has been drawn into a position he is not able to retain. He has left his rook by itself, while my pieces, few as they are, remain placed in support of one another."

"Yes, we all stand in awe of your words, but we will let Princess Maud be the judge of your design," Brian replied.

"Did William tell you that Uncle David gave me a *bestiarum?*" I asked Brian.

"I'm afraid not. He mostly discussed how wonderful his new dog is."

"Colin? I don't care for him. Whenever we are in the same room, he leaps on me and then licks me with his terrible tongue. I do not think I shall ever love dogs as William does."

"Ha, check!" Robert shouted, placing his knight in position to strike.

"One step ahead of you," Brian countered, moving his bishop to neutralize the threat.

"I thought it was I who was always one step ahead, at least when it comes to stalking."

"No one denies that you are physically skilled, but you must also occupy your mind with the task at hand," Brian replied, his eyes still searching the board. There was silence for about a minute until he finally let out a cry of, "Checkmate!"

Having examined the board one last time, Robert determined that he was indeed pinned down.

"I admit it: you have bested me this time. Even so, Lady Fortune shall not look on you so favorably next time, I'll be bound."

"Can I play now?" I asked the two of them.

"It is really more of a man's game," Robert began, but his vanquisher cut him off.

"As the reigning champion, I would consider it my honor to teach you a bit of the game."

He spent the rest of that time demonstrating to me the possible moves and which ones could be most beneficial. It was too much information to take in during one sitting, but I felt that with practice I could master the game.

"When you are older, this should become simpler for you," Brian told me. "For now, you can continue to practice with us whenever we are playing."

"I hope this rain is going to stop soon. I have a fierce desire to get back on a horse," Robert added.

Even so, the heavens continued to pour forth, and I was back in the study chamber the following three days for more brief lessons. I could not understand why my mother had never thought this a necessary skill for me to learn. It seemed to involve the very kind of thinking that would aid me in the future. More than anything, I enjoyed spending time with the king's lads and wished that the emperor's ambassadors would stay far away from England, at least for a little while longer.

CHAPTER SIX

T he arrival of summer was not so cheerful as it ought to have
been, for while the world seemed alive with joyous possibility, the changing of the seasons was for me a harbinger of doom.
The thought that I should very soon be taken away from the ones
I loved was almost more than I could bear. Even so, I was the
daughter of King Henry of England, and bear it I must.

The abbot of Westminster, Giles Crispin, used to say that the
will of God could be interpreted from the acts of nature, and
that in every storm cloud the hand of the Almighty could be
seen. Thus I received small comfort from the news that a strange
illness had struck the city of London that they named "the holy
fire." It was so called because the victim would first display a high
fever that would force him to bed, along with the most profuse
sweating. After his lying a few days in this manner, the afflicted's
limbs became discolored, in time turning black as soot. Few were
known to have survived this scourge.

The queen determined that the court must be moved to
Windsor, although the palace remained under construction and

was not as lavishly decorated, nor half as large, as the one in Westminster. The king planned to rebuild the castle entirely in stone, but many of the outer buildings were still made of wood and straw. Whenever it rained, the blacksmiths struggled to keep their fires lit. Even the animals seemed bitter at the less-than-perfect conditions. It was therefore a happy day when word reached us that the disease had abated and it was safe to return to our home downriver. It seemed that the Lord had decided to postpone the end of days, though for me it was still a kind of apocalypse, with word now reaching us that the emperor's ambassadors had traveled as far as Bruges and would soon be in sight of the white cliffs.

Although my experience of the outside world was poor, I had perhaps more knowledge of foreigners than the average Englishman on account of the many visitors the queen had received over the years. She was such a great patron of music and dance that she always welcomed the most gifted performers to her court at Westminster. She was particularly fond of the French minstrels, whose songs were filled with such words of love as would melt any woman's heart. Some complained that she was too free with her charity and should pursue a course of greater austerity, but to what more worthy cause would such men have deemed those monies fit to be sent? Better to lend one's gold to those things that build rather than those that destroy.

We received performers from the empire on more than one occasion, whether from Lorraine, Bavaria, Saxony, or even far-off Lombardy. They told great tales of snow-covered mountains rising to touch the sun, forests so dense that they were black as night, and the River Rhine flowing through the vineyard lands, its length dotted with marvelous cities that boasted some of the finest cathedrals in Christendom. They understood but little of our speech. Even so, we were able to converse in broken bits of Latin. Had I not feared the fate by which I was bound,

I think that I would have loved to visit the land of which these men spoke.

The imperial legates landed safely in Dover and proceeded north. King Henry intended to resolve the matter at his Whitsun court, and they evidently did not wish to keep him waiting, for a full day before they were to arrive, their banners were sighted on the southern bank of the river. Some of the flags had the crest of the imperial house, while others portrayed a great black eagle on a field of gold. Ambassadors they may have been, but they seemed to me an invading army.

The party made across the bridge into London town and then rounded the bend toward Westminster. Among those who received them were the king himself; the lord chancellor, the bishop of Salisbury; the Earl of Warwick; the constable Edmund fitz Hugh; and William D'Aubigny, who had lately been made chief butler in the king's household. The leader of these visitors was Adalbert von Saarbrücken, chancellor to Emperor Henry V. It was said that Adalbert had brokered an agreement with the pope in regard to the great controversy—that was, whether the emperor had the right to install bishops according to his choosing. Also in the party was the duke of Swabia, Frederick II, one of the most powerful German lords and a nephew to Henry V, his mother being the emperor's sister. He was still a young man at this time, but the emperor trusted him to represent the interests of the ruling family.

The remainder of the party included Adalbert's younger brother, the Count of Saarbrücken, and several clerks of the imperial court, the chief such man being named Burchard. *Ministeriales* they called them: masters of the law who carried out the business of the empire, enriching both their lord and themselves in the process. Not a few men of less-than-noble birth rose high indeed through such works, which became more essential by the year.

I was due to be presented to the ambassadors at the feast that night. Never before had I made such an appearance, and I was so eager to please that I gained a new respect for the promptings of Lady Beatrice. Long months of preparation had led up to this moment, and I was determined to make the best possible impression on our foreign visitors.

Ah, to be so young again! To possess that mixture of hope and fear that must accompany such an occasion! Across the span of my life, I would be involved in many such occasions, but none would ever be to me as that first moment when I heard my name called out: "Her Royal Highness the Princess Mathilda!"

The doors to the great hall were opened before me, and I saw England's nobility in all its glory. Rather, I would have seen it, had my view not been substantially blocked by the new veil and fillet that both the queen and Lady Beatrice had commanded I wear for the occasion. While my vision was clear enough straight before me, I could make out nothing to the right, to the left, or above without moving my head. I can only imagine what the ladies and gentlemen must have thought upon viewing such a girl, scarcely the height of a man's waist, her head adorned with such ornaments as befitted a woman twice as large.

I took one final breath from the air outside the hall. Then, with the determination of Caesar, I crossed the threshold and strode toward the dais. Members of the crowd were straining to get a glimpse of me, for they had as little experience with me as I had with them. I could barely see the king and queen standing up above the heads of the crowd. Privately I hoped that my determined pace would give off a sense of confidence that I did not truly possess.

Eleanor, my mother's chief attendant, was there to help me up the stairs to the dais. Ever since that sad incident the preceding year, Lady Beatrice had not trusted me to perform any great feat of movement in such attire without falling to the ground. The officials seated at the high table bowed as I walked past. Finally I reached the assigned point next to the king, at which a wood block had been placed, and, taking his hand, I stepped on top of it.

I could now see the full extent of the hall more clearly and became keenly aware of the hundreds of eyes fastened on me. Still holding my right hand, my father stepped back to display me to the imperial ambassadors seated farther down the table.

"*Hier ist meine Tochter!*" he proclaimed, using a line that I am certain he had practiced earlier in the day in order to impress the Germans.

I assumed from the looks of recognition on the visitors' faces that he must have been making some comment about my arrival. The king turned and motioned for all to be seated so that the feast might commence. A chair was now provided so I could sit between my mother and father. As we waited for the food to arrive, each of the ambassadors rose from his position and made his way over to examine the new arrival.

The first man was the tallest, and he was dressed in dark robes, which to my seven-year-old mind gave him a somewhat sinister appearance.

"Lady Mathilda! *Schön sie kennenzulernen!*" the man said.

Seeing the look of confusion on my face, he made an attempt in my own language.

"Lady Mathilda, I am pleased to meet you. Your appearance is most magnificent on this night! I am called Adalbert, chancellor to *Kaiser* Heinrich . . . Emperor Henry."

I nodded to show my understanding. "It is a pleasure to make your acquaintance, Your Excellency."

"*Was hat sie gesagt?*" the younger man standing behind Adalbert said. I assumed from his manner of dress that he must be Frederick, the Duke of Swabia.

"*Sie sagt, sie ist glücklich, uns kennenzulernen,*" the chancellor replied while looking right at me. I assumed that the comment was meant for his companion, as my ignorance of German was already quite plain.

The duke edged closer and examined me as one might eye an oddly shaped carrot at the local market.

"*Sie ist sehr jung, denke ich. Nur ein kleines Mädchen!*"

The queen had left the table for some reason and the king was caught up in another discussion, so I was left feeling rather helpless, unable to understand the strange words spoken by these two men. My only comfort was that the younger one did not seem to understand me either.

"You must forgive the duke," Adalbert explained, taking the empty chair to my left as his partner departed. "He has no experience with the English speech."

"I would like to know what he was saying about me just now," I told him. "I am afraid he does not like me very much."

"No, my lady, he simply told me what an excellent . . . consort you will make for his uncle, the emperor."

This was some relief, though I sensed that the chancellor had not revealed all to me.

"You know the emperor well, sir?"

"*Ja*, very well."

"What is he like? I have heard few reports from anyone who has been in his presence."

"He is just what you would hope, my lady. He is a great German prince like his *Vater*, the late emperor. He has . . . how do you say this? He has a good seat upon a horse, and he is an excellent commander."

"Yes, but what is his character?"

"*Persönlichkeit?*" He paused for a moment to consider his answer. "This is difficult to say in your speech. The emperor is a true Christian, and he is most serious about learning."

"So he is a lover of books?"

"No, not so much as this. He likes to ride or to joust. He must move or he grows weary."

"I see." The emperor sounded very much like the type of ruler my brother William hoped to become.

"Ah, do not worry! My master has many books in his library!" the chancellor responded, seemingly afraid that this was the origin of my concern. "When you come to live in the *Reich*, you will find that we have many things, good things. You will want nothing."

"Thank you, sir." I found it unlikely that I would want for nothing, but I held my tongue.

"If you wish to speak with my fellows, they all know Latin," Adalbert offered.

He could scarcely have designed a better way to shame me if he had tried. I was forced to reply, "I am sorry, Excellency, but I have not yet mastered the Latin tongue."

"No matter. Bruno will take care of this."

I was about to inquire about this Bruno when the queen returned and was eager to recover her seat. Providing apologies in three different languages, Adalbert moved to take his place at the other end of the table, even as the servants began placing the supper in front of us.

"I see you have met the imperial chancellor," Mother whispered to me.

"Yes, he seemed quite eager for me to be impressed by the emperor."

"Little wonder there, since his position likely depends upon the fate of this match," she replied. "The chancellor will do his utmost to use you to his own advantage, my daughter, as any official would. Embrace his advice and stay close to him, but take care, for a day may come when he will ask more of you than you ought to give."

"Yes, Mother."

I do not know how long our discussion would have continued in that vein had the large platter placed in front of me not contained a giant fish with a savage appearance. I moved back from the table as my father pulled out his knife and dug into its flesh with the ardent desire of a man more prone to hunger than the king surely was.

"Mother, the fish is looking at me," I said with concern.

The queen placed her arm around my shoulders and, without a trace of irony, replied, "You had better make yourself accustomed to it, Daughter. Everyone will be looking at you from this day forward."

On the day of Pentecost, on which the Spirit of our Lord descended upon his saints lo those many years ago, King Henry required of the imperial legates that they swear upon the name of the emperor that all the terms of the matrimonial agreement would be upheld, and that the two kingdoms would continue in perpetual peace and fidelity from that day forward. With solemn dignity they made the pledge and sealed it. Then the king sat upon his throne in Westminster Hall, the royal crown was placed on his head, and all who were present stood in awe.

It was agreed that I should depart for my new home after the following Candlemas. You will note that this feast came near my own birth date and would mark the beginning of my ninth year of life. The ambassadors departed for their native land, there to share with their master the news that his bride would be delivered to him as promised.

The age of eight being too early for a proper marriage ceremony, it was decided that the wedding must take place after I had attained the age of twelve, by which point I should be a full woman. Some wondered at the emperor's willingness to endure such a wait before undertaking the continuation of his dynasty, but others argued that his chief aim was to gain my dowry and make use of it in his dispute with Pope Paschal. Indeed, some whispered that King Henry had driven a bad bargain, for the taxes that he would now be forced to levy upon his subjects were such that they would surely result in rebellion. "Who is this emperor of the Romans that he should receive both the king's first-born daughter and the wealth of England in exchange for little of value?" they would complain. But the will of the king ruled all, and he was intent on ensuring the alliance.

Through all of this, I watched and waited. There was news from the east that the imperial army had been forced to retreat from its advance against the Poles, who had brought great torment to the peoples of Pomerania and Bohemia. This was a setback not only for the dispute in Bohemia, but also for the defense of that kingdom against Hungary, which had for its ally the same Polish king, Bołeslaw, wicked man that he was.

The tales of Bołeslaw's barbarous actions were well known: how he would cause enemy troops to be hung by the feet for days on end with their entrails cut off and fed to the dogs, how he did not shrink from using the children of his subjects as shields against the German advance, and how he'd gouged out the eyes of his own brother, Zbigniew, in his lust for power. Less like a Christian and more like a pagan, my mother thought him, though she still treasured the bear pelt that he had sent to her some years earlier.

It seemed that the empire was beset from all sides, but with the strength of this new English alliance, the fortunes of the young Emperor Henry could only improve, or so we hoped. When autumn arrived, the king decided that I should attend my first royal council when he made his court in the city of Nottingham. Upon arriving in the land of the Germans, I would be forced to act as mediator on my husband's behalf, overseeing grants of royal charters and matters at the imperial court. For such work I must be readied in advance.

We set out to the north in the first week of October, making our way along the road first to Saint Albans, where we spent the night on a goodly estate belonging to one of the local barons; I cannot remember which one. The next two nights we made camp along the path while the men sought game in the nearby woodlands. I had traveled only a little in my young life, but I made my best attempt to adjust to this continual motion, being planted one evening and removed the following morn. I was thankful at least that my mother the queen had decided to make the journey along with us.

On the third day, we glimpsed the walls of Northampton Castle rising above the River Nene, illuminated by the autumn sunshine. It had been built by order of my grandfather, King William, who had granted the lands to Simon de Senlis and made him the first Earl of Northampton. The earl was a great builder and deeply religious. Under his patronage the castle walls and those surrounding the town were raised, along with the new keep within the castle bailey. He also oversaw the creation of the Holy Sepulcher church in Northampton town—said to be a near copy of the one in Jerusalem—and the Priory of Saint Andrew.

Even so, the earl's greatest accomplishment was his highly profitable marriage to Maud, the Countess of Huntingdon, heir to the earldom of that northern land. When they were joined in wedlock, Simon de Senlis's possessions in Northamptonshire were joined with those in Huntingdon to form a territory exceeding that of most of the baronage. It was rumored that the earl had first sought after the countess's mother, Judith, for his bride, but was altogether more pleased to receive such a young beauty with which to build his dynasty.

As for the castle, it was surrounded by extensive dikes and ringed by a fence of wood pales almost three times the height of a man. The watchmen circled the interior on a scaffold, from which they must have received a superior view of the surrounding country. We entered through the north gate and made our way to the inner bailey, where the earl and his entire household had assembled to greet us. I watched through the carriage window as the king, the queen, Bishop Roger of Salisbury, the Earl of Surrey, and the king's lads moved to greet the rest of the officials in attendance. I might have been content to sit there for hours, but the door was now opened by one of the king's grooms, who bid me alight.

I did as I was asked, taking great care not to slip. I had been allowed on this occasion to forgo the traditional wimple in exchange for a gold diadem. The women attending me had been making their best efforts throughout the day's journey to perform this feat of adornment, while suffering from such motion as would send tremors through the carriage. More than one ill-timed pull of my hair produced a squeal. With my attendants in train, I was directed toward the Countess of Huntingdon for the usual introduction.

"Lady Mathilda, allow me to bid you welcome to Northampton Castle! We are honored to receive the king and his beloved daughter."

"And may I thank you, Countess, for your hospitality and great generosity," I replied, using the words I had learned beforehand.

The countess began to inquire as to the nature of our travel from Westminster, whether the road was in good condition for this time of year, and on what day we would make our departure for Nottingham, when a man whom I had not yet noticed interrupted us.

"Well, if it isn't my wee niece!"

"Uncle David!" I cried. "I didn't know you would be here!"

"But of course! When I heard the king was on progress in the North, I made haste to meet him. The English court is a far sight better than the Scottish one, and the welcome I receive is better as well." He then added in a low tone, "You must never tell anyone that I said this, but the food at the English court is superior to anything we receive up yonder. I suppose I should have come just for these delights, had there been no other reason."

Having knelt to embrace me, he now stood up and turned to face our hostess, who was standing patiently to the side.

"Apologies, Countess," he said with a bow of his head. "It was wrong of me to interrupt your conversation."

The look on her face was hard to read. "I have heard much about you, David, prince of Scotland. They say you are often with King Henry."

"As often as I can be, though I have my own affairs to attend to in the North."

"I have heard tell about that as well."

"I do not doubt that you have, Countess, but why ruin such a grand occasion by discussing matters of state?"

"You know that I am heir to my father's lands in Huntingdon," she said, her tone becoming more serious. "Rumor has it that you seek to build a kingdom for yourself in the marches of Scotland, and perhaps in England as well. You must know that I will not stand idly by the wayside should you threaten my ancestral lands."

For a moment the prince and countess simply stared at each other. It seemed that each one was straining to see within the mind of the other and determine how best to win this battle of wits. He was of higher rank than she, but her superior age seemed to set them on equal footing. Finally my uncle smiled and reached out to grasp the countess's hand. He raised it to his lips and then looked her in the eye as he gently kissed it.

"My lady, I doubt that any man could take something of yours which you did not willingly give. Have no fear!"

Something in the countess's face seemed to soften, and had the earl and the king not stepped forward at that moment to bid us all enter the hall, I suspect that the two of them could have carried on staring at each other for a good while longer.

Certainly they had forgotten my presence long before the conversation ended.

We spent but two days at Northampton Castle before proceeding north to the seat of the Earl of Leicester, Robert de Beaumont, which was next to the River Soar. We stayed a few nights there as the train of nobles accompanying the king continued to grow, among them the Earl of Warwick, uterine brother of the Earl of Leicester. The Earl of Surrey, William de Warenne, had already traveled with us from Westminster, while the Earl of Northampton had joined us only in the past few days. All made ready now for the final push toward Nottingham.

If the number of earls in this tale overwhelms you, Daughter, allow me to assure you that most of them will play little role in the remainder of our tale, for by the time I had cause to visit the castles of earls again, a new generation had arisen to supplant the companions of William the Conqueror.

We approached the River Trent upon the ides of October. I still remember the feeling of that autumn day as the cool wind brushed against our faces and seemed to sink through the layers of cloth and skin to our very bones. For the first time, the beaver furs were brought out to increase our comfort. The ladies wrapped a mantle around my shoulders and bid me be at ease, for we were almost there. I had never before traveled so far, and I found myself longing for the sight of Nottingham Castle, where a hearty fire would greet me. I closed my eyes and leaned my head against one of the pillows in the carriage, my imagination conjuring thoughts of hot cider and stew, fresh venison, and the last of the season's berries.

We made our crossing at the confluence of the waters, where the River Leen joins the River Trent. The former is little but a channel in comparison to the latter, for only small craft may pass through its waters. We continued our path along the Leen until we saw the cliffs rising up from its banks. On top of them the stone motte of Nottingham Castle rose high, encircled by its wood fortifications.

"The bailey entrance is around the other side," the bishop of Salisbury could be heard saying to the king. "We had best approach from that direction, by way of the town."

Having no reason to quarrel, King Henry and his men led the company along the main road that stretched through the town and up to the castle gate. As we passed, men quit their business and rushed out to catch a glimpse of the king in all his glory. Housewives bent out of windows on the right and the left to offer their regards, and children ran beside the horses, which more than doubled them in height. Every man, woman, and child cried out, "Long live King Henry! Long live Queen Mathilda!"

We soon reached the castle gates, which were opened with great pomp and not a little effort by the servants of Sir William Peverel, lord of Nottingham Castle. The company poured into the lower ward, and those on horseback alighted. The carriages were brought round so that they might be unpacked, and I was ushered to the ground by my attendants. Such a great number of people were there! It seemed that no gentleman or lady of the king's court had seen fit to stay at home. I was now brought to stand beside my parents as Lord and Lady Peverel received them.

"King Henry, Queen Mathilda—I bid you welcome to Nottingham. We have eagerly anticipated your arrival. Should you have the slightest need, my household stands ready to aid you, in order that your stay here may be as pleasant as possible. My home is your home."

"Thank you, Peverel, for your hospitality," the king replied.

"And this must be the lady Peverel, Adelina," my mother said.

"The very same," Sir William replied as his wife curtsied. "Allow me to also introduce my son, William." A man who appeared to be near thirty years of age stepped forward and made his bow. "He is fully trained for the knighthood now, and will do good service for the House of Normandy."

"Excellent," said the king, eyeing this prospect. "It is to you that the Honor of Peverel must fall, then. I trust you will safeguard it as well as your father has done these many years."

"I will do my utmost to retain its glory," the younger Peverel answered.

"Robert! Brian!" the king called out. "Come over here!"

The king's lads approached and stood to the right of my father, on the opposite side from myself.

"Sir William," the king resumed, "I wish to make use of the forests nearby. My companions and I have felt sorely the absence of decent game these past few days. I believe that your woods are far better stocked than those we have seen up to this point."

"It is as you say, Your Highness," Peverel the elder replied. "But my son is now the best guide that you might wish for on such a journey."

"It's settled, then: the lot of us will be off to the forest, there to have such adventures as will serve for the benefit of our manhood. I have longed for some real sport," my father concluded. "On the morrow, you shall find me at the break of dawn in this very place awaiting our departure." He paused for a moment and smelled the air, as a hound might when tracking a scent. "Yes, I do believe we shall meet with good luck here!"

"And we shall enjoy the peace and quiet," the queen said softly.

The king's council met two days later, after there had been time to bag such beasts as the king and his men pleased. This was the moment for which I had been brought all this way. With all the great lords of the land present, I stood beside my father as he signed a succession of charters for the granting of royal demesne to sundry individuals. As the future queen of the Romans, I made my mark beside his own.

There was much talk of matters across the Channel and what form the king's next advance against the French might take. Some wished to know the fate of the king's brother Robert, my uncle, who remained in prison after his pointless betrayal of a few years earlier, when he had risen against his rightful king.

"And what of your nephew, William Clito? Does he remain in the custody of the Count of Arques?" the Earl of Leicester asked.

"Indeed he does," the king replied, "though I believe that the last of Duke Robert's supporters may seek to spring him from that particular jail when the time is ripe. As you all know, the count is married into my brother's family and remains a firm supporter of that lost cause. I do not doubt that at some point he will seek to breathe new life into the old rebellion."

"Then we had best take charge of the boy before it is too late and transfer the element of control to ourselves," said Roger of Salisbury. "We cannot allow this danger to fester and feed the hopes of those who seek to do harm to Your Grace."

The Earl of Warwick now offered his opinion. "Yet there are those who already find fault in the handling of the boy's father, and to handle the son in such a manner would attract scorn beyond our own lands, I fear."

The conversation continued thus until the setting of the sun, at which point I was excused to make preparations for the feast that night. A truly marvelous occasion it was, with all the attendants in their finest apparel. Admittedly, the hall at Nottingham Castle was nowhere near as grand as the one at Westminster or Windsor. Yet on that particular eve it shone so brightly that even the residents of Constantinople would have been forced to admit its magnificence.

"Fantastic, isn't it?"

I looked to my right to see Robert sitting there with a goblet in hand. He was evidently taking a brief rest from the night's festivities. I had seen him dance with no fewer than five women already, and despite the cooler air, there were beads of sweat on his forehead and he was breathing deeply.

"I shall miss you, brother Robert, when I go across the sea," I told him.

"And I shall miss you too, Maud, as will Brian. You know we both favor you."

"Do you think we shall ever be in each other's company again?"

"We may yet, Sister. We may. Until then, let us always remember one another. Do you still have the stone of amber that Brian gave to you?"

"I carry it with me always," I replied, and it was the truth, for I kept it in a small satchel upon my person. I suddenly felt a tinge of fear and said to him, "When the time comes, will you say farewell to him for me? I think I should be afraid to speak with him again."

"Why is that?" he asked. "You have no difficulty conversing with me. Why should you feel so around him? Did we not enjoy many pleasant summer days together? Did he not show you brotherly kindness?"

"Yes, of course." I was not sure how to say what I was feeling. Finally I said, "I cannot explain it to you, but I would be very glad if you should do as I request."

"If you wish it, then certainly I shall," he replied.

I was eager to change the subject and made the first observation about the evening's proceedings that came to mind.

"Uncle David is dancing with the Earl of Northampton's wife. That is interesting—I did not think they cared for each other."

I turned toward Robert and was surprised to see him smiling in a manner that implied that he knew something more about the subject but was afraid to share it.

"What is it? Did Father force him to dance with her? Did he have a poor night at dice?"

"Nothing so honorable," Robert answered. "Can you keep a secret, Maud?"

"Yes, and anyway I am about to bid my final farewell, so no one will hear what I have to say."

He leaned close and whispered in my ear, "Uncle David has a passion for her, more so than I have seen in him with any other woman before. Were she not shackled to the old earl, I suspect he would have attempted to induce her into matrimony. Of course, the prince must covet her ancestral lands, but I do not think the lady cares about that as much as she lets on. She cannot seem to keep her eyes off him . . . or her hands."

I was appalled to hear my brother speak thus. "But she is a married woman! Surely you are wrong. I know my uncle is an honorable man. Perhaps he merely regards her from a distance and seeks to win her favor by performing mighty deeds. The poets often speak of such love."

"So they do, but believe me when I say that a man may be honorable in all other things, but the female sex is another matter entirely." He paused for a moment, then said, "The last night we were at Northampton Castle, I awoke to find that Prince David was absent from his bed. I had my suspicions about where he might have gone, but it was only confirmed to me by one of the servants the following morning: he spent the night in the lady's chambers."

"That is no way for a man to behave," I said, not wanting to accept what I heard. "I wish to God there was some mistake in what you say. Do you think that these rumors shall ever become public knowledge?"

"That is the danger, Maud, so you must promise me that you will never speak a word of this to a single soul."

"I promise, unless someone should ask me directly, in which case I would have no choice but to be honest."

"Then perhaps it is good that you are going to Germany after all, for no one there speaks our language." He laughed as he said it, but I still felt troubled.

"I think it is time that I went to bed," I responded and rose to make my way back toward the ladies, at least one of whom would be forced to break away from the festivities long enough to help me out of my gown. As I turned to go, Prince David happened to be standing in my path, and he moved to greet me. I suspect he must have been quite confused upon witnessing me turn my face away and continue walking without uttering a word.

CHAPTER SEVEN

February 1165
Rouen, Normandy

It is early morning, and outside my window a goldfinch is perched on a nearby branch, casting its small eyes here and there across the yard. Such a creature could be easily overlooked until one catches a glimpse of its red face and yellow wings, which set it apart from the common sparrows known only to God. The slightest movement of my hand attracts its attention, and for one brief moment it turns to examine my own feeble frame, which age has now stripped of what small beauty it once possessed.

"How fine you are," I whisper.

A sudden noise breaks the spell. It is Adela come with her usual morning gift: one glass of fresh milk, another of hot water, and a plate with some bread. As she sets this all down on the small table beside me, I notice that she has accompanied this small offering not only with the usual sample from the buttery, but also with some honey that she received from Jean, the beekeeper.

"Good morning, my lady," she greets me in her usual comforting voice. "I didn't know if you would be awake so early this morning." Immediately she begins moving about the room, arranging objects as necessary, replacing the spent candles with new ones, and starting the fire.

"I am not sure why that should surprise you," I reply. "It is my usual manner these days. Even if I wished to sleep until the rising of the sun, I doubt that my body would allow it. In any case, I like to join the monks for Lauds in the morning."

"Yes, the archdeacon tells me you have taken to walking to the sanctuary barefoot and in your robes, carrying your own candle. I think you ought not be out so early."

"If there is anyone who ought not to be out at such an hour, it is you, Adela. You have a family to attend to. I wonder what those poor boys must be thinking with their mother always slipping out before the break of dawn."

"My 'poor boys,' as you pronounce them, shall survive as they always do," she tells me with a knowing smile. "Have you been writing again? There is no need for that, or is Father Lawrence failing in his duties as your clerk?"

"Certainly not! He should come by within the hour to begin again. I have merely been scribbling a few lines before his arrival. There is no need for concern. I take pleasure in it, and I am not yet so decrepit as to suffer from such small labor."

"As you wish," she responds, having enticed the logs into a small blaze. "Now, if the archdeacon is coming, we must get you properly clothed."

As she removes the articles from my wardrobe, I glance back through the window. I know that I am fortunate to be so wonderfully placed. The guest rooms here at the monastery of Notre-Dame-du-Pré provide a perfect view across the Seine. In the distance I see the green hills, and before me the town walls of Rouen rising up next to the river. To the right is the Mont du

Sainte Catherine, upon which sits the nunnery that once housed my own Adela, if only for a short while.

At the southeast corner of the city, the great residence of the Norman dukes rises in splendor, the tower providing a handsome view. Incidentally, this was also the spot where my father once sent the traitor Conrad to his death, forcing him headlong onto the street below. That is quite a story, Daughter, but perhaps one for another day. Farther inside the walls is the Priory of Saint Gervais, where my grandfather William breathed his last, and the monastery of Saint Ouen. Towering above them all is the cathedral. As always, it arrests my gaze, its bright stones shining in the morning sunlight. I have not set foot within those walls for months, not since . . .

"My lady?"

Ah, Adela has caught me lost in thought once again. Here she stands directly beside me, waiting to assist.

"I am sorry, Adela. I was just gazing at the cathedral. It looks truly wondrous this morning."

"You were thinking about him again, weren't you?"

I pause to decide how to respond. Should I feign ignorance or admit that I was thinking of my son William, who lies buried in the very cathedral of which we now speak? The grief of his loss still plagues me—not so much the fact of it as the manner in which it happened. But should I admit this and expose myself to my friend's inquisition?

"I was thinking that it is bound to be quite cold again today. I had best put on something a bit warmer."

A slight frown shows upon her face that would be undetectable to most but is clearly visible to one who has studied her behavior these many years. She then smiles and moves to exchange the garments. Upon her return I request to be allowed to continue my preparations in solitude. She agrees and leaves me to adorn myself. As soon as the door is shut, I find myself repeating, "Time . . . time . . . time . . ."

On the nones of February, in the year of our Lord 1110, the long days of waiting finally came to an end, for it was time at last to depart for that land across the sea. An endless line of chests contained all that was necessary for a young bride setting out into the world. One was filled exclusively with linens of cloth, another with furs, and still another with precious silks. A smaller vessel contained the glistening jewels fit for a queen. At my mother's request, one chest was set aside solely for works of literature. Naturally, we needed several carts to hold the endless provisions necessary for such a journey: food enough to satisfy a small army, a supply of parchment and ink, an extensive array of healing herbs and cleansing drafts, and weapons fit for such an occasion.

Our party was to be led by the legate Burchard, a clerk in the imperial chapel who had arrived in Westminster a few weeks earlier. A small retinue of knights and *ministeriales* had accompanied him to England and would now join us for the return. A much larger contingent of Normans would later join our company, particularly once the rumor spread that any knights who traveled with the princess were likely to receive the emperor's beneficence for delivering unto him such a treasure. Chief among these was Roger de Clare, who, along with his brother, Gilbert fitz Richard de Clare, was heir of that great Norman lord who fought beside William I at Hastings and was rewarded with lands throughout England to accompany those across the Channel. The younger son, Gilbert, had lately received the lordship of Cardigan from King Henry, and I believe that his brother must have sensed that this was the time to achieve his own manner of distinction.

You must not ask me to remember the names of all those other knights who were with us upon that journey, whether they were Alain or Bertrand or some other such person. The span of years has swept such things from my memory. However, I shall never forget the best of those knights, Drogo, who was to become my chief guardian and protector through many dangers. He too was with us when we set out from Westminster.

I would be remiss if I did not mention Henry, archdeacon within the See of Winchester, who oversaw the Norman clerks and attended to the spiritual needs of all persons in the party. He joined us at the command of the king, who had made his acquaintance on several occasions and believed him to be a most upstanding gentleman. As fate would have it, the archdeacon was able to present himself in the best possible light to all manner of men. I wondered if he had not learned something of this from Bishop Roger of Salisbury. This Henry would later become bishop of Verdun.

That, my daughter, is a full accounting of the individuals in our company, but for the two maids who attended to my every need. Small comfort they provided to my soul in those hours, for I was filled with terror. I remember well how I lay awake in my bedchamber pondering the coming day, knowing for certain that I should never again pass the night in the same room as my brother, William, whose loud breathing no longer annoyed me.

Never before had the morning light seemed so unkind as it did that day. Never had the ordinary preparations taken on such an awful significance. I felt as if I were living in a dream, my body performing the actions my mind commanded, but my spirit unable to grasp that this was truly the last time I should be dressed by Lady Beatrice, walk these halls, and feel these embraces. Despite my dearest hope to be granted a reprieve, the moment had arrived, and as the palace doors opened before me, revealing the farewell spectacle I had so long dreaded, I was struck with a fear that threatened to undo me.

Although it was uncommon on such occasions, the queen was determined to take me by the hand and lead me out into the outer ward herself. We didn't speak as my mother approached and accepted me from Lady Beatrice, placing my hand within her own and offering me a smile that might have strengthened me under different circumstances. It was a cold winter day, and I was wrapped from head to toe in heavy garments. Since departing my bed that morning, I had become aware of a strange beating of my heart that grew stronger with every step. Now I felt that in spite of the chill in the air, my body was hot as burning coals and under intense strain. We had not taken ten steps past the threshold when I found it necessary to halt. The path toward the open carriage seemed eternal.

"Are you unwell, my love?" the queen asked, bending over to meet my gaze.

A thousand responses rushed through my mind, but I was unable to make a sound except to utter, "I feel hot."

As my legs began to quiver, my mother grasped me with both her arms so as to hold me still. I could see the great lords of England assembled before me: the Earls of Warwick and Suffolk, Bishop Roger of Salisbury, Brother Robert, Brian fitz Count, and all the other men of court and the king's household. At the center of my vision was King Henry himself and William beside him. Every eye was fixed upon me, and I felt an intense pressure to perform my duty, but I could not cause the fire to cease.

"Maud, look at me."

The command distracted me for a moment, and I did as the queen requested.

"Do you have the strength to walk?"

"I hardly know."

"You are overwhelmed, I think. Rest for a moment."

They were all forced to wait as I recovered my balance. I breathed slowly, and the cold air seemed to temper the fire. Somewhere deep inside, a force greater than fear was gaining ground: the desire not to bring shame upon my family and myself. Finally I was able to say in all honesty, "I am ready. We can continue."

I walked under my own power toward the carriage, stopping to bid farewell to a few officials. There were smiles from both Brian and Robert, some tears from the ladies of the queen's household—who seemed to like me now despite all my bad behavior—nods of blessing from several old men whom I had seen only in passing, and a deep bow from the bishop of Salisbury. Upon reaching William, I was somewhat surprised to see that his eyes too were filled with tears. Despite all our disputes, he must have sensed as I did that there was a bond between us, which distance would now seek to sever.

"I will miss you, Sister," he said with some great effort.

"And I you, William, more than I can say."

Although it was not altogether seemly, I embraced him for a brief moment. It seemed to be too much for the queen, who let loose the tears she had been holding back until that point. This caused the king to become most impatient.

"Why all the tears? This is a great occasion!" he protested, evidently displeased that a flood of human emotion was diminishing his moment of personal triumph. Perhaps he even feared that the emperor's men would gain the wrong impression from all this sadness.

"Come, Daughter," he said in a somewhat kinder voice.

As he led me up to the carriage, the queen stopped him and hugged me one last time. She kissed me and held my face between her hands, bringing it close to her own.

"Maud, remember the words of Saint Paul: 'Let us keep the profession of our hope, without wavering, for he is faithful that promised . . . The just shall live by faith.'"

"Mother . . . ," I said, but it was too late, for the king had pulled me once again into his own power, and he lifted me inside the carriage and closed the door. I attempted to look again upon those I loved, but my father seemed intent upon saving this last moment for himself and positioned his body so as to command my attention.

"Remember this, Maud: you must always strive your hardest, for us and for England. Godspeed!"

Enveloped in the relative darkness of the carriage, I could hear the grooms making final preparations and the driver yelling at the horses to begin their long march. The crowd cheered, but I dared not pull back the curtain to glimpse their faces. The tears were once again trailing down my small face, and I cared not that I gasped for breath, or that my body writhed with the pain of separation. I lay my head upon one of the pillows and wept for what must have been an hour before finally succumbing to weariness. I was keenly aware of what lay before me. "I am alone," I whispered to myself. "At last, I am truly alone."

I did not speak a word to anyone the rest of that day—not when the company stopped to rest, not when we ceased travel for the night in Rochester, not throughout the lavish supper that I hardly touched, and not when the ladies put me to bed. I responded to their instructions and answered through slight nods of the head, but was silent.

"She must miss them dreadfully, poor thing," one of them said to the other once they believed I was asleep. "A little slumber should set her right."

Oh, how they overlooked my capacity for despair! I proved myself quite able to remain mute even as we pressed on to Faversham and Canterbury. I mumbled a few words at the Holy Mass and accepted the host with fervor, but I admit that it was not the suffering of my blessed Savior that occupied my mind. Rather, my own tribulations took hold of every thought and maintained the bitterness of spirit that grew with each passing hour.

"Sooner or later, you will have to eat something," one of the women said. "You have a long journey until we reach your betrothed, and I am sure he has no wish to see you nigh unto death."

Little did they know how I could feed on the bread of loneliness, certain of my own righteousness and the iniquity of a world that would send young girls to live among the wolves. So I remained as silent as Zecharias, even as our trail led us along the River Dour toward the great port of Dover. It seems strange now to think that before this time, I had never beheld the sea. The world of my youth, lively as I believed it to be at the time, was limited to a rather small space. What I possessed in determination I lacked in experience, but that would soon change.

On account of the pleasant weather that day, the curtains on the carriage were pulled back, and I could see the cliffs rising on either side and feel the sea air upon my face. The town itself lies at the mouth of the Dour, near the harbor. Somewhere in that harbor was a ship ready for my own voyage, a prospect that filled me with dread. Though I knew that the king had sailed safely across the Channel many times, I was nevertheless troubled by the stories of men with a different fate, who were swallowed by the waters and never seen again.

Rather than pressing all the way to the harbor, our company climbed the hill on which sat Dover Castle, a perfectly placed fortress if ever there was one. Sadly, it was not so presentable in those days as it is now. The old Saxon fortress had suffered much damage when King William placed it under siege. Little survived but the chapel of Saint Mary and the remains of the old Roman *pharos*, whose twin sat upon the western hill. The new fortifications were made from wood, as was usual at that time, though there were a few hastily built rooms of stone that would be our refuge for the night.

I was given leave to move about the grounds—"But no farther than the church!"—and seized the opportunity to glimpse the sea for myself. Walking toward the cliff's edge, I saw before me the endless span of water. So massive was it that the town and harbor seemed minute in the face of such grandeur. Glancing toward the right, I could see the exposed white face of the cliffs and determined that they were every bit as magnificent as the tales of legend. I sat down on a nearby rock and stared in wonder. What secrets lay within those watery depths? Fish, certainly, and forests of weeds, along with the remains of sunken vessels and their wares, but this was not what worried me. I had often heard tales of great monsters of the sea, which would lie in wait for years before rising to the surface with a fury to feed upon doomed souls. As I watched I feared to see some leviathan springing up from its dark cage, but the only movement was of the endless waves pushing toward the shore.

I pulled my coverings tighter around me as the wind blew. My ears were beginning to ache from the cold, and I was considering turning back when I realized I was no longer alone. It was the knight Drogo who approached me, whom I recognized by his extraordinary height, and he carried a bound volume in his left hand. As he neared, I could see that it was the *bestiarum* given to me by my uncle David.

"Lady Mathilda," he said with a bow, "I took the liberty of retrieving this from the chest of books sent by the queen. I have noticed you often examining it in the past. I thought it might bring you some cheer."

This was so unforeseen that my former thoughts seemed to flee, as did my habit of silence.

"Thank you, I am much obliged to you, Drogo."

I accepted the volume from him and immediately opened it to examine the familiar drawings. I then noticed that the knight still stood there. I looked up, thinking that he had something else to say, but he remained mute. It was much like our earlier encounter in the king's presence, when he had been uncertain how to proceed in the presence of royalty.

"Was there something else?" I asked, hoping that I might draw out his thoughts and thus bring a quicker end to the conversation.

"No, my lady. That is . . . yes. May I be permitted to sit next to you?"

The request was so earnest that I had little choice but to answer him in the affirmative, though I had no sense of where our discussion was headed. Fortunately, the stone was large enough to hold more than one person. Drogo sat beside me and bent forward slightly, clasping his hands together and pondering his words.

"Forgive me, my lady, but you have been slightly melancholy since we left Westminster, and I wondered if you were in any discomfort, and if you were in such discomfort, if there was anything I might do to relieve you in your present situation. That is, if some action on my part might help to ease you along your journey."

I do not know why I smiled, whether I was once again touched by his earnest nature, amused by his overly positive description of my current condition as "slightly melancholy," or simply glad to see that he was finally able to put forth his request, even if it was somewhat drawn out.

"I thank you for your pains, sir, but I am merely sad to leave my home and a bit apprehensive about what lies ahead."

He nodded slowly but did not immediately reply. We both paused to look out toward the sea and listen to the breaking waves. The sun was once again visible from behind the clouds, and things seemed more pleasant than they had a few moments earlier.

"Do you like animals, then?" he asked.

"Why, yes! I do, very much."

"That seems like an excellent book for someone who loves animals."

"Yes, it was a gift from my uncle. It was made by the monks at Lindisfarne."

"Do you mean your uncle Prince David of Scotland?"

"Yes."

"Ah." He let out a slight laugh. "I cannot remember any of my uncles or other distant relations giving me so much as a pebble, but then again, none of them were of particularly high rank."

"But you are a knight of the king's household, so surely you must come from a good family."

"Oh, to me they were the best family one could have, but none of them was very rich in this world until my father came to this country and made a name for himself."

"I am sure he must be very proud of you," I offered.

"I wouldn't know. He passed from this world long before I completed my training. It was he who first advised me to take up this profession. For myself, I think I might have been happy in the Church, but I soon saw the benefits of this life and the adventures it holds. After all, not every man can say that he has conversed with royalty."

He turned and looked into the distance, his eyes straining to see something that I could only guess at.

"My eyes are not as sharp as they used to be. Can you see land in the distance?"

"Land?"

"Yes, they say that you can see the distant coast from here on a clear day, but I fear there are too many clouds at present."

I too strained my eyes, looking to see if I might catch a glimpse of a distant tower staring back, but there was nothing.

"I cannot see it either."

"What a shame!" he replied. "I suppose we will just have to wait until after we raise anchor and sail off to the South."

"Where will we make port?"

"At Boulogne in Flanders. It is a short journey, and I am sure you will be well received."

"Boulogne? I was not aware that we would land there. I thought we might put in at Calais."

"That is the shorter route, to be sure, but the Count of Boulogne and his wife were keen to receive us, from what I hear."

I then remembered where I had heard about Boulogne in the past. "The countess is my mother's sister, but I have never met her. They spent many years together in their youth living within the convent."

"Yes, Mary of Scotland, who is now Countess Mary of Boulogne. You will be able to meet her, as well as her daughter Mathilda, who must be a few years younger than yourself."

The prospect of seeing these relatives for the first time interested me. I had imagined the Continent to be completely foreign, but perhaps I was wrong.

The church bell rang and roused the knight from his thoughts. He stood up and had begun to take his leave when I stopped him.

"Drogo?"

"Yes, Lady Mathilda?"

"Thank you for the book. It was kind of you to find it for me."

"It was nothing. I was glad to do it."

As he made off toward the hall, I felt a new chill and determined that I too must return. Taking one last glance toward the sea, I walked back past the church and the tower, and was greeted upon my arrival by my two ladies, whose exclamations of "Where have you been?" fell on deaf ears as I felt for the first time in days something like hope.

The sky was clear for the next day's voyage, and a favorable wind put us in Boulogne by afternoon. At first I found the experience pleasant, but I soon fell victim to that sickness that so often plagues seamen, and I longed to once again set foot upon solid ground. The sight of the belfry of Boulogne was welcome indeed. Upon our dropping anchor, the servants began bringing the goods to shore in earnest. Not only the chests that had traveled with us from Westminster, but also the wares of all the English merchants who had made the journey as well. From where I stood, I had a clear view of the town. There were several shops and market stalls near the port, beyond which I could see the city walls.

One of the sailors must have noticed my interest, for he said to me, "It was an old Roman fortress, back when they mounted their invasions into Britain. The count lives within the ancient walls, but the town has grown beyond those bounds."

"So we are not to be received here at the pier?"

"No, my lady. The count and countess await your arrival at the castle."

Thus it was that I was removed from the boat along with my possessions and placed into the carriage that would bear me up to the city. I could see the walls before us, a mixture of gray and reddish stones piled one upon the other, with a succession of towers at regular intervals. They were not so tall as the ones in London and were worn by many long years. Nevertheless these walls would be a sufficient obstacle to any invading army. And to think that they were set down a thousand years before the present time!

The tall wood gates swung open before us and we entered into the lower city, moving through the square and onto the main thoroughfare, upon which sat the manor house of the Count of Boulogne, Eustace III. Arriving within the close, I made my first study of the noble family, the count and countess and their young daughter, Mathilda. My primary desire was to determine if I noticed any resemblance between the Countess Mary and her sister, who was my own mother.

The countess appeared a bit shorter than the queen. She wore a blue gown and matching shawl, with a long white veil in the Frankish style. She possessed the same fair complexion as her sister, though whether the countess's hair was of the same hue, I could not determine. The daughter was a slight thing, a bit overwhelmed by her own garments. I noted that neither of them had a smile on her face, though this may have been on account of the winter cold.

Count Eustace, in contrast, was a sturdy man, no doubt hardened by the many dangers he'd endured in the Holy Land with his brothers, Godfrey of Bouillon and Baldwin of Boulogne. It was said that the brothers fought valiantly upon the plains of Palestine, reclaiming the land of the apostles for Christendom and forcing out the Saracens. When the younger brother, Godfrey, became protector of the Holy Sepulcher—not king, for he refused to take a crown of gold where Christ had worn a crown of thorns—Eustace returned home to his seat in Boulogne with all the glory accorded to a warrior of his stature.

As I settled in for the evening, the countess and her daughter requested a private audience with me, and I made haste to arrive at the stated time. I found the room far smaller than the queen's chamber at the Palace of Westminster, though it was clear that the countess had attempted to compensate for this with much adornment. I also could not help but notice that, far from following the manner of feminine gentility, she had clearly made a concerted effort to impress anyone who entered. The tapestries bore not the pastoral and hunting themes my mother favored, but rather images of the history and victorious battles of the House of Boulogne. On each of the two longer walls hung a tapestry stretching the full length. One portrayed battles in the Holy Land, ending in the seizure of Jerusalem and the coronation of the count's brother. The other was of the conquest of Britain by my grandfather, King William. The count's own father, Eustace II of Boulogne, had been among William's companions at Hastings.

It is worth noting, Daughter, that the accounts surrounding Count Eustace's participation in this battle greatly varied. The one favored by the House of Boulogne portrayed him with all noble characteristics, persevering against strong odds and lending his own horse to Duke William when the other man's steed fell. However, the more common account, and indeed the one most likely true, was that Count Eustace, alarmed at the strength of Harold Godwinson's forces, sought to retreat and took up the standard once again only when Duke William witnessed his cowardice and threatened him with all manner of punishments should he fail to return to the line. It is an established fact that after this battle, the elder Count Eustace supported a rebellion of the men of Kent against their rightful king, though he escaped from this failure with a victor's rewards.

On the far wall was displayed a shield with the arms of both the House of Flanders and the House of Reginar, from which the counts of Boulogne descended. The black and golden lions formed a magnificent setting as Princess Mary of Scotland, now Countess of Boulogne, stepped forward to wish me well.

"My own niece, Mathilda, come sit and tell us of your journey."

She motioned toward two chairs by the hearth. I was moving toward the nearer of the two when the young Mathilda, who could not have been more than five years old, sat down upon that very spot, her legs so short that they hung in the air rather than resting upon the floor.

"Mathilda!" the countess called out, and I immediately turned toward her, only to recognize that the call was directed toward her daughter rather than myself. "Go sit next to the other ladies."

"It's too cold!" the girl replied, and before her mother could speak reason, she launched into teary protestations of the injustice of this request. She scorned the countess's calls for silence. I presumed that some harsh punishment was in store for my cousin, but instead the countess made a hasty retreat.

"Very well, very well! Maria, please fetch another chair for our niece."

The seat was duly fetched and placed slightly farther from the fire than the one filled by the young Mathilda, whose victory seemed to have brought about a sudden change of mood, as she now grinned with pleasure. "Had I ever behaved in such a manner, I should have been made to regret it," I thought.

"Mathilda, my sister-daughter, how do you find Boulogne?" the countess asked, having taken her seat directly across from me.

"I like it very much. It seems a pleasant city and well placed along the coast."

This was the best response I could make to her inquiry, as I was still rather distracted by the incident involving my small cousin, who now twisted in her chair, looking at me in a rather tilted manner. I found it most disturbing.

"What news have you of my sister, the queen?"

"She was well when last I saw her," I lied, for I knew her to have been in great torment of spirit at our parting. "Her court in Westminster attracts the most charming persons from far and wide."

"Yes, I am sure," Countess Mary replied. "My sister always excelled in such matters." Although the words she spoke were kind, I sensed a slight strain in her voice and wondered for the first time if the sisters had ever been at odds with each other. However, I quickly pushed the thought from my mind.

"Aunt Mary, I wonder if you might tell me a tale of the days in which the two of you lived among the holy sisters? I have heard stories from my mother, but I am sure you have much to add."

Young Mathilda had now abandoned the chair for which she'd fought so fiercely and was standing directly to the right of me, her eyes intent on my every move. Whether or not the countess disapproved of this action, she had apparently decided to overlook it.

"I am sure you know most of it already," she offered. "I was four years old when our esteemed parents sent us to live with our aunt Cristina at the abbey of Romsey. We received instruction fit for our station and were later sent to Wilton to complete our training. I left the abbey before my sister, of course."

Her tale seemed to end here, so I inquired once again. "What was it like living together in the convent? Did the two of you become very close?"

"As close as any two such sisters sent out to live in the world. We always shared a bed at Romsey, but at Wilton we were granted separate quarters." She paused for a breath, perhaps betraying some uncertainty, but then continued. "Our interests were somewhat different. My sister was always eager to seek out the farthest reaches of knowledge, the highest degree of spirituality, and all the delights of modern culture. For myself, I have always been content with a more quiet life. We each sought to serve God in our own way."

I thought she might cease her comments there, but I was wrong.

"As the elder daughter, she received many offers of marriage from several esteemed gentlemen. I have no doubt that you are aware of this."

"Yes, I have heard the story of how my parents met at the abbey. She was at first loath to marry, I think."

"That is correct. One by one they came, yet she turned them all away. Meanwhile, we both were tainted by the same rumor: that we were in fact consecrated sisters. That is to say, that we had taken vows of chastity. That never kept a suitor away from my sister, though I found it a more trying impediment."

"She must be jealous indeed," was the chief thought that echoed in my mind. I was not sure if or how to respond, so I tried to shift the conversation.

"Is it true that the queen incited King Henry to arrange the match between yourself and the count?" I asked.

The countess leaned back slightly and pressed her lips into a half smile. "Yes, once she had achieved her own place, she was good enough to make sure that I was provided for. And so you see, I am the most fortunate of women to be mistress of such a dominion."

I sensed that my aunt was not so glad as she let on, but I never had a chance to inquire further, for at that very moment we both noticed young Mathilda, who was perched near the fire and reaching out to grasp one of the pieces of wood—for what purpose I could only guess. The countess let out a yelp, and, not waiting for one of her ladies to act, dived forward to snatch her daughter from certain danger. The image remains fixed in my mind to this day: the countess holding my cousin, both of them twisting and turning in a strange kind of dance that ended with both of them falling backward onto the floor. The next ones to scream were the countess's ladies, with cries of, "My lady! My lady! Are you hurt?"

Young Mathilda broke free from her mother's arms and shunned the embrace of each of the ladies as she ran to hide behind my chair, gesturing toward me that I should not reveal her position. It was only then that we saw that the hem of my aunt's gown was burning. Shouts once again rose to the heavens as the desperate ladies attempted to smother the fire. The one named Maria went to fetch a water basin, but found it too heavy to lift. She was helped by a raven-haired woman, and together they brought an end to the flames.

The ladies moved to lift up the countess, whose gown was now soaked through, and restore her to dignity. Oddly, I had not strayed from my position throughout the entire ordeal, uncertain at every turn how to respond. My fright at that moment had seemed to freeze me to the spot. Never in my life had I witnessed anything quite like this. I believe that all involved had quite forgotten that I was there, except for my cousin, who seemed content to remain behind my seat. As most of the ladies knelt down to clean the mess and attend to the countess's scrapes, one of them did come over and ask if all was well with me and if I had seen where my cousin went.

"I am quite fine, thank you, though I wish to return to my room."

"Of course, I will take you at once."

"And my cousin is hiding behind the chair."

I know it is wrong to reveal another's secret, but I was now so repulsed by my cousin's behavior that I overcame any scruples that might have prevented my revelation. Young Mathilda responded by cursing in my direction, "*Faux ami!* I am better than you!" and then running off.

The maiden who had been speaking to me let out a sigh and took my hand to lead me back to my chamber. As we left, I could still smell the smoke coming from the countess's direction. She remained surrounded by three or four ladies, while the rest sought her daughter. Once we were alone, I asked, "I do not wish to be rude, but is this how things generally take place in the countess's household?"

The lady did not immediately reply. I could tell she was afraid to denounce her mistress. She waited until we reached a quiet corner, turned to glance in each direction, and then whispered to me in confidence.

"Usually it is not so bad, but things have become worse lately," she replied. "Mathilda is the countess's only child, and the doctors say that there shall never be another. As a result, she tends to dote on her, and I think this explains some of the . . . behavior." She quickly added, "Of course, you understand that this is not for outside ears."

"But I have never seen a noble daughter act in such a manner!" I protested. In all honesty, I was a bit beyond my bounds asking such questions, but my curiosity was raised to such an extent that I could not remain silent. "Does the countess never seek to impart discipline?"

The woman straightened her back and spoke more directly. "Now it is you who must understand something: The countess's daughter is a very strong-willed child. I do not believe that her mother is able to counter such emotion. There are few who can. All of us in her household do our best, but we are not in a position to improve matters to a large degree, for our powers are few and the count is occupied with more urgent affairs.

"I will also say this," she continued, relaxing her manner a bit. "The countess is not a bad woman, but she has faced many hardships in her years. Lately her health has declined, and she is unable to keep her daughter in check as she might have in the past. It is not normal for such a state of affairs to prevail, but I believe that my mistress suffers from a sense of helplessness at present. When she is well again, I am sure all will be set right."

Within a few steps, we reached the guest room in which I was to spend the night, and I thanked the woman for her assistance, apologizing if I had been too direct. After a final warning not to repeat anything I had heard, she returned to the audience room, where I can only imagine that chaos was still the order of the day.

There is a further side to this story. It was many years later that I was able to piece together the full truth. Princess Mary of Scotland was both the daughter and the sister of a queen, yet she was only able to attain the level of countess through her marriage. This was always a source of private ire for my aunt, who was determined that her own daughter should not suffer the same fate. Over the years, I believe the countess came to despise her older sister, who had received the greater honor and the lion's share of suitors. It is possible that Mary herself was in love with one of them, but I am merely guessing. My arrival in Boulogne perhaps brought forth this hostility that had lain dormant for years, for I was the daughter of Queen Mathilda and set to be raised even higher through matrimony with the emperor. I must conclude that this jealousy was the cause of some of the strange behavior that day, though there are parts of it I shall never fully understand. The countess succumbed to her illnesses a few years later. What became of her daughter, Mathilda of Boulogne, is a story for a later date, but I can at least assure you that she outgrew her wild state.

The next morning, we recommenced our travels through Flanders, pressing east toward the empire, where my betrothed awaited the arrival of his young bride. I little knew what was to come, but I hoped that the only fires ahead would be figurative.

CHAPTER EIGHT

S peed was of the essence now, for only a few days remained before the scheduled meeting in Liège. We moved quickly to Thérouanne and then followed the River Lys until we arrived at Lille. This took less than two days. However, on the morning we were to set out from Lille, there was so much rain that the roads turned into something resembling a bog. We had intended to make it as far as Tourneau before stopping for the night—a short day's work before a long push on to Mons. Fate, it seemed, had other designs for us. As twilight neared, we were only halfway to our destination. The wheels of both carts and carriages were all but useless under these conditions. Even the riders were forced to descend from their horses and lead them by hand through the mud.

Finally we decided that we must abandon most of the articles for the present and allow those who could to press ahead toward our goal. I stepped from the carriage, and the ladies fetched a cloak for me to wear. I doubt that the person who'd crafted it dreamed that it would end up covered in mud. The archdeacon, Henry, lifted me onto his steed, and we proceeded in that manner for the next few hours. Darkness set in and the torches became our only light, for the moon was hidden behind thick clouds.

Our company had begun as a merry bunch, but the rain seemed to lower the spirits of all, leading to a silence that could last for an hour with no sound but the fall of water, the footsteps in the slop, and the horses' heavy breathing. At first I attempted to sit in the womanly manner that I had been taught, but it proved difficult to maintain proper balance. After about a mile, the archdeacon said that I must place one leg on each side and remain as close to him as possible. He brought his arms around me and used both hands to tug the reins this way and that, harnessing all his strength to direct the animal along the devilish path.

I shall never forget the bitter cold of that ride, the constant pounding of the rain against my body. I did not understand how men could ride in such a way, for my legs screamed in protest against the way they were spread, and each step increased my discomfort. It was with great joy that we finally arrived at the city of Tourneau—not a moment too soon, for had I remained in that state any longer I think I should have been unable to walk for the following week.

Once I was received, I was given a most welcome bowl of stew. So weary was my body as I sat at the table that I struggled to keep my eyes open. Yet my hunger surpassed my weariness. Thus, in silence, I consumed every drop, only half noting the conversation taking place in the adjoining room.

"We cannot continue in this manner overland," I heard Roger de Clare say. "Even after this rain ceases, the roads will be well-nigh impassable for some time, and we are already forced to travel without the princess's dowry. Our only hope is to move along the river."

"It will be difficult to ferry such a company," the archdeacon countered. "Perhaps we should send a messenger ahead and warn the emperor that we are delayed."

"And suffer the shame of a late arrival?"

"We have no other option. I am sure that Burchard will convey our apologies to his master."

"No, the river is our best hope. As you say, it will be difficult to find enough boats, but difficult is not impossible. We must make a good first impression."

"Perhaps you misunderstand me," the archdeacon said, his voice lowered in tone but more intense. "The difficulty is not only a matter of physical movement, but also one of coin. The lords of England are already paying dearly for this endeavor. What clamor might commence when we are forced to rent half a fleet?"

"Better that than our other choices."

I couldn't hear the conclusion of the matter, but I surmised that Sir Roger must have carried the argument, for I awoke to find that several of the traders of Tourneau had been relieved of their boats for an ample fee, and we were to set out upon the River Scheldt. A light rain still fell upon us, but our progress was substantially improved over the day before, and we arrived in Mons on schedule. A short walk the following day brought us to Charleroi, where Archdeacon Henry procured even more vessels to carry us along the River Meuse. From that point on, the journey was a smooth one. Indeed, it was almost pleasant. We were once again united with all our possessions in Namur. The emperor's clerk, Burchard, was especially glad to receive the tools of his trade, which he had been forced to abandon in the deluge. I had achieved a kind of friendship with him along the way, made possible by his knowledge of the Norman tongue. He was eager that I should be ready for my entry into imperial court life, and I was no less desirous to satisfy the demands placed upon me.

I had begged him from the start to teach me something of the German speech, for I was well aware that my Latin was not up to the task of a full conversation. He created a game between us, in which he would tell me a new word each time I was able to correctly tell him another. As we sailed along the river from Namur to Huy, he began such a dialogue.

"Lady Mathilda, good morning to you!"

"*Guten Morgen!*" I replied.

"Excellent! Now, which word do you wish to know?"

"'Ship,' sir."

"Why, surely you mean *Schiff*?"

"Ah, *Schiff*. 'Ship.' *Schiff*. 'Ship.'"

I had a habit of repeating the words back and forth to aid my memory. I suppose it must have seemed comical to the others on board, but it was effective.

"Very good!" said Burchard. "Now, if you are so clever, then tell me, what color is the sky?"

"*Es ist wolkig.*"

"I did not ask about the weather, but about the color."

"Yes, but sir, today the color is cloudy!"

"*Grau*, then. But what color is it normally?"

"*Blau.*"

"Yes. And what color is the lovely raiment you are wearing today?"

"*Grün*. That is two questions! Now you must tell me two words."

"Certainly, I shall do my best."

"How do you say 'the king'?"

"*Der König*, and 'the queen' is *die Königin*. There, that is actually four."

"Is that what I will be, then? *Die Königin*?"

"Yes, you will be our queen: queen of the Romans and queen of the Kingdom of Germany. But you will also be more than that. You will be *die Kaiserin*."

I did not reply this time, but paused to consider. The words carried such great import that it seemed the weight would crush me, so small was I in comparison. How could I be their queen, much less their empress? I was barely able to speak the language, much less understand the people I was meant to rule. Of course, the emperor was the true sovereign, but I would have to carry out business on his behalf. Surely this was too much for me . . . surely.

"You need not fear us. We will welcome you with our whole hearts," Burchard said, as if he understood my thoughts. "No one is born a great ruler, but time makes of us what it will. You will not be thrown into the whirlwind. You shall be trained in every way possible. I am certain you will do well."

"Thank you, Burchard. I think I have grown a little tired of the game for the present. Perhaps we can start again another time?"

"As you wish. I stand ready for your command."

He walked back toward the captain and inquired as to the time of our arrival in Huy. It could not be long now. I glanced toward the passing field, which would have been a lush meadow in springtime, but presently remained a mixture of *Grau* and *Braun*. It seemed familiar, and yet I knew it to be desperately foreign.

"I am off the edge of the map, and there is naught to guide me but the hand of God," I whispered.

Silently, I pulled out the satchel that held the beloved stone of amber. I ran over it with my fingers, turning the object this way and that. I saw myself in the moth, trapped within its stony cage.

"I will make good. I must make good."

I continued to speak the words to myself, gaining what strength I could from each syllable. Then the old song came to my mind, the one my mother sang to me. I called it out now in my hour of need.

Now we must honor the guardian of heaven
The might of the architect, and his purpose
The work of the father of glory
As he, the eternal Lord, established the beginning of
wonders
He first created for the children of men
Heaven as a roof, the holy Creator
Then the guardian of mankind, the eternal Lord
Afterward appointed the middle earth, the lands for men
The Lord Almighty

As we moved closer to Liège, I could see a great forest and distant hills as far as the eye could see.

"Is that the Alps?" I asked Burchard. "I have heard so much about them."

I was a bit dismayed that he laughed in response. "The Alps? Hardly! No, that is the forest of Ardennes," Burchard told me. "If you were to walk in that direction long enough you would arrive in Trier, but I think only a bird should choose such a path, though the hills are minute in comparison with the Alps. The trees are very dense and do not allow fast movement."

"So the Alps are taller than those hills?" To my young mind, this was hard to believe. In the place where I was raised, the tallest object in any region was usually the local church tower.

"Far taller!" Burchard answered. "The tallest mountains on earth, with no equal in beauty. Trees cannot grow upon their heights, so cold is the air. They are continually coated in snow."

"Even in the summer?"

"Yes, even in the summer. Do not worry; you will see them before long, and a most wondrous sight they are to behold."

Suddenly, there was a sound of harsher hoof-beats. Burchard was riding directly by my carriage and we were conversing through the small window. Now I saw Archdeacon Henry upon his horse, galloping back toward our position. They slowed as they reached us.

"My lady," the archdeacon shouted, "we have just sighted the city of Liège and the emperor's messengers coming to meet us."

To tell the truth, I would rather have continued on our journey for another few days, conversing with Burchard or Drogo and delaying the inevitable. However, I was not to be granted the reprieve I desired, for the end of all our efforts stood directly before me, and there was naught that I could do but say, "Thank you, Archdeacon. Could you call for the ladies to come join me and aid in the preparations?"

"Most certainly," he replied and ran off to carry out my instruction.

"May I take my leave of you as well, Your Grace? I should go ahead to speak with the imperial heralds and discuss the entrance into the city," said Burchard.

"Of course, you must go. Farewell."

"And may the grace of God be with Your Highness," he replied, leaving me alone to await the two ladies.

The convoy had now come to a complete stop. I leaned out the window so that I might view the city. Liège is most famous for its many scholars, who come from the ends of the Christian world to study under the canons of the seven collegiate churches. Here, along the banks of the River Meuse, were shaped many of the greatest minds of our time. The chief of these churches is Saint Pierre, which lies in the center of the town, directly next to the church of Notre-Dame-aux-Fonts and the bishop's palace.

I could see the city wall stretching with the bend of the river. I did not find these fortifications as imposing as the ones in London, which I had gazed at so often from my window at the Palace of Westminster. Nevertheless the town was formidable, with its many spires, both within and without the walls, rising toward the heavens. The reddish stones gave off a more favorable light than the dark-gray ones I had seen elsewhere.

The ladies soon appeared and attended to me. My gown for this day was made of yellow silk and richly embroidered with the finest thread. They placed bands of garnet and gold on my tiny fingers and wrists, and set a great chain of pearls around my neck. My white veil was crowned with a golden crown in the shape of laurel leaves.

"You are a vision of loveliness, my dear!" they claimed.

For my part, I was not swayed. My future husband was a grown man, and it seemed impossible that he could see much to impress him in a young girl. Nevertheless, impress them all I must, for my whole future depended upon it. Entering through the south gate, we made our way down the narrow city streets. I was astounded to see the number of people who had turned out for the occasion. They pressed in so close that the carriage could barely move forward. All of them were reaching out their hands, and a few succeeded in getting through the window and actually touching me. They were shouting words that I could not understand, and I found the experience most distressing. I moved farther away from the window, only to be grasped by those on the other side. There was nothing left but to smile, which I did with as much feigned joy as possible.

As we entered a wider lane the imperial knights, whose ceremonial armor shone brightly in the afternoon sunshine, pushed back the crowds and prevented them from rushing forward.

"We must be getting close," I concluded.

No sooner had this thought passed through my mind than the carriage came to a halt and I saw before me the great episcopal palace. Eminent officials filled the front *porticus* and descending steps: knights and nobles, monks and bishops, attendants and women of higher rank arrayed in what was surely their best attire. Standing at the front, with a great crown upon his head, was the man I knew must be the emperor himself, *Kaiser* Henry. With the veil covering much of my face and a great distance still separating us, I could not make out his features clearly, but he appeared to be taller than most, with brown hair and a small beard. His blue robes were even more richly decorated than my own, and his jewels were just as fine.

I had little time to ponder all of this, for the carriage door was opened before me, and Archdeacon Henry reached out his hand to help me to the ground. The cheers swelled into a roar as the crowd caught sight of me. People were not only bending out of windows, but actually standing on the roofs of buildings in order to gain a better view.

"Take my arm," the archdeacon said, and I did as I was commanded.

We began to walk forward. I wanted to look at the emperor, but I was afraid to meet his gaze, so instead I made a careful examination of the figures around him. I recognized only two of them: Frederick, the emperor's nephew, who had come with the imperial party to England the year before, and Chancellor Adalbert, once again clad in black from head to toe. A shorter archbishop stood next to Adalbert. I could see that he must be powerful, for he was wearing some of the finest shoes I had ever seen. Before I was able to make out any other faces in the crowd, a man standing directly before us stopped our progress. His vestments revealed that he too was a bishop, though of a slightly lower rank. He bowed his head and even lowered his shoulders a bit in a sign of respect.

"Bishop Otbert of Liège," the archdeacon stated.

I tried not to show alarm, but my mind had made the connection. This was no ordinary bishop, but the one they called "the wolf of Liège"—he who had incited the fury of the Holy See to the point of excommunication, removing worthy abbots from their posts and replacing them with the highest bidders. While the ban of excommunication had since been lifted, it was generally accepted that the man was no fit apostle of the Lord. It was also said that the sacrament, when blessed by the wolf of Liège, was a curse that attempted to enter the unsuspecting through the arse rather than the mouth, consuming their insides with dark torments. Now he began to speak.

"*Libenter te, Principissa, Henricus imperator et urbs Liège accipiunt!*"

I gathered that he was welcoming me to the city on behalf of his master, so I gave my best reply, struggling to remember something from the endless sessions with Lady Beatrice.

"*Tibi gratias agimus, Domine.*"

The bishop smiled, and I knew that I had done well. Thankfully, he did not attempt to continue our conversation in Latin, but turned and led us the rest of the way toward the lords and ladies. At the last moment, the bishop turned to the side, and there we stood, face-to-face with the emperor. I had no choice now but to meet his gaze. His expression was rather sober, though not fully unhappy. Were I to guess, I would have said that he too was a bit nervous, though I could not think why that should be, since he was clearly the most powerful man in attendance.

The archdeacon let go of my arm, and I found myself standing alone. My heart began to pound even harder as I made a deep bow, lowering my head until my face was pointed toward the ground. I was not sure how long I ought to remain in that lowered position. It seemed like an eternity, but I am sure it was no longer than two breaths. As I once again rose, the emperor walked forward and extended his hand toward me. I gave him my own right hand. Due to our differing heights, I had to reach upward in order to grasp it. It was a strange feeling, my hand being inside his. I sensed the strength that rested in that hand, the strength of a man experienced in the ways of the world, or so I imagined. I had the odd feeling that we were acting out some sort of play, and at any moment someone would leap out from behind a pillar and declare it all to be a poor attempt at humor, the great emperor paired with a girl young enough to be his daughter. I wondered if he longed for a woman more equal to his stature, or if my dowry was enough to satisfy any scruples.

"*Ego Henricus sum,*" he said, loud enough for only me to hear.

It was then I recognized how silent the crowd had become, each person apparently caught up in the moment, even as I was. The silence was, to me, even more deafening than the earlier cheers. I took a breath, and, straining to remember everything Burchard had taught me, I replied, "*Ich bin Mathilda. Schön Sie kennenzulernen.*"

To my great surprise, those standing just behind the emperor started to clap, and cheers then spread throughout the crowd. It took me a moment to see that this was in response to the words I had spoken in their own language. This made me wonder if I had offered to do them some favor without being aware of it. Even the emperor seemed to smile.

"*Wir müssen reingehen,*" he said, motioning toward the entrance of the bishop's palace.

Although I did not know the meaning of *reingehen,* this small gesture had allowed me to interpret it. And so he led me slowly past all those happy faces, up the stairs, and through a great door carved with tales from the life of a saint whom I knew not.

"If it is all to be Latin or German, I will not last through the evening," I thought. "They will quickly discover that their new *Königin* is not the *Wünderkind* they first supposed."

I remember everything about that night: the wonderful painted flowers carved into the wood beams, the light of the flames as they sparked and danced, the joyous shouts of men who had imbibed a bit too much, and the massive portions of food. Platter after platter of meat dishes was brought forth—some that I recognized, and others that I did not. I knew it was essential that

I learn to enjoy the food of my new country, but I remained in such a state that I doubt even a bowl of gilded apples would have tempted me. Nevertheless I made my best effort as the servers continued to spoon different items onto the dish in front of me, often covering them with a mustard sauce that seemed to diminish rather than enhance their quality.

Although I was seated directly to the emperor's left, we spoke scarcely a word to each other, on account of both our lack of familiarity and the language difference. Though I knew enough to ask, "*Mehr Wasser, bitte*," the greater subtleties of conversation were lost on me, and the emperor certainly did not know a word of the Norman or English tongues. So it was that I sampled the new cuisine in relative silence, while my betrothed carried on a lively discussion with his two nephews: the Duke of Swabia and his younger brother, Conrad. Their mother, Agnes, was the emperor's sister.

Around the time that I felt I could not possibly eat another morsel, I received a divine reprieve in the form of Chancellor Adalbert, who approached to greet me along with the shorter archbishop I had noticed earlier, the one with the fine shoes. To tell the truth, I was glad to see them, for I knew that one of them, at least, knew some of my own native language.

"*Meister Adalbert*," I said, making use of one word I did remember from Burchard's lessons.

"Lady Mathilda, soon to be queen of the Romans, I offer to you congratulations for your espousal," Adalbert replied. "Here is His Grace Bruno, archbishop of Trier."

Bruno bowed his head and I bowed mine in return.

"It is an honor to meet you, Lady Mathilda," he said to me. "We have long awaited this blessed day. I trust that your journey was pleasant."

My mind immediately ventured to the lanes of mud, the seasickness, and my aunt's dress catching on fire.

"Yes, very pleasant," I replied.

"I am to be your tutor. We shall make our study in the ancient *burg* of Trier, which is my home. I think you will like it there."

"So I am not to be at the imperial court?"

"Not at first, no. That is, not once you have received your coronation in all pomp at Mainz. Then it will be time for your studies, until it is determined that you are ready."

"I am sorry, Archbishop. Ready for what?"

"For the marriage, of course."

"Pardon me, mistress," said the chancellor. "I must have words with someone over there."

We both watched as Adalbert moved toward another table, picked up a glass of wine, and began talking with a noble I did not recognize.

"He is a sly one, Adalbert," Bruno said.

"Oh?" I had not imagined that I would receive such an honest revelation.

"Yes, he may appear to be free of partiality, but at heart he is as fierce a broker as any."

"And you are not?"

He smiled at me and sat down in the empty seat to my left.

"I see you are wise beyond your years, Mathilda. In such times as ours, it is true that all men of the cloth find themselves bound together with the rulers of this age. 'Twas not always so, but the times require it of us. Here, I will teach you something. We have bishops here, as you do in England, but the bishops within the empire are not only men of God; they are also princes, and powerful ones at that. The temptation of worldly gain is great."

He must have guessed at my thoughts, for he continued, "Do not mistake me. There are many who resist this temptation, and not all contact with the secular realm is an evil. For myself, I seek to advise the emperor on how he might create a better world both for our holy Church and for the kingdom. Saint Augustine once spoke of two cities . . ."

"The city of God and the city of man," I ventured, hoping that I had remembered something correctly from Master Godfrey's lessons.

"Right you are! I see that you have been well taught."

I dropped my gaze as I was forced to admit, "I could not tell you the particulars of the book, but I do remember once seeing a magnificent drawing of the two cities, one all darkness and the other all light."

"Yes, well, things are not always so simple. The devil himself often comes to us as an 'angel of light,' as Saint Paul tells us."

"How then can one become a righteous ruler?"

Bruno smiled and said to me, "That is precisely what I intend to teach you, if the Lord should give me strength to do so. For now, rest and enjoy these moments. You have performed well on your first day and brought honor to your esteemed house. Once you have made it through the beginning stages of your journey, then we shall take up the study of these things."

Our conversation paused at that point, for the chancellor had returned with another man.

"Your Grace, I present to you Duke Godfrey of Lower Lorraine."

The duke looked to be a man of about fifty years, on account of which he had lost most of the hair on top of his head. He apparently made up for this by growing such a long beard that others at court referred to him as Duke Godfrey the Bearded. He wore a large hat that concealed any trace of his malady, but he was forced to remove it when paying his respects to the emperor's future consort, thus revealing his secret.

"The duke has a petition to make of you," Adalbert explained.

Before I had time to consider what possible petition the duke could make and what I, not yet an empress and much less a woman, might be able to accomplish on his behalf, he

159

launched into a passionate argument, none of which I could understand, save for a few scattered words. A full minute must have passed before he stopped to catch his breath and Adalbert offered a translation.

"The duke says he is hard pressed by the traitor Henry, who attempts to steal his rightful possession."

"The emperor stole his land?" I asked.

"No," said Bruno. "He means Duke Henry of Limburg. The man was once a supporter of the emperor, but then reverted to his father during the late conflict."

Now, Daughter, you will note that my betrothed, the fifth Emperor Henry, was at war with his own excommunicate father, Emperor Henry IV, during the last few years of the old man's life. This is a rather long story and not fit for telling at the present time. Suffice it to say the new emperor had felt compelled to avenge himself on the allies of his father once he had gained the throne. It was for this reason that Duke Godfrey labeled Henry of Limburg a traitor.

Duke Godfrey was once again speaking earnestly, and Adalbert was forced to add, "In fact, this Henry is duke no longer, but grants himself that title according to his own evil desires. The emperor has taken back Limburg from Henry and put him in Hildesheim."

"He is imprisoned in the North, near the palace of Goslar," Bruno clarified.

I did not understand where the problem lay. "If he is imprisoned and Duke Godfrey now controls the lands, then why does he come to me?"

Adalbert nodded and began speaking to the duke again in German. "*Was wollen Sie von der Dame? Sie versteht Sie nicht.*"

The bearded duke was a bit perplexed and seemed to beseech the chancellor. "*Er lügt! Er verbreitet Gerüchte!*"

"Yes, we know he spreads lies, but what do you want the lady Mathilda to do about it?" Bruno responded, clearly intending his comments more for my benefit than the duke's, for he certainly did not understand them. A further translation from the chancellor was necessary, after which the duke responded in German and Adalbert, having taken a moment to collect his thoughts, said, "Will you speak to the emperor and promote the claim of the duke, that their . . . alliance is strengthened?"

"Yes. I shall be happy to do so."

The duke, having guessed at the meaning of my reply, broke into expressions of, "*Danke! Danke!*" and was then ushered away by Adalbert.

"More than you hoped to deal with on your first night?" Bruno asked.

"Honestly, sir, I was just hoping to make it through," I answered.

We tarried in Liège a few more weeks. The emperor spent much of this time in the council of his papal ambassadors, including Archbishops Bruno and Adalbert. I was not made aware of the full extent of their discussions, but I surmised that the emperor wished to be crowned by His Holiness in the manner of his predecessor, Charles the Great. In addition, the issue of investiture weighed heavily, for the right to grant the bishop's staff is also the power to rule.

Throughout this time, there was no official espousal for Emperor Henry and me. That was to take place in the northern city of Utrecht. I used the time to acquaint myself with my new ladies; chief among them were Gertrude and Adelaide. All were of noble houses, but none were able to converse in the Norman tongue. Thus making their acquaintance was rather difficult. On the occasions when I despaired entirely, I sought out the company of my chief knight, Drogo, whose value as a friend had increased still further, as he was now one of the few people who could understand me.

At last the day of our departure arrived, and all the imperial vessels sailed north upon the River Meuse through the region of Limburg. Whereas the river flowed through green hills and rocky crags farther to the south, the land now grew smoother and we could see a few vineyards near the river's edge. We passed through the great trading center of Maastricht and continued north. It was seldom necessary to drop anchor, so well provisioned were the emperor's ships, but when we did so, I noticed a change in the speech of the pier workers: their words were neither Flemish nor German, but something else entirely.

Our boat was filled mostly with those who belonged to my own household: knights, ladies, a pair of clerks, and the chaplain Altmann, who was to serve the royal consort exclusively. More often than not, we sailed directly beside the emperor's ship. His was the most magnificent by far, with two great black eagle heads protruding from the bow and his imperial standard hanging from the mast. From time to time, I glanced in that direction to see my future husband standing forward of all the others, arms crossed and gazing always ahead. He seemed to survey his mighty kingdom with the surety of a cat that holds the mouse directly under its paw, for the look on his face betrayed naught but confidence.

What might he be thinking at this moment? What impression had he formed of his new bride? We had spoken little since my arrival in Liège. Entire days had come and gone without our sharing each other's company. His mind was apparently occupied with great matters of state that were beyond my comprehension. Perhaps he intended to wait until I was fully grown to pursue any kind of familiarity.

Once we had passed out of Limburg, it became necessary for us to cross overland to the Rhine, the chief river within the Holy Roman Empire. The land was not without canals, but none were of a sufficient size for that massive company. This process consumed a great deal of time and annoyed all involved. On we traveled, passing the mills and market towns, the boats of local fishermen, and the scattered church spires whose bells rang out with the music of village life. Peasants paused to stare in wonder at our procession, no doubt hoping to catch a glimpse of Emperor Henry and his future bride.

We were quite fortunate that the skies remained clear for our voyage. Spring had finally arrived and the pastures were turning green. However, with the warmer weather came the fasting season of Lent, and not a scrap of meat could be found anywhere on the emperor's ships. I believe this was a sore test for many of our company, though I was satisfied to eat little more than bread throughout the journey, or *Brot*, as I came to know it. I did not care for many of the fruits I was offered.

My new chaplain, Altmann, carried with him an extensive collection of books, most of which were written in Latin, save for a copy of the Gospel of John in the language of the Germans themselves. I was most eager to examine its pages and was able to inquire, "*Kann ich es sehen?*" He was happy to oblige and bid me sit down and hold the volume open in my lap. On the first page was written the title, *Das Johannesevangelium,* as well as a note about its origin at the monastery of Lauresham. There was a fine image of an eagle set against the rising sun. Below was the city of Jerusalem, with the Church of the Holy Sepulcher at its center. With great care I turned past the table of contents and read the first sentence.

"*Im Anfang war das Wort, und das Wort war bei Gott, und Gott war das Wort.*"

Here was a riddle to which I must set my mind. Two words I easily translated: *Wort,* meaning "word" and *Gott,* referring to "God." I was also able to quickly make out "the" and "was." This left me with little work to do.

"*Vater Altmann,*" I asked, "*was ist 'Anfang'?*"

"*Principium,*" he replied.

"Ah, so 'beginning.' *Danke.*" Then, to myself, I continued, "It must mean 'In the beginning was the word.' Yes, that seems right. 'And the word was . . .' What does *bei* mean? Oh, 'with'! So it should go, 'In the beginning was the word, and the word was with God, and the word was God.' I have it!"

I continued in that manner for approximately an hour, until larger buildings appeared on the riverbanks and we quickly moved into the center of Utrecht, the principal city in that region. It is famous for its *kerkenkruis*, five churches built to form a cross over the heart of the city. At the very center was the great *Dom*, or cathedral, of Saint Martin. The collegiate churches of Saint John, Saint Peter, Saint Paul, and Saint Maria formed the remainder of the cross. The Rhine flowed through the city center, with canals branching off to the right and left. The local residents used the waterways to transport goods, and also to prevent the flooding of their beloved town.

Our own destination was the Lofen Palace, residence of the emperors, which stood just north of the cathedral on the right bank of the Rhine and next to the manor of the bishop of Utrecht, Burchard. We dropped anchor directly at the imperial palace and made our way through a magnificent cloister and into the yard. As I walked, Lady Gertrude saw to the train of my dress, while my other attendants strode just behind us. The yard now teemed with Norman knights conversing with those of the emperor, grooms seeing the horses to their stables, servants of all kinds carrying objects from the river into the palace, noble ladies waiting to be attended, hunting dogs chasing one of the kitchen cats, the chief butler looking over some silver goblets, and Emperor Henry in the center of it all conversing with *Meister* Adalbert. It was a great deal for me to take in, and before I could complete my observations, Lady Adelaide ushered me inside.

As we moved toward the doors, I noticed a young girl, no more than five or six years old, holding the hand of one of the ladies of the house. The two of them walked up to the emperor, and upon becoming aware of their presence, he bent down and kissed the girl on the cheek, then stood to pat her on the head before walking off to some other business. I could not help but wonder at the significance of this small gesture and why the emperor would pay such special attention to a young girl. "Perhaps she is one of his nieces," I thought, making a note to inquire later about her name.

The weeks of Lent were almost complete. The next day would be Maundy Thursday, and soon after that the feast of Easter, at which point we could celebrate the grand espousal without austerity. As it was for Christ, Easter would be for me both an end and a beginning.

What must I say about the day of my espousal? Perhaps I should begin with the preceding night, for my dream upon that eve was of such a nature that I remember it to this day. I was transported not to that spiritual realm which is the privy abode of the saints, but rather to a place very familiar, and yet not. I was in England again, somewhere within the halls of my childhood home at Westminster. Still, it was not altogether the same, for the moment I opened one of the doors, the room transformed. Gone were the usual furnishings, the well-trod floors, and the worn gray stones. In their place were other objects, brought, it seemed, from places far beyond England's shores: vessels from the temple of Solomon, dark-skinned men from the lands to the south, strange flowers and fruits of every kind, and a *simia* with one child in its arms and another on its back.

"What are all these things, Mother?" I inquired.

No sooner had I spoken the words than she appeared before me. She was not alone either, for I also saw my father and brother William, Prince David of the Scots, Lady Beatrice, and, most strangely of all, Father Anselm, who seemed to have been raised to life again by divine power.

"I do not understand. How are you alive?" I asked him.

I received no answer. Indeed, there was no word from any of them, and the living presence of this man long dead seemed to have no effect. I was thinking about how utterly strange it all was, when suddenly I heard the words, *"Mathilda, es ist Zeit, aufzuwachen!"*

My eyes opened to a very different sight: a bedchamber at Lofen Palace in the city of Utrecht, with Lady Adelaide looking down on me and several other ladies entering the room and busying themselves with the morning's affairs. I tried shutting my eyes and opening them again, hoping that this was all another dream, but life was stubborn and forbade me to make it all disappear. Moreover, my mind knew this to be the place where I had last been awake.

"Es ist Zeit, aufzuwachen!" Adelaide repeated.

"Es ist nicht die Zeit," I muttered in reply.

"Was?"

"Es ist Zeit zu schlafen," I said with greater determination, rolling over and turning my back to her.

Rather than allowing me to sleep a bit longer, this incited passionate rhetoric from all the ladies in the room, who exhorted me in no uncertain terms about *Verlobung,* a foreign term that I determined must refer to the espousal set for that very morning. I understood no more than half of their words, but that was enough to prove that resistance was pointless. So it was that within the space of a few hours, I stood before the altar of Saint Martin's Cathedral, my small hand clasped within that of the king of the Germans, listening to the words of Bishop Burchard of Utrecht. It seemed an overly long time to stand so, with every person of note within a hundred leagues in attendance. I prayed that the emperor would not notice the sweat forming upon my palms, the blush upon my cheeks, or the dust that had made its way onto the hem of my gown in my short walk to the church.

We spoke the words that I had set to memory over the past week, pledging ourselves to each other. The approving smile of the bishop assured me that I had performed the task as was desired for a future queen. My future husband was another matter. He endured the entire ceremony with an air of solemn determination. I sensed that he was quite decided upon this course of action, but that he did not allow it to alter his soul or touch his heart, if indeed he possessed one.

As we took our leave of the cathedral, I knew the heavenly die was cast. The laws of the Church required that I be twelve years of age before entering into matrimony, but for all intents and purposes, the deed was already done. I, Mathilda, was now joined to Henry V, emperor of the Romans. The significance of this fact, and the way in which it would alter my life, were beyond my ability to comprehend in that moment, but one thing I did know: I must become a full woman, for the world was determined to treat me as such.

CHAPTER NINE

Mark my words, Daughter: there is nothing that sets men against one another more easily than that demon Mammon. At his feet the lords of this world daily prostrate themselves in worship, though they often know it not. Our final days in Utrecht saw this principle borne out time and again. Of course, the emperor had agreed to the marriage only for want of coin, which was duly transferred to him upon our espousal. What he intended to do with this newfound wealth was equally well known, for rumors of the emperor's great expedition to Italy had spread like wildfire.

Yet Emperor Henry would have been remiss had he not acknowledged his future bride with such gifts as befitted her new position. He bestowed raiment of the finest quality upon me, along with jewels of the imperial house, few of which were fit for a young girl of my stature. There was armor also for the knights of my household and weapons to match, magnificent fabrics for my ladies, and a dozen horses sired by the most vigorous forebears in the kingdom. Of the knights who had traveled with our party from Westminster, there were many who sought gifts from the emperor's hand in the form of demesne or position. They were frustrated on both counts. I shall never forget the looks on their faces as the emperor and his chancellor bid them return to the land whence they had come. Yes, the lure of Mammon is powerful indeed.

Around this time, Count Robert of Flanders came into Utrecht, he who was often called Robert of Jerusalem on account of his exploits in the East. The count was no friend of the emperor, or of King Henry of England, for the usual reasons: disputed territories, unpaid tribute, and the displeasing alliances of the other two men. His arrival could hardly have been more opportune—or less, depending on one's opinion—for it was during the same week that the imperial council was forced to deal with a highly delicate matter: namely, the apprehension of one Gerulf, a Frisian of low origin, in the northern city of Groningen. He was brought to Utrecht with all haste, having been charged in connection with the murder of Conrad, the former archbishop of Utrecht who had been viciously killed in his own cathedral some ten years earlier.

It was rumored that the man who actually wielded the knife, a mason who had been dismissed from his work on the collegiate church of Notre Dame by the old archbishop, might have harbored some other motive beyond wanting vengeance for the aforesaid expulsion. Many believed the murderer was in the pocket of some noble with whom Archbishop Conrad had had a dispute, and here the mind naturally leaped to the Count of Flanders, whose forces had clashed with those of the archbishop on several occasions. However, there was no direct evidence of such a plot, and some who held the archbishop in low esteem did little to suppress whisperings that it was a crime of passion.

In light of this, it was rather extraordinary that Count Robert should have been in town at the very time that this Gerulf was sentenced. They say that the count showed no emotion as the man was dragged to the block, the ax was raised, and the blow was dealt that severed body from spirit. If the count did have any remorse, he never displayed it. Mind you, I was not there, but I heard such things from others. I do not possess that peculiar fondness for public execution held by so many.

Having concluded all necessary business with the Count of Flanders, the emperor made known his intent to set out upon the Rhine in three days' time. With nothing further impeding his venture to the Holy See, he was impatient to begin his southern descent. By poor chance, my health had begun to decline. Day and night, I experienced a constriction of breath accompanied by a most irksome discharge from my nose. A physician from the abbey of Susteren in Limburg happened to be in town, and was fetched with all haste to examine me. He made an extensive study of my anatomy, muttering to himself on occasion but never conversing. He felt around my wrists, looked into my eyes, inquired of Lady Gertrude as to my diet, and made a great show of placing his nose to several objects in the room in order to detect any odd smells. Finally he instructed me to breathe deeply. When I did so, I once again broke into a coughing fit.

"*Schlecht, sehr schlecht,*" was his final analysis.

I understood enough by that point to determine that this was not a favorable conclusion. "*Was? Was ist es?*" I pleaded.

Rather than answering me directly, he turned to address my ladies.

"*Sie hat eine Lungeninfektion. Es gibt zu viel Schleim, glaube ich.*"

Before I could inquire as to just what he meant by "lung infection," the physician was directing the women to remove all flowers from the room, on account of the potentially deadly fumes they released. Such harmful smells, he contended, were one of the chief causes of infection. I did not believe the scents to be particularly malicious, but I knew I had little choice in the matter. He also instructed the ladies not to allow me to leave my bed until we were to set out from Utrecht. Finally, he had some stern words for me.

"*Sie soll kein Wasser zu trinken! Der Schleim wird dadurch noch mehr.*"

"*Aber ich habe Durst!*" I protested, for my throat was already parched, and I doubted that this instruction would improve matters, unless the water itself was polluted.

He did not take kindly to this. "*Ruhe! Sie müssen tun, was ich sage!*"

With that the doctor gathered his things and departed the premises, leaving me in a rather dour state.

"I think I shall die here," I complained in my native tongue. A few of the ladies looked at me oddly, but as they did not understand my words, there was no response. Of the mystery of the four humors I knew little, but that a lack of water would put me in ill humor I was quite certain.

I passed the afternoon and evening miserably. As the all-knowing physician had forbade drinking water, the ladies would bring me only a small cup of milk from noon until suppertime. There was great pain in my throat, which felt as if it were actually burning. A great debate ensued around sundown as to whether or not I could consume quail eggs without worsening my condition. They finally determined that I should simply take some bread and wine. For the food I was most thankful, but the wine seemed to burn my insides, and I refused to drink more than a few sips.

My sleep was uneasy that night. I had a fever that would not abate and woke me every hour, shaking from head to toe. I felt weak in my members and found myself beginning to fear. I wanted my mother's consoling presence. Indeed, I would have settled for Lady Beatrice, for though I did not care for her severe methods, I never doubted her skill. I could see the looks of concern on my ladies' faces and the uncertainty with which they undertook their tasks. For a while I succumbed to sleep, and then I was roused by the sound of Adelaide's voice.

"*Mathilda,*" she said. "*Mathilda, wach!*"

Whether or not I provided a response I cannot say, but it could not have been more than a mere whisper, so weak had I become.

Adelaide turned to Gertrude and commanded, "*Holt den Erzbischof! Bruno—finden Sie ihn!*"

The morning light was just beginning to break when Archbishop Bruno of Trier arrived. He immediately pulled a chair over by the bed and began his work, questioning the ladies in German.

"Archbishop, am I going to die?" I asked him, wishing to know the truth.

"Certainly not!" he assured me, "but I do question your physician's instruction." He placed his palm on my forehead. "You are quite hot, and yet I see very little sweat. How much water have you had this night?"

"None, my lord."

"What? *Verdammt!* That physician is worse than useless. Madame Gertrude, *Wasser—jetzt!*"

"Is the water clean, sir?" I asked.

"Yes, the well water is clean. I cannot speak for the river. Here, I brought you something."

The archbishop pulled out three yellow fruits that were rounded on the ends, larger than an apple and with thicker skin. I was about to ask what they were, when he told me, "These are called *citrus* in Latin, or *turunj* in the language of the Saracens. They grow in the South, around the great sea. My servant bought them from some sea merchants yesterday. A friend who spent time in Jerusalem said they are used there for medicinal purposes. Sadly, the plant cannot survive our harsh winters."

He called for a small knife and a bowl, and then proceeded to cut each of the fruits in half. Beneath the skin was a thick white layer, but the yellow center was filled with liquid. This part the archbishop pulled out with his fingers and bid me to consume. Its taste was unlike anything I had ever known—as strong as wine, but less sweet. I confess that I didn't like it, but as it seemed to be the first decent remedy presented to me, I tried to digest it.

"Eat!" Bruno said. "With luck, it will help revive you." He accepted a cup of water from Adelaide. "Now, Mathilda, I want you to drink a full glass with each passing hour. Lady Adelaide will fetch it for you."

"So, then, you do not think that I have too much phlegm, Archbishop?"

"No, this is a common disease that affects those who come into contact with other diseased persons, though beyond that it is not well understood. It should pass within the week. The trouble, of course, is that we set sail in two days, but I am sure that you will feel well enough to walk by that point, and if you are well enough to walk, then you are well enough to travel."

He then turned to leave, but halted to provide one last instruction: "*Sie sollte aufrecht im Bett sitzen. Dadurch wird die Krankheit weggedrängt und es wird ihre Lungen frei machen.*"

Not for the last time, Archbishop Bruno was correct, and by the end of the day I had substantially recovered. I was still weary the morning we set sail down the Rhine, but I no longer struggled to breathe. As an added benefit, I had actually grown to like the *citrus* fruit, provided it was covered with a bit of honey.

Having set out from Utrecht, we departed the region of Friesland and moved up the river. The spring rains had caused the river to swell past its appointed bounds, and we saw not a few newly planted fields flooded as a result. The men strained at the oars against the water's flow, pressing hard to arrive by sundown at the imperial palace of Nijmegen. It was known as the Valkhof, the court of the falcon, commissioned by Charles the Great himself. As the sun began to set, we could finally make out the small hill upon which sat the *Kaiserpfalz*—that is, the emperor's palace. My household knight, Drogo, with whom I had scarcely been able to converse since the royal espousal, greeted me as I left the boat.

"God save you, my lady!" he said.

"Well met, Drogo. I am glad to see you."

"I heard you were ill and taken to bed, but I see you are looking well now, if a bit tired."

I could see the response of Lady Gertrude, who appeared to be offended by the familiar manner of our conversation, though she could not possibly have understood all the words. I decided not to address her.

"Thank you, I am quite recovered, except for the weakness you mentioned, and I do continue to cough at regular intervals," I replied.

"Is there anything which I might do that would aid your relief?"

"No, nothing at all."

"Very well, then. I received a letter for you sent by your royal mother, Queen Mathilda."

My eyes must have grown large as he retrieved the bound letter from his coat. The parchment was of the highest quality and carried the royal seal.

"When did you receive that?" I asked, fully amazed.

"The day before yesterday. I would have given it to you sooner, but as you remained in your chambers and I was then set upon a different boat, this has been the first opportunity."

"*Sollte ich das, meine Dame?*" Gertrude offered.

"*Nein, danke,* Gertrude. I will keep it," I said immediately, taking the letter in my own hands before she had an opportunity. It was perhaps irregular for me to respond in such a manner, but to such things the ladies would need to accustom themselves if they were to remain by my side.

"Thank you, Sir Drogo. I am indebted to you for delivering this."

"Not at all, Lady Mathilda."

Once I had been directed to my private chamber inside the Valkhof, I was able to gain a moment alone to examine the letter's contents. I had not understood until that point how dearly I would treasure the smallest token from home and the chance to read any news of the goings-on in England. It allowed me to keep some connection to the land of my birth, however small. I knew that on most occasions, the queen would speak to one of her clerks, who would then write down all she said and ensure that the Latin prose was perfect. However, upon breaking the seal I could tell that my mother had written this in her own hand, in the Norman tongue.

"Clearly she did not want me to have to use a translator," I thought.

I still possess the letter to this day, and it reads thus:

To her most beloved daughter, Maud, queen of the Romans: Mathilda, by the grace of God queen of the English, to whom he also saw fit to grant the fullness of maternal blessings, wishing that you may come to know "what is the breadth, and length, and depth, and height" of the love of Christ, "being rooted and grounded in love."

I will have you know how I have remained on bended knee day and night, beseeching the Lord's goodness, that he may safeguard you, my daughter, my jewel. At times, I thought I never longed for anything as I now long to see your face again. That you should be removed from my side . . . this was a thing too frightful to bear, or so I believed. Nevertheless, my prayers have not been in vain, for the perpetual ministry of the Spirit and the Virgin Mary, who suffered the loss of her only child, has become as real to me as the hand with which I now write. Thus, you must know that my pains are few and there can be no cause for concern on your part, my dearest daughter.

We received word of your safe arrival in Liège from Burchard, goodly man that he is. Such consolation this brought to my soul! There was also a note from my sister, Mary, upon the subject of your visit to Boulogne. Rest assured, she had nothing but praise for you and wrote that your respite there was free of the slightest adversity. How fortunate that she was available to offer you hospitality!

Now, write to me, Daughter, and tell me how you do, for I desire to hear all of your news. The briefest word would cause my heart great cheer. It is a wicked fate that we should not find ourselves always in the company of those we hold most dear, but the Lord provides us with the strength to overcome.

"Unto him therefore that is able to do exceeding abundantly above all that we ask or think, according to the power that works in us, be praise in the Church by Christ Jesus, throughout all generations for ever, Amen.

MATHILDA REGINA

I confess that by the time I finished the letter tears flowed freely from my eyes. Perhaps she had known this would be the case and sought to spare me the shame of public tears by avoiding the need for a translator. If so, she had done me a kindness.

"My pains are few," she had written. I wanted to believe it, but suspected that she merely sought to raise my spirits at the thought of her good humor. I could not help but remember the indifference shown by my father at our final parting, and it certainly seemed to be, in the words of my esteemed mother, "a wicked fate."

But this was interesting: Countess Mary of Boulogne had reported that my visit was one of complete tranquility! For myself, I could hardly think of anything less so than the brief audience I shared with my aunt and cousin that day. "The tales of men are oft deceiving," was my final conclusion on the matter.

"Virgin Mary, grant me the strength to overcome," I prayed, "for I am not my mother. Her faith exceeds my own as the light of the sun does that of the moon."

With that frank admission, I bid the ladies bring me some small morsels from the kitchen and then ready me for sleep. It was to be another early morning the following day. Indeed, I had forgotten the last time that it had not been an early morning.

Once he had satisfied himself that all was in order, Emperor Henry's ships set stern to the north and bow to the south, continuing their course upriver. Our progress was helped by calmer winds than on the preceding day. In addition, the emperor employed more men at the oars to ensure that we would reach the great city of Cologne with all haste. It was not long before we passed Cleves, and all in all it was a pleasant day for travel. I had the good fortune to be placed on the same vessel as Archbishop Bruno, to whom I addressed not a few questions regarding that region. I mentioned some ruins that I had seen near the palace in Nijmegen, and he explained that they were all that remained from a time long ago.

"The Roman emperors of old built a great wall along this river, only a few remnants of which now survive. Little is known of those days, but there are stories passed down from father to son and a few chronicles that speak of the coming of the Romans to Germania. We know that the great river, the Rhine, marked out the line between Germania Inferior and Magna Germania, as they were then named. When you come to Trier, or Augusta Treverorum as it is known in Latin, you will see evidence of their stay here. East of the Rhine the empire was absent, or so it seems. That was the land of the *barbari*."

With the word *barbari*, he raised his brows with a mischievous look, as if he seemed to take pleasure in it.

"You act as if you prefer that designation," I said.

He laughed softly and then replied, "It is best that I explain this to you, as you ought to understand the people that you rule. There is a contradiction within the minds of the Germans. On the one hand, we have the glorious Holy Roman emperor, descendant of Constantine. He is ruler of not only the Germans, but many other peoples as well, even as was the case with the great Caesars of Rome. Here in the Rhine Valley, the past merges with the present and speaks to the connection between one empire and the next. It is a sign of our ancient lineage, from which we draw great pride."

He paused slightly, took a drink from the goblet set before him, and then continued.

"There is another story which also shapes us as a people, and that is the story of those east of the Rhine, the ones who withstood the Roman advance. Think of it! Rome was the most powerful empire the world has ever known, conquering everything from Babylon in the East to your own Britannia in the North. Yet in the tribes of the Germanii, the Romans met their deadliest foe. In these forests and upon these hills the warriors of old fought the imperial legions, gladly spilling their blood to defend the land of their fathers. Their paganism is a mark against them—that I will grant you—but even so, there is something laudable about it."

"And what meaning should we take from this?" I asked.

"Well, history is always a matter of interpretation," the archbishop admitted, "but in light of the present disagreements between the bishop of Rome and the emperor . . ."

"The Kingdom of Germany is eager to once again declare its independence," I concluded on his behalf. "So the emperor is both the heir of Rome and its foe?"

"As I said before, it is a contradiction, but I think you will find, Lady Mathilda, that the world is full of such contradictions."

"My mother the queen always believed that the princes of the Church were charged with administering spiritual authority, and not the lay members, however exalted they might be," I replied. "Is it not enough that the emperor is lord over his own lands? Must he, in the manner of his father, also defy our holy Church?"

The archbishop's brows were raised once again, but this time the look was not one of humor. Indeed, he appeared to be taken aback, and I feared that I had been too forthright in my assertions.

"I am sorry, Archbishop Bruno. I did not mean that the emperor is not a good Christian prince."

Fortunately, Bruno relaxed his features and broke into a smile. "No harm done, my lady. The words you speak have been echoed in the mouths of many a man from Paris to Pisa, and several persons within our own kingdom as well. I think as you spend more time with us, you will come to understand how difficult the matter is. I could certainly never find fault in your honorable mother, who is known far and wide as a true disciple of Jesus Christ. However, I think it best that in the future you refrain from making such assertions publicly, particularly in either the emperor's or his chancellor's presence."

"That I should never do, Your Grace, not as long as I live," I answered.

"I have no doubt that you speak the truth. Now, we are but an hour or so from Neuss, and I need refreshment. Is there anything I can retrieve for you?"

"No, I am quite content. Tell me, how long until we reach Cologne?"

"Not until the sun sets, I fear. It is a long way and against the current."

"*Danke, Bruno.*"

"*Gott sei mit euch, Mathilda.*"

We did arrive in Cologne by sunset and were received by Archbishop Frederick. I found him highly different from the archbishop of Trier; there was a seriousness in his manner that lent a greater sense of import to certain matters than was strictly necessary, though he was not without humor. Building was one of his chief passions, and even at that time he was already overseeing the construction of the Volmarstein Castle on the River Ruhr. Other fortresses and monasteries would follow throughout the course of his tenure.

Tradition dictated that the archbishop of Mainz oversee the coronation of each new German king and any royal consorts. However, the seat was vacant at that time, as Emperor Henry had not yet named a successor to the late Ruthard, a man who found himself at odds with the fourth Emperor Henry when the Jews of that city were slain on his watch. Ruthard had attempted to seize the property of those poor souls for himself, although it was the emperor who had all authority over such persons according to the principle of *Kammerknechtschaft*, which is called in Latin *servi camerae regis*. Whether by divine judgment or the workings of nature, Ruthard soon departed this earthly realm. Because there was no archbishop in Mainz, it was decided that Frederick, the archbishop of Cologne, would take over the coronation duties.

Also in Cologne we received news from afar that the forces of Christendom had prevailed against the enemies of God in Beirut. We were glad to hear of it, for there was not a child in the Lord's Church who had not heard the tales: how the heartless Saracens had brutally overtaken the land in which the Messiah once walked, aiming to force their idolatry on others and striking down pilgrims to the holy city in a most cruel manner. This continued for many long years before the Byzantine emperor sought out the help of His Holiness Pope Urban in retrieving that which had been lost, healing the breach between the papal court and the eastern bishops. In the year I arrived in the Holy Roman Empire, the kingdom of Jerusalem gained control of not only Beirut, but Sidon as well, the latter with King Sigurd of Norway's help.

Forgive me, for I have once again diverted from the main purpose of my tale. After departing Cologne we passed through a section of the river where the hills grew high on both sides and vineyards multiplied. The men of that region were exceedingly proud of their wine, the earth providing desirable conditions for growing grapes. The river then took a turn just before we reached the city of Mainz, which was to be the site of my coronation. I understood that we would cease our travels there, but we were back in the ships the following morning, this time pressing on to Speyer. It seemed that the emperor had business there regarding the upcoming Italian expedition.

Although I tired of this continual travel, it was an extraordinary time in my life. I was able to gain in a few short months a substantial knowledge of the kingdom that had become my home. While I was still apprehensive about some of the foods placed before me, I found that my palate was gradually adapting to the changed conditions. Each new day provided an opportunity to converse in the German, and in accordance with the wishes of both Archbishop Bruno and my chaplain, Altmann, I renewed my effort to learn Latin. I much preferred the language of the empire to that of Rome, but I was well aware of the necessity for Latin in government affairs.

It was still rare for me to speak with my betrothed beyond a few words exchanged over supper. As always, he spent most of his time talking with his counselors or in different pursuits with his nephews, Duke Frederick of Swabia and his brother Conrad. I understood that the emperor's sister, Agnes, mother of both those young men, would be present in Mainz for my coronation on the feast day of Saint James. This was a high honor for me, as it required her to travel from her home in the Eastern March, where she lived with her second husband, Leopold of Babenberg. I was most eager to meet any female relation of my future husband, even if she was considerably older.

I shall never forget those days in which, for the first time, I saw the great cathedrals of the land. Emperor Henry's predecessors built many works along the Rhine, designing new houses of worship more grand even than the one in Aachen. The principal construction was in Speyer, and upon this model they built equally grand cathedrals in both Mainz and Worms, though on a somewhat smaller scale. The Mainzer Dom had been officially consecrated in the preceding year, but the Cathedral of Worms was only just completed. Thus the imperial party halted there during the progress south in order to consecrate the new church.

Allow me now to tell of those days in Mainz. We had been traveling down the river from Speyer, which was a welcome change, as it allowed us to move with the current. Only the scores of merchant ships sharing the waterway slowed our progress. We sighted the piers of Mainz within a day of our departure, and after we navigated past the confluence with the River Main, the ships were all planted within the shadow of the great cathedral. As usual, I waited for the men to make everything ready, then made to alight with my ladies. The plank was quite slick—indeed, while they did not say so at the time, I suspect it had been used earlier to move barrels of fish. I was almost to the bottom when my right foot began to slide. I tried to recover my balance, but was uncertain which way I should fall in order to avoid the water. As you might suspect, this indecision proved my undoing. My foot turned to the side and my weight tottered, carrying me forward toward the stone pavement.

Fortunately, Drogo was there to break my fall, even as the ladies behind me let out a collective gasp. He held me for a moment and allowed me to slow my breathing.

"Are you hurt, my lady?" he asked, even as the crowd pressed in around us.

"I think not, thanks to you," I replied with some difficulty. "I feel a bit sore . . . and stunned, but I hope nothing more serious."

The knight then let up his grasp, and I once again bore my own weight. I felt a sudden pain in my right foot and had to reach back and place a hand on Drogo's shoulder.

"*Geht es Ihnen nicht gut?*" Lady Adelaide inquired, but Gertrude started yelling, "*Nicht laufen! Nicht laufen!*"

"What is she saying?" Drogo asked.

"She says I should not be walking, and I think she is correct," I answered.

Another voice then broke into the conversation. "*Was ist los?*"

I looked over to see that the emperor himself was now standing among us, the tumult having caught his attention. Before anyone could reply to his question, he strode forward and bid me sit down. He then asked me what hurt, and I pointed to my right foot.

"*Kannst du laufen?*" he asked, to which I quietly replied, "*Nein.*"

Lady Gertrude began to speak quickly in German, and though I could not understand it all, I gathered that she proposed some manner of transporting me. The emperor apparently did not agree with whatever she proposed, for before she was able to finish, he said to me, "*Pardon,*" and lifted me off the ground and held me in his arms.

"*Machen Sie den Weg frei!*" he yelled, and the crowd moved back to clear a path before us.

He carried me a short way before we came to a waiting carriage. Without a word, he placed me inside and commanded the two ladies and Drogo to join me. Once all were aboard, he said to the driver, *"Bringen Sie die Königin in ihr Quartier,"* and we immediately began moving up the hill in the direction of the *Dom*. I suppose I ought to have been considering how extraordinary was the emperor's assistance, but instead there was only one thought troubling me: "How will I ever be able to walk down that aisle?"

We soon arrived at the quarters normally reserved for the archbishop of Mainz, which were just across the square from the cathedral. The royal physician felt no broken bones, but declared that my ankle had been strained. It was impossible for me to walk, so we compromised: I would be aided as necessary at different points in the coronation ceremony. Given that I was already dreading the occasion, this added difficulty was most unwelcome.

The bells were ringing in the cathedral of Mainz that morning, and all around there was a sense of hope. The very stones seemed, from the way they reflected the sun's light, to join the festivity. For on this day the emperor's young consort, the Roman queen, was to be crowned, and it would be a glorious moment in the kingdom's history. So must most of the people in Mainz have experienced that day, but to me it was more than some monument to tradition. Rather, it was a test that I must pass. This very necessity provoked my spirit that morning—knowing as I did that under no circumstance must I allow myself to falter. To this day I might find myself in the long watches of the night dreaming of that morning, and though it was completed so many years ago, I experience again that rush of fear that might torment a woman of eight or eighty years upon this earth.

In spite of that fear, I found myself at the appointed moment seated upon one of the grandest horses I had ever seen, legs placed carefully to one side, my body clothed in purple silk, my head adorned with a simple white covering, ready to receive a diadem fit for a queen. We proceeded across the yard to the church, with Drogo leading the horse and the Duke of Swabia walking in front of us as crown bearer. It was a very short walk, but we moved slowly on account of the throngs of people on either side, a sea of cheering voices branching off in all directions and down every nearby street. At the end of our path, the great red walls rose up toward the heavens, capped by a tower on each side, with arches carved into the stones at each level.

With some effort we reached the eastern entrance to the church, where the archbishop of Cologne and the archbishop of Trier awaited us. The horse halted, and Drogo, in whose embrace I felt most safe, carefully helped me to the ground. Maintaining my grip on his arm, I took a few carefully placed steps toward the archbishops, trying to favor my left foot as much as possible without appearing lame.

"All this work, and I am only at the door," I thought to myself.

Archbishop Frederick recited the sacred words writ in ages long past. He bid the crowd declare if they would accept as their queen "Mathilda, daughter of the king of England, come here today to be crowned, and pledge to serve her in perpetuity, according to the laws of God and man." They answered back either, "*Volumus!*" or, in the German tongue, "*Wir werden!*" raising their right hands in a show of fealty and devotion. Scattered cries of "*Salve regina!*" echoed around the square.

Archbishop Bruno stepped forward now, as it had been agreed that he would carry me down the length of the nave to the western front. It was an inelegant solution, but the most practical one.

"Permit me, Your Highness," he said, and bent down as I placed my small arms around his neck. He lifted me up with the greatest care, being sure not to leave the hem of my gown askew.

"Are you ready?" he asked.

I answered in the affirmative, and Archbishop Frederick motioned toward the open door, which was set underneath an arched portal. With the utmost caution we crossed the threshold and entered the great *Dom*. We were now in the northern aisle, and I could not see the entirety of the church for the large number of men and ladies crowded among the great pillars, which seemed endless.

"So many people," I whispered.

"*Ja*, and they are all here for you," Bruno replied. "You must take courage from that."

Whatever I took from that, I doubt that it was courage, but there was no time to ponder such concerns. The heralds' trumpets were already playing, and after a brief pause for all my ladies to take their places, we turned to the left and began to move in procession—first the standard bearer, then Archbishop Frederick, followed by the Duke of Swabia carrying the crown, then myself and Archbishop Bruno, and finally the ladies. We quickly arrived at the nave, which presented a view much like that of the *Dom* in Speyer, though of a slightly different style. Light poured down from the high windows, illuminating our path in a kind of heavenly glow.

We passed people of great import from all parts of the empire, lords and ladies of the royal court, ambassadors from countries near and far, and a great number of clergy. At the very end of the line, just before we reached the stairs, was Emperor Henry, standing next to a woman I could only conclude must be the Margravine of Austria, his sister Agnes. Her younger son Conrad and Chancellor Adalbert sat farther down. Agnes smiled at me as I caught her eye, and thus my first impression of her was a positive one.

"Perhaps she is more personable than her brother," I mused.

At last Archbishop Bruno placed me upon the royal seat, and the archbishop of Trier was free to resume his ceremonial role.

I tried with some difficulty to fix my mind on the words that the archbishop of Cologne spoke, though I was perpetually aware of the many eyes staring at me. Could I really rule over them, and how might such a thing be accomplished?

"*Accipe hunc sceptrum cum Dei benediction tibi collatum, in quo, per vitutem sancti Spiritus resistere et eicere omnes inimicos tuos valeas, et cunctos sancte Dei ecclesie adversarios regnumque tibi commissum tutari atque protegere castra Dei, per auxilium invictissimi triumphatoris domini nostri Iesu Christi.*"

So the archbishop pronounced the sentence, even as he placed the golden scepter into my right hand. This was the usual moment at which the imperial sword was given to the new king, but such a weapon of justice was not deemed proper for the weaker sex, or so I was told. Instead I was granted the scepter and orb, each of them covered in jewels of equal magnificence. Now Archbishop Bruno brought forth the golden ampulla, which stored the holy oil of anointing. While all nations may anoint their rulers in such a manner, the Germans do so twice. This was the first anointing, in which Archbishop Frederick dipped two fingers into the oil and then made the sign of the cross on my forehead. As he did so, I could almost sense the divine presence enveloping me with that sign, setting me apart for God's work and covering me with a layer of protection. I do not know whether this experience was authentic or imaginary.

Then came the fated moment. In a manner both careful and determined, the archbishop of Cologne lifted the royal crown and carried it in great ceremony toward the throne. All was silent, so much so that it was possible to hear the sound of a stray bird that had found its way into the heights of the cathedral. It seemed that all nature had come to witness this. The archbishop lifted the crown high above my head, and as my eyes moved upward I saw the briefest of flashes as a ray of light from one of the windows landed upon the diadem. No sooner did it appear than it was gone, and he set the crown into place. It was a bit too large for my small head, though the craftsman who had first shown it to me claimed that it would match my fully grown frame. The people then chanted the hymn "Laudes regiae," proclaiming Christ as the king of kings and beseeching him to grant the new queen help.

"To Mathilda, crowned of God, great and pacific queen of the Romans, life and victory!"

They recited it in Latin, but I knew the words according to the Normans. There followed then "Te Deum laudámus," that much-beloved hymn so familiar to me, though it did go on for an inordinate amount of time.

"Holy, holy, holy, Lord God of hosts! Heaven and earth are full of the majesty of thy glory!" they chanted.

We then came to the Mass, and I was forced to stand up from my seat and walk the few steps to the altar, once again doing my utmost not to betray any weakness or constraint. Undoubtedly the crowd had guessed at my malady when I was carried to the western front, but I could not allow this vision of their queen to be weighed down by a sense of ill health—not when the choir chanted the glories of the anointed monarchy.

I slowly dropped to my knees on the colored tile, taking care to keep the crown steady. This was the one point in the ceremony where I could express my wishes, for I had been asked in the days afore which hymn I would prefer for the sequence. My mind had immediately turned to one that Father Anselm taught to me: "Veni Creator Spiritus." As the choir chanted, I raised up my own prayer to the Creator that he might indeed send forth his Spirit to rest upon me and grant me heavenly aid. As the host was lifted up, I prayed that the Savior would cause me to ascend to some higher realm where the treasures of divine wisdom were stored.

In such a manner the ceremony progressed until "Spiritus Sancti gratia" was sung and Bruno carried me back the way I had come. Such a feeling of relief swept over me that even the pain in my ankle seemed to lift and my whole body felt lighter. My bearer also seemed to enjoy the moment, for he said to me with a smile, "The thing has been accomplished, and it is well done."

The following day, the archbishop's quarters were being emptied as quickly as they had been filled. Those things belonging to the emperor's household were made ready to be carried down the river to Speyer, whence my betrothed would depart to the South: first to visit *la Grancontessa*, Mathilda of Tuscany, on whom the affairs of that land largely depended, and then to attend His Holiness Pope Paschal at the church of Saint Peter in Rome. My own possessions were loaded onto carts for the journey over land to Trier, where Archbishop Bruno was to take up my instruction, preparing me for the day when I would wed *Kaiser* Henry and reign with him as *Kaiserin* Mathilda.

As I waited for all to be made ready for our departure, I asked to return to the *Dom* and see it in its natural state. It was agreed that my chaplain, Altmann, should take me hence, as he was familiar with the grounds. I had not yet been able to explore the entirety of those chambers, and my guide was more than happy to answer my questions about the carvings, parchments, tapestries, and sacred vessels. Whereas some may have found my childish zeal disagreeable, he seemed to embrace this chance to inform others about the inner workings of that world. Finally we came to a small chapel just off the threefold nave, a room set up for private devotion more than public spectacle. Lovely tapestries upon the walls portrayed the life of one of the apostles, though I could not make out which one.

"*Wer ist das?*" I asked in my best German.

"*Dies ist Jakob, der Apostel von Christus.*"

"Ah, Saint James. I suppose I should have known that."

Sure enough, each panel portrayed a different tale from the saint's life: the falling of the Holy Spirit upon the gathered saints, the great council at Jerusalem, the writing of his epistle, and finally his martyrdom. Silver thread wove through the large fields of blue, and the saint's eyes looked perpetually toward heaven, even to the very end.

I had paid so much attention to these works of craftsmanship that it was only after thoroughly examining each one that I noticed what was at the center of the room: a square glass *reliquiarium* upon a marble stand. What I saw inside, my eyes recognized before my mind could accept. It appeared to be a human hand, but unlike any other I had seen. If it was indeed a real hand, it must have been very old, for it was of no natural hue, but rather a dark gray that spoke of death long ago, or perhaps the effects of fire. It was repugnant, and yet I found myself stepping forward to view it more closely. The fingers curled inward, but the nails were mostly intact.

"I see you have found the hand of Saint James," a voice behind me said.

It was Archbishop Bruno, who had apparently entered the room when I was not aware. His presence was a great surprise. My imagination had, for the space of one second, been certain that the matching withered hand was coming to seize me from behind and pull me to some dark place.

"Archbishop," I said, with a small bow of the head, "is what you say true? Did this hand belong to the apostle?"

"That is the story, yes."

"But I thought he was buried in Santiago. Why else do the pilgrims flock to that site?"

"His body lies there, but the city was able to gain this relic for display in the cathedral. For a man whose words have been studied as much as his, the hand is of special significance."

"So they cut it off?"

"Perhaps it broke off of its own accord."

I turned to look again at the withered member. I had seen many relics in England, but none as exalted as this. Yet I still felt somewhat disturbed by the sight of it. I tried instead to imagine its power.

"'Blessed is the man that endures temptation: for when he is tried, he shall receive the crown of life.' This very hand must have written those words," I said. "It is a strange thing to be so close to that which seems so distant."

"The past often reaches out to us, to illumine that which we cannot understand," he replied.

Altmann must have grown tired of this conversation in a foreign tongue, for at this point he begged leave of both of us and returned to make preparations for our departure. I guessed that Bruno had not come merely to speak about relics, and when asked he informed me that it was time for us to depart if we were to make the most of the remaining daylight.

"But I have yet to meet the emperor's sister," I protested.

"Margravine Agnes has already departed Mainz with her sons."

This disappointed me greatly, and the archbishop must have sensed my regret, for he quickly changed the subject of conversation.

"*Ich habe ein Geschenk für Sie,*" he said, revealing a parcel that he had kept hidden behind his back.

I attempted to quickly shift my mind to the new language, but the longest phrase I could assemble was, "*Danke, Erzbischof.*" I accepted the book from him and opened it to the title page, which read, "*Commentarii de Bello Civili.*"

"Civil wars? Is this a book about warfare?" I asked.

"*Ja und nein.* This is the commentary of Julius Caesar regarding his battles against Pompey." As if pointing out a redeeming feature, he added, "It will provide an excellent opportunity for you to study Latin!"

"I know this book."

"*Ja?* You have read it? I am most impressed."

"Strictly speaking, it was read to me. Master Godfrey included selections from it in our daily lessons."

"Who is Master Godfrey?" Bruno asked.

"He was my first tutor, save for my mother and her ladies." I suppressed the desire to add, "He was a complete idiot."

"Do you remember anything from the book?"

"No, not a word. For one thing, he was not very skilled at explaining, nor did he set much store by it. For another . . . I was rather easily distracted."

"I see. Well, any worthy endeavor deserves a second attempt."

"I suppose."

"You suppose rightly," he concluded. "Now we must be off to Trier, ere the candle burns too low! Come, there is much yet to learn, and too little time in which to learn it. The philosophers of old will be our guides, for we must be as innocents in our actions, but wise as serpents in the ways of the world."

CHAPTER TEN

Augusta Treverorum, northern capital of the Roman Empire of old, jewel upon the River Moselle, crowned with nobility down to the present day. Long before the legions of Rome walked those streets, the Treveri laid down the ancient foundations—they the descendants of the great prince of Assyria. As a sojourner from the East founded Rome itself, so its northern twin came into being. Here Constantine the Great first revealed his power and oversaw the creation of the magnificent Trier that lives on today. 'Twas he who strengthened the walls, built the imperial palace, and constructed the bathhouses that yet stand. The greatest remainder of those days is the Porta Nigra, the Black Gate, which for some time the local residents stripped of its dignity, believing it to be the perfect quarry for their more modern ambitions. It was only of late that a monk by the name of Simeon sought out that structure as a place of meditation, and in so doing hallowed the very ground. A monastery was then adjoined to the gate, and men named it the Simeonstift. Now the Porta serves as a place of worship for our Lord, and may it continue to do so for as long as the city stands.

In mighty Trier was Archbishop Bruno's seat, and there he taught me the language and customs of the German people, as well as general matters of philosophy that he believed a royal consort must understand. Here it seems proper, Daughter, that I should carry on solely in our own tongue, for were I to set down such dialogues in their original form, they should be so foreign to you as to prevent your proper understanding. Suffice it to say I knew the German language by the end of that year, hearing little else from sunrise to sunset.

The Aula Palatina, palace of the Roman emperors, was by that time in the hands of the Church and the archbishop. Having fallen far from its former grandeur, it was hardly a proper residence for Trier's most esteemed inhabitant. Instead Bruno had his private quarters nearer the *Dom*, just to the south of the Simeonstift. A chamber was set aside for me in the monastery with a window overlooking the cloister. It was my first time living among men of the cloth, and I found the experience strange indeed.

Though I was among them, I was not one of them. I watched them moving to and fro, some to the *scriptorium*, some to the rectory, and others to the gardens. They did not allow a moment to pass without putting it to some good purpose, save for some mild revelry in the evening. They followed the office of the blessed Virgin to the letter. It was a life unlike that in a royal castle, for the inhabitants were always busy but never appeared so.

I too followed a regimen. You will remember Archbishop Bruno's gift to me upon my coronation, the volume of commentaries by Julius Caesar. Master Godfrey had read to us from such works for an hour at a time, and in those days I could scarcely think of anything duller. However, upon my arrival in Trier, Bruno determined to provoke in me a love for the ancients.

"Do not think of this merely as an example of Latin text," he instructed me. "Here before you is a guide for those who would ride into battle. Moreover, it speaks to the primary instincts of human nature."

"But Archbishop, as a royal consort, why do I need to learn about warfare? In what tale does a queen lead men into battle? I have never heard of such a thing."

"*Die Schildmaid* is praised in legends and songs," he replied.

"That is not the same as a queen, which is what I am."

"Shall you be satisfied if I provide an example?"

"Perhaps."

"Well, then . . . Herodotus wrote of Queen Artemisia of Caria, who under the command of Xerxes led a fleet against the Greeks at the Battle of Salamis. I trust this satisfies your query. Now I think you must translate for me ten lines in payment."

"I do not think that should count, since it took place on the water," I countered, but noticing the look in the archbishop's eye, I decided to surrender. "Which lines?"

"Here at the top of the page. First in your own language, then in German."

"I doubt Queen Artemisia was forced to perform such a task," I muttered to myself.

I began to read out as Bruno had instructed. It was a section near the beginning, starting with Caesar's address to the men under his command.

"What is happening here?" Bruno asked when I had finished.

"Caesar blames Pompey for the state of civil war, and Pompey blames Caesar."

"And who do you think was to blame?"

"How should I know, sir?"

"The text provides clues, does it not?"

"Yes, but . . ." My voice trailed off.

"What is it?"

"This was written by one of the combatants."

"Yes."

"So is it entirely credible? Men are apt to praise their own actions."

"Quite right you are. This is what you must decide. Caesar makes his case for crossing the Rubicon. Do you think him justified?"

I stopped to ponder for a moment, then replied, "To break the peace is a hateful thing, as Scripture teaches us."

"Yet the Lord commanded the Israelites into battle."

"I suppose you are right. This is like asking if the emperor is justified in his quarrel with the pope."

"Ah, now we come to it!" He seemed oddly delighted to broach the subject. "Your future husband has gone down to Italy to treat with His Holiness."

"Why are you not with him, sir? You served as his ambassador to Rome in the past."

"It is more necessary that I am here," he answered. "I must see to your training, and in any case, it would not do to leave the sheep behind when the wolves of Saxony are ever on the prowl."

"Wolves of Saxony?"

"Yes, if there is any rebellion in the Kingdom of Germany, you can be sure that it comes from Saxony."

"Why should that be so? Does the emperor treat them poorly?"

Bruno reached toward a dish full of apples. Taking one in his hand, he pulled out a knife and began cutting it into pieces as he spoke.

"Ruling an empire as immense as the one over which your betrothed now sits is a delicate balance. One must always be aware of contentions between different factions: the nobles, the bishops, the lower classes, the *ministeriales*, all the members of the ruling family, the church in Rome. As you can see, there are a lot of them, and I have yet to mention the divisions between houses and regions. There is our present position—the Rhineland—and then Burgundy, Swabia, Lorraine, Lombardy, Bavaria, the lands to the east. Suffice it to say, there is no end to the number of factions."

"Surely all these that you have mentioned owe their allegiance to the emperor?"

"Would that it were that simple," he said, handing me a slice of the apple. "Eat this."

"Thank you," I answered, gladly accepting the sweet morsel. "Archbishop, you often speak of the men of the church here as if they were even more powerful than the nobles."

"In a sense they are. Their earthly possessions are substantial. Many emperors have sought to use them as a check against the noble houses, for when an unwed man dies, his property may revert back to the state rather than being handed down in perpetuity. The difficult thing of it is, a man of the Church always seeks to serve two masters: one at home, and one far away in Rome."

"You fail to mention service to God," I objected.

"If God may be served, so much the better—quite right you are. However, the facts of life force us into a hard position. The city of man and the city of God are too often at odds, as in the case of investiture. Rome would give the emperor no say in selecting bishops within his own kingdom, even though they receive both land and power within the secular realm."

"What does the emperor intend to do?"

"He will offer His Holiness a great compromise, wherein the church will retain all its rights of investiture, but it must renounce its imperial grants, from the time of Charles the Great down to the present day."

"Is the pope likely to agree to that?"

"He has already said that he will, but even the pope must contend with factions of his own. The Gregorians will surely oppose such an agreement, in which case we shall see how powerful Pope Paschal truly is."

"I suppose it is a noble principle: poverty for the sake of Christ, allowing the Church to see to its own business, and so on. Still, do you think it is likely to work?"

"Only time will tell," Bruno concluded. "The slightest act might set all our devices to ruin. As Caesar says, 'Great events often depend on small changes.' That is written in this very volume. Let us proceed with it."

I knew that I would rather continue discussing the emperor, but in resignation I replied, "Yes, sir," and set about the task of translating the next lines, dismayed to see the number of pages that were yet to be addressed. It was to be a long endeavor.

As the year of our Lord 1110 grew old and the sky took on a constant gray, we received two letters on the same day. One came from the South and recounted the exploits of Emperor Henry against the Lombards, along with the progress of his discussions with the Holy See. Accompanied by the royal counselor David, the imperial chancellor, and a native Welshman, the emperor had made substantial progress in his efforts. The Kingdom of Italy was pacified, and his counselors had every reason to think that the coronation would take place early the following year. Over cries of outrage from the Gregorians, His Holiness Paschal II seemed ready to place his seal to the agreement, which would end the great controversy that had plagued both church and empire for decades. As for Adalbert, he had been assigned the archbishopric of Mainz.

"Let us hope that he does not use this new position merely to favor his House of Saarbrücken," Bruno commented, revealing mistrust for the man who shared with him the emperor's affections. Indeed, I sensed that he begrudged Adalbert his place as the chief imperial counselor, for that was a position that had once belonged to Bruno.

The second letter was from England, and I assumed that it must be from the queen until I saw the parchment's great red seal. It was no royal emblem, though perhaps its originator felt he was very near that degree of majesty, for Bishop Roger of Salisbury was its author. I was surprised to receive any communication from him, and thus it roused my interest for whatever revelations might follow. I broke the seal and read the words before me.

To Mathilda, queen of the Romans,

Roger, bishop of Salisbury sends his greetings and best wishes for your good health and welfare. Your esteemed father, King Henry, wished me to inform you of all that has taken place here in England. Rest assured that the king is in good spirits and ever beloved by his subjects. His efforts to improve our own cathedral in Salisbury have created a deep affection in the people here, to the extent that they all look to the king as if he were their own father, so precious do they count the gifts they receive from his royal hand. In everything, the king proves himself to be the true heir of his father and an equal of all the rulers of elder days.

Prince William has also progressed in his studies and is the image of his honorable father. He is ever among the king's men and benefits greatly from such true companions. In the fullness of time, all of England hopes to see him take up his father's place with a comparable degree of distinction. May God continue to grant this land such good fortune in its rulers!

Sadly, the same cannot be said for Fulk, Count of Anjou, who has continually goaded the king in word and deed. He now holds the County of Maine by virtue of marriage and is determined to pillage the land of Normandy.

Thus your father makes preparations for another journey across the Channel to defend his inheritance. May God grant him victory! Amen.

I would be remiss if I did not also mention the other reason for the king's restoration, namely the birth of his son, who is called Reginald. Despite the failure of the queen to bring forth more children, the Lord has seen fit to grant these further blessings. Know that it is not from any desire of the flesh that the king behaves in such a manner, but rather to avoid the chaos brought on by an uncertain succession. Fear not, for your brother William, being the only fully legitimate offspring of the king, is in no danger of being deposed, for the bonds of matrimony are the proper breeding ground for future kings. However, in such cases, one can never be too careful.

We rejoice to hear of your coronation and hope this letter finds you in the center of God's blessing. Grace and peace to you.

"So the king has forced his second in command to reveal this news to me," I thought. "Pity he did not tell me himself. It might have been more proper. And to think that the bishop should excuse his master's indiscretions so! What kind of a man would write such a letter?"

The ladies had gone for the night. I set the letter on the bed and lay down next to it. My mind wandered through several considerations. How long would my father continue to seek out such trifles? Who was mother to this particular child? Would the king choose to recognize this son officially, as he had Robert? What feelings must be coursing through my mother's heart? How would she recover from such continued evidence of her husband's lack of devotion?

Another thought entered my mind, namely that my own future husband might be the same. Did he intend to seek comfort outside the bonds of matrimony? Had he perhaps already done so? How many bastard children would I be forced to smile at, and to how many mistresses must I grant hospitality on his account? The questions continued until I found myself growing tired, my mind endeavoring to count and recount the number of trusses holding up the roof overhead.

"This is no good," I said aloud. "I must not allow myself to be ruled by such thoughts. I ought to rejoice that I have a new brother, though it seems unlikely that I will ever make his acquaintance."

My father had more than a dozen such bastards, and of those I had only ever seen two. Robert, the eldest, was the only one with whom I had achieved a fraternal bond.

The weeks continued to pass, and at length February arrived. I was nine years old. As it happened, we had not received any word from the emperor for more than a fortnight, but on the fifteenth day before the kalends of February, we finally saw a messenger on horseback approaching from the south. He was received with all haste and brought before the archbishop, with whom I happened to be studying in the Simeonstift. The doors to the chamber opened and the man, still in his riding boots and cloak, entered and performed a great bow.

"Your Excellency, I bring news from Rome," the messenger said.

"Well, out with it then," the archbishop replied.

The man stood upright and recited his message from memory. "His Royal Highness Henry, king of the Romans, reached an accord with His Holiness Pope Paschal, the third day before the ides of this month. The king is to renounce all rights of investiture, and the bishops are to return the *regalia* granted by both the present emperor and his predecessors. My informer declares that when he left the city, all of Rome was preparing for the ceremony in Saint Peter's Basilica the following morn. Emperor Henry is to be crowned in the presence of all the princes of the Church, and the edict shall be signed and read out for all to hear."

The messenger thus ended his tale, and Bruno asked, "Is this the entirety of the message?"

"Every word, Your Grace," he replied.

Bruno stepped toward a nearby chair and sat down, his eyes staring at the floor and his mind apparently deep in thought. The royal messenger continued to stand there, evidently uncertain whether he should say something else or simply take his leave. Closing his eyes, the archbishop took a deep breath. Opening them again, he said, "This is excellent news! Things are unfolding precisely as we had hoped. It will be difficult for the bishops to accept, myself included, for it will require a great many changes, but I believe we can survive on the people's offerings. The emperor may have the more laborious task ahead, as he will no longer be able to select his own men for service."

Another pause, then Bruno asked, "What day did you say this agreement was reached?"

"The third before the ides of February, sir."

"That is four days ago! The best horses in the empire run faster than that."

"So they do," the messenger replied, perhaps sensing the danger of this line of questioning, "but I was delayed on account of some poor weather and an injury to one of the horses. Furthermore, I was set upon by thieves not twenty miles hence, and but for some clever thinking, I should not have made it to Trier unscathed."

"You can certainly find ill fortune in all manner of places," Bruno replied. "I hope the next man from Rome does not encounter such issues, for I long to hear how the Gregorians will take this news."

As fate would have it, the archbishop was not forced to wait long, for even as they spoke, the door burst open and another messenger entered without proclamation, taking his stand next to the first.

"Are you from Rome too?" I asked, thoroughly surprised.

"Yes, I come with urgent news on which a great many things depend. Archbishop," he said, looking earnestly at the older man, "I am sorry for my rough manner in entering your presence so, but I had not a moment to lose."

"What is it? What has happened?" Bruno asked, his voice betraying his concern as he rose from the chair. "Was the ceremony canceled after all?"

"Not as such. The emperor entered the church of Saint Peter in great pomp. All who looked upon him were amazed. He took his seat upon the royal throne, and the agreement was read out. At first all seemed well, until they reached the point of inevitable conflict. 'We forbid and prohibit any bishop or abbot, either now or in the future, to hold *regalia*, that is, towns, duchies, marches, counties, rights of mint or toll, imperial advocacies, rights of low justice, royal manors with their appurtenances, armed followings or imperial castles.' Well, the assembly did not take too kindly to that. Several of the bishops leaped out of their seats and cried in turn, 'Heresy! Abomination!' They refused to accept it. It was a terrible spectacle."

"Oh dear!" I said, without stopping to check myself. The archbishop was even less restrained, and turned his back to the rest of us, muttering, "*Scheiße! Scheiße!*"

"I fear that this was not the worst of it," the messenger added.

This caused Archbishop Bruno to once again become aware of the others in the room. He walked several steps forward, until the two men stood face-to-face.

"What could possibly be worse?" the archbishop asked in a low voice that almost seemed to threaten. When the messenger did not immediately reply, he yelled, "Answer me!"

"Excellency," he replied, "when the emperor saw that the pope would not go through with the agreement, he returned to his original demand of the full rights of investiture. This was too much for Paschal, who refused to crown him. Then the emperor . . . the emperor . . ."

"Spit it out, man!" Bruno demanded.

"The emperor and his men seized both the pope and the cardinals by force of arms and fled the premises. They broke through the city's defenses. The emperor himself was wounded in this action, though he sustained no serious damage to his person. Last I knew, they had retreated with their prisoners and camped not far from the city. It is likely that they shall remain there until one side is forced to back down. I rode day and night to bring this news to you, with few stops for rest. I hope you can accept it."

The archbishop looked as I had never seen him before and never would again. All color had fled from his face. He was utterly astounded and unable to speak. His eyes stared ahead into those of the messenger, his lips quivering. Abandoning all custom, I ran to him and placed my small hand upon his arm.

"Archbishop! My lord Bruno!"

He looked down at me, then back at the other two men standing in the room.

"I must sit down," he finally said, and both men moved to help him toward the chair. He pushed them away and was seated under his own power, covering his face with his hands.

"This is a calamity," the first messenger whispered to the second.

"It is worse than calamity," Bruno said, his voice muffled by his hands. "This is a tragedy worthy of Sophocles. They will say now that he is no different from his father, and his father died an excommunicate. This is a gift to his enemies."

Another moment passed in silence, then the archbishop looked up and continued. "It would have been better if I were there—then I might have advised him. Perhaps it is still possible for me to do so. You, messenger," he said, gesturing toward the first man, "I will bid you take a message to the emperor on my behalf. This fellow here needs rest if his tale is true. Be sure that fortune smiles on you this time, for I can brook no delay."

"It shall be done, Your Grace," the messenger replied.

"Leave me now," Bruno added, looking in turn at all three of us. "I must return to my quarters and provide what written instruction I can. May the saints guide me, for I can think of no precedent for this."

The messengers left as swiftly as they had come, but I tarried just a moment longer.

"Archbishop?"

"Yes, Lady Mathilda, be quick about it."

"Do you think that Pope Paschal will excommunicate the emperor?"

"I cannot possibly know that."

"But if he does . . ."

"My lady, there is a time for questions and a time for silence, and this is the latter," he responded rather bluntly.

"Forgive me," I said, and departed from the chamber.

I couldn't fathom what Bruno might possibly do to improve the situation. The emperor's actions seemed monstrous. He had committed a deed from which his reputation was likely never to recover. The pope could hardly submit to compulsion, and even if he did, such an agreement could be annulled after his release, as it would have been made under duress. If Bruno was right about the animosity already present within the empire toward their anointed ruler, then all of this would likely strengthen the chance of rebellion.

"My mother was right in her foreboding," I thought. "This is even worse than she feared from this villainous man. Emperor or not, who is he to raise his hand against the heir of Saint Peter? No, it cannot be borne. It shall not be."

Throughout the remainder of that day, I held on to the stone of amber and rubbed my fingers over it, wishing more than anything that I could return to that place whence I had come. But not even that stone of help could stem the tide of worry that enveloped me, as I knew that my entire future was in jeopardy and my husband was now likely to be declared *anathema*.

"Perhaps he will die before me," I hoped, allowing the anger to consume my soul.

My meetings with the archbishop were suspended for the remainder of the day, and even when he was able to resume our lessons, it was only in the most ill humor. At intervals I noticed his sight drifting to some object, his eyes open but his mind occupied elsewhere. I heard him ask on many occasions "whether there be any news from the South," referring to the situation in Italy. One, two, three days passed without so much as a word. On the morning of the fourth day since the messengers gave us the dreadful news, I visited the archbishop in the usual chamber. I found him seated at the table, with a letter spread out before him. He was leaning his forehead upon his right hand for support, or perhaps as a sign of frustration. His lips silently formed the words on the page.

I took the seat opposite him and waited until his attention was drawn hither. At length he looked up and addressed me.

"You wish to know what I am reading?" he asked.

"I did not inquire, my lord, for I believed it to be a private matter."

"Private for the moment perhaps, but in the fullness of time all things shall be brought into the light of day. The subject is public enough; this is a letter from His Royal Highness."

"The emperor?"

"Yes, he shall be emperor in full if the pope crowns him, though for the moment he remains most truly king of the Romans. Should he conjure some victory from this current situation, then most rightly we shall name him Holy Roman emperor, anointed of God and crowned by the vicar of Christ."

I was uncertain of how much the archbishop intended to reveal, but I sought to try my luck. "And what does King Henry have to say?"

To my surprise he handed the letter over to me and instructed, "Here, read it yourself. There is nothing that needs hiding, and it provides an opportunity for you to practice your translation skills."

"You wish for me to read it aloud, then?"

"All of it, if you please. It is not overlong."

I allowed my eyes to pass over the parchment. The markings were somewhat slanted and had clearly been written with a firm hand and in some haste. Whether they were the work of the emperor himself or one of his many clerks, I could not determine. I began to read as Bruno had commanded.

Henry, by the grace of God king of the Romans, to Bruno, archbishop of Trier, we send greetings from Tuscany.

You have no doubt heard the news of our interrupted coronation, for we sent our messenger thither upon solemn oath to relay to you the state of things, namely that we have here the bishop of Rome within our camp and several leading cardinals of our Church, and we have every reason to believe that an accord can be reached.

To this blessed state all our hopes are now bent, and know for certain that we should never have undertaken this course were it not for our firm opinion that His Holiness Pope Paschal has been subject to the most abominable counsel from that company of men who call themselves the sons of Gregory. Verily, we declare that they are no descendants of Gregory who misuse his successor in such a manner.

Though the pope be well disposed toward our person and ready to agree with us, he remains ever at the beck and call of these soothsayers, these perverse men of the world who wear the cassock as a disguise against their true natures. We sought in removing the pope from his Roman prison to grant him the freedom to choose what most pleases the Almighty rather than men.

Even so Jacob wrestled with the angel of the Lord and boldly proclaimed, 'I will not let you go, except you bless me.' May that same Lord who appeared to Jacob, and out of him made a great and powerful nation, come to us again in this present age and proclaim the justice of our cause. For we are most abused by that faction of clergy who seek to glorify themselves at the expense of all honor and comely brotherhood. Very soon, we foresee that the pope shall agree to our demands and see this justice be granted to our descendants and us.

Do not think that we act without conscience, for only after pursuing all those chances for peace which were made available to us did we take up arms against the city of Rome, which has lately sunken into such lechery as to make even whores blush. We heed not their protestations and wait only for the Lord's command. 'If God be on our side, who can be against us?' Rest you in the knowledge

that all will soon be set right, and relay our greeting to the young Mathilda, whom we have left in your especial care.
HENRICUS REX

"A fine letter," Bruno said, "no doubt recorded from the lips of Adalbert. Let us hope that his counsel of the king is not that of a fool."

Another two weeks passed before we received the news that an agreement had indeed been reached. This was the conclusion of the matter: The pope would not seek to inhibit the sovereignty of King Henry on account of the issue of investiture, nor would he excommunicate him. Rather, he would crown him in the same manner that had been earlier arranged. For his part, King Henry made the following pledge:

"I, Henry, the king, will, on the fourth or fifth day of the ensuing week, set at liberty the sovereign pope, and the bishops and cardinals, and all the captives and hostages, who were taken for him or with him; and I will cause them to be conducted, safely, within the gates of the city, beyond the Tiber; nor will I hereafter seize, or suffer to be seized, such as remain under fealty to the lord Paschal: and with the Roman people, and the city beyond the Tiber, I will, as well by myself as by my people, preserve peace and security, that is, to such persons as shall keep peace with me.

"I will faithfully assist the sovereign pope, in retaining his papacy quietly and securely. I will restore the patrimony and possessions of the Roman church which I have taken away; and I will aid him in recovering and keeping everything which he ought to have, after the manner of his predecessors, with true faith, and without fraud or evil design: and I will obey the sovereign pope, saving the honor of my kingdom and empire, as Catholic emperors ought to obey Catholic Roman pontiffs."

Of course, none of this touched upon the real issue of debate, that being the question of who possessed the right to invest both bishops and abbots with their offices. They compromised on that score, the pope pledging that the emperor might bestow the ring and crozier upon those chosen for office—men freely elected without suspicion of violence or simony—and maintain the right to refuse his consent. Thus he would oversee the task of investiture, while the Church would select and consecrate. This acknowledged both the spiritual and temporal powers given to these men of God, who were both citizens of the empire and of the heavenly kingdom.

In due course the pope crowned the emperor in a most glorious ceremony in Saint Peter's church, placing upon his head the symbol of imperial power and anointing him with the holy oil, which served as proof of divine blessing. Having achieved that for which he'd set out, Emperor Henry returned to Germany in a state far superior to that which many had conceived of only a few weeks earlier.

We received word of his coming near the beginning of summer and were called to meet him in Speyer, for as part of the agreement set down at the Lateran, the ban of excommunication was lifted from the emperor's departed father, Henry IV, he who on account of his sins was buried not inside the imperial cathedral, but in the unconsecrated chapel of Saint Afra. No longer in communion with the Church of Christ at the time of his death, he was denied the right to sleep beside his ancestors. However, the reversal of the papal edict now allowed for the late emperor's body to be reinterred within the heart of the royal *Dom* in Speyer.

I had no proper concept of what would take place on such an occasion, as I had not commonly attended any form of Mass for the dead, let alone a secondary burial. Adding to my unease was the current emperor's former state of rebellion against his father, which had resulted in open warfare. It seemed to me strange that, given the degree of hostility he had displayed toward his forebear in life, Emperor Henry V should show such concern for that same man's immortal soul in death. Such is the way of things, it seems, for even those who spurn the path of righteousness in waking days may find themselves placed among the saints in the minds of men *post mortem.*

We set out overland on our southeastern course, traveling past a number of small towns and the remains of an ancient fortress built by tribes of old. At length we skirted along the northern edge of the Wasgen Forest. That wood is immense: an infinite line of dark-green hills, and beneath the trees a secret world where all manner of life teems. When we were within a short march of the River Rhine, we turned south and spent the night at Limburg Abbey, that monastery particularly favored by the emperors. From there we had but one day's travel to complete along the banks of the Speyerbach.

Once we sighted the town of Speyer, I noticed how humble it appeared in relation to the great cathedral, which towered over it even as a mighty oak might a farmer's field. I wondered that the emperor's great ancestor, Conrad II, should have selected such a site on which to build the most magnificent church in the kingdom, save perhaps for the great *Kaiserdom* of Aachen.

"Would it not have been more apt to place it in one of the chief cities of the empire?" I inquired.

"Hardly!" Bruno replied, "For there is nothing a ruler desires more than to build something new, a testament to greatness that will stand for generations, even as Constantine the Great founded the city which bears his name. The greater the ruler, the greater the monument, methinks. Better to take a small city and make it the envy of men."

The summer rains had created backwater to the west of the city, but we persevered as best we could. Passing through the western gate, we found ourselves on the main thoroughfare leading directly to the cathedral. A true vision it was, larger than any church in Christendom, or at least any that I had seen. Its twin towers looked as if they might equal that of Babel. I felt in that moment as the shrew must in relation to the cat. We made our lodging in the bishop's palace very near the *Dom*. Several rooms had been built just for the imperial visit. The emperor's party had been there for some days before our arrival, and the main act was to take place the following morning. Both Gertrude and Adelaide were on hand to dress me for the occasion. I was to be clothed entirely in black, save for a golden belt and a few ornaments. The two of them worked to comb out my hair, the dull brown curls unyielding. At last they worked it into a tight braid they then gathered at the top of my head and hid with a dark fabric. They set a small diadem that had belonged in years past to the emperor's sister, Agnes, in its proper place.

"All is ready. Now to church!" Adelaide said.

I was all obedience as I joined the procession filtering into the *Dom*. A few hundred distinguished people attended, a sizable crowd, but not enough to fill the cathedral by any means. Bishop Bruno of Saarbrücken, the bishop of Speyer, greeted me upon my arrival. He was, by chance, brother to the new archbishop of Mainz, Adalbert. I say it was chance, but I am sure you know as well as I the power of certain families to see their children elevated into positions of power, thus enriching both themselves and their progeny.

"God save Your Ladyship!" the bishop said. "It is a pity that we should meet again under such circumstances, but nevertheless we are most privileged to receive Your Grace into our cathedral of Speyer."

It was true that I had briefly met the bishop at some point in the past year, though I suspected that his memory of the occasion was far stronger than my own.

"Bishop, would you be so good as to explain to me how the service will proceed?" I asked him. "It seems odd for a burial to take place under such circumstances."

"That is true," he answered, "but given the extraordinary situation, we must all adjust accordingly. You are aware, I am sure, of how my predecessors fought the good fight on behalf of the former emperor, always pressing his case to the See of Rome."

"Yes, I am well aware. The tales reached even to my native England."

"Then you will understand how dear we count this opportunity to lay a great man to rest in the cathedral which he built almost with his own two hands. First the relatives of the deceased shall meet in the Afra chapel to exhume the body, and then we shall proceed into the cathedral and bear the emperor up to the king's choir, where he will be buried beside his father, Emperor Henry III. Now, come follow me, for the family is assembling near the chapel portal."

I followed the bishop down the northern aisle, my eyes tracing the columns of many-colored stone up to the vault high above. The air smelled of incense, and the choir's chanting was not enough to drown out the sound of our footsteps upon the stone floor. We came at last to the single door that marked the entrance to the chapel. Margravine Agnes was already there, along with her sons and daughters, including the Duke of Swabia. The margravine was the last remaining of the emperor's siblings after the death of their brother Conrad some ten years earlier. She was speaking with Archbishop Bruno of Trier, while Archbishop Adalbert of Mainz stood to the side. A few other priests were also in attendance, as well as several lay assistants.

It was not long before the King Henry arrived. It was the first time I had seen him since he went to Italy. There appeared to be little difference in his personage, though his hair was a bit longer and his beard a bit thicker. With several nods of the head, he acknowledged each of us, and then turned to the bishop of Speyer.

"It is time?" he asked.

"Yes, it is time. Let us proceed," the older man replied.

The bishop led the way into the chapel, swinging his censer of incense, while his brother Adalbert followed directly behind, bearing a large golden cross in which precious gems were embedded. Not sure of my place, I slipped into the line of mourners entering one by one, just behind the emperor's nieces but ahead of the remaining churchmen, including Archbishop Bruno.

The chapel was larger than most, but not so much that it could have held all who might have wished to witness the moment. The late emperor's body was kept in a rather plain sarcophagus. We formed a tight circle around it. Emperor Henry stood nearest to the bishop, who was chanting from the psalms, ending always with the phrase *"Requiem aeternam dona eis, Domine, et lux perpetua luceat eis."*

In the wall just behind me, I could not help but notice a small circular window not far above the floor. The room on the whole was dark, for curtains had been pulled over the larger windows, and light was provided only by the many candles placed throughout the chapel, save for a few beams of light drifting through this small opening.

"Archbishop, what is that window for?" I whispered to Bruno, who stood beside me. "It seems out of place."

"That was installed that the common people might look upon the resting place of the late emperor," he responded.

"Do you mean to say that on their way home from the market they stop to look through that hole?"

"Yes, the emperor's father was much beloved of the city folk and lower classes, but now is not the time for discussion," he enjoined.

We had reached the point where the body was to be removed from its resting place, and I suddenly felt a chill of fear. There had been so much to do beforehand that I'd had no time to consider the fright that might come with exhuming a corpse. Never before had I been close enough to a long-deceased body to experience it fully, but those who had done so had told me tales that might have terrified a grown man: bloating, mold, maggots, and indescribable smells. As the men moved into position to remove the stone lid, I had a sudden desire to be anywhere on God's earth except where I currently stood. Bruno must have noticed the look of fear in my eyes, for he broke his own rule against conversation and bent down, placing his arm around me.

"Never fear! You are not going to see the body. It will remain in the coffin."

He could not have known the relief that his words engendered. I watched as they lifted the marble slab with the greatest care and set it down, revealing the oak coffin lying inside. This they raised with a system of ropes, on account of the lead container inside, which housed the body. I do not know how long we waited there as the men strained at their work, but it seemed an eternity. Nevertheless, I was thankful that there was no foul odor. They placed the coffin on a specially made cart and the bishop sprinkled it with holy water, continuing to chant the burial prayers. As we processed back into the church, he raised his voice and proclaimed, "*Et exultabunt ossa humiliata!*" That is, "The bones you have crushed shall rejoice!"

We came at last up the stairs near the high altar, the coffin borne upon a wood ramp. I found myself observing the faces of my fellow mourners. The bishops and other members of the clergy showed little emotion, but went about their business in a most solemn manner. The emperor's nephews appeared dour, while their mother and sisters wept softly, leaning on one another for comfort. Then there was the emperor himself, my own betrothed, who seemed deep in thought. For a long time, he would stare at the coffin, then look into the distance, then back toward the floor, then again at the coffin. He broke this pattern only when there was some change in the service.

At last the time came for the second burial. A new vault had been cut directly beside that of Emperor Henry III, so that father and son might rest together until the Day of Judgment. The site having already been blessed by the priests, there was little left to do but place the coffin in its new home. Having sprinkled this with holy water once again, the bishop of Speyer recited the blessed words that the Lord spoke unto Martha before the tomb of Lazarus, which in our own language read, "I am the resurrection and the life. He that believes in me, though he were dead, yet shall he live. And whoever lives and believes in me shall never die."

Before lowering the coffin, the bishop turned to the emperor and asked in a low voice,

"Have you anything to say? If you wish, you may take this moment."

All in attendance seemed to hold their breath as Emperor Henry V stepped forward toward the coffin of his father, the man with whom he had fought so mightily in life but whom he nevertheless sought to honor in death. He paused in front of it and set his hands on the side where the head must have lain. He leaned slightly forward and looked down at the carved wood, as if he could see through the layers of covering directly into his father's eyes. He stood in that manner for the space of a few breaths, speaking not a word but arresting the attention of all. When he did utter something, it was in a tone so low that even I, who was standing within a few strides of him, could barely make it out.

"Rest well, Father," he said. "May your soul find its way to heaven." He paused, then added something that I could not make out, but the tone was pleading, almost as if he were asking for help . . . or perhaps forgiveness. There before the great men of the land, the emperor bowed his crowned head until it touched the wood coffin, his eyes closed, his hands planted palms down upon the lid, his lips forming words we could not hear. It was a time I would always remember, when all ceremony and custom seemed to stop, all history was set aside, and at last it was just a man and his father sharing one final moment together.

At the beginning, many doubted that the young Henry possessed the same sense of purpose as his father. They scoffed at the idea that he might follow in his father's footsteps. But what I saw at Speyer that day seemed to overthrow such talk, for I witnessed a deep connection that still remained, and took it as proof that he intended to carry on his father's work rather than reverse it.

The remainder of the Mass completed and the coffin safely placed in its vault, we left the cathedral and walked back toward the bishop's palace. As luck would have it, I walked next to the emperor's sister, with whom I had been unable to converse the one time our paths had crossed.

"Dear Mathilda, my heart rejoices to finally become acquainted with you!" she said. "Bruno assures me that you are excelling in all your studies."

"Thank you, Lady Agnes, I hope that is the case," I replied. "I do try my hardest to please everyone."

"You will be marvelous!" she concluded, smiling in my direction. "I only wish that we could be in each other's company more often, but as you know my husband dwells far away in the Eastern March, and to him I must go."

Seemingly out of nowhere, a young girl ran toward the emperor crying out in delight, her golden hair flowing in the wind. Her minder trailed just behind, calling for the child to come away. However, the girl would not be stopped, and she arrived at her destination, wrapping her arms around the emperor's legs. Rather than turning her away, he bent down and brought her into an embrace, lifting her off the ground and kissing her on the cheek.

"Apologies, my lord, she broke away from my grasp, so pleased was she to see you," explained the woman who had been in pursuit.

"No apology is necessary," he said, "but I must be away for now. I will see you later today," he told the girl, giving her a final kiss and returning her to the attendant.

As we entered the palace and I was led back to my chamber, my mind turned over what I had just seen: First, this was the same young girl whom I had seen with the emperor in Utrecht the year before, though at the time I'd thought little of it. Second, she had referred to the emperor as *Vater*.

CHAPTER ELEVEN

"Who was that girl?" I asked as soon as the door to my bedchamber was safely closed. "The one who was with the emperor—who is she?"

Only Adelaide and Gertrude had entered with me, and both of them halted their work, looking first at each other and then at me. Without speaking a word, they evidently decided that Gertrude should answer, for she stepped toward me even as Adelaide continued sorting my garments.

"Whatever do you mean?" she answered. "There were many people in the streets today."

I was incensed. "Do you take me for a fool? I may be young, but I have eyes enough to see and ears enough to hear, even as you do. How many of the emperor's subjects call him Father as this girl did?"

"Why, all of his subjects naturally look to him as their father!" Gertrude began, but she was interrupted by Adelaide.

"You might as well explain, for she will find out in time."

"My dear Adelaide," Gertrude replied in a rather mocking tone, "since you are so eager to advise, perhaps I should let you handle this."

Gertrude then walked toward the window and lifted the pot from the floor. "Excuse me, my lady, but this needs emptying," she explained, leaving the room with a flourish. As it had been emptied earlier in the day, I assumed that this was a mere ploy. I turned my glance toward Adelaide and kept it there until she began to speak.

"The child you saw is named Bertha. She is a ward of the emperor."

"She is the emperor's child," I countered.

"Yes, it is as you say, but I assure you, there is no reason to fear."

"No reason to fear!" I could not believe my ears. "How can you say such a thing? Who is this child's mother? Will I soon see her at court?"

"I should think not. She died giving birth."

I had not foreseen this answer, and was thus rendered mute. Adelaide seized the opportunity to clarify the situation further.

"I understand why you are troubled at this revelation, but the child is merely the product of a fleeting dalliance on the emperor's part. Since the death of the child's mother, who was a woman of little consequence and ignoble birth, he could not simply leave Bertha without some means of support. He assigned her to Mistress Hildegard's care, and she is most often in Utrecht, though I suspect the emperor wished her to attend her natural grandfather's burial. He seldom sees her, choosing most often to send her gifts and, on occasion, a letter. Believe me when I say there is no reason to fear. The child is a bastard. She could never compete with any of your own royal offspring."

"That is not my concern," I replied, sitting down upon the bed. "What I must know is whether or not I can trust my future husband."

"Oh, that you can, most assuredly!" Adelaide said. "He is a grown man now and many things have changed. I suspect that kingship has placed within him a new zeal for righteousness."

"Most kings tend in the opposite direction," I thought, but I did not speak the words aloud. I sensed that there was nothing further to be gained from our conversation. Still, I had one more question. As Adelaide returned to work I called after her. "Adelaide!"

"Yes, my lady?"

"The child Bertha—how old is she?"

She paused for a moment to consider. "I cannot be certain, but I suppose she would have to be very near in age to yourself, or maybe a bit younger."

I nodded my head in acknowledgement and the conversation came to an end. For a long time, even after Adelaide departed, I remained seated in that position, my mind deep in thought. Perhaps there was truth in what Adelaide had said. Maybe it was best to forget the whole incident and continue as if nothing had changed. Young I may have been, but even I sensed that I could not easily adopt such a policy.

Some may consider the revelation of my betrothed's child to be a subject worthy of concern, and so I also did at first, but I soon forgot it. Even as the emperor basked in the glory of his Italian conquest, forces were already in motion that would shake the foundations of the kingdom that he and his predecessors had built. I remember one particular storm that passed through early that year. No longer dismayed at the sound of thunder, I peeked out of one of the monastery windows to see the sky alight with flame, great streaks rending the heavens from north to south, east to west. As I watched, one such bolt landed very near the town gate. The sound of it was as nothing I had ever heard before: first silence, then the sense of an earthquake and a noise like the trumpet of God. The power of Thor was on display, or so the Germans of old might have concluded, and it seemed to be a harbinger of divine judgment.

Within a few days of this incident, word came from the French city of Vienne that a great synod of bishops had been held, naturally led by Guy, bishop of Vienne. He was one of those men who know all too well every inch of their own significance, and he had long been an adversary of the Salians—that is, the imperial household. Of all the men in Christendom, none had felt the alleged slight of the pope's agreement with the emperor more deeply than those in the Kingdoms of Burgundy and France, and they were determined to set matters right.

They declared Emperor Henry to be an enemy of Christ—"a second Judas" in the words of some—and pronounced the sentence of *anathema* against him. This seemed to confirm those earlier fears, when Bruno had bemoaned the possibility that my husband might become excommunicate in the same manner as his father. Still, despite the bishop of Vienne's boldness, the pope acquitted Emperor Henry of any guilt regarding his actions in Tuscany, and pledged not to pass a sentence of excommunication.

Thus the meeting to which we all looked forward was the one at the Lateran in late March, when the pope himself led an assembly of bishops, most of whom were Italian. The sons of Gregory in attendance carried influence of equal weight. Without the presence of the German king and his army, there was little pressure brought to bear that could equal that being applied by the Gregorians. They succeeded in revoking the agreement, thus reversing the promises made to the emperor. In this one thing did the pope stand firm and refuse to relent: he would not excommunicate Henry V, believing that his word was his bond. In this, at least, Pope Paschal was able to surmount the obstacles laid before him and establish his rule.

They say that the leopard cannot change its spots, but it is my experience that when men become bishops, they may undergo a profound change in character, either to their benefit or to their doom. Such was the case with Adalbert von Saarbrücken, who had lately been made archbishop of Mainz. Ever had he been in the emperor's counsel in former years, his words heeded more closely than those of any other, even Bruno of Trier. The emperor rewarded him with an archbishopric that befitted a true prince of the Church, but the harvest that he would reap from this action was a bitter one indeed. No sooner had Adalbert taken up his seat then he and the emperor were caught in a dispute as fierce as that which my own father had maintained with Father Anselm. The cause was that old devil Mammon, who ever seeks to put at odds those who ought to rightfully move in harmony with one another.

Within the Wasgen Forest lies the fortress of Trifels, which once belonged to a relative of the old archbishop of Mainz, Siegfried I. The man's name was Diemar, and upon his death Trifels Castle passed into the hands of the imperial dynasty. Emperor Henry V was eager to make improvements to the fortress, which was perfectly set upon the crest of the hill called Sonnenberg. It lay within the Rhine Valley, which was the main center of support for the Salians. The emperor had great designs to transform Trifels into a *Reichsburg*, or imperial castle, but he was forced to contend with Archbishop Adalbert, who claimed that the castle was his by right on account of his spiritual descent from the former Archbishop Siegfried, who as I mentioned was a relative of the onetime owner.

If this causes you confusion, my daughter, it is perhaps understandable, for claims of inheritance are often a source of much vexation, particularly when they take place between an emperor and an archbishop. That friendship that had survived so many hardships became fractured as questions of estate divided them further. The emperor was furious that this man whom he had raised up should defy him in such a manner, while Adalbert claimed that his position required of him a renewed devotion to the will of God and the sanctity of Church affairs, which were inviolable even by princes. Within months the situation regressed to such a point that the emperor ordered the archbishop be seized and imprisoned within the very castle at the heart of their dispute, Trifels. This angered the archbishop's allies, and most of all those in restive Saxony, who cried out against what they believed to be a breach of justice. The usual methods of judgment had been set aside, they said, in favor of outright tyranny.

All around me the world was thrown into chaos. Those men, Henry and Adalbert, were as two great titans who in their fighting cause the very earth to shake. The reverberations of this battle were felt far and wide.

"What shall become of us, Bruno?" I asked one day. "The emperor seems caught between enemies on all sides."

"What always happens under such circumstances," he replied. "The parties will be driven on until one or both of them finds that to continue is more costly than whatever they are hoping to gain."

"And what is it they are hoping to gain?"

"Primacy."

I let out a sigh, for I found Bruno's view of life a bit too bleak for my taste.

"In truth, you are asking the wrong question," he said, reclaiming my attention.

"Oh? What is the right question, then?"

"In such moments of weakness, a prince may become overly consumed with the danger directly before his eyes. But the world does not wait for us to rise from our falls before dropping the hammer once again. The question we ought to ask is, whence does the next blow come?"

"Well, from whence does the next blow come?"

His features transformed into a grim smile.

"Saxony! It always comes from Saxony."

"You are awfully harsh on that duchy, sir. One might almost think they had breathed some slander against your mother."

This at least drew a laugh from the archbishop. "Harsh or not, it hardly matters. I am no longer in the emperor's counsel. Forgive me for saying so, but I believe he is in danger of becoming a toy of lesser men."

"I hope you are wrong," I replied, and with that we returned to the lesson at hand.

The crisis did not abate with the beginning of a new year. Bruno's prophecy that the next blow would come from Saxony was entirely correct, for the emperor was forced to remove Lothair of Supplinburg as duke of that realm and instead appoint Otto, the Count of Ballenstedt. The dukedom had been thrown into question a few years earlier with the death of the last male of the ruling House of Billung. This Lothair had been able to gain control of many of the Billung lands, making himself the natural choice to succeed as Duke of Saxony. However, he quickly became the fiercest of all the emperor's enemies, siding with the thankless archbishop of Mainz. He even led his troops into battle against the imperial army. In light of this challenge to his own authority, Emperor Henry decided to impose his will on the dukedom and elevate the Count of Ballenstedt in place of Lothair. With so many fires springing up throughout the empire, one feared that the emperor might lack sufficient means to smother them all. Even the emperor's nephew, the Duke of Swabia, found cause for dispute.

It was at this moment of extreme stress that I received a letter from my mother, Queen Mathilda. It seemed that the Earl of Northampton and Huntingdon, Simon de Senlis, whose hospitality I had enjoyed not three years earlier, had contracted the bloody flux while abroad in France. His death had left his wife, Mathilda, in control of his substantial estates throughout the north of England. This news excited my interest, for I knew that my uncle, Prince David, had been involved in a secret affair with the lady the last time I saw them, at least according to brother Robert. As my mother made no mention of this connection in her letter, I assumed that either she was ignorant of her brother's conduct, or she was choosing not to acknowledge it. For my part, I suspected that the earl's death was not an occasion of mourning for either the prince or the lady, who would now be free to woo in the open, assuming that they still desired each other.

Another year came and went. By that time I was well into my eleventh year. Relations between the emperor and the pope had not improved, nor had he restored his friendship with Archbishop Adalbert, who continued to defy the emperor from his lofty prison. Every so often, word came to us that another person had offered himself as ransom, demanding the archbishop's release. All such offers were met with swift action on the part of the imperial guards, and none achieved their desired end. In Saxony discontent continued to brew, though by God's mercy it did not spill over into violence.

None of this was of particular import in comparison with that which was to take place shortly after the Advent season: namely, my marriage to the emperor. Our espousal had lasted almost four years, during which time I had dedicated myself to study in preparation for my future life as empress. I would be just shy of my twelfth birthday when our hands were bound in matrimony. At such an age, only the children of kings marry, and most particularly the daughters, for I never heard tell of peasants giving away their daughters at such an early age. Nevertheless, I felt that my extensive preparations would stand me in good stead.

In due course I received a message from the emperor summoning me to join him in Bamberg for the feast of the Nativity, after which point we would progress to the west for our marriage in the city of Worms. This journey brought me farther east than I had yet traveled during my time in the empire. We departed Trier and moved along the Moselle until reaching the Rhine, at which point we turned south and sailed through that charming valley that leads to Mainz. There we changed course again, setting east upon the River Main. By the time we arrived at our destination, I felt I had never been so happy to set foot on land, having spent most of the past week within the confines of a boat.

We were blessed with a warm Advent season that year, and there was no sign of snow anywhere in the town. The emperor was already busy when we arrived, so the ladies set to work unpacking my possessions and arranging them throughout the manor house built for the emperor in the city center. As we were in the midst of this, there was a knock at the door, and a steward by the name of Arnulf entered the room.

"Hail Mathilda, queen of the Romans!" he proclaimed. "I am here to inform you of Emperor Henry's will regarding the evening festivities, but first allow me to welcome you to the great city of Bamberg and to eastern Franconia. I understand this is your first visit?"

"Yes, that is true. Until now I have spent most of my days in Trier, which is quite far to the west, as I am sure you are aware."

"Your Royal Highness is correct. The empire is massive. I myself have only ever set eyes on a small portion of it. If you ever have the opportunity, I would heartily recommend that you travel south of here to the Duchy of Bavaria, for that is my home. In the city of Salzburg I was born . . . But I have forgotten the purpose of my visit!"

"Yes, do tell us," Gertrude uttered, her face betraying a lack of patience.

"Emperor Henry requests your presence at supper, which is to be held in three hours' time, after which we will all proceed to the cathedral for the night's festivities."

"Festivities?" I asked. "What do you mean?"

"The emperor has arranged for some of the men of Freising to travel here to Bamberg and delight us with a performance of the *Officium stellae*, that is, *Order of the Star*."

"Oh, is it about the Magi?"

"Yes, my lady. They have been performing it in Freising for many years, and now they will provide us with a recitation that is sure to bring joy to the listener. Does it not fill you with delight?"

"Oh, we are filled to the brim!" Gertrude answered in a tone that belied her words.

The messenger overlooked her comment. "Remember, supper in three hours, and then on to the cathedral!"

"I will be there!" I replied. The idea of attending such a performance excited me, even if it was not to Gertrude's liking.

My dear mother had summoned companies from near and far to perform at Westminster, and though my grasp of Latin was rather dismal at such a young age, I was able to guess the meaning of much of what I saw based on the players' actions. Given my improved understanding of Latin, I reasoned that I would now understand any such performance. We gathered in the hall for supper, a truly merry affair. Boughs of fir and holly hung from the trusses, such that the room had all the appearance of an enchanted forest. Had there been any lack of good cheer, it would soon have been banished by the wealth of beer consumed by the revelers. I attempted to drink a small cup, but found it was not to my liking, so I accepted wine instead.

It was at this supper that I met Otto, bishop of Bamberg, for he sat very near me. Although he held a title below that of an archbishop, his influence was just as great, for the bishopric of

Bamberg was accountable directly to Rome, unlike most of the empire. Bishop Otto was thus very powerful.

I was seated directly to the right of the emperor, while the bishop had the position of honor to his left. Also in attendance were Bruno of Trier and David, the imperial chancellor, the emperor's nephews, and Duke Welf II of Bavaria. The emperor talked for most of the meal with the bishop and the duke, and, having little to add of any value, I simply listened.

"Tell me, Welf, how is your wife?" the emperor inquired.

I knew this to be at least half mockery, for the duke had lived apart from his spouse, Countess Mathilda of Tuscany, for far longer than I myself had been alive. It was said that their dispute had sprung from the revelation that the *contessa* intended to bequeath her inheritance to the papacy rather than the House of Welf. Fortunately, the duke was game for the emperor's teasing.

"It is hard to say, Your Grace. If you happen to see her in your travels, do pass on a good word for me, and let me know how she does."

"Yes, for you would not suffer the trial of visiting her," the emperor replied, laughing heartily.

"My wife and I have a strange but truly beneficial understanding," the duke protested. "I do as I please, she does as she pleases, and only under the harshest of extremes must something be done between us."

"You might have done for the life of a monastic," Bishop Otto said. "It seems you share in their suffering already."

This prompted another furor of laughter from the emperor, which drowned out the duke's protestation of, "I do not suffer so much as you suppose!"

"Peace, man! It was kindly meant. Go to the lady Wulfhilde and get something to quench your desire," the emperor replied, gesturing in the direction of a rather buxom woman who was dispensing drinks.

With a scowl the duke moved on to another table, leaving the other two men to speak freely. I think that they had forgotten my presence beside them.

"Would that all men of the House of Welf were of the monastic type, for then I would have fewer of them to contend with!" the emperor muttered. "Even so, they have done us a good turn lately."

"Sire," the bishop answered, changing the subject of conversation completely, "you might be interested to know I have received a new letter from my old acquaintance, Anselm of Laon."

"How go his affairs?" the emperor responded with a notable lack of excitement.

"Quite well, for the most part, though he reports some trouble with one of his pupils who, in spite of his undoubted talent, possesses a rather irksome demeanor. Always he seeks to challenge the established order and shows no respect for his teacher. As it so happens, he was sent away from the school of Paris for this very reason, and now Anselm fears it may be necessary to repeat that judgment."

"What is the fellow's name?"

"Pierre Abélard, Your Grace."

"I have never heard of him. He cannot be of any great import. I have now in my household one Norbert from the town of Xanten, a bright young man by all accounts. I am sure he could easily thrash this Paul in any matter of debate, and with more respect for his elders, I daresay."

"Pierre."

"What?"

"His name is Pierre, Your Highness, not Paul."

"What of it? Why do you trouble me with such things? I have an empire to command. Come, bishop, let us lead the procession to the cathedral!" the emperor said, striking the older man on the back and rising from his chair. He then turned in my direction and added, "You as well, Lady Mathilda. Everyone, up!"

We walked the short distance to the cathedral. The other ladies and I made use of our warmest robes, but in an apparent demonstration of fortitude, the men determined that such external apparel was needless. At the very least, the emperor decided not to put on any further garments, and the rest of the men followed suit. The noon sunshine had brought warmth to Bamberg, but in the dark of evening our breath was visible, illumined by the torches. Though I looked forward to our night's festivity, I was sad to leave the warm fire of the hall; I knew that the church would provide no such comfort.

The cathedral seemed an odd place for such a private performance, but it had been determined that there were no proper rooms in the imperial quarters, and in any case the men of Freising were accustomed to performing under such conditions. As I followed the others through the nave and toward the eastern end, I could see that a scaffold had been erected on each side of the transept. Before the high altar was a simple feed trough, such as a farmer might use. Chairs were brought out for the most important guests, while all others stood behind. Not having to stand on such occasions was one of the privileges of high rank that I eagerly embraced. We waited as everyone took their places, and then the play began with a small but eager choir singing the opening lines.

Let the King mount and sit upon the throne.

Let him listen to opinion.

From himself he takes counsel.

Let an edict go forth

That those who detract from this sovereignty

Shall perish instantly!

"I like this play already," declared Emperor Henry to roars of laughter from the audience.

We watched as the shepherds encountered the angel who would point them to the Christ child, and then the three eagerly awaited Magi made their appearance, walking down toward those of us who were seated as they recited their lines.

Tell us, citizens of Jerusalem,
Where is the one awaited by the nations,
The newly born King of the Jews,
He whom, revealed by heavenly signs,
We are coming to adore?

"In yonder manger!" was the reply of more than one of the "citizens of Jerusalem."

It was then time for King Herod to enter the story, welcomed by the usual mockery. I could not remember the listeners responding in such a manner in England, but I surmised that the rules must be different in the empire, or at least at the court of Henry V. They laughed as they watched King Herod give orders to his poor messenger in an overly pompous fashion. Finally the Magi entered Herod's throne room.

"Hail, Prince of the Jews!" the three men cried out.

"What is the cause of your journey? Who are you, and where do you come from? Speak!" Herod replied, drawing yet more delight from the audience.

"A King is the cause of our journey; we are kings from Arabian lands, making our way here," the men answered.

"There are a great many kings in this play; too many, I think," the emperor muttered to those sitting nearby.

The remainder of the plot, I suppose, is well known to you, Daughter: how the Magi came upon the resting place of the Christ child, the angel appeared and warned them not to return by way of King Herod's palace, and the evil king then ordered the destruction of the youth of Bethlehem, repeating even the work of Pharaoh. But as with Jochebed's son, our Lord was saved from Herod's snare. Thus the performance ended with the choir proclaiming triumph for the babe.

This day has given us what the mind could not have hoped:

It's truly brought a thousand joys in answer to our prayers,

Restored this kingdom to its King, and peace too to the world,

To us it's brought wealth, beauty, singing, feasting, dancing.

It's good for him to reign and hold the kingdom's scepter:

He loves the name of King, for he adorns that name with virtues.

When all was completed, the audience broke into great cheering. As we rose to depart, Bishop Otto of Bamberg approached me.

"My lady Mathilda, how did you find the performance?"

"I liked it very much," I replied in all honesty. "My mother used to tell that story to my brother and me for the feast of Epiphany. Thus it is most dear to me."

"On this feast of the Epiphany, you and the emperor will be wed!" he told me, though I was already well aware. "Please know that I speak for all of my brethren when I say that we look forward to serving our empress as faithfully as we have her husband."

"Thank you," I replied, uncertain how else to respond, and not wanting to raise doubts as to the truth of his claim. After all, Bruno had made me well aware of the struggle between the emperor and his bishops. If there could be such enmity between lords, then I had no reason to suppose it might not be transferred to myself.

"Did you notice the resting place of Pope Clement when you came in?" Bishop Otto asked.

"No, I didn't know that one of the popes was buried here."

"Clement II, or Suidger von Morsleben as he was called at birth, was a native of this very town and a predecessor of mine in the episcopal seat. It was his dearest wish to be laid to rest in this cathedral, which was like a second home to him."

Having arrested my attention, the bishop forbade me to leave until he had not only shown me Clement's tomb, but also pointed out a number of elements of the cathedral's design. Most of these features were obscured by darkness, but that did not suppress his desire to describe them. He told me of the great repair works, which had become necessary after a fire some three decades earlier. His passion for such things was clear, though I gathered that his greatest desire was to return to Pomerania so that he might continue his work among the pagan peoples of that region. Feeling that the night had gone on far too long, I declared my admiration for his work and then begged leave due to weariness.

As I walked back to the manor with my ladies, we noticed that snow had begun to fall from the night sky.

"Finally, snow for Advent!" Adelaide said in delight. "How many years have passed since that was the way of things?"

"Not enough," was Gertrude's reply.

Once in my travels, I happened by a small village church where a wedding was taking place. There was no pomp, no glorious procession, and no great degree of solemnity. The bride and bridegroom simply entered the church, took their vows before God and man, and then returned to their abode. The bride's dress was quite plain, for she was a mere peasant girl, and rather than a glistening diadem, her head was crowned with flowers that had quite clearly been plucked from a nearby meadow. Such a ceremony held little in common with my own, yet there was a kind of quiet dignity in it—the ease, the good humor, the warmth of familiarity.

On the morning of my wedding, I may well have wished for such simplicity, for the weight of duty hung upon me like a yoke, or a rein forcing me this way and that. To my great dismay and that of all the ladies, my face took on a rough complexion in the days leading up to Epiphany. When Adelaide first saw the red dots covering my chin, she feared that I was suffering from some strange affliction, but the wiser Gertrude discerned that these blemishes were no different from those that affect many young ladies. Whatever the cause, it presented another challenge to my attendants, and they ordered me to wash my face with rose water five times a day.

Our nuptials would provide the grandest imperial court in living memory. All of the archbishops were to attend, save for *Meister* Adalbert, who remained locked inside Trifels Castle, and the archbishop of Salzburg, who was unable to make the long journey. The dukes and lesser lords would be there as well, including Lothair of Supplinburg, who would ask Emperor Henry to restore him as Duke of Saxony. Given his insurrection and treacherous plotting with the archbishop of Mainz, even the most casual observer saw that Lothair must make a fantastic effort in order to recover his place in the emperor's good graces. And then there was the Duke of Swabia, whose fresh peace with his uncle had yet to produce the same degree of affection they'd had earlier.

I could brook no complaint as to my apparel, for it was as fine as any bride could wish for: a gown the color of red wine and an outer robe of gold with precious jewels. There were bright stones on my fingers, upon my wrists, tied around my waist, hanging from my ears, and sitting within the royal crown upon my head. Best of all was a brooch of gold and garnet that the emperor had sent ahead to me as a wedding gift. No bride could have been adorned better.

The wedding itself was much like our espousal ceremony. The words of the Mass were almost the same, though they took on an increased significance. The Cathedral of Worms is the smallest of the three *Kaiserdome*, and it appeared even smaller that day on account of the number of officials in attendance. After we had spoken our sacred vows, the bishop of Worms declared us to be lawfully wed, and the whole city rejoiced.

We then moved to the hall built for this particular occasion within the palace outside the city walls, for there was no dwelling in Worms that could hold such a large number of guests. I had wondered why this city was chosen over one such as Aachen, site of a grand imperial palace, but it was explained to me that the emperor's famous ancestor and founder of the Salian house, Conrad, Duke of Lorraine, was buried within the cathedral—a clear point in its favor. Sadly, the new hall did not remain long in its place, for it was destroyed in the uprising of the following decade.

Two thrones stood on a dais at the far end of the hall, and there my husband and I sat to receive our many guests from both near and far. The Duke of Bohemia acted as chief cupbearer, a duty to which I assume he was not accustomed, for in his own house he was surely waited upon by an entire legion of servants. Such was the occasion, however, and those nobles pressed into service performed their duties with all propriety. Among the first to appear before us were the five archbishops in attendance. To each one, the emperor made a gift of a statue carved by the craftsmen within his household, one each of the four evangelists and a fifth of the Madonna and child.

"I suppose the archbishop of Mainz will be sad to hear that he did not receive one of these," I thought, "though I reckon it is the least of his worries at the present."

Each of the men was called forward in turn. First was the archbishop of Cologne, Frederick, who had overseen my own coronation.

"God save Your Royal Highnesses, and may I offer my blessings upon your marriage!" he said. "We are most indebted for your kind gift and shall use it to adorn our cathedral."

He then called forward two servants, who displayed an image painted upon a wood panel. "To one who gives so freely, much must be given in return. Here is an image composed by one of the citizens of our great city."

"Let me see it," the emperor commanded, and the two men brought it closer for him to examine.

The image showed a king sitting upon a throne and another man standing just to the side, with a finger pointed in the direction of the king. I looked at my husband, who frowned in apparent confusion as to the meaning of the picture.

"What is this, Frederick?" he asked.

"Your Excellency looks upon the image of King David, the most glorious ruler of Israel," the archbishop answered.

"And who is this other man, the one in plain clothes?"

"That is the prophet Nathan."

Emperor Henry stopped looking at the picture and cast his gaze instead upon the archbishop. There was a sudden strain between them, the origin of which I could not determine. After a long pause, the emperor spoke.

"I wonder, Archbishop, that out of all the deeds performed by this great king, you should choose to dignify this one. It seems a curious choice."

"I think that as Your Highness meditates upon the meaning of the image, you shall find that all becomes clear," Frederick answered. "I hope that it is to your liking."

"Yes, yes," the emperor replied, and then said to his chancellor, "Place it with the other gifts."

"Certainly, Your Grace," Chancellor David answered.

The archbishop of Cologne then returned to the revelry at the other end of the hall, but I could tell by my husband's countenance that he was vexed. We proceeded through the line of archbishops until we arrived at the archbishop of Trier.

"Bruno, my friend!" the emperor greeted him. "It has been too long!"

"Any separation from Your Grace is always a sad cross to bear," the archbishop concurred. "We thank you for the gift. It shall bring great joy to our flock." There was a short pause, and then Bruno continued. "Emperor, I wonder if I might approach more closely, for I have one or two private words which I wish to share."

"You may."

The archbishop then climbed the steps to our position and knelt beside Emperor Henry, placing a hand upon the arm of his throne.

"My lord, you know that for some time I have desired to be more in your counsel, as it was in the old days," Bruno said in a low voice. "Before now, that would have been rather an impossibility, as there was another person closer to Your Grace . . . if you take my meaning."

"I do take your meaning, and I am well aware of your desires, but it was you who first distanced yourself from us, and not the other way around."

"Only because I was provoked by that traitor who now sits imprisoned!" Bruno replied. Although he still whispered, his tone was quite marked. "I regret that it has taken so long for you to see in him what I have known all along, but such things are all in the past, and now that this impediment to my presence has been removed, surely there would be no reason not to restore me to my former place."

"Do you think me blind, then?"

"No, my lord! I merely state that he has abused us all in a most vicious manner, and I am sorry to see it."

"Well, I too am sorry, Archbishop. I am sorry that, despite your reputation for wisdom, you have reduced yourself to begging before me, and on such an occasion as this. I would have thought you more discreet."

"Sire," Bruno continued, attempting to restore calm to the situation, "I never sought to cause you distress. I would be perfectly content to discuss this on another occasion."

"Yes, let us do that," the emperor said, motioning with his hand as if to shoo the older man away.

Sensing the need for a hasty but honorable retreat, Bruno offered his thanks for the gift one more time and quickly presented his own offering before taking his leave.

"Who is next?" the emperor asked.

"His Excellency the Count of Nordheim!" the herald proclaimed.

"Excellent he is not," the emperor muttered to himself even as the count stepped forward.

I could not believe my eyes. Although the man was undoubtedly noble, he appeared before us in a simple tunic and barefoot. I turned to Adelaide, who was standing just behind, and asked, "Who is this man, and why is he dressed like that?"

"'Tis the former Duke of Saxony, come to beg for the return of his title."

"Ah, I see."

Now within a few paces of the dais, Lothair of Supplinburg, for such was his Christian name, sank to his knees and with both hands ripped open the upper portion of his garment, revealing a hair shirt underneath. The skin around it was raw, with traces of blood. The count then began to plead.

"My emperor, I come before you as a humble penitent, ready to confess my grievous sins against Your Grace and to beg forgiveness for the same."

I looked to my husband and could see that he appeared calm, but I doubted not that his spirit was inflamed.

"The pardon of a king is not lightly granted," the emperor replied. "We find the charges against you to be great indeed." He then looked at the officials standing nearby and asked, "Friends, tell me, if you were to sit in the seat of judgment, as I do even now, would you countenance such behavior from a man of noble birth, one who has offended both God and his anointed ruler through unnatural rebellion, who has stirred up the passions of our subjects against us and plotted with men of our holy Church to bring death to our person?"

He looked from face to face, but not a one was brave enough to reply. The man at the center of discussion continued to cower in his low position, hoping perhaps that if he stayed in such a state long enough, the rain of verbal blows would pass over him. Finally, the emperor descended from the dais and stood directly before the count.

"Stand up!" he commanded with a firm clap of his hands, and the count obeyed. "Tell me, Count, do you read Scripture?"

"I do, sire."

"Are you familiar with Saint Paul's letter to the Romans?"

"As familiar as most, though I am no scholar," he replied.

"Bishop Otto," the emperor called, "perhaps you could enlighten the count on what Saint Paul says regarding the establishment of government."

The bishop took a moment to remember, then quoted, "'Let every soul be subject unto the higher powers: for there is no power but of God, and the powers that be are ordained of God. Whoever therefore resists the power, resists the ordinance of God: and they that resist shall receive to themselves condemnation.'"

"Apt words, think you not, Count?" the emperor asked. "Do you acknowledge before this assembly that you have rebelled against your rightful prince, ordained by God, and are thus bound to be damned for all eternity, except the Lord have mercy on your soul?"

"My emperor," the count answered, "there is no reply which I can offer unto you which might excuse my actions. Whether they were the product of some foolishness of youth or the undue influence of lesser persons, I cannot say. There is naught which I can do but declare in the words of Job, 'I abhor myself and repent in dust and ashes.'" He then knelt again at the emperor's feet. "I beg of you, by the grace of the Virgin Mary, take pity on this pour soul!"

For a long time, both men were silent, and I could not see which way things would turn. At length my husband smiled and said, "Arise, Duke Lothair of Saxony. I have heard your petition and grant you pardon. More to the point, the man who took your place is a fool. Nevertheless, if you prove false, do not presume to receive mercy from our hand a second time."

"I cannot thank Your Highness enough! You shall never have a more faithful subject!" Lothair declared, then departed to another part of the hall to celebrate his escape from imperial wrath.

Emperor Henry continued to follow the man with his eyes even as the herald declared, "Rabbi Ezra ben David, of the school of Rashi, representative of the Jewry of Worms."

The feasting went on well into the night. Such was the wealth of food and drink, of couples joined in dance, of jesters and musicians filling us with mirth, that I would never again see its equal. It was also on that night that Drogo joined me once again; he had remained in the emperor's service during my espousal. With my own household expanding, he was to become my closest guardian and remain by my side at all times. This encouraged me as much as anything that night.

As luck would have it, Drogo also brought me the latest news from England: Prince David of Scotland had wed Mathilda, Countess of Huntingdon, just as I had assumed he would. What was more, she was due to give birth to their first child any day. Even my frail powers of logic discerned that this was far too short a time for a woman to carry to term, but for once I decided to forgo moralizing and simply delight in the promise of new life.

When the feast ended and the revelers either lay down for the night or departed for home, my new husband took me by the hand and led me toward our adjoining chambers within the palace. He had bid all others remain behind and grant us this time of privacy, despite their protestations that only in their witnessing the act might any rumors be put to rest. In the weeks leading up to the wedding, I had mostly succeeded in putting any thoughts of this moment out of my mind. I sensed, perhaps by instinct, that there was nothing I could do in preparation and nothing to be gained by fretting. The thing must simply be gotten through. However, as we took those final steps toward the threshold, my beating heart betrayed me. The emperor pushed open the door to my bedchamber and led me inside. I could see that all had been made ready; one of the ladies had even set out a change of clothes. He let go of my hand and shut the door.

"Do you require any assistance removing your garments?"

I still am not sure how I found the confidence to speak, but I let out a rather meek "No."

"Very well then," he said.

He strode toward me and took one of my hands, at which point I impulsively recoiled, my own will to persevere now faltering at the moment of truth.

"There is no need to worry," he told me. "I know what the world requires of us, but we have plenty of time to bring forth heirs. We are both young, you more so than me."

He leaned down and kissed my brow, then let go of my hand. My mind began to accept what had just taken place. I was to be reprieved after all, and I felt that I ought to offer him something in return.

"I shall do everything in my power to be a good wife to you," I said. "You have shown me kindness in all my time here, and I am most obliged to you."

He did not respond, but moved toward the side portal that led to his own chamber, turned one last time to bid me good night, and then disappeared. Having achieved my solitude, I braced myself with a hand to the bedpost and let out a flood of tears—for once, tears of relief rather than despair. I had made it through possibly the most important day of my life. I had finished the race. All was well.

When I had mustered my strength, I changed into my nightclothes—what a strange joy to dress one's self!—and fell directly into bed, content to drift off into blissful sleep, my new life awaiting me with the morning sun.

CHAPTER TWELVE

"For what can there either be, or be committed, more disgraceful or more unrighteous in human affairs, than to refuse to show fear to God or affection to one's own countrymen, and without detriment to one's faith to refuse due honor to those of higher dignity, to cast off all regard to reason, human and divine, and, in contempt of heaven and earth, to be guided by one's own sensual inventions?"

Such were the words of Gildas as told to me by Master Godfrey of Bayeux. Much as I might have desired to forget them, those lines seemed to return to me in moments both timely and untimely, a final warning from some long-ceased conflict intended to mock my living ears. No stable kingdom, removed by long years from any substantial threat to its borders, can properly understand the continual fear of rebellion. Indeed, I did not know this fear then, but I have been forced to learn of it by many years of toil.

Tyranny is a great evil, to be sure, but what of its opposite? What happens when a ruler can no longer maintain power, when it drains from him as water through a sieve, only to be seized by men of inferior rank and ideas? Could such an evil be greater even than the first? One may argue that rebellion is rather a necessary evil when a ruler comes to power in an unlawful manner, or when his conduct so offends as to draw the wrath of God down upon him. As to the truth of this, you, my daughter, must come to some conclusion. I can tell you only the things that I have seen and done.

There was little joy in the year following my marriage. The Duke of Saxony's penance proved only momentary. His public humiliation at the marriage feast surely did little to help the situation. In a matter of months, Duke Lothair returned to his plotting, drawing many others in with him. His growing roll of supporters included many who had somehow felt the imperial slight. Duke Henry of Lower Lorraine had long since been deposed from that position in favor of Godfrey of Louvain, but he would not consent to this lessening of his dignity. Although he was not a man of Saxony, the rebellion there became the perfect means to show his discontent.

Then there was Count Wiprecht of Groitzsch, an early supporter of the rebel Lothair's cause. He was taken prisoner in 1113 and transported to Trifels Castle—the same that housed Archbishop Adalbert—where he was condemned for his treacherous behavior. The count was spared from execution only when he agreed to forfeit all his lands to the crown. Even this was not enough to gain his release, and he continued to languish in Trifels. Meanwhile his son, Wiprecht II, vowed to avenge his father.

Count Ludwig of Thuringia was a sometime adversary of the emperor. His support for the rebellion was both open and secret by turns. From his high fortress, the Wartburg, he reigned over the center of the Kingdom of Germany, his influence much sought out by all his neighbors. The count had experienced his own imprisonment long before Henry V ever ruled as emperor.

He was said to have stabbed Count Palatine Frederick III. They held Count Ludwig in Giebichenstein Castle far to the east, nestled upon the banks of the River Saale. When he was threatened with death, the count carried out the deed for which he was ever after remembered, leaping from a window and plummeting into the river below. From the time of his escape, he was known as "Ludwig the Springer."

Perhaps the greatest surprise among the Duke of Saxony's allies was Otto, Count of Ballenstedt, the very man who for almost a year had held Lothair's dukedom, until he too fell out with Emperor Henry. Such was the disdain of these two Saxon nobles for their rightful overlord that they set aside their own quarrel to join forces against him.

These were the circumstances in which my husband found himself at midyear. In addition he had interpreted the riddle of the archbishop of Cologne's painting all too easily. Even as the prophet Nathan had accused King David of heinous sin, Archbishop Frederick now stood with his finger pointed directly at the emperor, becoming bolder in his opposition with each passing day. While Saxony had been a boiling pool of dissent even in the time of my husband's father and grandfather, the city of Cologne marked the entrance to the Rhineland and a region that Henry V could ill afford to lose.

The city of Mainz was likewise restless over the imprisonment of its own archbishop, Adalbert, whose brother bishops throughout the empire were quickly adopting his cause. Even Bruno of Trier began to counsel the emperor that Archbishop Adalbert was at least as dangerous in prison as he was outside it. With his enemies moving to encircle him, my husband determined that it was necessary to attack. His first step was to move his court north to the Kaiserpfalz Goslar, a fortress built up by the emperor's grandfather, Henry III, who had waged his own struggle to establish his authority over the Saxons. Set on the northern edge of the Harz mountains, it was not only well-nigh impregnable, but it also placed the imperial forces in a good position to strike out against any uprising.

The road to Goslar was not an easy one. There was no convenient water route that could carry us from the middle Rhine all the way northeast, so we were forced to travel overland through the region of Hesse. We followed a sequence of valleys through the hills, making do with such dwellings as we could acquire. There were none along that path as luxurious as those that lay within the centers of Salian power, but my companions pledged to me time and again that the comforts of our final destination would make amends for any hardships along the way. Fortunately, the weather remained very pleasant throughout the course of our march.

Skirting around the western edge of the mountains, we finally came to a plain that continued as far as the eye could see. My chaplain, Altmann, was traveling beside me.

"Are we well into Saxony now?" I asked him.

"Yes, we have been traveling in that duchy for the past two days. Beyond us, to the north, are the lands of the House of Billung, which stretch even to the sea."

"Shall we be safe here, Altmann?"

"Oh, never fear, my queen! As you can see, we travel along with all of the imperial household knights, and the emperor has already sent troops ahead to meet us at Goslar. Even more shall join them in the coming months, maybe several thousand men in total. Moreover, there is no more able commander than he who carries the imperial banner, Count Hoyer of Mansfeld."

"What, will the emperor not join his men in battle?"

"No, that would not be prudent," Altmann explained. "The peril would be far too great."

"But surely his men will want to see their leader, to know that he stands with them."

"I beg your pardon, my lady, but I am sure the men are quite ably led. They have no need of further inspiration. The emperor may be chief in their thoughts, but their commanders in the field know them each by name. It is to those leaders that they shall look if and when the time comes."

"Forgive me, sir, but I disagree. The kings of England have always gone to war. Not to do so would be considered a sign of cowardice. My own father would never dream of such a thing."

"Do you call your husband a coward then?"

I had evidently overstepped the bounds, and aimed to retract. "Well, I am not so familiar with the customs of this land as I am with those of England. Perhaps such a thing is more common here, yet I seem to remember that the emperor and his father both accompanied their troops in the past."

"You are correct," Altmann admitted, "but you forget that Emperor Henry has no direct heir. There is no son ready to take his place, as was the case with his own father. Were your husband to be struck down even now, still in the prime of his youth, it would be the end of his line, and another would be raised up. Surely, as his consort, you could not desire that?"

"No, of course not," I answered quickly. I recognized that I must have seemed rash in my earlier comments, and sought to make amends. "Altmann, I am but a young woman who knows little of the ways of war. If I have erred, forgive me."

"My lady, you need not beg my forgiveness," he replied, "for you are as high above me as the stars are above the earth. However, I would hate to think that you should doubt your husband, for he is worthy of your respect."

"I respect him," I said in a quiet voice. Whether he had intended to do so or not, the chaplain had, in the midst of his flattery, accused me of forgetting my proper place. It would not be prudent for me to press the matter still further.

In the space of an hour, we came within sight of the town of Goslar. The palace sat at the foot of the mountains, where the ground begins to gently incline. The town was directly below it, slightly to the north. Under normal circumstances, the Duke of Saxony might have received us, but that was clearly outside the realm of possibility.

Now, this is how the palace grounds are arranged: The main gate lies to the north, and it was well defended, for any invading army would of necessity come from that direction and not over the mountains. In this manner the builders ensured that the fortress's residents would always possess the high ground. There was a large, open site in the center in which many tents were placed. On one end of this field stood the Kaiserhaus, which was then undergoing a period of construction that would bring more living quarters and a new chapel dedicated to Saint Ulrich. The Liebfrauenkirche—that is, the Church of the Beloved Lady—adjoined this structure on the north side. Across from the Kaiserhaus was the collegiate church of Saints Simon and Jude, along with supporting structures for stabling the animals, preparing food, and housing the armory, among other uses.

The Kaiserhaus was divided into two levels, the upper one reserved for the emperor, his family, and those who received his special favor, and the lower level remaining open to the rest of the court. One could walk from my private quarters and those of the emperor to the highest floor of the great hall, and then on to the upper floor of the Liebfrauenkirche.

"I think I shall like it here," I said to Adelaide once we had reached my private chamber. "The climate is not too hot, and the view of the mountains is magnificent. 'Tis a pity that we should be driven here by civil unrest, for in times of peace I am sure that it would be as pleasant as any place on earth."

"Your cheerful spirit is a welcome balm," she replied. "I have spent half the journey listening to some of the young maids complain that they ought to be enjoying these summer days in the shade of their own roof rather than entering a region of conflict." I was about to respond, but she quickly added, "Do not worry, my lady! I made sure to inform them of their duty to Your Highness and the high honor of accompanying you, even under such circumstances."

There was a knock at the door, and Adelaide went toward it. Upon opening it she cried, "Emperor!" and bowed as he strode into the room. The rest of the ladies, who had all remained bent over their work, immediately stood and responded in kind. I was already upright, but made a bow of my own.

"My lord, to what do we owe the honor of your presence?" I asked.

"Be about your business," he said, casting his glance toward a few of the ladies and then back to me. "I have no desire to interrupt. I simply wished to determine if everything was to your liking."

"It is very much to my liking," I replied. "Indeed, these might be some of the finest quarters in which I have resided."

"I am glad to hear it. The steward of the house, Herman, will see to any of your needs. Do let him know if there is anything you require."

"Thank you, sir."

He paused as if trying to remember something, and then said, "The knight Drogo wished me to tell you that, should you desire to join him for a tour of the grounds, he will be at his leisure this evening."

"Thank you. I am most beholden to you."

I turned to Adelaide to request that she inform Drogo, but the emperor added, "There is no need to send word. I shall tell him myself, for I am sure to see him below."

His words caught me by surprise, for I was not aware that the emperor was in the business of carrying messages to persons of lower rank. I presumed he would take his leave, but he stood there long enough that I felt the need to ask, "Is there something else, my lord?"

"Do you walk often, Lady Mathilda?" he asked.

"As often as I can—that is, when the situation allows. I try to take the air once a day. Is that a problem?"

"No, no! I was merely curious." He paused for a moment and then added, "We should go for a walk sometime, you and I. You may bring a few of the ladies, of course."

"Certainly, sir, if that is what you desire."

"It is," he said. He then bid me farewell and departed as suddenly as he had arrived.

The ladies and I all looked at one another, each of us considering this most odd discussion. It was Gertrude who finally spoke.

"Well, there is something I've never seen before! The emperor would usually send one of his underlings to convey such a message. I wonder at his true purpose."

"Could not his true purpose have simply been to make sure I was well?" I asked.

"I suppose, but asking you to take a walk with him—that seems odd indeed. For a start, I cannot imagine when he will find the time. Second, the emperor does not go for walks. He goes off riding into the mountains—maybe to his lodge at Bodfeld, but other times elsewhere—and he has been known to take part in sports within the confines of the palace grounds. I have never seen him walk, though, except perhaps from one building to another."

"Perhaps he feels guilty that we have been married half a year and still barely speak," I thought, but as on so many occasions, I did not share my feelings with the ladies. Instead I said, "This is none of our concern. Please find me something to wear for supper. These travel clothes will not do. They are covered in dust."

As the ladies undertook their new assignments, I cast my gaze out the window toward the lands of Saxony, in which I reasoned that the great lords were at that very moment conspiring against the emperor. What did I know of such a dispute? Were it not for my attachment to my husband, I might have seen merit in the rebels' cause. After all, the emperor had not behaved in an entirely Christian manner. Yet I sensed that, in truth, their motives were no more righteous than those of their ruler, and I did not believe that much good could come of the conflict.

"From whence does the next blow come?" I asked myself. "From whence do the rebels strike?"

In the month of October, Archbishop Frederick of Cologne and a force of rebels attacked an assembly of imperial soldiers near the town of Andernach. In so doing, the archbishop made his treachery complete. He had used not only the weapons of the Church, but also the weapons of war. As had been the case during the time of the emperor's father, he used Henry V's feud with Rome to scorn his will. However, what likely disturbed these bishops as much as any conduct on the part of the emperor was his policy of granting more freedom to the towns, which had long been subject to the direct rule of their bishops. In championing the growing classes of *burghers* and *ministeriales*, the emperor was creating enemies within the noble elite.

The conflict at Andernach revealed the delicate nature of his position. Losing the sympathies of the people of Cologne substantially damaged his cause, but the worst was yet to come. Despite further measures taken to bolster imperial control within the towns, there was another rising in the city of Mainz. In the shadow of that same cathedral where I had been accepted as their rightful queen, the public gathered in ever-growing numbers, calling for Archbishop Adalbert to be returned to his rightful seat. The situation quickly degenerated into chaos, and several of the emperor's men suffered injury attempting to restore stability.

It had all become too much. Even the most powerful emperor could not long countenance such a sustained assault from several quarters. He finally made the fateful decision to release the archbishop from his castle prison, having decided that keeping him locked away was more harmful than granting his freedom.

"But do not release that traitor Count Wiprecht," I heard him yell, "for while I may rue the quill of Adalbert more than the sword of Wiprecht, I think we shall find that the count has fewer friends!"

The story would later be told that Adalbert walked out of Trifels on the verge of death. In truth, few of those who claimed to have witnessed his departure were actually on hand that morning, and certainly the archbishop's claims of ill handling were somewhat amplified. Nevertheless, the emperor had sent a powerful message to every man who wore the bishop's miter: to violate his command was to incur a dreadful punishment. Still, some would argue that this truce between archbishop and emperor was only the third most notable act that year.

A few days after Candlemas in the year 1115, as the last winter snow still lay upon the fields of Saxony, word came to Goslar that the duke was gathering his forces just to the south, between the eastern edge of the mountains and the River Saale. Count Hoyer of Mansfeld had led the larger share of the imperial troops farther to the north, hoping to counter any challenge from the Billungs' lands. This left Goslar open to a westward march by the duke's forces, and Emperor Henry immediately sent his swiftest riders to bid Count Hoyer bring his men south and cut off the route of attack.

The count was quick to carry out the emperor's command. After gathering his full strength at Wallhausen, he marched his men twenty-five miles in less than a day, finally sighting the rebel forces near the town of Welfesholz. A few skirmishes took place that night before the men retreated to their camps. Because of the short distance between the imperial palace in Goslar and the battlefield, the messenger carried these tidings to us by sunrise the following morning. It was then the third day before the ides of February.

Oh, the dreadful hours of waiting! As morning passed into noontime, and then noontime into afternoon, I waited along with the rest to hear of the battle's outcome. The two armies' meeting presented a perfect opportunity to strike at the forces of Duke Lothair once and for all and project imperial power in the North, but a great deal depended on the skill of the marshals in the field. The number of troops on both sides was, by most accounts, fairly equal. Their weapons of war were much alike, as were their styles of attack.

Sensing that the outcome rested upon a knife's edge, and knowing that the consequences of defeat were too dreadful to consider, the emperor even sent some of his own household knights the day before the battle, hoping that their skills gained through years of training would overcome the hastily formed rebel forces. So it was that the palace of Goslar remained eerily quiet on that February afternoon; even the birds seemed to await the news. As the sun began to sink low in the western sky, a rider could be seen approaching from the east. I had been attempting in vain to set my mind to the written word when I glimpsed the frenzy taking place outside, with every guard at arms scrambling onto the battlements, awaiting the appointed sign. In my excitement I rushed down to the lower level of the hall and ran out the door before any of the ladies could assail me. The chancellor was already standing in front of the Kaiserhaus, his eyes fixed upon the guards.

"What is it, Chancellor?" I asked. "What do the men see?"

"They look to see the color of the banner that the rider carries. Once he is close enough, he will display it."

"But what do the colors signify?"

"Red for victory, black for defeat, and white if the battle yet rages," he answered. "We are very near the moment, I think."

"Oh dear! I hope it is red!" I said, taking little care to check my emotions. "I fear defeat would place us in serious danger."

"Quiet!" the chancellor instructed, and then corrected himself. "I am sorry, my lady, but I must hear what the men have to say."

I nodded in assent. In fact, I was perfectly willing to forgive his overstepping, believing it to be the product of a moment's fear rather than a mark of contempt. All of a sudden, the guards turned back toward the palace and began waving their arms wildly.

"Black!" they cried. "The banner is black!"

Again and again, they repeated the horrible word, and I could hardly believe my ears. I looked to the chancellor and found that he was stone faced. Finally he uttered, "I cannot believe it . . . I . . . I cannot believe it. I must tell the emperor, but how can I?"

I had no words to offer him and continued standing there even as Chancellor David turned and made his way back into the hall, where it would likely fall to him to inform Emperor Henry of the defeat. My husband had until that point spent his day on several random matters, hoping to distract himself from worry. There would be no chance of that now, for all haste was necessary.

As it happened, the messenger carried more than a banner. In time we heard from him how the battle at first seemed to favor the imperial side, and the rebels endured heavy losses. It was at that point that Count Hoyer of Mansfeld found himself facing Wiprecht the Younger, the son of the long-imprisoned count. Of that meeting great tales have since been told, each more fantastic than the last. Different words have oft been attributed to one combatant or the other. A particularly common addition is that when their blades met, a shower of sparks flew into the air. Such things hardly seem possible, but perhaps in the memory of battle they ring true. Regarding one thing all tales agree: the count's superior skill proved no match for the young man's desperate yearning for vengeance. His blade found its mark and struck a fatal blow, and thus Hoyer of Mansfeld met his end.

Those around them were oblivious to what had taken place, so locked were they within their own struggles: swords clashing against shields, mud flying here and there, horses falling to the ground along with their masters, and hails of arrows meeting their targets. Seeking to proclaim his feat, the young Wiprecht is said to have lifted up the head of his enemy and proclaimed, "Servants of the heathen emperor! Look upon the face of your leader!" I hope to God that this is also mere fiction.

Naturally, their commander's defeat dealt a harsh blow to all those fighting on the emperor's behalf. Fear filled their hearts, and as the enemy struck forth with a renewed confidence, many of the imperial troops fell back. All too soon, they were in outright retreat. From there the remaining horsemen under Duke Lothair chased down the scattered remains of much of the imperial army, cutting down those they could and sending all others to flight.

The emperor did not wait to hear this full story, or to say a prayer for the fallen. Soon the enemy would be upon us, and with his main force destroyed, there was no choice but to flee Saxony with all speed. We left a small contingent behind to guard the fortress, but all those who could took horses and went in one of two directions: the main party that included the emperor, the members of his council, and the remainder of his household knights went west, while the court ladies and their guardians took a harder path through the mountains. The rebels had no quarrel with them, and in this manner it was less likely that they would be caught in a skirmish, or be seized for ransom, or fall prey to the outlaws who frequented the lower elevations. They carried with them as many goods as possible, but as the carts would not manage that rocky path, they left less important items behind to be pillaged.

There was some question as to which way I must be sent, for although I was a woman, I was also the imperial consort and thus might provide a better prize for anyone with ill intentions. With very little time to make a decision, the matter was left up to Drogo, who said he felt more comfortable riding with the emperor's party. He loathed the whole idea of traveling into the mountains, as he feared we might come across large numbers of rebels lying in wait on the other side. As ever, I trusted his judgment.

In this too my faithful knight proved his value, for he had demanded during my stay in Goslar that I be trained in the delicate art of riding. By the time of our flight, I was able to keep my seat directly in front of him, with his arms enclosing me and gripping the reins. Whereas I had at first found it painful to ride in the manner of men, I now felt quite at ease. Having disguised myself under a dark cloak, I allowed Drogo to place me upon his stallion. Without further discussion we departed into the growing darkness.

There would be no rest for us that night. I could scarcely make out the figures around me, for we did not dare light a torch. How we found our way along that path, I don't know. Perhaps the animals sensed it by instinct. The only sounds were pounding hooves upon the ground and heavy breathing of both horses and riders. Once or twice, I turned to look behind us and imagined that I saw lights in the distance. I dared not ask whether they be friend or foe, for what good could come of such an inquiry? What was to be would be, and that was the end of the matter. I may have drifted into sleep at some point, but at certain times

the mind reaches that place where the dream is scarcely different from waking. Such a night was that one on which we fled into
the darkness, praying each hour that daylight would bring with
it safety.

I have yet to speak of everything else that took place that year,
but first allow me to complete this story. Our nighttime flight met
with good fortune: the following day, we passed into the Duchy
of Franconia, and thus into relative safety. As it turned out, the
rebels could not match our speed, and they did not seek to harry
the party that traveled through the mountains. As for those poor
men who fell at Welfesholz, the enemy was not content merely
to send them from this life before their time. There was a man
among the Saxon ranks, Bishop Reinhard of Halberstadt, who,
despite his claims to piety, gave no sign of Christian benevo-
lence. He declared that as the imperial soldiers fought under
the banner of one who was rightly excommunicated, they too
were removed from God's favor. He compelled the captains to
have all the dead of that side—whether great or small, noble or
common—piled in a heap and burned, for, he argued, they were
not worthy of Christian burial. This caused exceeding pain to
many poor widows throughout the land, and it belied any claim
that the rebels acted with honor.

Had those traitors felt any lack of justification for their actions, the archbishop of Cologne was only too happy to provide
it for them. In April of that year, he pronounced the sentence of
excommunication within the empire's very heart, thus granting
succor to any who sought to forsake their allegiance to their rightful lord. Now that he had lost the support of such a respected figure, it was essential that the emperor reconcile with Archbishop
Adalbert, as I have described.

With the north of his kingdom all but lost, Emperor Henry's
options were few. His two surest supporters were still his nephews

Duke Frederick of Swabia and Conrad, soon appointed Duke of Franconia. The count palatine of the Rhine, Gottfried of Kalw, also had an essential role in maintaining the South's security. There was little more fidelity to be had throughout the empire.

Then something unforeseen happened. In the weeks following Midsummer, word came north to Germany of the death of the famous *contessa*, Mathilda of Tuscany. Long had she reigned over her lands in Tuscany, Emilia, and Lombardy. Between the great mountains and Rome there had been none more powerful than she. That region was rightly under imperial control, yet for as long as the *contessa* lived, the emperors were forced to defer to her judgment on many occasions. As a practical matter, it was difficult to maintain a base of power on both sides of the mountains, and the Salian emperors often cared more for their native land.

Mathilda of Tuscany was as rich in territories as any man, and in the years that preceded her death, she was apt to change her mind as to who should inherit them. Her husband, the Duke of Bavaria, was long estranged from her, as I mentioned before, and he held no rightful claim to her lands; neither had their union produced a male heir. Instead the lady wavered between leaving her possessions to the emperor and bestowing them upon the Church. As her friendship with the Holy See was of long standing, Emperor Henry was well aware that he must move quickly to grasp that which had been promised to him, ere the pope attempt to claim it for Rome.

When all is chaos in the land, it hardly seems the right time for a king to go abroad. Yet under the circumstances, the emperor believed that it might turn out to his advantage. He sensed that the rebels gained their greatest cause for disputation from his own difficulties with Rome, rather than from any popular opposition to the imperial throne itself. In traveling south, the emperor might acquire the lands of Italy and use this advantage to obtain a new agreement with Pope Paschal. In so doing he would return to Germany a new man, endowed with authority beyond what he already possessed.

He thought the potential benefits thus exceeded the hazards, and took counsel as to how he might achieve such an agreement. He brooked no delay and was unwilling to wait until the following spring to set out upon the road. By good fortune a letter survives from that period, which I must have received from my mother late in the summer. As it is filled with information of interest, I produce it here in its entirety:

Mathilda, by the grace of God queen of England, sends this token of her love and affection to her dearest Maud, queen of the Romans, wishing it Godspeed across waters and kingdoms, that it might find its way into well-beloved hands.

My daughter, I have heard of your afflictions in that far land. The emperor's defeat in Saxony is often discussed here in Westminster, as it is throughout the kingdom. It pained me greatly to hear that he has been cast out of communion with our holy Church, even if the pope has not seen fit to extend the ban by his own hand. It was my firm intention to write to your husband and beseech him to repent of his deeds rather than following the path set down by his father, but I thought the better of it for fear that it might cause you harm.

I wish that I could extend my arms across those endless miles and even now wrap you in a maternal embrace. From time to time, I imagine your face, considering how it might have changed these last five years. As I cast my gaze into the looking glass, I perceive the passage of time in my own visage, more careworn now than ever it was in youth, whereas I am sure you grow only in beauty. How could you not?

There is much to tell of our affairs here. My brother's wife, the Countess of Huntingdon, gave birth to a son whom they named Malcolm after our mutual father, but the child was not long for this world. Such sorrow they must have known! Yet God in his mercy granted that within the year she might be delivered of a hale and hearty prince. They christened him Henry in honor of your own father. I have not yet been so fortunate as to see the child, but I offer up prayers for him daily, that he may grow even in the manner of Christ, increasing "in wisdom and stature, and in favor with God and men."

They say that my sister, the Countess of Boulogne, is very ill and nigh unto death. If this be true, then all that remains of my esteemed parents will be the king of Scotland, the Earl of Huntingdon, and myself. From eight we are thus reduced to three—oh, unhappy fate! Yet it is wrong that I should speak thus while my sister remains among the living. I fear for my niece, who will be bereaved of a mother.

The king is shortly to be in England again after his latest foray into Normandy. Your brother counts these visits dear. He was robbed of his father's presence for most of last year on account of the battles in Wales, in which King Henry forced the allegiance of the Welsh lords and brought peace to us all. Normandy is likewise tempered thanks to the imprisonment of that scourge of men, the rebel Robert of Bellême, as I mentioned in my earlier letters. It seems that England's chief quarrels are now with King Louis of France and the Count of Anjou, but absent of any action on those fronts, we should enjoy the king's presence for some time.

Prince William continues to excel in all the martial disciplines. I daresay he will be the equal of his father. I would rather he spent more time in study and less within the lists, but in this matter I have frequently found myself entirely devoid of influence. His closest brothers in arms are the same as always. Stephen of Blois is grown into a superior gentleman, his skills exceeding those of most. The king lavishes favor upon him and is soon to bestow on him the County of Mortain.

Your eldest brother, Robert, is contracted to Mabel fitz Hamon, the Countess of Gloucester, as you well know. It remains uncertain when their marriage will be solemnized before God, but as a matter of law their union is settled. I have heard no rumors that the lady is to begin her lying in, but I suspect it is only a matter of time before the Earl of Gloucester is able to produce offspring within the marriage bed, even as he already has outside of it. Earl Robert is ever in the company of Brian fitz Count, who is well respected at court. Of the four lads, he is the cleverest, methinks. But though he is perfectly able in battle, I believe it is Robert who possesses the superior skill in that realm.

The king delights in their company as if all four were his own sons, though for William he holds an especial devotion. The prince would follow his father in everything. Although I feel a twinge of motherly regret when I think that I should lose my boy, I am filled with pride at the man he has become. There is constant speculation at court as to which ladies will be so fortunate as to enter into wedlock with one of these young men. For myself, I hope that William might be united with a woman of good Christian virtue when the time comes. Though he is still too young for such things, King Henry has already ensured that all the nobles of the land pledge fealty to the prince as his rightful successor.

So many words I have written to you, and yet I have scarcely begun to tell of all that has taken place here in England. I would much rather hear from you about conditions in the empire. Is it true that the emperor will lead an expedition south to recover the territories of the late countess? Oh, the agony of ignorance threatens to drive me mad with longing to hear from you! Yet I remember the words of Saint Augustine: "Thou hast formed us for Thyself, and our hearts are restless till they find rest in Thee." Even so may you find your rest, beloved daughter!

In the name of the Father, and of the Son, and of the Holy Ghost—

MATHILDA REGINA

Such letters were a welcome relief from the troubles that pressed down upon us daily in the empire. I took pleasure from the news that they provided, even though the sentiments contained within were not always pleasant. Only in my mother's letters did I receive such unabashed love, and though I began to see how her advice would at times miss the mark, I was ever glad to receive it. I knew not whether I might ever see her again, but in her writing I was given a chance to commune with her spirit, and that was some consolation.

With the coming of another Advent season, the imperial court moved to Speyer to celebrate the feast and arrange for the emperor's second journey to Italy. Whereas I had formerly remained behind under the care of the archbishop of Trier, I would now be accompanying my husband over the mountains and into the kingdoms of the South. Despite the stress, I found myself looking forward to such an adventure. Though I was certain that the journey would be treacherous, I longed to experience some new land, and even perhaps to set my eyes upon the center of Christendom in Rome. But let us speak no more of the days of preparation. We must be on to the march!

CHAPTER THIRTEEN

April 1165
Rouen, Normandy

There is a place in the garden where I often take my repose and ponder the workings of the day. It is not so far from the great house as to put me beyond a comfortable walk, and yet it grants me the privacy I crave. On a spring morning, even as the one that we now enjoy, it is a welcome respite from the deeds of state I must perform. I once again find myself alone this morning, for my trusted companion, Lawrence, was inclined to set out for the mountain of Saint Michael, there to converse with our dear friend, Abbot Robert of Torigny. I bid him inform the abbot how much I respect his historical writings. So much rubbish is set loose on us now in the guise of history! One or two things I might correct in his accounts, but in general I find the abbot more just than most of those lofty chroniclers. Happy men they are to sit in judgment over us all, well after the fact and many miles away.

Thus I am left this morning to take the quill into my own feeble hand and compose such few lines as come to mind. I know you will forgive me this indulgence of my own scattered thoughts, for I feel it does me some good. I have been sitting under this sun for half an hour, and yet I find myself no more able to express its beauty in words than I was when I began. See now how I babble on about matters of little consequence, unworthy to be preserved by future generations. But here is Adela now, come to meet me upon the green. I see she bears the day's letters in her hand. What news might they contain?

"My lady," she says upon reaching my position, "I received several messages this morning for Your Grace. I wondered if you might care to read them."

"Surely you can inform me of their contents, or at least those which are most urgent," I reply.

"What do you mean?"

"Adela," I say, "I am well aware that you examine any letters I receive before passing them on, so do save us both the trouble and tell me now whether there is anything of great import."

Her face takes on a shade of red that the morning cool does not demand, and I sense that this simple teasing has set her on edge.

"I am sorry, Lady Mathilda," she responds, "I do not examine them in the hope of gaining any privy information, but rather to make things . . ."

"Easier? Yes, I believe you. What's more, it has been a long while since either of us had any secrets from the other. In any case, there is nothing in my letters which requires the powers of concealment, at least not from you."

"Thank you for your understanding, my lady," she answers. "Shall I provide you with a summary, then?"

"Yes, please."

"Abbot Suger writes from Saint Denis. He has heard of your interest in the improvements to the abbey church and wishes for you to visit at your earliest convenience so that he may provide you with a personal tour of the grounds."

"Oh, that I were fit for such a journey!" I respond. "I have longed to see the new quire there since it was first completed twenty years ago. Alas, I never had the time, and now that I have fewer demands upon my schedule, I fear that I no longer possess the vigor. A true pity, for I have heard such tales of what the craftsmen have spawned there. They say it is a new vision of construction."

"Then I am truly sorry that you cannot make the journey. Should I have one of the clerks reply to him and request some drawings? That would at least allow you to understand the design."

"Yes, this seems a good idea. There is already a messenger bound for Paris who will depart tomorrow. Leave it with him."

"Certainly. You also received a letter from Queen Eleanor."

"Oh . . . And what does my daughter-in-law require?"

"She wishes to visit before her final lying-in at Angers."

"That will be soon. The children are with her?"

"Yes, Richard and little Mathilda, though the others remain in England."

"Write and tell her I accept, though I am sure she does not ask merely to see me play the role of doting grandmother."

"You have heard the gossip, then?"

"What gossip?" Truly, Daughter, I do not care for such whispering, but when it concerns my own family, I find that involvement is all but inevitable.

"Why, that King Henry has taken up with a new mistress."

"According to whom?"

"That I cannot say. I heard it from one of the monks, who heard it from a traveling blacksmith, who heard it from God knows where."

"Well then, that is hardly a trusty source."

"Trusty or not, it would be no surprise if a king should attempt to get his fill of all the rare delicacies placed before him, now would it?" she says with a sly smile.

"As a matter of principle, I agree with you, Adela, but you must remember that this subject touches me rather near. I hold no illusions about my son. I think he is half his father and half my own father, and neither of those men was known for his chastity. Even so, I regret to hear that there might be anything that should force me to pity the queen. God knows she has no need of it."

Perhaps I should mention that Queen Eleanor was not so beloved in my heart, for reasons that I shall not delve into on this occasion.

"No more talk of that," Adela instructs. "Let us think of happier subjects. What is that book in your hand?"

"It is the latest work by the mystic Hildegard. She sent it to me some weeks hence at my especial request, and I have scarcely been able to tear myself away from it ever since."

"You believe what they say, then—that she receives visions from the Almighty?"

"I cannot claim to be a proper judge, since I have never met her in the flesh, but much of what she writes has the aura of truth about it. She is clearly learned, and I have no particular reason to doubt her claims. But in all honesty, my interest arises in part from that which we have in common. We both know what it is to press against the bounds of convention. In any case, it is far more beneficial than most of the volumes that now abound."

"I shall leave you to it then," she concludes, turning back toward the house. No sooner has she done so than a change of mind sweeps over her, and Adela says to me, "Wait! I forgot! There was another letter for you, but this one even I was unwilling to open. I think you had better look it over now, though I doubt it will bring you any pleasure."

"Some recommendation! Let me see it."

She hands me the rolled parchment and I set my eyes upon the seal. This message is from the archbishop of Canterbury, Thomas Becket.

"Again he writes to us?" I ask in frustration. "Honestly, what does he suppose I can do for him? He must truly be desperate if he seeks my good opinion—I who warned the king from the beginning that he was not fit for high office. I swear to you, Adela, that man is everything that is wrong with the Church! Such a hypocrite, pretending to piety, but allowing the priests of England to rape and murder in broad daylight without so much as a word of condemnation! What kind of Christian is that? Yet here he is, begging me to whisper a fair word on his behalf in the ear of the king. Well, Pope Alexander might humor him, but I cannot."

"Perhaps he merely seeks out your wisdom, which is known to be great indeed," Adela offers.

"I think not, but bless you for saying so. No, if I know Thomas Becket, he hopes to employ what advantage he can over the situation, and what better means to do so than a beseeching mother? Vain man! He seeks to make me a tool in his own hand, but he would never lift a finger on my behalf, I'll be bound. He never has. Even so, this rancor must not continue. No king can afford to set himself at odds with the Church without great detriment to his rule, to say nothing of his immortal soul."

"What will you do then?"

"Well, as you say, I shall offer such pearls of wisdom as I can muster, but I fear the situation has grown beyond my power to heal. I do not believe we have seen its equal since I was in Germany. Speaking of which, King Henry has sent his ambassadors out to meet with the emperor and discuss this marriage alliance for the girls."

"Really? What is your opinion on the matter?

"Ah, once again you seek to know my mind rather than revealing your own. A shrewd decision, no doubt, for it frees you from the shackles of an opinion. If you must know, I am happy for any alliance that brings us closer to the empire, and I suspect it will be greatly to the princesses' benefit—but at such a young age! I cannot help but worry. And the support of the emperor for the false pope offends me greatly. I fear that this is an alliance that will do my son ill."

"I suppose it is only natural that you should fear, given your own experience."

"Yes, and it shows how little Queen Eleanor regards my advice, that she should not seek me out before deciding upon this course of action, despite the fact that my connections within the empire remain strong, perhaps even stronger than those of King Henry. Sadly, I think she only values my counsel when it might help in quarrels with her husband."

"At least that is something," Adela replies with a smile. "I must be off now. No matter how much I strive to train them, it seems that the men of my house are unable to feed themselves."

"Go then, with my blessing."

"Thank you, my lady."

Having now recorded much of our conversation, I find myself growing rather tired of this stone bench. A return to the house is in order, but not before another brief amble through the park, a chance to ponder the memories that I intend to set down upon the return of Father Lawrence. Give me leave to set down my quill and bask in these first days of warmth, for I know all too well that they cannot last.

Imagine now those days of yore, when Emperor Henry V and his young bride set out against the dying days of winter to claim the lands of the late *contessa* for their posterity. Emilia, Tuscany, Lombardy, Verona: to all these lands the winding path summoned the imperial party. They passed first through the river towns of the North, where endless fields of grain grow within the flood-plain and punters float to and fro along the canals. Then, traveling by way of the western vale, they came at last to the city of legend, the glowing beacon that draws men thither from the far reaches of the earth.

I set out upon that road with little in the way of experience to guide me. It would take more than a crown to create in me an empress. Yet that sojourn did leave its mark upon me, and were I to have revealed the inner thoughts of my heart upon returning north, I might have been so bold as to declare myself no longer a girl, but a woman ready to fulfill her duty. Ah, the blessed ignorance of youth! Even so, I cannot deny the effect those days had upon me.

We had all gathered in Augsburg shortly after Christmas to make our final preparations for the journey south. I will grant that the word *all* implies a more extensive company than was gathered at the time, for with rebellion still raging in the North, my husband was unable to spare his thousands of men-at-arms to accompany the imperial convoy. Instead we made do with a small force composed mostly of the emperor's own household knights, a good stock of secular and church officials, and two men of particularly noble blood: the Duke of Carinthia, Henry of Eppenstein, and Count Henry of the House of Welf, brother to the Duke of Bavaria. The former owed his presence to the plain fact that his lands abutted the March of Verona, which Emperor Henry hoped to retain. The latter was brother-in-law to the late Countess Mathilda of Tuscany, and he was in charge of overseeing his family's claims south of the mountains.

With such a small force at his command, any chance of victory for the emperor would depend upon his ability to influence others. He would first need to gain the support of the northern Italian regions just below the mountains. Having ensured their allegiance, he could then proceed south and bring pressure to bear upon the papal lands. My chaplain, Altmann, was in no fit state to ride, and thus it was determined that he ought to join me in the carriage for the duration of our travel. Although some might have objected to such an idea, I was glad of the company.

We made our way along the Via Imperii, the ancient path leading from the northern sea to the mountains. Passing through them along the narrow way, the road descends through the Italian hill country to Rome, from which there is easy access to the Middle Sea. That was no easy road, but it was easier than any of the other paths that led either through or around the mountains. I was eager to see those hills that men call the Alps. On many occasions Bavarian minstrels who sang of those high meadows, falls of water, and gray heights crowned with snow had graced the emperor's court. The mountains seemed to live within their very souls, and they claimed it was only the brave who dared set foot in the lowlands.

Before long we climbed through the rising hills, and for the first time I could see mountains in the distance. A sense of wonder came over me—I could think of nothing so magnificent as these lands. Only the eternal sea, with its unbounded power and unfathomable depths, also provoked such awe.

"She is a great wonder, is she not?" Altmann said.

"Yes, but why do you address the mountain so?" I replied.

"I should think it would have been evident. Who can know the mysteries of those heights? Only the men of Babel were bold enough to tread there. I feel that one could stare at those mountains day upon day, yet still not comprehend them. Such is the case with a woman, no?"

"Perhaps, but I might have guessed that you would see in those fierce hills a picture of the masculine."

"It is not the sole dominion of the sons of Adam to be fierce," he countered. "Have you never heard of the great lady Brünnhilde? She was as fierce as they come."

"That name is wholly foreign to me," I admitted, "though I may have heard it spoken in passing."

Altmann didn't respond immediately, but cast his gaze out the window at the Alps, apparently seeking inspiration. At length he spoke.

"You are perhaps aware that in the ancient days, before the gospel of our Lord Jesus Christ traveled to the wild regions of the North, the people of that land made their homes among the trees, with the starry heavens serving as their roof. The manner of their worship remains largely a mystery, but we know they served many gods. Not as you and I serve God, mind you. Their deities had none of the goodness of the true Creator, being mere creations of human fancy, the alleged power behind every snapping twig and crashing wave. In such a manner savage men still live today in the far corners of the world, enveloped in the darkness of ignorance, having no knowledge of the light. Great tales were told in those days, passed down from generation to generation, and the greatest of all I will tell you now.

There was a *Schildmaid*, Brünnhilde, a daughter of the gods, who lived in the farthest reaches of the Northland, condemned by the high god Wotan to be imprisoned within a ring of fire in punishment for some misdeed . . . I remember it not. It is said that the warrior Siegfried, a man without fear, passed through the fire by aid of sorcery and released her from her bondage. Freely they gave their hearts, pledging eternal devotion one to the other, and for many happy nights walked together beneath the stars. At last Siegfried was forced to set out, but swore that he would return and marry none but her. Are you certain that you have not heard this all before?"

"No, indeed, I have not. I bid you tell me more," I replied, enchanted by his tale.

"Very well, then. When he arrived in her realm, the witch Grimhild placed the faithful Siegfried under a spell that caused him to forget all he knew of Brünnhilde, even the pledge of love that he swore to her. He was married instead to the daughter of Grimhild. That crafty mother! She purposed in her mind to have her son, Gunnar, wed to the shieldmaiden instead, but was forced to muster Siegfried's help to win her. Brünnhilde, not knowing that Siegfried was troth plighted to another, was all too happy to go with him. Only too late did she understand that her love was lost to her for all eternity."

"So she married Gunnar?"

"Yes."

"But why?" I protested. "If Brünnhilde was indeed a powerful warrior, surely she could have escaped. She did not have to bind herself to an inferior man."

"Ah, but you see, her heart was broken by the one she loved, and all her hopes had faded. Once she could no longer have Siegfried, she felt herself dead to the world, no longer possessing the will to resist."

"This is dreadful. How does the story end?"

"The way all such tales must. Siegfried was brought down by the sword of a jealous foe, his body placed upon a fiery bier; and Brünnhilde, for want of succor, threw herself upon the flames, wishing rather to die than to live ever after in despair."

There was a moment of silence, and then I said, "Altmann?"

"Yes, my lady?"

"I have never before heard such a story of woe as the one which you now tell me. But why must all the queens of legend suffer at the hands of love? Did not the Carthaginian queen, Dido the Fair, also surrender her body to the flames when parted from noble Aeneas? Did not Cleopatra offer her breast to the asp, that its venom might rid her of her love for the Roman general?"

"Yes, it is as you say," he replied.

"Why must it always be so?"

"There I am obliged to grant you a straight answer, Your Grace. It is in the nature of the female to make great outward displays of emotion and to allow herself to be guided by the feelings of the moment rather than the cold hand of reason."

"I do not think that is true," I objected. "A woman may give way to emotion from time to time, but it need not control her. And in any case, are not men borne off by the fury of war to commit deeds that, in sober judgment, might seem rather monstrous? Yet how the poets praise them for doing so!"

"Perhaps, and being pledged myself, I am glad to see that you set little store by the demands of the flesh and that odd yearning which tends to drive even the most reasonable of young ladies mad."

"I give you my full assurance, sir, that I would never throw myself on a fire for any man, nor would any woman of sense do so! We must acknowledge that some dishonor our sex through flights of fancy leading to despair. But a woman may be ruled by reason as much as any man."

He smiled in return. "It is right that you should think so, my lady, for I believe it will serve you well in your role as consort."

I leaned my head back and gazed out the window. Soon enough we would come upon the city of Innsbruck, of which I had heard only good things. From there we would take the Brenner Pass through the mountains and down to Lago Garda and the town of Verona, which was the portal to Italy. As I looked upward, I thought for a moment that I glimpsed an animal of some kind standing high above. It had a brown coat and stood on four legs, perched rather dangerously on a narrow ledge. I strained to gain a better view, but was too far away to make out its figure properly. I asked Drogo about this later, and he concluded that it must have been one of the highland goats basking in the afternoon sun, oblivious to the great movements of men taking place far below, with only the choughs for company.

They say that the Carthaginian general Hannibal once marched his army over the Alps and into the river plains of Lombardy accompanied by a band of fighting elephants. How he accomplished this, I cannot fathom. Truly, the skills of the ancients must have far exceeded our own. It was enough for us to come at last to that lake the Italians call Garda and to rest upon its banks with naught but dogs and horses to tend.

We spent a few happy days in fair Verona, home to a stadium built by the Romans of old. I was rather impressed by the structure, both for its sheer size and for its magnificent design. Even so, I was assured that it was as a child's toy in comparison to the Colosseum of Rome.

"Wait until we are in the holy city, and then you shall see a true wonder of the world built with human hands," Chancellor David said.

From there we moved east, taking the road that leads between the mountains and the Adriatic. We paused briefly in Vicenza and Treviso, and on each occasion the emperor met with the local officials to ensure their fealty. As it happened, most of the people in those towns were only too happy to receive such regal visitors from the North, hopeful that the imperial visit would bring with it an abundance of royal favor.

We descended into Venice on a clear day, the fifth before the ides of March. The emperor was to be the guest of the doge and dogaressa. The doge at that time was Ordelafo Faliero, heir to one of the city's great families. His father had supported Emperor Henry IV throughout his dispute with the pope, and thus the son was viewed as a friend of the empire. The dogaressa was a distant relative, being a daughter of the counts of Boulogne, the most recent of whom had married my mother's own sister, Mary of Scotland.

Lying in the center of the Laguna Veneto, the island city had long been known for the extent of its trade, and by the year of our Lord 1116, it had become a point of transit not only for goods, but also for pilgrims on their way to and from the Holy Land. Even as our convoy progressed along the highway, we passed men and women traveling in both directions, some hoping to gain respite for their souls and others hoping to line their purses with coins of gold. "Venice is the entrance to Jerusalem," they used to say, and every day the ships arrived with foreign wares to sell.

Having arrived in the port town of Mestre, we boarded crafts that would carry us across the *laguna* to Venice itself. It was close to high tide when we made the crossing, and the water moved to overtake some of the smaller islands. A cluster of these isles contains the city, while the one they call Lido guards the entrance to the Adriatic. A more perfect harbor one is unlikely to find in all the kingdoms of Europe. We sailed to the isle of Rialto and laid anchor next to the doge's *palazzo*, which lies at the heart of the city. The houses there were built upon the very edge of the water, and at high tide one might step from the canals directly into any one of them, taking a small step upward and through the front door. Merchants moved along the water in vessels of every imaginable form, some large and ornate, others so plain as to remain unnoticed. It was a strange and wonderful thing.

The doge and dogaressa waited upon the *palazzo* steps to receive us. Emperor Henry was first to climb out of the ship, and he lent his hand to me as I followed. We ascended together. I could see clearly that the dogaressa's attire was of a different style from that favored in the North, and for a moment I wondered if she would find my own raiment overly rustic. My good ladies had made every effort to place as many of the royal jewels upon my person as possible, but nevertheless I feared that before the dogaressa I was bound to suffer in comparison.

"*Benvenuto mio signore!*" the doge proclaimed, stepping forward to embrace the emperor. "*E 'passato troppo tempo da quando ho visto la tua faccia!*"

Based on the experiences of the past few weeks, I knew that my husband was not very skilled in the languages of the Italians, and thus it did not surprise me when he responded in Latin.

"A parting too long, but one that we will now remedy. The city is even fairer than I remember. You must be commended for receiving us in this manner, and for your continued friendship and allegiance."

"Everything has been made ready for Your Grace," the doge replied. "Several of the rooms have been decorated in the new style. We hope you like them."

"Truly, that is a great relief!" the emperor said. "Do not ask me to recount for you the many hours upon this journey that I have spent in agony of spirit, wrestling with this very question: how are my rooms to be furnished? Never mind the pope—it's the tapestries I've come to see!"

For a moment, both the doge and dogaressa simply stared at him with looks of confusion, and I thought perhaps the emperor's meaning was lost on them. Finally the Venetian let out a hearty laugh and said to his wife, "*Sta scherzondo!*" She immediately joined him in laughter, though I sensed a lack of ease about her person.

"Come!" the doge declared. "We have food and drink made ready for you inside, the best that our city has to offer. The Byzantines and sultans of the East shall find their repast no finer than that which we present to Your Highness."

As we made our way up the stairs and toward the entrance of the *palazzo*, the doge placed his arm around the emperor's shoulders. It was an odd degree of familiarity, but I reasoned that it must be based upon experience.

"We have many things to discuss," the Venetian said with some excitement. "You will tell me of your war with the Saxons, and I will recount my battles against the Hungarians."

"I do hope there will be some time to judge the current matter at hand," the emperor replied.

"Ah, yes, yes! All will proceed in due course."

Of all the great houses I entered during my time in Italy, the ducal *palazzo* of Venice was by far the most magnificent and certainly different from the rest. It was built of a kind of light-colored stone, with marble columns supporting a chain of arches into which were carved images of birds, beasts, flowers, and stars—seemingly whatever had caught the mason's fancy. There were large windows in every room looking out toward either the canal or the main *piazza*. Rich fabrics, all of them acquired from eastern traders, were draped from the windows and the ceilings. The carpets, I was told, had been crafted in Persia; the ivory for all the carved figures brought from Africa; and a scimitar covered in jewels, which was displayed in the dining hall, had apparently been seized during the doge's siege of Acre a few years earlier.

Most extraordinary of all were the mosaics that covered both the walls and the ceilings. Plants and birds, the like of which I had never seen, danced upon a field of gold leaf. I wondered at their beauty. One of the largest displayed the crest of the *famiglia* Falier, with its blend of silver, blue, and gold. High above, the four patrons of Venice—Gabriel, the Virgin Mary, Saint Mark, and Saint Theodore—looked down on us, bestowing a silent blessing.

As we sat down to eat, the doge called for the wine to be brought forth. It was of a good Tuscan vintage and somewhat sweeter than that of the Rhineland. Thus I found it more to my liking. There were several creatures living in the house that appeared to be small apes, and one of them perched itself on its master's shoulder for the duration of our meal, receiving from the doge's hand a few small morsels. It was a strange little thing, perpetually twitching and examining each of us in turn. I wondered if this might be the *simia* from my book.

The servants continued to present dishes seasoned with diverse spices, their names often a mystery to me. One of these was so divine that I summoned the courage to inquire as to its origins.

"What you are tasting is known as *kinnamon*," the dogaressa told me.

"It is wonderfully sweet," I replied. "Where is it grown?"

"There is little agreement on the subject. Some say that it comes from Ethiopia, where the traders drag it in from the sea with their nets. Others believe that it is used by the birds of Arabia to build their nests, but no one knows where they find it."

"But the traders of Venice have traveled throughout the world," I argued. "Surely they have discovered the answer to this riddle."

"If they had, it would hardly be in their interest to tell, now would it?"

"I cannot guess your meaning."

Smiling, she said to me, "Have you never heard the saying, 'A man will sacrifice all he has for a rare stone, but will give nothing for the pebble outside his front door'? Those who sell this *kinnamon* know that it is better to leave its source a mystery, thus encouraging public interest. In any case, I doubt that even the men of Venice know for certain where it comes from."

"Where do you think it is grown?" I asked the doge, turning to face him. "Is it like any other plant, or does it descend from heaven itself?"

"You must forgive the lady Mathilda," the emperor said. "She is very forthright in her manner. It is the English way, I think."

"It is no matter," the doge answered. "If you were to ask me, I would say it comes from the east; very far to the east. But God knows that the merchants will not surrender their secret."

"Speaking of things to the east, how goes it with the Hungarians?" my husband asked.

"Well, for the most part. I have only lately returned from finishing that conquest. It is necessary, of course, in order to ensure that our shipping routes remain open. The Byzantines will attempt to counter us, as they always do, but they are much too occupied with the Saracens at the present time to put up a strong fight. Thus in subduing the Hungarians and their king, Coloman . . ."

"You have achieved near domination of the Adriatic."

"Yes, well, we still have the Normans of the south to contend with, but they have their own problems. Together, you and I will ensure that their ambitions are held in check, and the Normans are far too corrupt to serve as a permanent solution for *il Papa*. If he throws himself under their protection, they will tear him to shreds."

"Some might say that would suit you," the emperor replied.

"And it would suit you even more, I should think! But let us not get ahead of ourselves. Tell me, how do you intend to obtain the lands of *la Grancontessa*? I see you have left your army at home."

"I assure you, *Signor* Faliero, that it was a necessary precaution. In any case, the thing is of little matter. I intend to win over the northern provinces and offer proof of my claim. The lords of Tuscany cannot afford to let *il Papa* seize control of their land bit by bit. A master north of the mountains is less irksome than one next door, I daresay."

"You speak reason, but without the consent of the Holy See, you cannot hope to succeed for long. Surely the past few years have taught you that." As he said this, the doge fed the animal another piece of fruit.

"They have indeed," the emperor replied, the tone of his voice becoming harsher. "But you forget one essential thing: Paschal is not my enemy. He has fallen under the spell of the Gregorians, who speak of reform but have revealed they are hypocrites. They seek reform so long as it does not trespass their own interests, but their time is coming to an end."

"So you believe you can win the Holy Father over to your cause?"

"I would have done so before, had the circumstances been more in our favor."

"So now you will back Paschal into a corner. What if he attempts to declare the order of excommunication from Rome itself?"

"I do not think he would be so foolish. Had he the slightest intention of that, it would have come already. In any case, he took a solemn oath before God not to do so, and I would prefer to think that such a pledge is still worth something when it comes from the lips of the pope himself."

"We shall see," the doge concluded, and with a wave of his hand, his servants cleared the table and the ape returned to the ground with a great leap. "Come," he said to the emperor. "You must see our great production."

We set out toward the eastern edge of the island, where the doge presented the mighty shipbuilding works, which were his pride and joy. A great deal was said about the rising merchant class, taxes and profits, shipping routes, and his vision to build the greatest enterprise of industry known to man.

"This is the way of the world now," he told us. "The great race has begun, and we shall be among the leaders. The world will no longer be run by armies, but by the power of the purse."

"The world has ever belonged to those who hold the purse," the emperor replied.

"Yes, but not to such a degree. The Lord God will honor the works of our hands, of that I am certain."

As the two men continued to debate these grand movements, I could think only of the London wharf and the merchants I had watched from afar setting out upon the river and returning in boats filled with wealth. They would surely have approved of the doge's venture and sought to create its equal on the River Thames.

"How long has it been since I glimpsed those shores?" I thought. "What must they think when they hear of us now?"

When we had spent but two days in Venice, we were called back to the mainland, where my husband once again set about the task of winning the northern lands. With a stay in Padua, he gained the allegiance of the last major town in the March of Verona, and the time had come for us to move into those lands that had been under the late *contessa*'s direct control. The first such object of his concern was, in many ways, the most important. Almost forty years had passed since my husband's father, Emperor Henry IV, crossed over the mountains in the depths of winter and came as a humble penitent to the fortress of Canossa, stronghold of Mathilda of Tuscany. It was there that Pope Gregory had come to stay, and there the emperor sought him out, for only absolution by the heir of Saint Peter could stem the rising tide of rebellion against him.

Such a tale was sure to join the great legends: two lords of men standing in opposition, each anointed by God to rule over his own realm, each as immovable as the pyramids of Egypt, and yet each oddly dependent on the other. Fate had appointed the hour of their battle. At Canossa the fourth Henry suffered humiliation for a time so that he might secure his imperial reign. In this he was only partially successful, for though the tide did turn for a time in his favor, he was to be humbled once again by an enemy far closer to home: his own son.

Now Henry IV was long dead, as was the pope who so greatly vexed him. Even the *contessa* had gone on to her eternal reward. Instead it was our small company that rode through the hilly passes to Canossa. Those who had once been rather joyous now took on a certain solemnity, which I reasoned was due to the nature of the occasion. We each of us sensed that the visit of the son to this site of such significance for his father marked a turning point in this Italian journey and was the first time the emperor was likely to face any substantial opposition, for the hereditary claims of the Tuscan lords were strong indeed. But as Wipo said of Emperor Henry III, "Next after Christ he rules across the earth," and so Henry V hoped it to be.

The *fortezza* sits upon a hill with a visage equal to that of Janus. To one side it is green and welcoming, but on the other the jagged gray rock has a frightful appearance. Even so the southern lands held for us the promise of change, but whether victory or defeat none could be certain. With some labor we made the final climb to the castle gates, where a host of officials waited to receive us, three of them standing forward of the rest.

"Altmann," I asked, for my chaplain remained within the carriage, "what can you tell me of the three men standing there? The ones of great significance?"

"Ah, well, that man on the left is Philip of Ravenna. He serves as imperial chancellor in all the regions of Italy. He will have come to join the emperor for the remainder of his journey south. Next to him is a certain Count Rabado of German origin. I am not sure what his business is here."

"I see. And their fellow? The one in the brown cowl?"

"I know him not, though by his attire I would guess he is one of the Cluniac order."

The man was indeed from one of the Cluniac houses, as Altmann had guessed, but he was no ordinary monk. This surprise visitor was none other than Abbot Pontius of Cluny, chief representative of the most powerful monastery in Europe. There was no greater champion of Church reform in those days than Cluny, although it has since fallen upon harder times. Through its immense collection of priories, it promoted the rule of Saint Benedict and advocated for a more vigorous, purified papacy.

Three monks of Cluny had so far become popes of Rome. First there was mighty Gregory VII, who lent new life to the papal throne with the force of his person. Then came Urban II, who proclaimed the first holy pilgrimage to the far corners of Europe, beseeching men to take up the sign of the cross and march to Jerusalem. Finally there was the pope in those days, Paschal II, a close personal friend of Abbot Pontius. One could see why the pope would send his ally Pontius to treat with the imperial party, hoping to reach an accord before the emperor advanced into the heart of Tuscany and within close range of the Holy See. His coming was nevertheless a surprise, and I cannot say that the emperor greeted it with anything but the smallest measure of hospitality. Both men would be forced to act peaceably if they were to reach an agreement.

We were ushered into the great hall, where a pair of thrones stood ready to receive us. I could not help observing that this was a better welcome than we were likely to receive from the Roman *curia*. The musicians performed for us a new song, which had been written particularly for the occasion. Players came forth to add to the reception, each one receiving the gratitude that was his due. The lords and bishops paid their respects to the visiting emperor. At length the clamor ceased, and Emperor Henry V arose to make a speech.

"Good people of Canossa, lords of Lombardy and Tuscany, friends both old and new, and servants of the Church of our lord Jesus Christ, we thank you for the manner of our reception, which touches our spirit beyond the power of words. Many days we have traveled to stand before you, with the object of offering you comfort in this difficult time. The Countess Mathilda was known far and wide for her piety and devotion to the Church, as well as the excellent manner in which she administered the regions under her care. We have seen how, in word and deed, she has left an everlasting mark upon the hearts of those who loved her.

"Fear not! For even as our Lord assured the disciples, you shall not be left as orphans. Though your mistress has reaped the rewards of a long and glorious life and rests now with her fathers, a new Mathilda comes before you: my queen, the empress of these lands and daughter of King Henry of England."

Here he pointed in my direction and the eyes of all in attendance found me. I smiled and gave a slight bow of the head, acknowledging the emperor's high praise. Yet as I did so, I doubted that the residents of Canossa would see me as a proper substitute for the woman who had ruled over them for some forty years.

The emperor continued, "Do not suppose that I have been unmindful of the recent difficulties. Only four years ago, I had the countess crowned as imperial vicar and vice-queen of Italy, titles of honor fit for her person. She was to me a second mother, even as she had been to my father, and her passing has grieved me deeply. Yet there are forces at work even now which would see her final wishes denied and her inheritance divided among men who hold no true claim.

"It is for these reasons that I come before you: first, to offer comfort to one and all in the hour of grief, and second, to ensure that the lands of Tuscany remain within the Holy Roman Empire ordained by God. From the reign of Constantine the Great down to the present day, it has been the duty of emperors to act as the protectors of Christendom, doers of the Lord's work upon this earth. I pledge to you that I shall continue to do so in a manner that respects the rights and traditions of the people of this land.

"Now is not the time for fracture, but for unity. Therefore, we are much pleased that as your emperor, we have received the fealty and respect due to our person. God be with you, and may he continue to show us favor!"

His words were met with great cheers, and it appeared that Henry V's visit to Canossa was to be far more glorious than the ordeal undergone by his father many years before. I noticed Drogo standing off to the side and motioned for him to come to me.

"That was an excellent speech, no?" he said.

"Yes, though I think this audience is a bit more friendly on the whole than the one which awaits him farther south. I have noticed just now that Abbot Pontius did not seem to be enjoying himself."

We both looked in the direction of the abbot as he pushed through the crowd to speak a word in the emperor's ear.

"They will hold a secret parley, I suppose, and there the real work will begin," I continued. "I do hope that they can agree. I would hate to think that you or anyone else should be asked to come to blows on behalf of this cause."

"I can see that your mind is more cunning than mine," Drogo replied.

A thought suddenly came to me. "Drogo, why are we speaking in Latin?"

Although I have not made it clear, Daughter, we had until that point been proceeding in the language with which we were forced to conduct most of our daily affairs at that time. How long it had been since I had spoken in the words of my own land, I could not remember. Seemingly struck with the same desire, we both started speaking those words, one at a time.

"Eagle."

"Blue."

"Village."

"Family."

"Cat."

"Royal."

"I rather like this," Drogo said.

"Ah, but how much do you know of the English tongue?"

"Hardly a word. You will remember, I was raised in Cornwall, and they have their own manner of speaking."

"Then say something in the Cornish speech."

He paused a moment, then said with a smile, "*My'ternes.*"

"What does that mean?"

"'Queen.'"

"I think it is much like the language of the Scots. My mother used to speak it to me when I was young, but most of it was a mystery even to her."

"So go on, then. Show us your English speech," he teased. "I have yet to find a Norman lord who owns it."

"You might have been better off trying a Norman lady," I replied, unwilling to be mastered. "I will speak Caedmon's *Hymn* for you."

There was still much noise in the hall, but I closed my eyes and strained to recite.

Nu scylun hergan hefaenricaes uard

Metudæs maecti end his modgidanc

Uerc uuldurfadur swe he uundra gihwaes

Eci dryctin or astelidæ

He aerist scop aelda barnum

Heben til hrofe haleg scepen.

Tha middungeard moncynnæs uard

Eci dryctin æfter tiadæ

Firum foldu frea allmectig

When I opened my eyes again, I could see Drogo standing dumb before me, evidently taken aback by my words.

"I do not see why you should be so surprised," I told him. "I am, after all, my mother's daughter."

CHAPTER FOURTEEN

Though it aided stability in the imperial realm, hereditary privilege was a weapon that cut both ways. The passing of honors from one generation to the next ensured the existence of an able, learned class and served to prevent much of the destructive warfare that is so common in nature. For if men have no lords, then might every man become a lord unto himself, and thus would the words of Scripture be fulfilled: "Every man did that which was good in his eyes."

The emperor was well aware of the benefits of inheritance. Yet there was an equal danger, for noble families proved to be fickle allies of their rightful king, ever intent on advancing the cause of their own descendants. Such ambition too often resulted in the continual violence that their ennoblement had sought to prevent. My own father, King Henry I of England, was of the same opinion as my husband: that men who are raised up by the king often prove far more steadfast than those who benefit from fortunate descent. Given the state of affairs in Tuscany and the absence of an undisputed heir to the *contessa*'s title, the emperor knew that he must seize the opportunity to install a man of his own choosing, thus breaking the line of dominion by this single family, which had made full demonstration of its changeable nature over the course of generations.

Count Rabodo proved to be just the man for this purpose, being only a minor noble within the Kingdom of Germany and rather pliable to the imperial will. Before departing Canossa, the emperor appointed him as Margrave of Tuscany and bid him maintain the fidelity of the people to their anointed sovereign. There was some complaint on the part of Duke Welf of Bavaria, who was the *contessa*'s lawful husband despite the long years of separation, and thus had a claim on her estate when she died without issue. But any hope the duke held for authority over the wider region was disappointed, as the imperial jurists were quick to ensure Rabodo's elevation. Thus the House of Welf was diminished in Tuscany for a time.

The next target in Emperor Henry's sight was the ancient city of Mantua, which sits upon the River Mincio just north of its confluence with the Po. It was here that the infamous ruler of the Huns, Attila the scourge of God, met with the beloved pope, Saint Leo the Great, a man whose spiritual genius was more than equal to his enemy's skill in battle. In all humility the bishop of Rome appealed unto the mercy of the cruel Hun. Then a miracle took place, for behind Pope Leo there appeared the figures of Saint Paul and Saint Peter with drawn swords, warning Attila that if he dare advance upon the holy city, he would suffer the fate of Alaric, whose fleet and body were both destroyed after he pillaged Rome. Filled with holy terror, Attila withdrew his forces to their ancestral lands, whereupon he gave up the ghost.

Stories such as this caused me to fear when I considered how my wedded husband now sought to bend the will of the vicar of Christ to his own. I understood the arguments put forth by the emperor and his substantial force of printers. He seemed to be a man of both sense and conviction. The longer I remained in his company and that of his counselors, the more I saw the justice of their cause. Yet my feelings were ever held in check by that great respect which is due to ours. To the emperor the Gregorians were a menace, yet they served as an inspiration for many, including my mother. Thus my spirit was torn within me, and I wished most of all for a peaceful and happy outcome.

As we approached the surroundings of Mantua, much of which were marshland, I remained as ever in the company of Altmann, whose infirmity remained. On this particular day, weariness showed in his every feature. I reasoned that he must have imbibed too fully during the previous night's feast.

"Altmann?"

"What?" he muttered, a bit startled. "Yes, my lady, what is it?"

"They say we are to make our stay at the castle of Governolo."

"Yes, so I have heard."

"That is very close to Mantua, is it not?"

"Yes, very close." He rested his face upon his right hand and allowed the lids of his eyes to sink farther and farther downward.

"Do you know who was born there?"

There was no answer, but merely a snort from my companion.

"Altmann!"

"What? Yes! Yes! I agree with you." His eyes strained against the light, and it was clear that he had not taken in my words.

"You agree with what?" I asked.

"Why? What did you say?"

"Do you know who was born in Mantua?"

"I must admit my ignorance."

I was a bit displeased with his lack of interest, but pressed on in spite of it.

"Virgil! You have heard of the famous poet, have you not? He was born very near here."

"Virgil?"

"Altmann, did you take any sleep at all last night?"

"Not a bit, my lady," he replied, perhaps too honestly. His eyes were threatening to close once again.

"Sleep, then. I can see you are no good for conversation today."

"Thank you," were his final words, as he slipped again into blissful slumber.

I contented myself the rest of the journey by attempting to remember the words of Virgil. Bruno of Trier had ordered that I make a study of the *Aeneid* to improve my understanding of Latin. This work of Virgil now seemed rather apt, as the emperor journeyed onward to Rome in the manner of Aeneas, driven on by the same force of purpose.

Before long the walls of Governolo's castle rose above us, and the local nobility stood ready for our arrival. I lent my attention once again to my companion.

"Altmann! Wake up! We are here."

"What? Oh, yes, I see."

"Did you enjoy your repose?" I asked with a smile.

"You mistake me, my lady. I was merely in deep meditation. As your spiritual counselor, you could hardly fault me for taking a few moments each day to make my peace with God."

"Certainly not, though I suspect the Lord may take offense at your boisterous snoring."

Having discerned that there was no purpose in maintaining his pretense, he answered, "What penance would the lady have me perform for this grave misdeed?"

After considering for a moment, I replied, "Speak well of me before the emperor, if you can. I wish to remain in his good graces."

"Have you reason to doubt his regard?"

"I suppose not, but for all of my observation, I fear that I still know him little."

"I will see what I can do," he concluded.

Now, Abbot Pontius was still in the imperial company in those days, and though he did not treat with the emperor as often as he must have desired, the mediation continued apace between the opposing camps.

One evening, I happened to stray into a chamber that was connected to the emperor's private quarters. I certainly cannot remember the purpose of my visit, but what I heard through the door, which had been left slightly ajar, remains fixed in my memory to the present day. I noted the voices of three men: one was plainly the emperor, another I guessed by his tone to be Abbot Pontius, and the third, mostly silent member of the party seemed to be Philip of Ravenna attempting a reconciliation between the two men. Their speech was a mixture of Latin and a few scattered words in each of their native tongues.

"I warn you, the Holy Father will not accept any threat against the papal territories," the abbot said. "He has not forgotten your last infamous visit, and though His Holiness Pascal is a forgiving soul by nature, I think you will find that the memory of your actions fills all Rome with loathing."

I did not imagine that Emperor Henry would respond kindly to such a comment, and he offered a rather cutting discourse in reply.

"If any harm was done to the blessed city, if any freedom of movement denied to His Holiness, and if any harsh measures were taken with the local people, it was due to no fault of our own, but rather the actions of the citizens themselves, who war eternally against one another, family against family and sect against sect. I think you will find that it is your own allies within the alleged reform party who are most at fault for this strife, for though they sing the tune of peace and benediction, their true intent is to subjugate the holy Church in such a manner as they see fit and to gain for themselves the wealth of this life rather than the next. Do you suppose that I have not seen how even the houses of Cluny, which espouse the values of righteous simplicity, have amassed riches beyond that of any order which is now or ever has been? I say, remove first the plank from your own eye!"

"That is a baleful slander!" the abbot protested. "The pope lends us his esteemed ear because he sees that we are not afraid to defend the truth, even if rulers such as yourself see it as a thing of burden to be lightly thrown aside. If you possessed the smallest part of wisdom, you might mend your ways before you suffer the same fate as your heretic of a father."

"*Das ist zu viel!*" the emperor yelled, apparently abandoning all attempts at civil Latin discourse. "*Sie und alle deine Brüder sind diejenigen, die Buße tu müssen!*"

"What in God's name is he saying?"

The abbot had apparently directed this question to Philip, for his was the next voice I heard.

"I think the emperor would prefer that you not speak of his father in such a manner."

"Ha!" the abbot replied with some incredulity. "*Ce n'est pas le même Henri qui est allé à la guerre contre son père?*"

There was then a period of silence in which I can only guess that one or more of the men whispered to the others, for upon resuming communication they seemed to have moved beyond their former dispute.

"Excellency," Abbot Pontius began, "it seems we argue to no purpose. I do not believe that either one of us wishes for open warfare. In fact, I have come upon an errand of peace."

"Who speaks of war but yourself? I am merely here to claim what is rightfully mine by law." The emperor clearly intended to surrender nothing, though I felt his confidence was rather brash under the circumstances.

"The Countess Mathilda was quite clear in her final days that she wished for her possessions to be transferred to the Church for God's work," the abbot replied.

"And we are equally certain that she promised them to this holy empire, but even if you are correct in the matter of her personal estates, the *Grancontessa* had no power to bequeath all the cities of the North to whomever she pleased," my husband continued. "But are you saying that our actions in Tuscany, which are entirely in line with civil and church law, will provoke an armed response? From whom? I was not aware that the men of Cluny waged war with swords; machination is more common among your kind."

"God alone knows what must happen by and by," the abbot replied, choosing to overlook the slight against his order, "but His Holiness bid me make it clear to you that, should you take any hasty actions, he may be forced to enter into an alliance with the Normans of the South, for the protection of his person and the city of Rome."

"I disagree with your implication! I am no foul pagan! The heathens of old may have sought to strip bare the churches of Rome, but I come to strengthen the bond between God's anointed priest and his anointed emperor."

"So this is the message you would have me carry back to our mutual father?"

"You may send him all of our best wishes," Philip said. "I do believe that the emperor means no harm to the pope, but merely to acquire his inheritance, as he has stated."

"*Nous verrons,*" the abbot concluded. "*Nous verrons.*"

There followed the sound of chairs being pushed back from the table, and I moved to depart ere I be seen listening in on their private conversation. I slipped back into the inner passage and quietly returned to my assigned chamber. It appeared that there would be no reconciliation anytime soon.

Here it seems necessary to inform you of what was happening in Rome, for even as the imperial forces continued to gather strength in the North, Pope Paschal found himself in the midst of a dispute the like of which that city has seen far too often. For though the bishop of Rome ruled over the Vatican and Lateran hills, the Romans were loath to see any but their own magistrates placed in charge of the town, and they were suspicious of undue ecclesiastical involvement.

Thus, when the reigning prefect of the city died, the question of who should succeed him began to consume all involved. Paschal favored a son of the Pierleoni family, which had served him faithfully for many years and raised itself to the pinnacle of Roman nobility from the basest of origins. It was said that their line descended from those Jews who lived within the confines of Trastevere, a fact that their enemies were all too eager to mention. Many believed that it was no business of the pope to select a prefect over Rome, and that the duty fell instead to the city elders. An opposing choice, a nephew of Count Ptolemy of Tusculum, was put forward, and when the pope acted of his own accord to install the Pierleoni son upon Maundy Thursday of that year, the citizens rebelled. A number of the papal attendants were seized in the coming days, and Paschal himself was met by a hail of stones upon his departure from the Lateran church.

Soon violence seized the entire city, with the pope's enemies mounting an attack against the towers of the Pierleoni and not even fearing to pillage the city's churches, nor to attack members of the clergy. It was all too much for Paschal, who fled the city and made for the refuge of the Alban Hills. The pope then attempted to purchase the fealty of Ptolemy of Tusculum with a grant of the lands of Ariccia, but it was to be a short alliance, for when the papal forces recovered a footing in Rome and imprisoned the count's nephew in a most cruel manner, Ptolemy scorned the false promises with which he had been caught and again entered the fray on the opposition's side.

Throughout that summer Rome was in a state of siege, the pope banished from his own see and many of the surrounding regions rebelling against his authority. The emperor was well aware of these circumstances, but he was also keen to bide his time before striking out. I surmised that he must be awaiting greater strength of arms.

Summer faded into autumn, and still the emperor marched on through the cities of Italy, his cause gaining ground with each new day. The Norman counts seemed in no haste to aid the Holy Father in his struggles, so he relied on the Pierleoni, his truest remaining allies within the city of Rome. Although Paschal had withdrawn his offer of lay investiture from the emperor, such actions seemed hollow in light of the challenge to papal authority upon his very threshold.

Count Ptolemy of Tusculum wrote to the emperor assuring him of the fidelity of both himself and his house, not failing to mention that the imperial authority could be helpful in bolstering support for the new prefect within the city. Furthermore, he told of others who were willing to declare for the emperor, including the *famiglia* Colonna, the *famiglia* Frangipane, and Abbot Berald of Farfa Abbey, the monastery that had aided Emperor Henry during his last visit to Rome. Yet for all this, the emperor did not charge to the south.

It soon became clear that we were to stay through the winter and well into the following year, for as the end of the year 1116 approached, the mountain paths back to the north were surely becoming too treacherous. Instead we were to travel east to the old city of Ravenna, which sits near the Adriatic coast just a few days' journey south of Venice. The climate there was rather pleasant considering the time of year, for we had grown accustomed to the colder heights of the mountains. The old palace of King Theodoric had been utterly destroyed long before, and its remaining pieces of value taken with papal blessing by the Emperor Charles the Great to build his royal chapel in Aachen. Once a jewel of the Romans, the Goths, and the Byzantines, Ravenna has in our own time surrendered its high position to the Venetians, though it remains a city of some import. The palace in which we lodged for those few weeks seemed a rather pale imitation of that of the doge, but it had its own charms.

Now, you may remember that almost two years earlier, on the occasion of the emperor's stay in Goslar, he had asked me to join him for a walk about the grounds. Despite the tumult of the days that followed, we had on occasion found time for such pursuits, always with a great many attendants following behind. Our conversation was usually limited to odd trees, the state of the weather, and the many imperial hunting tours. Seldom did we stray into matters of state, unless I had lately received a new letter from England, in which case I would report the news and answer any questions that he put to me.

It happened that the emperor found himself at liberty one day in late December and decided to come to my quarters. I was attempting to help some of the local ladies—for my usual attendants had remained in the North—with a tapestry that was, in truth, well beyond my level of skill. Setting out to craft the figure of a lamb, I willed my hands to perform their actions with vigor, but I let slip my needle and pierced the end of one of my fingers. I tried to conceal my gasp for breath but was dismayed to see that despite the trifling nature of the injury, it seethed with pain and let forth a flow of blood I couldn't hide.

"Francesca!" I said, for so the chief maiden was called. "Is there a towel?"

"*Cosa intendi?*" she replied in her own tongue.

Uncertain of how to best explain the situation, and being as I was in need of some haste, I simply held up my hand for her to see the trickle of blood. Having grasped my meaning, she fetched a scrap of linen that had been intended for some work of embroidery and pressed it into my hand.

"*È necessario tenere su questo molto strettamente!*" she told me.

I had little time to consider these strange words, for the door opened and Drogo stepped into the room.

"What is it, Drogo?" I asked.

"His Excellency Emperor Henry," he said, his eyes shifting from my face to the bloody cloth in my hand with a worried look.

"This is nothing," I assured him, quickly making my bow along with the rest as the emperor entered.

Before I could offer a word of welcome or recognition, my husband expressed his own concern regarding my condition.

"Are you bleeding?"

"Yes, but it is hardly the first time," I responded. "I seem to be prone to injuries of this sort."

"Let me see," he said, taking my hand into his own and unwrapping the cloth to reveal the damage. He seemed to study it as one would an odd-looking stone.

"My lord, there is no need for concern. It will stop bleeding any moment now."

"I think you are right," he replied, once again wrapping the cloth around the wound, "but it seemed best to be certain."

He relaxed his grip on my hand and looked me in the eye, making a study of my face even as he had my finger. At length he said, "The church of San Vitale is the finest in this city. Indeed, it is one of the finest anywhere. I have never set foot in it, but I have heard many tales. Would you care to join me there? They will not have Vespers for a few hours, and I have arranged for the place to be emptied so we might enjoy its wonders without all of this . . ."

Here he motioned broadly to the many people in the room, and I took his meaning.

"I think I would like that very much."

"Very well. Let us walk, then."

As we made to leave, Francesca and the other ladies began to follow us, but my husband turned to them and said, *"Bleib hier! Das ist . . . hic!"*

Whether or not my attendants could comprehend either the German or Latin instruction, they apparently understood that they were to remain.

"My lord?" Drogo asked as we turned to leave without him, but the emperor repeated, "I will not require assistance from any of you. Remain here, and we will return within the hour."

I placed my hand on my husband's arm, and we strode down the steps and out to the street. More guards and officials offered their company, but each time the emperor refused. As his men occupied the surrounding region, it was of little consequence, but even so it felt strange to be walking along *absque consortio*.

We made the walk to the church in silence, and a kindly old priest stood there to greet us. He bowed and led us through the main portal and into the outer gallery.

"Does Your Excellency desire a tour?" the priest asked. "I have made a long study of the church's history. It was laid down by Bishop Ecclesius in the days of . . ."

"Thank you, Father, but I was hoping rather to ponder its beauty in silence, which most befits a spirit of worship," the emperor said.

"Ah," he replied, with great sadness in his voice. "Perhaps then you desire a recitation of some mystic work? We have here an excellent young minstrel—Giovanni is his name."

"Silence would be the most blessed sound to my ears," the emperor repeated.

As the priest continued in his attempts to make the most of the imperial visit, I left the two men to their bartering and entered the center nave, the better to study it all.

What a sight to behold! I found it at first to be rather small and in no way comparable to the towering monuments of the Salian emperors. Indeed, it could not even match the old cathedral of Winchester in scale, and certainly not the great hall at Westminster. Yet in the dim candlelight I began to see the treasures for which the church of San Vitale is known: a host of rich mosaics covering the walls, columns, and ceilings. The church was built in the Eastern style, with an inner circle surrounded by eight outer walls. A line of columns supported an upper gallery, and on the eastern end stood the magnificent sanctuary to which the eye was naturally drawn.

The discussion behind me had ceased, and I turned to see the priest, a pair of deacons, and a woman with a basket full of Advent ornaments leaving the church, while the emperor was walking toward me.

"No need to worry. There are men stationed at all the entrances outside. We are perfectly safe."

I then recognized that this was the first time my husband and I had been in a room alone for quite some time; yes, since the day we were wed and he had brought me to my chambers without the usual royal watchers, only to leave me there alone.

The emperor had apparently noticed my keen observation of the stonework, for he added, "If you would prefer for me to fetch someone who can explain things to you, then I will. For myself, I know little about mosaics. I merely sought to grant you some privacy."

"I am glad you did. I spend every day in the company of people who explain things to me."

"I guessed as much."

He had now come to stand directly beside me, and together we gazed upon the walls, our eyes registering every aspect.

"These figures here, around the entrance to the sanctuary—they must be the apostles," I finally said, walking closer to the subject of my comments. "See, there is Peter, and Paul, and Thomas!" I pointed to each of them in turn.

"They say it was made to resemble the throne room of Emperor Alexios in Constantinople."

"Then his palace must be grand indeed."

As I continued to look toward the front of the church, I saw two great murals: one of an emperor surrounded by counselors, and the other of a great lady and her attendants.

"Who are they?" I whispered, more as a comment to myself than an actual question, but the emperor had heard me.

"That is Justinian to the left, one of the greatest emperors that ever reigned in the East, and that to the right is Theodora, his empress."

"She looks as if she must have been very pretty; at least, the craftsman wishes us to think so." I glanced at my husband, whose own eyes were fixed upon the image of Justinian. After wavering for a moment, I finally said, "You too have the chance to be remembered, even as he was. An opportunity lies before you, if only you would take it."

This seized his attention, and he turned back to face me.

"You refer to the efforts with Paschal."

"I do."

"And you think I take too hard a line with him?"

"I did not say that."

"So what did you mean? What is this opportunity of which you speak?"

"The opportunity to forge a peace for your kingdom that could last for generations. The opportunity to be seen as a ruler who wished for something better for his subjects."

"I do seek a better life for my subjects, but the matter is not so easy as you suppose." For a moment he seemed to search for the correct words, and then he added, "That the pope has authority in spiritual matters, I do not deny. Indeed, it must be so, according to the word of our Lord. But it is only in this present generation that Rome has sought such power over kings as it now possesses. Never before has a bishop been so bold as to seek control over every aspect of life in the kingdoms of the North. It is a strange thing never before heard, but begun in the time of my father, and I believe it to be as dangerous for the purity of our holy Church as it is for the powers of the temporal realm. I seek a greater freedom for my kingdom, for the German lands. We have our own manner of doing things, and that must be respected."

"So why not go to Rome and make your case to Paschal directly?" I asked. "If your cause is just, then perhaps the two of you may reach an accord that will prevent any blood from being shed."

"Paschal cannot even enter Rome under the present circumstances. The people have turned against him. It is best that we wait for the opportune moment. When the time comes, they will beg for us to come and restore order. Just wait, and you will see how our position is strengthened."

I thought that he must be angry with me, but instead he smiled and concluded, "I see that my friend Bruno has affected you."

"How so?"

"Here you are lecturing me about warfare. Surely you know that queens are meant to concern themselves with affairs of court and not those of state! But I see he has made a scholar out of you, and I suppose I should be glad of it. Better a wife who is of real use to me. In fact, I am depending on you in the coming days to take a greater part in our dealings. Do not think that your acts are unseen. I believe you are able to fulfill any request I might make of you."

"I am honored that you should deem me worthy of your trust. I do wish to be for you as Theodora was for Justinian." This was perhaps an odd thing to say, Daughter, but it was my earnest desire. Knowing I had gained the emperor's trust justified my efforts.

He stepped forward still farther, coming so close to me that I was forced to look upward to meet his gaze. The emperor was a tall man, and though I had by this time grown very near my full height, I was not much past the level of his shoulders.

"Mathilda," he said. "You have grown much since we first met. Do you remember the day?"

"How could I possibly forget?" I thought, but instead merely nodded my head. Such close proximity had robbed me of speech.

"And now here you stand before me, a young woman worthy of esteem."

A suspicion had been forming in my mind, and now seemed warranted, that the emperor had not been thinking purely of mosaics when he asked me to accompany him there. Indeed, the fact of our solitude was now of far greater import than I had guessed moments earlier. I had always known, since that first night when I was granted a reprieve, that my husband would not be content to act as a brother toward me much longer, not if the Salian line was to continue. Therefore the present situation did not come as a surprise, yet it incited a kind of fear in me. I was not troubled by the idea so much as the pressing fact of it all.

He placed his hands around my waist and pulled me closer to himself. He must have sensed my concern, for he paused for a moment and asked, "Are you afraid of me?"

"No," I replied. This was mostly true, but my uncertainty as to what would come next did make me nervous.

There was no further time to consider the matter, for he leaned down and kissed my mouth. Although I said nothing, I was thinking that this was not such a bad thing after all, if a bit awkward. Then something happened that I did not quite understand. He seemed to let out a kind of groan and pulled away from me, wincing in pain.

"Did I do something wrong?" I asked without stopping to consider. The words immediately sounded rather childish to my ears.

"No, I am quite all right," he told me, recovering his tranquility. "I just had a slight pain. I must still be sore from riding."

I was not sure whether or not to believe him, as this "slight pain" seemed to have come on rather suddenly and with some degree of violence, but I decided that I should not press the matter.

"I think it best that we return to the palace now. It is almost time for supper."

"Yes," I answered without thinking. I took his arm once again as we proceeded out of the church. If he was in pain, he hid it well.

We made our return journey without any further conversation, and when we reached the entrance to my chamber, he said, "Farewell for now, then. I hope you enjoyed the church."

"Yes, I did," I said honestly, still trying to understand what had happened.

"I shall see you at supper," he replied, and departed without waiting for me to enter the room.

With whom does one speak concerning love, or if not the substance, at least the outward forms of love? To whom should a young woman look for advisement? To female peers? An empress has no peers. She might have friends, but true friendship is hard to come by when one is the mistress and the other the minister. The women who surrounded me in my youth were of a decent sort, but we did not share that equal disposition on which confidences are so easily built. To men? Surely not! To a mother? Mine was a world away. No, in such matters, I had none to counsel me. Nevertheless, I remained undaunted, for although the land I entered was a strange wilderness, it was not the first time I had trod the path with none beside me.

Christmas came and went, and we entered those days leading up to the feast of the Epiphany, which were filled with one grand occasion after another. I believe it was a Wednesday, the third before the nones of January, when the imperial company traveled just south of the city to the monastery of San Severo. That house was particularly favored by Archbishop Jeremias of Ravenna, and as a favor to the old man, Emperor Henry was set to grant San Severo new privileges and rights.

We arrived in the morning and were welcomed in the usual manner. I remember that we were ushered inside by the abbot, who on account of the hour chose to bring us in by a side door, for the monks had not yet finished the prayers of terce. He led us—that is, me, the emperor, Archbishop Jeremias, Philip of Ravenna, and a contingent of the imperial guard—along the walkway that surrounds the abbey cloister, there to await the proper moment. Suddenly I felt the ground beneath me begin to shake and I became unstable on my feet. I saw that the others were also knocked about. I clung to my husband for support, and he in turn grasped one of the nearby columns. The other members of our party were also forced to brace themselves as the ground continued to pulse more violently. The poor archbishop, who had been walking with the aid of a stick, was unable to move to safety in time and fell to the ground, receiving bloody scrapes on his hands when he moved to catch himself.

Dust fell from the ceiling above, and as I looked out across the cloister, I saw some of the weaker stones give way and tumble from their lofty heights. Screams came from the church, the refectory, and the fields beyond. Then, as suddenly as it had begun, the quaking ceased, and it was only our hearts that continued to tremble. One by one, we looked one another in the eye, our silent gazes revealing the terror we all felt.

"Good Lord, what judgment have you sent upon us?" the archbishop finally said as he struggled to reclaim his footing.

Even as Philip moved to help the older man recover his balance, he continued, "What is this? My cane is broken to pieces!"

We all looked at the spot to which the archbishop had pointed with his outstretched finger. The fractured remains of his walking aid lay underneath some bricks that had come loose.

"Never mind it," Philip replied. "You may lean on me until we can find a new one."

"I was so afraid," I admitted. "I thought the whole building was going to give way."

"That is a common response from a foreigner," the abbot replied, dusting off his robes with a few swipes of the hand. "We here are accustomed to these movements of the earth, though I admit this one was far stronger than usual. Perhaps we ought to pray for absolution if God is displeased with us."

"Think you that this is the work of God?"

We all turned to look at the emperor, who had made the inquiry. None of us offered an answer.

"Come then," he continued, "are none of you man enough to say what you really think? I know what you must suppose: that I have brought the wrath of the Almighty upon us all!"

"Sir," Philip began, but the archbishop quickly cut him off.

"What he means to say, my liege, is that no such thought had entered our minds. Who knows why God allows such calamities, whether for our own sins or those of another? But know for certain that such things do not befall us without reason! For we have the words of Job, which read, 'Who has been fierce against him and has prospered? He removes the mountains, and they feel not when he overthrows them in his anger. He removes the earth out of her place, and the pillars thereof do shake.'"

"But the sin may well be on the part of Your Grace's enemies," the abbot quickly added.

I found this discussion of the mysteries of divine judgment a bit superfluous in light of what had taken place over the past few minutes, which had left me in some anguish of spirit. I think the emperor noticed my discomfort, for he said, "Abbot, look to your house and make certain that none are hurt. Do you think we should continue with the ceremony today?"

"I see no reason why not," the archbishop interrupted, apparently feeling that he could speak on behalf of his subordinate. "Unless further tremors are to visit us, there is nothing which should stand in our way. The church does not appear to have suffered any substantial damage."

"Very well, then. On we go."

Having concluded that all was well in the monastery, the abbot led us through the remainder of the day. It would be some time before I felt safe once more beneath a roof, and for the next few weeks we did feel the ground move to and fro to a lesser degree than it had in that first hour. Word reached us from the North that this trembling of the earth had been felt for many miles, from the town of Pisa in the West up to Augsburg in the North and Venice in the East. Worst affected was the city of Verona, which we had visited only a few weeks earlier. Almost all the buildings in the city were destroyed. The cathedrals of Padua and Cremona also tumbled to the ground, and in general it seemed that the worst devastation was north of our position.

The earth's shaking kindled a further cycle of changes, which threatened to dislodge the sphere of government in the same manner. That very month, Archbishop Jordanus of Milan—no friend to the emperor—held a counsel that was attended by clergy from across the region of Lombardy. Spurred on by certain meddlers, they made their own declaration of excommunication against the emperor, with the support of many local consuls and a large portion of the citizens.

I could not help but remember the many difficulties facing my husband, for although he had spent most of the past year winning over the provinces of Italy, he had not won the loyalty of those western regions around Milan and leading into Savoy. There the pull of the Gregorians and Cluniacs was stronger, due in part to the nearness of the Kingdoms of France and Burgundy, both of which were the emperor's natural enemies.

Yet this new declaration of excommunication did not achieve what its authors intended, for despite increased support from the southern Normans and a band of new troops, Pope Paschal was unable to recover the city of Rome. The longer such a situation continued, the more legitimate it would become in the eyes of many.

At last, as the winter frost began to melt away, Emperor Henry V sensed his opportunity and marched his troops back through the land of Tuscany and down the southern road that leads to Rome. In so doing, he placed himself beyond the point of possible reversal—much as when Caesar crossed the Rubicon, thus beginning the civil war that led to his elevation. Bruno had told me about it once.

"Notice, when he discusses the *casus belli*, Caesar omits his own action in crossing the river," my tutor had said to me during our study of the *Commentarii de bello civili*. "He is quick to blame his foes, whether they be Scipio, or Cicero, or the great Pompey. But here, where a mention ought to be made of his departure from the provinces and unlawful entry into Italy itself, the account is entirely silent. Men are apt to remain silent upon the matter of their own faults."

"But Archbishop, did not Caesar have good reason to take up arms? Surely he believed that he would be attacked himself if he did not strike the first blow."

"Or perhaps he saw the opportunity to gain an advantage," Bruno countered.

I struggled to form a reply, knowing that my tutor wished to see me mount a challenge that displayed the workings of my mind. Finally I arrived at one.

"Well, Caesar defeated Pompey in the end, so I suppose that the question of who struck first was of little consequence. Victory was its own justification."

"Yes," Bruno replied, rising to my challenge, "but what sort of legacy did he leave behind? His life was ended in a pool of blood, betrayed by those he loved! The empire he created was torn apart by war. The great Roman *republica* of legend had come to an end."

"So you believe he seized power to no purpose, then?"

"Only God knows that," Bruno concluded. "Time makes of us what it will."

I could not help thinking as the imperial company made for Rome that the words of Bruno would be proven true yet again: time truly does make of us what it will.

CHAPTER FIFTEEN

I once possessed a book of sentences given to me by Bruno of Trier for the furtherance of my study. With so many of the ancient works lost to us, these small proverbs were all that remained of most of the Roman fathers. Time and again I read those words and committed them to memory, always uncertain if they were truly the product of those famous minds or merely the invention of a clever scribe. Among them was one quote by Livy that I thought of often during my travels in the South: "Rome is overwhelmed by its own greatness."

Such a declaration befits the city that has long declared itself to be both *Caput Mundi* and *Civitas Aeterna*. Whether it can honestly lay claim to either of those titles in our present age is perhaps a matter worthy of disputation, but the Romans care not; the pillars of the ancients may lie in ruins, but upon such a perch they will always place themselves. They are not content to be subjected. Therefore it was with some degree of caution that the emperor proceeded toward Rome, knowing as he did that the mood of the crowd might be turned in an instant. And it must be said that the Romans are more fickle than most, for long before they carried out their rebellions in our own time, they displayed much the same temper in former days to that famous general Coriolanus, who the writers tell us was betrayed by both consuls and citizens long before he lent his support to the Volscian cause.

Emperor Henry hoped for a happier result as the party crossed back over the Appenines and toward Tuscany, whence we would set out along the Via Cassia toward Rome. We were traveling through that region known as the Futa Pass when a rider approached bearing the ensign of a gold cross upon a field of red. Chancellor David rode his black steed ahead of the company and within a few paces of the stranger.

"Who is this that approaches the imperial company? Declare yourself!" the chancellor bellowed.

"I am Sancho, my lord, servant of the bishop of Braga!"

"Why come you hence?"

"My master wishes to parley with the emperor."

"On what grounds?"

"On the matter of his discussions with the Holy See."

"And what does the bishop of Braga have to do with that?" Emperor Henry asked, bursting forward of the line and joining the discussion.

The man, Sancho, leaned slightly backward in response to emperor's swift approach. Even his horse appeared to sense that the stakes had just been raised, for it neighed and beat its hoof upon the rocky ground.

"My lord emperor . . . ," the messenger began, clearly flustered by the presence of his superior. "The bishop was sent here on an errand for His Holiness Pope Paschal. He has been tasked to settle this affair in a way that is . . . favorable to both sides."

Upon his great brown horse, the emperor moved in a circle around the startled Sancho, his eyes making a careful examination of the man from head to toe. At length he replied, "Why is your master not in his own country? Has he forsaken his duty?"

"With all due respect, nothing could be further from the truth," the herald replied, once again finding his courage. "He cares deeply for the concerns of his flock, which he was appointed to shepherd by God and our holy Church. In fact, he sought a papal audience to address the undue favor that has been granted to Santiago de Compostela. The pope saw many good qualities in the bishop and placed this charge upon him: that he should strive to succeed where others had failed in bringing this matter to its conclusion in a peaceful manner."

"We have heard from many of the pope's messengers," the chancellor said, "but to a man they have been unwilling to meet our demands or acknowledge the ancient rights of the empire."

"In other words," the emperor continued, having caused his horse to halt directly in front of the messenger, "unless your master has something new to say, we have a rather urgent errand and cannot brook delay."

Sensing his chance slipping away, Sancho became more resolute in his disposition.

"Please, my lord, the bishop has come all this way! He awaits you now in the city of Florence and desires to speak with you in all earnestness regarding the issue of investiture. Any proposition will be treated with due consideration. My master is not like other men; you will receive a fair judgment from him."

There was a pause while the emperor considered the man's suggestion. He exchanged a few whispered words with his chancellor, then responded, "Very well. We will see your bishop. But do not mistake me; if we find ourselves misused, we shall depart immediately. I will have satisfaction."

"To Florence then?" the herald asked.

"No, that is the other matter. Florence is full of heartless men who value coin over conscience. They have not shown us the proper respect that is our due, and they have heaped verbal abuse upon the man to whom we have granted authority. No, we shall meet in Arezzo, where the roads come together. We shall not bestow the mighty gift of our presence upon the Florentines at this time."

So the matter was settled, and the messenger departed to inform the bishop of Braga of all that had come to pass. True to his word, the emperor avoided Florence and made his way south to Arezzo, where he took up residence in the bishop's palace and awaited the arrival of the papal ambassador.

As was true in many of the towns of Tuscany and Lombardy, the people of Arezzo had small regard for their bishop, one Guido Boccatorta. Their complaints were of the usual kind: unjust taxation, the imposition of onerous rules upon the marketplace, and the pompous manners of their ruler, which had as their crown jewel the fact of the bishop's wasteful spending. Even his name, which in the local speech means "wry mouthed," implied that Bishop Guido was less than honorable.

Thus the people of Arezzo, like so many of their Italian fellows, sought to create a free commune accountable to the emperor alone. By this point in his travels, the emperor had granted these or equal privileges to all the cities between Venice and Pisa, and in so doing ensured for himself the allegiance of many. However, no such charter had been arranged for Arezzo, and as the imperial party was in some haste, it was determined that the citizens of that town must content themselves for the present with that which men call the *status quo* or *praesenti fortunae*.

At length the bishop of Braga arrived, plain to all in his vestments and upon his white horse. His train of attendants was as nothing compared to the emperor's, the latter having swollen over the past year to include troops from many of the cities that had been granted imperial favor and now stood ready to defend their lord's cause. Had the bishop possessed any visions of greatness, they must have been quickly abandoned in the face of such an array. The imperial force was camped just outside the walls, but the knights and officials tarried along every road of the city, creating a feeling of martial occupation.

My husband had testified to his trust in me, and this was revealed by the fact that I was summoned, along with a few of the emperor's chief counselors, to attend the forum with the bishop. How glad I was to hold a proper seat at such a meeting rather than straining to eavesdrop as would a small child! When we were all settled—myself, the emperor, Philip of Ravenna, Chancellor David, the bishop, a few of the bishop's men, and a jurist from Bologna by the name of Irnerius—it was time for matters to commence.

Emperor Henry said, "I bid you, do not waste our time with trifles, for we are in sore need of haste."

"Thank you, Excellency," the bishop replied. "Allow me to introduce myself properly. I was born by the name Maurice in a small village along the French coast. I studied at the school of Cluny and under the archbishop of Toledo. I was granted the pallium of Braga by His Grace Paschal II, almost ten years hence. No doubt you have heard of my quest to Rome."

"Yes, this is all very interesting," the chancellor said with some derision in his tone, "but we have not ceased our march to hear your personal history. Tell us what the pope has to say for himself, and it had best be something new."

"As a matter of fact, I have nothing new from His Holiness," the bishop admitted. "However, things in Rome are changing quickly. The pope is not blind to your advance. When he heard of it, he retreated to the South, back to Benevento. I fear he does not wish to repeat the actions of former years."

No one spoke, but we all knew that the bishop referred to the emperor's past visit, when he ended up taking the pope and cardinals hostage and holding out for an agreement to his own benefit.

"Now then," the bishop continued, "as the pope has departed his seat, it falls to me as his legate to conduct business on his behalf."

The members of the imperial party looked up from behind their folded arms, suddenly more interested in the words coming from the bishop's mouth.

"Do you mean to say that you seek to make an agreement with us purely upon your own authority?" Philip asked.

"No, you misunderstand me. The Holy Father has delegated his power unto me by removing himself from the situation. I do not think that I err when I say that it is rather obligatory for me to carry out such duties on his behalf."

The emperor leaned forward, placing his weight upon the table that lay between him and the ambassador. There was a flicker of excitement in his eyes.

"My lord bishop, I am soon to depart for the holy city, there to restore order and once again proclaim my divine ordination. I will need the support of the clergy in order to do so. Are you saying that you intend to lend me that support?"

"Excellency," the bishop replied, "this matter has gone on long enough. I have all respect for our mutual father, but for the Gregorians I care not. In the name of reform, they have abased our holy Church with the affairs of this world. The Church has always worked in harmony with your esteemed ancestors, the Holy Roman emperors, and I see no reason why that must change. Why should you not have some say over the men who are appointed to shepherd your own people, over whom God has allowed you to rule?"

For a moment the rest of us merely watched as the emperor exchanged hushed words with his jurist, and then finally said, "Bishop, we are to leave now for Rome, and along the way we shall join forces with the abbot of Farfa, the Frangipane, and the Count of Tusculum. I would very much wish for you to make that journey with us. I can see that your presence in the company will be highly beneficial for us all. Please ride along with me."

"As Your Highness commands, so I shall do," he answered.

As the men arose and set about their business, I touched the shoulder of the chancellor and begged his attention.

"Yes, my lady?"

"Chancellor, I am clean amazed. What can account for this behavior? Given all that has taken place over the course of this past year, I cannot believe that the pope has approved such a course of action. I think the bishop does him poor service."

"Why are you so alarmed?" he answered. "You sound as if you agree with the sons of Gregory. I can sense it in your voice."

"You mistake me, sir," I quickly responded. "It is my strong desire to see this matter settled amicably. My fear is that the bishop of Braga acts of his own accord and thus may draw the emperor into a false sense of victory. The support of one bishop should not be equated with that of the entire Church."

"The support of the entire Church, as you put it, is something the emperor cannot hope to obtain. We must make do as we can, and the bishop provides us with an opportunity."

"I suppose you are right," I offered, "but that still does not explain why he should act in such a way. He has just earned the favor of the pope and now will surely lose it with this ruse. And while the emperor may smile on him now, what will he do once his patron has departed? No man can serve two masters, and if the bishop plays both sides he is likely to please no one."

"Perhaps you are right," he admitted, "but that is a debate for another day."

With the bishop of Braga now in our company, we continued south along the Via Cassia for most of a week, until we were within one day's journey of Rome. Our final resting point was near the shores of Lago di Bracciano, a lovely site surrounded by hills and an abundance of trees. A few small fishing villages lay along the water's edge, and the boats set out daily in search of a fine catch. There were also towers of the sort one sees throughout that country—fortresses of stone meant to guard the most powerful families—but no city of great significance could be found upon those shores. I imagine that such an abode might have been quite restful under other circumstances, but we found no solace there, for the day of reckoning was at hand. We awaited only the arrival of the emperor's pledged brothers in arms: Abbot Berald of Farfa Abbey, Giovanni Frangipane, and the Count of Tusculum with his ample force of men fit for war. What the citizens of Rome were thinking upon the eve of our arrival, I can only guess. It was uncertain how they, having been in the midst of tumult for the past year, would respond to such a courtly invasion.

Some of the gentlemen in the party seized their chance to bathe in the waters, and I must say that I envied them. Though spring had only just begun, the weather was strangely warm. I would have welcomed the relief, but even if I could have remained afloat in those watery depths, there was no place for women among a crowd of naked men. Instead I remained under the shade of the trees, the ladies taking it in turn to fan me. In such circumstances I might have dispensed with my usual veil, but the climate had produced such an effect upon my hair that it was not fit to be seen.

The emperor having sent for his esteemed allies to join him, the entire company was impatient for their arrival. In the late afternoon of our second day there, I was sitting once again beneath a large chestnut tree surrounded by the ladies, with a volume open upon my lap. Perhaps it was the *De consolatio philsophiae*; I cannot say for certain. We were roused from our serenity by the arrival of Philip of Ravenna.

"Empress Mathilda," he said with a low bow, "I have come to inform you that riders have been sighted upon the road."

"I am glad to hear it! Which of the parties is it? The men of Farfa? Count Ptolemy?"

"No, gracious lady, it is none of those. It is but a small company of riders approaching from the north."

"What is their appearance?"

"Men of the cloth, by the look of it, though not from any land nearby."

As he spoke I saw Drogo approaching in the distance, waving his arms in the air in a manner not entirely proper for a knight, effective as it was. With little thought spared for gentility, I abandoned the rest and set off in the knight's direction, if not at a run then at least with a determined walk. He in turn increased his own pace until we met in the middle of the nearby glade.

"Drogo!"

"Your Highness!"

"What is it? That is, who is it?"

"Archbishop of Canterbury."

"Truly?" I was in wonder at this news.

"Yes, the new one, Ralph d'Escures."

"What on earth is he doing here?"

"I did not have a chance to inquire as to all that. I saw him, asked his name, and then ran here to inform Your Grace."

"Does he bear some message from the king?"

"Once again, I cannot say. Let us go meet him together and hear what he has to say."

I did not need to be commanded twice. Even as my ladies had almost caught up with me, I set off at a vicious pace once again, my mind inflamed with suspense. As I neared the camp, I saw clearly a small band of men at arms standing outside the emperor's tent, their weapons laid aside and their horses gnawing on the grass. The signs on their banners were familiar, yet I did not see their master.

"*Equites!*" I yelled out in Latin, but received no response. "Friends! Knights! You there!"

They turned at the sound of their native tongue, bent low, and removed their helms.

"Lady Mathilda! Empress!" said one of them who had the look of a captain.

"I see your eyes at least serve you well. Tell me, where is the archbishop?"

"In there, my lady," he replied, pointing toward the imperial pavilion.

"Thank you. I am obliged to you."

I approached the two mute soldiers who stood guard at the entrance of the tent.

"Let me pass!" I commanded.

They did as they were told, and I stepped into this most lavish of temporal dwellings. On the opposite end sat a pair of royal thrones, the emperor seated upon the larger of the two. Clerks, counselors, priests, and all manner of servants seemed to fill that space as bees in a hive, and I could see my husband only on account of his high position. Between us stood a thick wall of men with their backs turned toward me. I found myself quite annoyed and was about to bid them part as did the waters before Moses, but a herald noticed my plight and proclaimed, "The Empress Mathilda!"

With that the crowd duly made way and a lane opened leading directly to the emperor, who stood to acknowledge my entrance.

I strode down this hastily formed aisle until I came face-to-face with the man whom I knew to be archbishop of Canterbury. He did not bear the full ornaments of his office, having chosen instead to robe himself in clothes more fit for travel. Nevertheless, his position was impossible to mistake. He moved to make his obeisance, but I bid him cease.

"My lord, it is I who wish to honor you, after you have traveled so many leagues over land and sea to stand before us today. Tell me, what is your errand?"

"Sadly, it is the dispute betwixt Canterbury and York," he said. "They refuse to submit to the See of Canterbury according to ancient tradition, and the king—that is, your father—permitted me to seek out an audience with Pope Paschal, that we might resolve this issue. He also said that if I came across the imperial camp, I was to stop and make my presence known, the better to aid the continued friendship between our two kingdoms."

"The pope has quit Rome," the emperor replied, stepping down from his throne to stand beside us. "He fled when he received news of our approach. Therefore, any conversation with him may prove quite difficult."

"I see. Well, this is strange news indeed, though I cannot say I am entirely surprised." The archbishop reached into a bag that hung over his shoulder and retrieved a collection of papers bound with cord. "Empress Mathilda, these are for you."

"Letters from England?" I asked eagerly.

"Yes. A few are from the bishop of Salisbury, others from the king himself, and there is one also from the queen, your mother."

As I traced my fingers over the edges, I resisted my desire to break the cord and read every page without delay.

"We hear that King Henry is at war with the king of France again," the emperor said.

"Yes, he fights on behalf of his nephew, the Count of Blois. Theobald is his name, and his younger brother, Stephen, is

among the king's trusted warriors." Then, turning to me, he offered, "I would be happy to share with you all the latest news
from our land. You no doubt heard of the sad destruction of
Peterborough Abbey in the flames."

"No, I did not, but I am far away. Tell me, how is my brother
William?"

"As fine a prince as ever there was, my lady. You have good
reason to be proud. He may even exceed his father in greatness,
which would be a singular feat."

"And my mother?"

Here the archbishop demurred, and for a moment I feared
the worst.

"Is she unwell?" I asked. "Tell me! I have no patience for riddles."

"Forgive me, Your Grace," he replied. "She is in no danger, I
assure you. She was enduring some form of malady before my departure, but I do not think that it was a sickness unto death. After
all, she was able to compose the letter you hold in your hands."

"Nevertheless, you must tell me everything," I ordered.

"Yes, but now is not the time for that," the emperor said, placing his arm around the archbishop. "There are some matters
which need our expert touch."

"How right you are!" the archbishop obediently declared.

I looked from one man to the other, my suspicions raised. I
hoped to God that the archbishop did not intend to keep anything from me, but I could not properly judge his character. I
finally submitted with a short bow and allowed the two of them
to walk out in each other's company, no doubt to spend the next
few hours in contemplation while traversing the wood. For myself, I knew there would be no chance of rest until I learned of
my mother's condition.

"I must simply read what she has to say and decide for myself,"
I concluded, departing the pavilion for my own tent, in which I
intended to discover the full truth.

As I made for my quarters, Francesca the handmaid was trailing behind, pronouncing orders in her own language that I should not have heeded even if I understood them. Upon reaching my quarters, I entered and found the tent empty of any other persons. There was a pair of wood benches that had been crafted particularly to be easy to transport. I took my seat upon one of them and, seizing a small knife from one of the girls' baskets, I broke the tie that bound them. I was sorting through the bundle, hoping to discover the queen's letter, when Francesca burst through the entrance, having finally caught up with me.

"Out! Out!" I shouted, in no mood for company. "*De!* Oh, what is the word? *Fuori!* Yes, *fuori!*"

The lady looked downcast as she slunk away, but I could not explain. In the work of a moment, I found the letter, smaller than the rest and sealed with the mark of Her Royal Highness Queen Mathilda of England. I broke the seal with such eagerness that I ripped through a section of the parchment.

"No matter," I told myself. "I can still read it."

My eyes passed over her words searching for some note of comfort. Here was news of the birth of a child to my brother Robert, the loathing of the king's subjects for taxes and strange weather, and an assurance that the nobility had placed their support behind William Ætheling and not that traitor, William Clito. Nowhere did my mother mention her own health as a subject of interest, stating only that she had attempted to introduce *citrus* into her diet upon my suggestion. Being that this was a letter from the queen, there was also an abundance of spiritual wisdom included, but nothing that could soothe my spirit. Here was one last note, perhaps added at a later time.

"I beseech you, Daughter, to embrace your high station and bid the emperor make peace with our holy Church. He has it within his power to reach an accord like that that was granted to this kingdom, the better to bring about peace in our time.

I confess myself ignorant as to the degree of your influence at court, but who is to say that the Lord himself has not placed this charge upon you so that you might aid the work of reconciliation? All Christendom awaits the outcome of this present debate. Better that we should unify ourselves against that enemy which awaits at the eastern gate than to drift into conflict unending."

"What would you have me do?" I said aloud, but there was none on hand to witness it.

In resignation, I placed the queen's letter to the side and proceeded through the rest one at a time, finding little there to hold my interest. At length the promised guests arrived—first Count Ptolemy and Giovanni Frangipane with their bands of knights, then finally the men of Farfa Abbey—and we enjoyed one last evening together before setting out the following morn for that object of all our desires, Rome.

I have heard it said that whatever road one takes, it is certain to end in Rome. I never set much store by this even in childhood, for I reasoned that on an island such as my beloved England, there were as many roads as one could wish for leading only as far as the coast. But if one does seek to enter Rome by the northern road, it is necessary to cross over the Milvian Bridge. That name is famous throughout Christendom, for upon those banks Constantine the Great, having received a vision from the Lord Jesus, took up the Holy Rood as his standard against the forces of the tyrant Maxentius. And though the enemies of Christ set upon the army of Constantine, they behaved as true men, preferring fight to flight. For even as the arrows rained down and blade clashed upon blade, the lances striking this way and that, God himself led the host of Constantine to victory, even as the chronicler Eusebius recorded in describing the end to which Maxentius was reduced.

"He turned back before the God-given might of Constantine, and began to cross the river in his path, having himself constructed a perfectly sound bridge of boats from one bank to the other, contriving thus an instrument for his own destruction."

And then he writes again, "In this way, through the breaking of the floating bridge, the crossing collapsed, and in a moment the boats, men and all, went to the bottom."

It was with some pleasure that I observed that the Tiber, or Tevere as the Italians name it, was now bridged by a more firm construction, as sturdy as one might desire. Such a large company does not move with haste, and it took the greater part of an hour before the thousands of soldiers, clergy, jurists, nobles, and servants of the royal household were able to cross. We had with us by that point all the forces of Count Ptolemy of Tusculum, as well as those of Giovanni Frangipane, in addition to all who had ridden with us from the lands to the north. I could not count their full number, but I imagine that it would have equaled that host which was fed by Christ, if not exceeded it.

I had until that point occupied my usual place in the carriage, stepping out only for a brief time while we waited for the company to cross the river. As I made to return to my seat, I heard a voice calling out my name.

"*Frau Mathilda!*"

I turned and saw the emperor approaching on foot. He motioned for me to come near, and I did so without delay.

"I wish for you to ride beside me when we enter the city. There is to be a great procession through the streets, and it is proper that the empress should be there for all to see."

I was taken aback by this request, for I had not been notified that I was to display my riding skills in public. Alas, Daughter, I did not possess such talents as seemed necessary for the wife of an emperor. When by myself, I preferred to ride as a man would, even as Drogo had taught me. But to ride in the manner of a woman—this was not to my liking, for it offended my sense of balance. Thus I made the best excuse that my mind could create.

"Surely such an action would only detract from the glory due Your Highness!"

He was not taken in, but seemed determined to counter my every word.

"I will not hear such folly from your lips! Your presence could only add to my glory. In any case, it has already been decided. You will ride, and that is the end of the matter."

I opened my mouth to protest, but he would hear none of it, silencing me with a raised hand and then moving to speak with one of his grooms. I felt a sense of dread come over me. The chance of falling from a horse in full view of the entire city, thus lending humiliation to the emperor's hour of renown, was rather a certainty in my mind. I looked in all directions for the one person who could help me.

"Drogo! Drogo!" I called out, each cry growing wilder. "Drogo, where are you? I have need of you!"

A few frantic moments passed before I finally saw him, his figure plain due to his unnatural height. He paced in my general direction, but was apparently deaf to my cries.

"Drogo!" I cried again with such fervor that he was forced to take notice, quickening his steps until he reached my position. "Where have you been? I trust you have a sufficient excuse!"

Poor Drogo really did not deserve such censure, but I was in a rare mood.

"I would rather not say, Your Highness," he replied.

"On what account? Tell me or I shall have you scalded!"

"You would never!"

"Just tell me."

"Well, if you command it."

"I do."

"I was taking a piss."

Ah, a well-laid trap I had set for myself! I was uncertain of how to respond, for I might as well tell you, if you do not know, that it is not the custom of men and women to discuss such things. After a few seconds of consideration, I determined that I would simply press on as if this revelation had never happened.

"Drogo, the emperor wishes me to ride next to him through the city."

"And you feel less than certain about this?"

"I know neither the horse nor the road."

"And you would prefer not to end up in the mud?"

"Precisely."

"Fear not! I shall walk beside you and hold the reins. You will not have to worry about the horse. If you feel unstable, speak to me in our own language and I shall help you. No one will understand."

"But I still think . . ."

"Think nothing, except that you will be magnificent!"

A sense of calm returned, and I found myself saying, "What would I do without you, Drogo? I think I should not last the week."

"And without you, I might be plowing some field in Cornwall."

"Barons never plow fields!"

"I might have been the exception. My father has a love of dice."

Soon we made our way to the head of the procession, and I was lifted with great care onto a gray mare draped with the colors of the imperial household. The ladies had dressed me this day in the brightest red garment they could muster, for they said that it would allow the people to see me more clearly amid the throng. They placed the finest crown of gold, which I had not worn since my wedding day, upon my head. As if to prove to the Romans the extent of my spiritual devotion, I was furnished with a crucifix of such weight that I feared it might pull my neck to the ground.

At last the mighty company began to move south in a ponderous manner. We could see the Porta San Valentino directly
ahead. The workings of the Frangipane had ensured that the
gates would be open to us. There was but one arched portal
through which man and beast could pass, and on account of the
long years since its construction, its base had become buried to
the point that some of the taller banners had to be lowered to
permit entry. So narrow was the opening that only two horses
could walk through side by side.

Once inside the walls, we found the road lined with cheering
citizens, the buildings decorated with garlands of flowers, and
the general spirit such that it must have approached the Roman
triumphs of old. But even as we began to enjoy this reception,
our progress was suddenly halted.

"What is this?" the emperor complained to the men in front
of us. "Keep moving!"

"Sire," one of them answered, "there are three men in the
road—bishops, by the look of it. Perhaps even cardinals."

At once, the emperor alighted from his horse and started
moving toward the site of the disturbance.

"Drogo," I said, "lead us up toward the front of the line."

"My lady?"

"I want to see what is happening!"

After what appeared to be a moment of deep consideration,
he signaled to the mare to follow his lead around the soldiers and
heralds until we could see the emperor with Philip of Ravenna
standing beside him. Walking toward them were three cardinals
of varying rank, each with his hands clasped, as if in prayer.

"Who are they? Did the pope send them?" I asked, but Drogo
had no more answers than I.

Finally, Philip called out to them in Latin, "Who is this that
hinders the emperor's progress?"

"Most Serene Highness," the senior cardinal replied, "I am Giovanni da Gaeta, chancellor to His Holiness Pope Paschal II, who is currently visiting with our dear friends in Benevento."

"You mean that he has fled to Benevento like a wounded deer," Drogo muttered, but I silenced him.

The cardinal continued, "Here with me are the bishop of Ostia and the papal vicar here in Rome, Bishop Pietro of Porto."

"Yes, we are familiar with them both," the emperor answered. "On what account do you come before us now?"

"First," Cardinal Giovanni answered, "we wish to welcome you to Rome and express our dearest wish that the days of your visit might pass in peace and tranquility."

"That has ever been my aim," Emperor Henry responded.

The look on my husband's face was one of part weariness, part annoyance, while the cardinals seemed doubtful of his claim of peaceful intent. I imagined that they must have been remembering the result of the last imperial visit to Rome.

"Second," the cardinal continued, "we bid you hearken unto these words of the Holy Father, who is your lord and ours in all spiritual matters. He is ready to make peace with you if you would only renounce this supposed right to invest the bishops of this Church with ring and crozier. Such a thing was never written in the Holy Scriptures, nor did the esteemed fathers, to whom we all look for wisdom, declare it. It is not right that the hand that bears the sword should also grant the staff. Surely you can see how this is a perversion of divine intent!"

"I see no such thing," my husband responded, his frustration clearly increasing. "If I do claim any right, it is only that which has been passed down from the days of my ancestor, Charles the Great, to the present time. Do not think that I am some heathen! I am as much a servant of Jesus Christ as you, and I think it only right that these men who are to be raised up within my kingdom should profess fealty to their king, even as the Apostle Paul teaches us. Yes, my lords, I too read Scripture!"

"But this is a scandal against the Church and against all propriety!" the bishop of Ostia declared. "How can you stand there and speak to a prince of the Church in such a manner! Consider that your obstinacy has already imposed great damage upon Christendom, placing the Church in danger from those wolves who would afflict it. If you would but accept the pope's gracious offer, then the state of the Church would surely be improved in all things."

"A neat argument," the emperor replied, "but I find fault with it. It is the Gregorians who first created the present situation when they sought to overreach the divinely ordained bounds. I have been anointed by Pope Paschal himself!"

"Only under the most vile duress," the bishop of Ostia answered.

Clearly inflamed, the emperor yelled, "Bishop Maurice!"

The bishop of Braga, he that had joined us in Arezzo, stepped forward from the crowd of officials.

"Brother Maurice!" Cardinal Giovanni called out, "I see that your mediation has failed."

"Not failed, brother Giovanni, but perhaps this is not the best time to discuss such things. Stand aside and let the emperor pass, the better to gain his good will."

The look in the cardinal's eyes was one of great suspicion, but he finally said, "If you have your orders from the Holy Father . . ." With that the three men relented and made their way to the side of the road, melting into the crowd.

"Thank you, Your Grace," the emperor said to the bishop of Braga.

"Never fear, my lord! The people are on our side. It is only a matter of time until they relent," Philip proclaimed.

I could not imagine on what grounds he made such an assertion, but it seemed to satisfy the emperor, and within the space of a few minutes, we were once again proceeding down the Via Corso, past the ancient mausoleum in which were once buried the remains of Caesar Augustus and his family.

"They say it was pillaged long ago by the Visigoths," my husband told me.

"Truly?" I replied. "So much for the mighty Augustus! *Sic transit gloria mundi!*"

"What was that?"

"*Sic transit gloria mundi.* The glories of this world are fading. It is something that Bruno taught me. They used to whisper it in the ear of the victorious generals as they marched through the streets in triumph, and it is now used for papal coronations."

"And so you whisper it unto me?"

"I was not implying anything about Your Highness."

"No, perhaps not, but your words may yet prove true. Ah, there is the Pantheon!"

Rising high above its neighbors was the dome of that famous church, shining boldly in the sunlight.

"I have never seen such a thing," I murmured. "There is such a sense of awe . . . One is struck with wonder."

"Yes, Rome has that effect on the visitor," the emperor said with a laugh.

Before long we had come to the site of the ancient Forum, the very heart of Rome. Here was the Arch of Severus, now partially buried, but nevertheless a fine sight to behold. The site was littered with lone columns, partial walls, and piles of rocks that would no doubt make their way into buildings of the present age. We alighted and began to walk through this maze of stone that was now overgrown by all manner of plants, the marble pillars wrapped in wild vines. More than one stray animal could be seen climbing upon the ruins, and it seemed that the city's beggars had taken up residence there.

"Is that it?" Emperor Henry called out to the bishop of Braga, pointing to the area next to the Arch of Septimius Severus.

"Yes, this is where the ancient *rostra* used to stand. The great orators would make their speeches here."

"Perfect," my husband replied, mounting the small hill along with several officials. I had no intention of joining them, but was beckoned thither by the emperor. "The empress must be seen!" he told me yet again.

The crowd was now pressing in on all sides, men and women struggling to move closer to the supposed dais. At last, when the clamor had lessened, the emperor spoke.

"Citizens of Rome, I, Henry, Holy Roman emperor, anointed by God to do his work, descendant of the emperors that were, lord over the kingdoms of Germany, Burgundy, Bohemia, and Lombardy, and all the duchies which lie therein, do declare the great esteem in which I hold this jewel of cities, the seat of our holy Church, the heir of the greatest empire the world has ever seen, which lives on even now in our own dominion.

"We have heard of your subjugation, how men who would seek to trample your freedom and make this city naught but a vessel for their own ambitions have denied your ancient rights. Not that we mean to offend His Holiness the pope, but rather we see that he has been ill advised by men who do not know their place and who lead him along a path which bears no resemblance to the teachings of our Lord or the decrees of the councils.

"Honorable Romans, we have heard your cries of distress and come hither to deliver you from the state of chaos that has prevailed for this past year. With tender love we wish to treat with you, and to establish a friendship between the lands of the North and those of the South; even between our self and you. We shall install Prefect Peter, your own appointed leader, in his rightful place. We shall bestow upon you blessings from the wealth that God has so richly granted to us. We shall oversee the creation of a restored Rome.

"Following the advice of our princes, we seek to appease the very serious conflict between Romans and the pope. We have heard the joyous testimony of the clergy and the people and visited the places of the apostles; and because we have not found the apostolic lord, who has fled out of his dread of the Roman people, we present our judgment to those in the Church. We thank God that there was none found who sought to accuse us either in secret or in public, but rather the voice of praise and joy was heard, which has commended them to their imperial lord, to God, and to the blessed apostles Peter and Paul.

"Three cardinals visited us and offered to us complete peace, arguing that we should cease to grant investiture by ring and crozier, and testifying that it was a scandal against the Church. We answered them thus: that it was set out as part of our right that we should grant the *regalia* of the ring and crozier. Yet they say that the Church is shaken and in danger, and they assure us that if the battle over investiture were to cease, the state of the Church would be 'improved in all things.'

"I beseech you, dear Romans, what peace can there be which is not based on the truth? Can a man be one day a tyrant, and the next a messenger of reconciliation? Even so are they who seek to rule over you, but their time is at an end! Rome for the Romans; that is what we say! In this manner, we shall restore the holy Church. What say you?"

The shouts of the people rose to the heavens. With the last pillars of ancient Rome rising behind them, this was a sight worthy of remembrance, even if those cheers were certain to die out once the emperor departed again for his own lands. Yet even in the midst of that spectacle, I was filled with doubt, and I wondered how this act of defiance would be perceived abroad.

Still, this moment was for the emperor, and he moved to embrace his counselors in turn. As the celebration continued around him, Henry covered his face with his hand as if in a moment of contemplation, the lines on his forehead betraying pain. I was about to move toward him, when it all seemed to pass, and he once again waved to the crowd, as if nothing out of the ordinary had taken place.

CHAPTER SIXTEEN

O n the anniversary of Christ's birth, in the year of our Lord 800, Charles the Great, king of the Franks, knelt before the high altar in Saint Peter's Basilica. There, upon the tomb of the apostle, Pope Leo III placed a magnificent crown on his head and proclaimed him to all as *imperator Romanorum.* Such an occasion might have swollen the pride of any man, but Einhard declares that Charles bore the title with great humility.

"It was then that he received the titles of emperor and Augustus, to which he at first had such an aversion that he declared that he would not have set foot in the church the day that they were conferred, although it was a great feast day, if he could have foreseen the design of the pope. He bore very patiently with the jealousy which the Roman emperors showed upon his assuming these titles, for they took this step very ill; and by dint of frequent embassies and letters, in which he addressed them as brothers, he made their haughtiness yield to his magnanimity, a quality in which he was unquestionably much their superior."

Whether Emperor Henry V could bear such laud with the same absence of vanity was yet to be seen. It had been six years since Pope Paschal placed the imperial diadem upon his head, but this action had done little to silence the murmurs of the discontented. The *privilegium* bestowed by His Holiness had been christened anew as a *pravilegium* by the sons of Gregory, which is to say a false privilege. Scarcely a man alive believed that the pope had not been coerced, and one by one the grants of Paschal were drawn back by the same hand. The single pledge to which the Holy Father remained true was his promise to refrain from issuing the ban of excommunication.

For this reason it was necessary that my husband should be crowned again in the basilica, as was the custom for kings and queens on such festive occasions. From the time of our arrival in Rome, this ceremony had been at the fore of the emperor's thoughts. It was not a simple matter of walking to church, for though we resided safely in a *villa* of the Frangipane family near the Colosseum—the emperor not being so bold as to attempt to possess the Lateran Palace—the land nearer the river remained under the control of the Pierleoni, chief adversaries of the imperial party. In addition to their towers on the bank of the Tiber and a stronghold upon the river isle, the Pierleoni held the main bridge, the Ponte Sant'Angelo. Although the imperial forces were far greater than those of the papal allies, he and his council hoped to avoid any violence. The day was Easter, the feast of the resurrection of our Lord, and thus a time for Christian unity. There would be strife enough without a call to arms, and the emperor had not forgotten how the people of Rome rose up against him after his last visit to Vatican Hill.

We mounted the horses at an early hour, knowing that it would take some time to reach our destination. The emperor and I were positioned at the front as usual. Directly behind us came the Count of Tusculum and his beloved nephew, Prefect

Peter, along with Giovanni Frangipane and other members of that household. The intent was to display that the civil governors of Rome were fully in support of the emperor.

Farther behind was Abbot Berald of Farfa, who along with the count was the subject of a papal ban, though he nevertheless held a position of power as head of one of the chief abbeys south of the great mountains. The land and possessions of the monks of Farfa were large indeed, as they controlled much of the territory north of Rome; in addition, their connections with the abbey of Cluny, which one might call *domus maxima*, ensured their place within Christendom. Also representing the clergy were the bishop of Braga, Philip of Ravenna, Bishop Burchard of Münster, Bishop Gebhard of Trent, and several priests of the imperial household, including my own chaplain, Altmann.

I am proud to report that I had finally acquired some small amount of courage in regard to my riding and was intent on proving my aptitude. Though Drogo offered his services, I bid him depart and declared that I, Empress Mathilda, was to command the reins. Fine words these were, but as I sat ready to depart, I suddenly felt ill and wished to God that I had not been so headstrong. I suppose we are all brave in our own imagination.

"Let us make haste!" Chancellor David declared, and no sooner had the words escaped his lips than the whole train began to move.

Now, the Pierleoni held the space near the Theater of Marcellus as well as the Tiber Island. Farther north, the bridge was also in their hands. Thus they held almost the entire bend of the river, and Giovanni Frangipane recommended that we ford to the north or south. However, the walls of Pope Leo enclosed the Vatican on three sides, and there was some threat that, were we to approach overland from either direction, a siege might be necessary to break down the gates, or perchance it would become a second Thermopylae. If we were to enter by way of the river, there would be no such opportunity for the guard to hold off our superior numbers.

The emperor thus endorsed another path that carried with it some peril, but which was nevertheless our best hope. We would attempt to cut through the middle of the Pierleoni territory, remaining equally distant from the towers to the south and the bridge to the north. This would place us beyond the range of most weapons. In addition, several of the Frangipane spies arranged for the entire route to be lined with adoring residents, as they knew the Pierleoni would be loath to attack such a gathering.

Our travel was pleasant enough as we rode through the city, even once we passed by the Pantheon and into the heart of the Pierleoni realm. Philip of Ravenna rode up next to me and asked if I was pleased with everything.

"Yes, all is as I had hoped," I replied, though I did not mention my joy that I had thus far stayed on the horse without incident. "I wonder, where are all these Pierleoni men that I have been hearing about? I thought they might appear from every window and door, ready to pursue us."

"It seems they have decided it would be better not to fight," Philip said. "They know there is little to be gained from conflict. Long after the emperor is gone, they will remain in their towers, lords over all around them, servants of the pope." After a moment had passed, he continued, "This ride is not what merits your concern. I am most worried about the river crossing."

"Why?" I asked, unhappy to hear of this new cause for alarm. "Will they shoot at us from the bridge?"

"No, what I refer to has nothing to do with the Pierleoni. It is merely a legend in this place, dating back to that time when the papal court was something less than what it ought to be. Dark days those were, and there was one descendant of Peter who proved particularly wretched. Formosus was his name; at least, that was his royal title. He established his reputation working among the Bulgarians, where he was much beloved. However, once he was made pope, he moved from one tribulation to the next, feuding with the eastern bishops, the king of France, and the Holy Roman emperor. During his papacy, this land was even attacked by the Saracens, God curse them! It was no surprise that he lasted less than five years in that exalted office."

"Why should this make us afraid of the river?" I asked, growing impatient in my attempt to make out his words over the noise of the crowd.

"Here you will find one of history's oddest tales. Pope Formosus was not long in the grave before his successor, Stephen VI, revived some old charges against him. You see, the new pope was allied with the House of Spoleto, and they shared a mutual hatred of Formosus's policies. It was ordered that the former pope must stand before a *tribunal*, so his corpse was removed from the earth and carried to the Basilica of Saint John, where they propped it upon a mock throne and brought charges against it. They determined that Formosus was never the rightful heir of Saint Peter. The corpse was then stripped of the honors of office, and Pope Stephen severed from the right hand those fingers that had been used to bestow blessings upon the faithful. All the acts of Formosus were declared to be void, and the body was placed into a common grave. However, so mad with vengeance was Pope Stephen that he pronounced one final censure upon his predecessor, ordering the corpse to be exhumed once again and cast into the Tiber.

"Well, by the end of that summer, Stephen himself was thrown out by the people of Rome and put to death, while the reputation of Formosus was restored. For the dishonor imposed on his remains, the bones of Formosus placed upon the river a terrible curse, and you often hear tales of swimmers drowned on a summer's day, boats run aground, or fishers contracting some fearful disease. I only hope we do not become the latest such victims."

I had until that point maintained a firm grip on my emotions, but upon hearing this story, I was filled with dread. I was familiar with tales of the supernatural. Indeed, in the years of my childhood there were men who saw blood bubbling up from the earth, were haunted by the cries of the damned at night, and saw the work of the devil in the eyes of a black dog. The Italians, I soon learned, were even more prone to such beliefs. In that moment the words of Philip of Ravenna provoked a frenzy in my soul, and I dearly wished that we could have traveled across the Ponte Sant'Angelo rather than entering the boats.

How I mounted the courage to board that vessel, I cannot say. The emperor must have noticed my lack of ease, for he made a comment in that regard.

"Is all well, Mathilda?"

"Yes, of course. Why?"

"Your hands are shaking."

I quickly clasped my palms together and willed them to be still.

"It's only a little cold, that is all."

"Here," he said, placing his own cloak around my shoulders. "I have no need of it. The sun is out and the heat has risen."

"Even as our Lord," I replied, wishing to distract myself from the movement of the boat across the water, fearing that we might plunge to the river's bottom at any moment.

"What do you mean?"

"Even as our Lord has risen . . . because of the day, you see."

"Ah," he said, apparently uncertain of why the comment was clever, but attempting to disguise this.

He must have noticed that my hands were still shaking, for he moved closer and held them in one of his own. We sat in that manner until reaching the other side, at which point I was most relieved to step onto solid ground. I suppose Philip's story was helpful inasmuch as it distracted me from the thought of the

Pierleoni archers upon the distant bridge, perched just out of range of my very head.

There was a large contingent of the Roman *curia*—that is, the papal court—waiting to receive us. Evidently they had been well aware of our coming and had chosen to accept this unwelcome visit for the present. I noticed among that number the three cardinals who had met us on the road earlier: the papal chancellor, the bishop of Ostia, and the bishop of Porto.

One of the ladies saw to the train of my gown, while another tucked any stray hairs under my veil.

"*Sorridi!*" she said cheerfully.

"What does that mean?" I asked as she walked away. "I still cannot understand a word you say!"

I placed my hand within that of the emperor, and together we strode up the hill. It was a truly glorious day. All throughout the city, bells were ringing in the celebration of our Lord's resurrection. A large flock of doves scuttled across our path, their musical sounds of "Coo coo!" echoing around us. Off to the right was the Castel Sant'Angelo, resplendent in the morning light.

Then I saw it: the jewel of all Christendom. The only surprise was that it was not the grandest of the churches in Italy, or even of the ones in Rome. In fact, the Basilica of Saint Peter dates from an earlier time. It was Constantine the Great who sought to erect such monuments over the most sacred places of our holy Church, and the apostle's grave was such a treasure. The building is of the old Roman style, and it has none of the magnificent towers or domes of the German imperial creations. The grand stairs lead up to a rather simple gatehouse, beyond which is the basilica itself. Just through the gate is a pleasant yard surrounded by a cloister, and a fountain in the center brings to mind the words of Christ, "But whoever drinks of the water that I shall give him, shall never more thirst; but the water that I shall give him shall be in him a well of water, springing up into everlasting life."

What a strange Easter morning that must have seemed to all the church's attendants, for rather than the usual papal Mass, they now struggled to ready themselves for a hastily called council of the imperial and papal parties. Once inside, I was granted a chair next to my husband, but most of those present were forced to stand. The air was filled with the chatter of hundreds of bishops, clerks, monks, knights, and all the rest. The emperor then stood and began to speak, the attention of all turned to his words.

"My lord chancellor, cardinals of our holy Church, bishops from near and far. We have come here today in pursuit of peace, a peace that shall bring stability not only to our empire, but to all of the Christian kingdoms. We are saddened to find that His Holiness Pope Paschal II has departed his see and left you to treat on his behalf, for we believe the pope to be the most honorable of all men and know that, were he here, his heart would yearn for peace as much as that of any man present. But as he is not here, it falls to all of you to come to terms with us and reach a settlement that shall be mutually beneficial.

"I bid you now consider how an accord between the secular and religious orders would appear. The glory of one would be the glory of the other, and the union of the two forces would inspire universal dread! Senates, consuls, and nobles, all good citizens of Rome and of the world, would regard us with satisfaction. Goths, Gauls, Spaniards, Africans, Greeks and Latins, Parthians, Jews, and Arabs would fear or love us. But ah! Other are our actions and other the fruits which we reap if we refrain from doing that which is incumbent upon us.

"Any such agreement must be accompanied by recognition of our divinely granted authority. We wish to be crowned here even as our predecessors were, for it is traditional to do so when the emperor is in Rome. In truth, I ought to be crowned by the father of the Roman Church, the lord pope, and his absence is a misfortune. But now I desire that one of you may do so in the name of peace. If that is your wish, then let it so be done."

The emperor then sat upon his great chair once again, and all present waited to hear what answer the cardinals would give. At length Giovanni de Gaeta, chancellor to the pope, rose to answer the younger man's declaration.

"Excellency, we are, of course, honored by your presence," he began. "Moreover, our hearts are moved by the words which you have spoken of the Holy Father, His Grace Paschal. We are glad to hear of your desire for peace. Indeed, it is the desire of every person here."

Then his speech took the inevitable turn toward the subject of disagreement.

"You know full well that there is nothing which the Church would not willingly bestow upon such an ardent son, provided it was in our power to give. Yet far be it from us to grant what the Lord has held back, or to take those keys from the hands of the apostles and hand them to Caesar. Did not our Lord say, 'Give therefore to Caesar the things which are Caesar's, and give unto God those which are God's'? Would you then instruct the Lord as if he were a servant to do your bidding? Heaven forbid! May God pardon you for such iniquity!" he finished, making the sign of the cross twice for an added flourish.

At this, many of the bishops let out shouts of assent, while those of the imperial party began hurling abuse and shaking their fists angrily. I turned and saw upon the emperor's face a look of complete enmity. He started to move forward in his seat, and I could not say whether he would utter some slander or move to strike his adversary. Without taking time to consider, for no such time was provided, I placed my hand firmly upon my husband's wrist, bidding him remain in his seat. While this did prevent him from mounting an assault, it also drew his anger upon me. With a cry of "Get off me, woman!" he removed his arm from my grasp and stood, his piercing eyes directed upon my defenseless frame. Still, I remembered my mother's plea for peace.

"You must remain calm! This will help nothing!" I said, my words filled with far more confidence than I truly felt.

To my great relief, he seemed to accept what I had to say, and raised his hands to quiet his supporters, who obeyed for the most part. He then turned back toward the cardinals, his eyes fixed upon the person who had just accused him.

"It is the custom of the emperors when present in Rome on occasions of high festival to allow themselves to be crowned by the pope, and thus crowned to walk in procession through the city." He paused for a moment—perhaps for effect, or perhaps to allow his anger to decrease—and then continued. "As His Holiness has not seen fit to join us, we will speak with our counselors about the best way to proceed. Allow us a moment to consider."

The cardinals were content to stand patiently while the emperor conversed in hushed tones with Chancellor David, Philip of Ravenna, and the lawyer Irnerius. There were murmurs throughout the room. On the opposite side of the nave, Chancellor Giovanni and some of the other cardinals allowed their faces to break into sly smiles. They were sure that the emperor had been backed into a corner with no way out. But upon other faces I saw looks of concern. They might have been afraid that the emperor would seek to overcome them through force of arms, even as he had six years earlier. After a few minutes of this, the discussion was finally abandoned, and my husband returned to his seat.

"Well?" the papal chancellor called out. "What is it to be?"

"I call forward the bishop of Braga," the emperor answered.

Every eye turned to look upon the bishop, who had until that point been standing with a few others in the space between the two camps, no doubt wishing to appear neutral. Suddenly, I recognized what was about to happen, and that it had likely been agreed upon long before. The bishop strode forward boldly, keeping his gaze fixed on the emperor and not heeding the calls of his brother bishops, many of whom appeared to be quite displeased.

"Here is our brother, Maurice Bourdin, bishop of God's holy Church, appointed legate of Pope Paschal," Emperor Henry proclaimed. "He has been with us for these last several weeks and can testify to our good intentions."

"Good intentions?" Chancellor Giovanni interrupted, leaping to his feet and shaking his head. "Oh, what is this jester who comes before us to speak of his good intentions? We have seen your good intentions, Your Grace: how you have launched this invasion worthy of your barbaric ancestors, molested and robbed churches of God, how you have in your embrace of simony made vile ordinations, and a number of other actions which are not fit for discussion in this sacred place!

"No sooner had you entered the region of Lazio than you wrought war upon its people on behalf of those excommunicates—the abbot of Farfa and the Count of Tusculum—who stand even now within your contemptible company, despite both being under the ban! You may be a king, sire, but you are not above the King of Kings, which is God Almighty! Even if we were disposed to consent to your demands, we could not do so, for we can have no intercourse with excommunicates!"

"Giovanni, you devil! Would you like me to cut out that mouth for you?" Count Ptolemy yelled, striding forward with his sword drawn. He was subsequently restrained by a pair of his fellows, but not before the situation descended into chaos.

Persons on both sides were yelling at their fellows across the way. I had never witnessed such a spectacle and did not care to ever again. My opinion of the male sex, I am sorry to say, was not particularly high at that moment. Then came a cry: "Silence!"

I was amazed to see that it was the bishop of Braga, displaying an unforeseen capacity for noise.

"Now, listen well to the words I say, for God knows I have heard little enough of reason this past hour. I was elected by the pope himself to see to this matter. Cardinal Giovanni de Gaeta"—here he looked toward the papal chancellor—"I have heard your high accusations, and it pains me to see that a man of your noble standing should be in such poor possession of the facts, for I testify to you that in the time I have spent with the emperor, I have witnessed none of the supposed injustices that you mentioned. While I know well Your Grace's fervor for the law of the Lord—the law by which we all are bound, whether emperor, peasant, or cardinal—I believe that on this occasion, Emperor Henry asks for nothing more than that which has been the standard practice for hundreds of years, and it is no danger to the Church."

Having heard these words, many of the cardinals began to yell, "Traitor!" "Blasphemer!" and "Portuguese bastard!" However, the papal chancellor said nothing, choosing instead to channel his loathing through a look as furious as the one Master Godfrey had lavished on me all those years ago, nostril flare and all.

"It is therefore my opinion," Bishop Maurice continued over the shouts of his enemies, "that I, as the papal representative, may place the crown upon the imperial head in good faith and without causing jeopardy to this Church, for it is only in keeping with tradition and the teachings of Scripture, which commands the utmost respect for civil authorities, and declares that there are none except those which are established by God. It is no crime to honor the head which the Lord himself has anointed!"

The bishop then bid the emperor walk toward the altar, before the very bones of Saint Peter. There was a large rounded tile of porphyry embedded in the floor, and upon this red circle the bishop bid him kneel. The imperial guard moved to block any of the cardinals who looked as if they might hinder the proceedings. As it turned out, most of them chose to march out in anger, proclaiming that they would have no part in such a profane act. Those who stood with Emperor Henry moved to gain a proper view. I too was conducted forward, the better to see and be seen. As Bishop Maurice began the ceremony, I could think of nothing but the reception we would receive upon leaving that place.

"Even now, the cardinals are surely conspiring with the Pierleoni to turn the whole city against us," I thought, "and if the pope has succeeded in gaining the arms of the Normans to the south, then he might arrive any day at the head of a large procession. There is as much to be lost from this act of rebellion as there is to be gained."

Bishop Gebhard of Trent brought forth the imperial crown. What an object of beauty! I had only witnessed it sitting upon the emperor's head once before, and that was on the day of our wedding. Jewels of every color under the sun covered its eight sides, and the symbol of the cross was set at the front. With great reverence the bishop of Braga accepted the crown and placed it upon Henry's head.

"To Henry the Augustus crowned of God, great and pacific emperor of the Romans, life and victory!" he cried, and all present repeated the words still louder. They echoed through the hall and seemed to cast their spell with ease, turning a bitter gathering into one of joy.

The emperor arose and led me out from that place, every person bowing before us. When the gate opened, I was relieved to see that there was no army waiting for us. Apparently the opponents had scattered farther afield. Still, I knew they would not be gone for long.

"That was a good service the bishop of Braga performed for you," I said so that no one else could hear. "I do hope you intend to reward him."

"Am I not a man of honor?" he replied. "The bishop has acted of his own free will. Even so, as you say, I shall find some way to thank him, for he has taken great pains on our behalf."

We traveled in the boats across the Tiber, then mounted the horses for our journey back through the city. The crowds cheered to see the emperor again, this time with the glittering crown upon his head. It was almost enough to distract me from those moments when I saw traces of pain upon my husband's features. I had marked them out for the past few days, particularly when we were riding. I was not aware that anyone else had noticed, and I was not yet courageous enough to broach the subject. I strongly suspected that he suffered from a stomachache, for I had seen him once or twice pressing his hand against his belly.

By the time we made it back to the *villa*, there was neither man nor woman among us who did not know some weariness of the body. Even the emperor intended to rest before the feast that evening. However, before he did so, he motioned me aside to have a private word.

"What is it, my lord?" I asked.

"Have your ladies bring you to my room tonight."

"My lord?" I repeated, wondering if perhaps I had misheard.

"I want you to come to my bed. We have been married now three years. You are a grown woman."

My mind struggled to form a reply, but in the end all I could say was, "I see. Well, if that is what you wish."

"It is what I wish," he said. "See that you do not forget."

As he left me to attend to his own matters, I was for a moment frozen in place, lost in thought. I was uncertain about a great many things, but this I much knew: it was not a conversation I was likely to forget.

Have you ever noticed, Daughter, how the very hours of the day take on certain lethargy before a dreaded moment? On such occasions I often find myself wishing for a quick conclusion that might place my concerns in the past, but time is not so kind as that; it prefers to torment us for as long as possible, drawing out from every moment the greatest share of misery.

Let me assure you, Daughter, that I was not ignorant regarding the subject of wedded relations. Indeed, my father's conduct and the wealth of offspring it produced required that I be granted an explanation at an early age. Then there were the words of Scripture to consider, along with the precepts of the Church. Thus what troubled me upon that day was not so much the thought of such intercourse, but rather two more practical fears: first, that my husband might find me wanting in some way, and second, that it was to take place on a holy day.

The clergy in England had often said that it was forbidden for a man and his wife to have relations on any feast day, along with a number of other occasions. On the other hand, the churches in the empire were somewhat different, and even within England there was disagreement on the subject, with some claiming that a Christian ought to abstain on every Monday, Wednesday, and Friday, while others claimed it was only the Lord's Day that required such consideration. And while Easter was among the holiest of days, it was also the end of the Lenten season, and thus an hour for rejoicing rather than austerity. Indeed, was not the bringing forth of new life an apt endeavor for an occasion that celebrated resurrection?

As the hours passed and my mind continued to work over these diverse arguments, I concluded that it was one of those matters about which a person could not be entirely certain, and thus my conscience was somewhat relieved. This left me with the mere problem of proving myself an able wife, a fear which did not abate even as I stood in my bedchamber that evening with the ladies preparing me as usual for the hours of sleep.

However, this was not to be like any other night. The emperor had informed Francesca that I should come to his quarters in a discreet manner. When the rest of the women had been dismissed, Francesca performed her usual duty of lighting a candle for herself and one for me. She then led me out of the room and into the short passage that connected all the private chambers. The rest of the house's residents had long since made their beds on the floor of the hall below, and I dearly hoped that they remained ignorant of what was taking place above, for I shuddered to think that I might become the subject of unseemly gossip.

Francesca knocked on the door ever so lightly, and I presumed that I would see my husband standing there when the portal was opened. Instead it was one of his attendants, who quickly ushered me into the chamber, which I immediately observed was far larger than my own.

"Why should he receive the grandest room when I am forced to carry twice as many garments?" I thought, but then censured myself for giving way to pointless distraction.

"The emperor will be with you shortly, after he has finished attending to a necessary matter," the man whispered.

I wished to thank him by name, but my memory failed me, so a simple word had to suffice.

His departure was welcome only in that it gave me a moment to adjust to my new surroundings in solitude. I was deeply troubled in spirit, to the point that I had to set down the candle that I was holding, for my hand was shaking badly. I was about to address a prayer to the Holy Virgin, then thought the better of it and instead directed my plea to Saint Helena, who knew her husband most truly.

"Lady Helena, make haste to help me, for I am in sore need!" I whispered. "I am ready to perform my duty. I wish that even as you bore the blessed emperor, I might bear children who fulfill their divine calling."

I tried to assure myself that this was a good prayer, but I strongly suspected that Saint Helena would not be impressed. Before I could make a second attempt, the door opened again, and my husband stood before me.

What followed I have no intention to relate, for there are some matters a woman must keep to herself. In any case, it is of little consequence except for what happened afterward. The deed itself was almost completed, and I was inwardly rejoicing that this first test had reached its end, when he pulled back from me and cried out in pain. In the moments before this, I had been so worried about my own actions and so ignorant of how a man might act in such situations, that I did not notice the warning signs that were undoubtedly there. I watched in dismay as he moved to brace himself and continued to groan. I could see now that his disorder did not afflict his bowels, but rather his secret place. Having spoken scarcely a word since he entered the room, I now had no choice but to break the protection of silence.

"Are you hurt, my lord?" I asked. "Should I fetch the physician?"

"No! No!" he said rather desperately, still crouched over in distress. "I do not want anyone else to see me in this condition! It will pass."

"I don't understand," I replied, by this point clothing myself once again, as I did not then and never have since found it possible to have a serious conversation in such a state. "I have been watching now for several weeks as you have tried to hide this pain, thinking it beyond anyone's notice. Well, it has not escaped my notice, and as your wife, I demand that the physician examine you! I will not hear your protestations!"

I said this with such authority that he seemed to be struck dumb. Not waiting for him to recover his sense of control and bid me stay out of his affairs, I reached for my outer robe and made to leave the room.

"Mathilda!" he called, as I was about to leave. "See to it that no one else knows what has happened here. No one must see you!"

"Of course," I replied, retrieving my candle and departing.

The feasting that evening had been even more unruly than usual, as the members of the court had consumed an inordinate amount of meat and beer, their fasting period having come to an end. Truth be told, more than one of them had wandered astray during the weeks of Lent, for I did not think that I could have imagined the smell of bacon. Now I felt my bare feet sticking to the stone floors on account of all the drinks that had been spilled; it was a most displeasing experience. The air itself smelled of beer.

I tried to place these thoughts out of my mind and instead pondered how I should go about finding the physician. Surely he would be lying in the Great Hall along with his fellows, but how was I to gain his attention without being noticed? No one must guess the cause of my errand. I came to the open doors and moved into the hall. The fire was little more than embers at that point, and it did not give off enough light for me to see the sleepers' faces clearly. I thus made my way around the room with all caution, taking care not to step on any hands or feet. It was slow work, for I was forced to stop more than once to make sure that all were really asleep. The heavy dinner seemed to have worked its magic on most, though the sleep of some was spottier, and I waited for them to settle before moving further. At one point my foot accidentally caught an empty goblet and I was sure that I would be discovered, but there was no response save for the squeak of a mouse that wended its way among the bodies in search of a night meal.

Finally I recognized the physician by his rather odd appearance, clothed as he was in robes unlike those of the other men. I considered how best to wake the good doctor without causing him to make a sound. I decided to place the light of my candle before his eyes and hope that it would perform its work slowly. When this had no effect, I tapped him on the shoulder.

The lids of his eyes slowly opened, and he instantly sought to establish the source of his disturbance. He looked in my direction, but his vision must have been poor in the dark of night, so I held the light near my face to illumine my features.

"My lady?" he whispered. "Is that you?"

Rather than speaking, I nodded and motioned for him to be silent. I then beckoned him to follow me out of the hall. This was somewhat of an ordeal, for the physician was not as light of foot as myself. It was with some relief that we reached the open door and made our way toward the stairs. Then I heard someone walking down toward us, followed by a voice.

"Who goes there?" the voice asked as its owner rounded the corner.

I held the candle aloft to glimpse this inquirer. From what I could make out, he seemed to be one of the Frangipane men keeping watch.

"It is I, Empress Mathilda," I said in a hushed tone. "Please lower your voice."

For a moment he gave no reply, and I began to wonder if I had exceeded his knowledge of Latin. He moved closer to us, and I could see from the light of his torch that he carried a flask of some kind.

"You know what I think you are?" he finally said, louder than I would have preferred. "I think you are one of the empress's ladies, sneaking down here for a bit of a midnight pick-me-up. If it's more wine that you seek, you can have some of mine here. A pretty face like yours deserves a good drink!"

I was incensed at his suggestion and immediately pushed the flask back in the direction of its owner.

"Do not assume that because you are a drunk, we all must be!" I answered. "I tell you I am the empress, and this is the emperor's physician, and I am in need of his assistance, for I have felt ill since supper. Now move out of the way at once, or I shall have you thrown out on the street ere morning comes!"

"Ah, so you need the wine for your stomach!"

"No, you fool! I want you gone this instant!"

"Very well. I can tell when I'm not wanted," he muttered, stumbling down the remaining stairs and passing back the way we had come.

"Are you really unwell? Is it your stomach?" the physician asked.

"No, sir. It is not I who need your help. Please follow me."

Feeling it was a miracle that the entire house was not awake, I preceded the physician through the narrow passage that led to my husband's room. As I placed my hand on the latch, I turned and whispered, "You are not to tell anyone of your visit here, do you understand?"

"Yes, my lady," he said without restraint.

I opened the door and found my husband seated on the bed, this time fully clothed, with his arms crossed and head down.

"My lord, here is the physician. What was your name, sir?"

"Bernard," he answered.

"This is Master Bernard," I repeated.

Without looking up the emperor beckoned for the man to come near. When Master Bernard was no more than a single pace away from him, he bowed and asked, "Your Grace, with your permission, what is the nature of your problem?"

At this the emperor finally raised his head and let out a sigh.

"We will no longer be requiring your presence," he told me.

"Very well. Good night, my lord."

I turned and left the room once again, walking back to my own chamber. I opened the door to find Francesca sitting in a chair near the fire, fully awake and staring at me. Without a word I closed the door and set my candle down on a nearby chest.

"Have you been sitting here this whole time?" I asked, but of course the lady did not understand me.

She rose and helped me remove my outer garments. Before departing, she turned back to me again.

"Did he?"

"What?"

She lifted her fingers and made a crude gesture.

"Get thee to bed! I have no more need of you or your perverse questions!"

Francesca only shrugged and left the room, granting me the solitude I so dearly craved. Yet I was not to be blessed with sleep that night, save for a few brief moments. Instead I lay in the darkness contemplating all that had taken place and wondering what it could mean. My husband was ill; that much I guessed. But of what nature was this illness? Would it pass quickly or remain? Did it pose any danger to his life?

There were no answers for me as I lay there staring up at the eaves, wishing for better days.

CHAPTER SEVENTEEN

The sun did not show its face the following morn. The rain clouds had pushed in from the sea, and now the fall of water could be heard upon the roof tiles—striking, pooling, and then rushing toward the ground in a stream just beside my window. The noise was comforting, or it would have been had my mind not been otherwise occupied by my night ordeal. As soon as I could, I called my ladies out of their pleasant sleep to begin the day. Candles must be lit, food must be consumed, the body must be cleansed, and clothing must be worn; such were the usual tasks of those early hours. Upon this dawn I would brook no delay.

At the earliest opportunity, I called for Drogo and bade him fetch the doctor for me. Many in the hall below had yet to stir from their slumber, but I was in need of answers, so any disturbance to the sleepers would have to be borne. A few minutes later, there was a knock at the door, and as one of the ladies—a girl, in truth, for the poor thing had no breasts—went to open the door, I imagined I would see in the light of day that same man with whom I had spoken in the night. But alas, it was not the physician, but rather the chaplain, Altmann, who stood before the threshold waiting to enter.

"Come in," I called out. As he bowed before me, I asked, "What is it?"

"My lady, you had asked me to come hither for our morning Scripture reading. I am certain that you said so last night at supper."

"Did I? Very well then, but I am to have another visitor at any moment."

"Ah. Perhaps it would be better if I came again at a later time?"

I was about to answer him when the door was opened once again for Drogo and the physician. From the look in his eyes, I guessed that the doctor had achieved no more sleep than myself.

"Master Bernard, please do come and sit!" I said to him, motioning to an empty chair.

"Do you wish me to leave then?" Altmann asked.

"If you would, just for a few minutes," I replied.

He duly departed into the adjoining room, and once the ladies moved to join him, I was left alone with the man whose confidences I so desired.

"Master Bernard, I cannot thank you enough for your assistance last night," I began. "I know that I can trust you to be discreet about all of this."

"If Your Highness has called me here for that purpose, you need not be worried," he answered. "I would never betray your trust."

"For which I am most thankful. Now, I wish for your opinion as a physician. After I left, what did you speak of with my husband? Is all well?"

He paused, eyes moving to and fro as if to search for any hidden eavesdropper. Finally he said, "I conducted a thorough examination of the emperor's complaints. He was in pain; that much was clear. At first he bid me not to touch the point in question, and I did not see anything that gave me cause for alarm. However, I felt it my duty not to leave him until I had also been able to feel for any deformity, if you understand me."

"I think I do," I replied.

"Yes, well, he finally consented that I should feel his . . ."

"His what?"

"Forgive me, my lady, but it is hard to know how one should speak of such things."

My patience was by now in short supply. "Sir, you may speak in plain terms with me. I might appear young to your eyes, but already my own have seen things which the aged man in his bed can scarcely comprehend, and though I may yet be ignorant of more than I care to tell, I must be informed of everything regarding the emperor's health, for you and I may be the only ones permitted to aid him."

After a moment of reflection, Bernard seemed to accept my request, for he said, "Very well. I felt that part which we call in Latin *testis*. You know of that which I speak?"

Now it was I who was left to feel the fool, for though I had boldly proclaimed my knowledge of the world, I was forced to admit to myself that this was one subject where I was less than expert.

"You refer to his member?"

"No, not quite," the physician replied, clearly beyond his level of comfort. "The other thing, or perhaps I should say, things."

"Oh. Go on, then."

"Yes. All was as it should be, except that I felt a small point which was . . . hardened."

"Hardened?"

"As if there were a pebble lodged within the flesh, and all around it was inflamed."

"And what was it?"

"That is the trouble. It may be any one of several things. I have observed such masses of varying sizes on every part of the human body. Some fade away over the course of a few months. Others remain as they are for years. Still others continue to grow and become more painful until surgery is necessary."

That was a word that sent a chill through my bones. I knew enough of surgery to be well aware of its perils. From what I could tell, a man was as likely to die from it as receive healing.

"Do not be troubled," he told me. "As I said, there are many kinds of masses, and there is no way to tell which one the emperor, that is, your husband might have. In some cases I have made a small cut and found them to be formed entirely of liquid, but others are as flesh. I think it quite possible that surgery will not be necessary. For the present, he will simply have to deal with the pain."

"So you are certain this is what has led to his condition?"

"Quite certain. I believe he thought it might have been some disorder of the passions which should have been cured through the usual manner, but I am afraid that is not the case."

I struggled to believe that this news was not as grave as it seemed. With great effort I told him, "Thank you, Bernard, for your care of my husband, and for informing me as to his condition."

"With pleasure, my lady. I instructed him to keep watch for any changes, and to tell me immediately if the pain worsens. In the meantime I proposed that he take some wine to help lessen his discomfort. He was most intent that this matter should remain a secret between the three of us."

"Yes, I am sure he is right. Farewell then, and please send my confessor in when you depart."

In the space of a moment, the doctor was gone and Altmann appeared, prayer book in hand, ready to receive my penitence. He sat in the newly empty chair and offered me a few words of joyful greeting that seemed entirely out of line with the gloom that had settled upon my spirit.

"My child, I am ready to hear your confession, if you wish to give it."

I fought to restrain the tears that threatened to break forth from their bounds and run down my cheeks with vigor. Though my iniquities were ever present, I felt more in need of divine comfort in such a dreadful hour.

"I confess that my spirit is addled," I answered, uncertain of how to proceed. "I have had some news which troubles me."

"No matter escapes the notice of God," he replied. "Empty yourself of these fears, and he may grant you the comfort which you desire."

"Would that it were so simple, but I fear this is not something that I can share with others—not even you."

"It is not an issue of sin then?"

"No, at least I do not believe so. Merely one of misfortune."

Altmann nodded his head slowly, as if to show that he shared my concern. At length he said, "Perhaps it would be better if we were to skip over the confession and move on to the reading."

I made no reply, but silently consented to this new order. He retrieved a large volume from the stand near the bed and opened it to a passage he deemed proper. As the raindrops continued to pound on the roof overhead, he recited words that were quite familiar.

"'Comfort you, comfort you my people, will your God say. Speak comfortably to Jerusalem, and cry unto her, that her warfare is accomplished, that her iniquity is pardoned: for she has received of the Lord's hand double for all her sins.'"

How these words to ancient Israel might be applied to my own life, I was not sure, but they did seem to lighten my mood. In fact, I was enjoying the sound of his voice when he came upon a few sentences that gave me pause.

"'He sits upon the circle of the earth, and the inhabitants thereof are as grasshoppers; he stretches out the heavens as a curtain, and spreads them out as a tent to dwell in. He brings the princes to nothing and makes the judges of the earth as vanity, as though they were not planted, as though they were not sown, as though their stock took no root in the earth. For he did even blow upon them, and they withered, and the whirlwind will take them away as stubble.'"

"Some comfort this is!" I thought to myself, suddenly aware of an unspoken longing to sit beside my mother, there to release the cares that had weighed me down. Then I remembered the last words she spoke to me, words of which I now had great need: "The just shall live by faith."

We remained in Rome for another forty days, the same as Christ dwelt in the wilderness when he faced the temptations of Lucifer. The devil had offered the Son of God all the kingdoms of the world, but alas, the emperor would have to content himself with lands already acquired, most especially those in Tuscany.

You may wonder how the Romans came to hold Emperor Henry in such high regard, for only a few years earlier they had risen in armed rebellion against his claims. It was the violence of the past year, combined with the lavish gifts he'd made to the people of that city, that allowed him to gain their devotion, at least for a time. In the interest of maintaining his influence over that region, it was resolved that his daughter, Bertha, was to wed the son of Count Ptolemy of Tusculum. A happy prospect this was for my husband, and I suppose I should have been pleased that she was to be sent far from us. Yet I could not but feel sorry for her in this, that her plight was not unlike that which I had experienced at such a young age, to my own perturbation. Thus I hoped that the match would grant her some measure of comfort.

All was proceeding as intended, until we received news from the South that the pope was to hold a synod at Benevento. There was a sense of apprehension among the company, for there could be only one purpose to this action: namely, to denounce the emperor and all those who sided with him. My greatest concern was that His Holiness might at last pass the order of excommunication against my husband, which would not only place his immortal soul in danger of everlasting torment, but also lend comfort to his earthly enemies, particularly those who had risen against him within the empire.

A few days later, we received a letter from Abbot Pontius—who continued to act as arbitrator between the opposing sides—saying that the pope and his allies had condemned the action by the bishop of Braga, declaring it to be an utmost betrayal. The bishop was placed under the ban of *anathema*. Yet there was the sole mercy that the emperor himself was once again spared from that chief reproach of excommunication, the pope having stayed true to his pledge granted in their past encounter. Small comfort this was, for Bishop Maurice could no longer claim any papal authority, nor could the emperor long hope to maintain the support of the Roman public once the full measure of the church's censure was made known. To make matters worse, Paschal was said to have won the full support of the Norman lord Robert of Capua and his army, and he could soon be marching at the head of an invasion. Therefore it seemed best to Emperor Henry that we should not remain in Rome past the feast of Pentecost. After all, it was not strange for emperors to leave the city during the heat of summer.

That was to be a day I would never forget. We set aside the hardships of the past month and proceeded once again to the Church of Saint Peter. This time there were two thrones placed within the chapel of Saint Gregory, and I was to be crowned along with my husband. This was customary for a visiting monarch, though the pope's opposition and that of all his cardinals meant that the bishop of Braga was forced to do the deed once again. I was not in favor of this decision, for as an excommunicate it hardly seemed fit that the bishop should set foot within the basilica, let alone perform the ceremony. But what was I to do? We queens are not as sovereign as men might suppose. What power we have must be exercised within the bounds the world has placed upon us. Were our kingdoms truly subject to our commands, what visions we might achieve! It is that belief which creates this madness within us, even as we know ourselves to be subjected as much as subjecting.

Thus, if my coronation was not by the hand of Paschal, but was performed by another as a matter of necessity, and I desired in all things that which was pleasing to the Lord, for surely the pope bore no objection to my humble person—if all these things were true, then we might say that I was crowned by the pope indeed. And if in later years men reported that it was Paschal who crowned me on that day, and I have taken no pains to correct them, it was for this very reason. Think not ill of me, for in anointing my husband six years earlier, the true pope had already bestowed his blessing on our reign, and therefore my crowning was acceptable before God.

After the passing of Whitsuntide, we departed the city almost immediately, having heard a report that Robert of Capua had marched his troops into the region of Campagna as far as the southern hills. Already they had laid siege to Piglio, burning and pillaging as they pleased. Within one or two days, they might stand before the city gates, and my husband did not wish to test his forces in battle, though most thought it certain that he could achieve victory.

"I am not here to crush the Normans, nor even the pope, but to safeguard my inheritance," he said, and these seemed to be words of wisdom. "If they come after us, we will behave as great lords and show them of what metal we are made, but we must not allow for the impression that we have come as invaders."

We made with all haste for the town of Sutri, which lies just north of Lake Bracciano. The town was well within Count Ptolemy's territory and this should have placed us out of danger, but when we were still a half day's march south of our destination, a messenger approached our train with all speed, carrying most unwelcome news.

"My lord! My lord emperor!" he cried out. "Where is the emperor?"

I had been lying in the carriage, mind in a state near dreaming, when these words pierced into my ears and woke me with sudden violence. I opened my eyes and immediately looked out toward the source of this tumult. Our progress had ceased and there was a whirl of men and riders moving about, consumed in hectic discourse. I could not make out their words, but it appeared that the men belonging to Count Ptolemy were preparing for a hasty departure, along with a contingent of those from Germany and the other imperial lands. I noticed the clerk, Burchard, passing by, and called out to him, "Burchard! Come hither!" When he merely turned to look in my direction, I yelled once again, "To me! Quickly!"

He was coming now upon his black horse, and I could see from the look in his eyes that he was in no mood to suffer interruptions. Still, interrupt I must.

"Yes, my lady?" he said upon arriving at the carriage.

"What is happening? I heard the messenger approach, and now there is chaos."

"Robert of Capua has been sighted not five miles from here and moving in our direction. Several of the men are breaking off to face him."

"What? I thought he was south of Rome!"

"So he was, but it appears that he has grown bolder in the past few days. We cannot always account for such things."

I looked once again at the men preparing for battle. "Who will go then?" I asked. "Is the emperor to lead the charge?"

"No, that would be just what the enemy desires. The Count of Tusculum is more than able to put off this attack, I think."

"You think or you hope?"

"Will all due respect, my lady, I should be about the emperor's business at the moment."

"Wait! What about Drogo?"

"Who?"

"Sir Drogo of Polwheile."

"I know not this Polwheile, but if you mean that giant of a knight, I believe he is joining the attack."

"No! He is of my household. I forbid him to go!"

"You forbid him to defend you? Forgive me, Your Highness, but it is the emperor's command."

I began to grow desperate at the thought that I might lose the one person with whom I shared the greatest affinity, the final link to the home of my youth. An unnatural fear now took hold of me: that were he to go to battle, he would surely be killed, and a part of myself should die with him. It was surely unreasonable, but I could not escape from that feeling.

I pushed open the door and strode out into the field. Burchard's eyes opened wide, so stunned was he by my action. I had it in my mind to argue further with him, when Chancellor David rushed up on his horse, intent on ending our conversation.

"Lady Mathilda! Return to the carriage!" When I merely looked at him, no doubt with a scowl upon my face and an oath forming in my mind, he called all the louder, "My lady! I command you to return to safety!"

"You would command me?" I stammered. "Upon what authority?"

"Upon the emperor's," he answered, placing himself between the clerk and me.

I could see in his manner that to disagree would yield nothing, so I made to walk back to the carriage.

"We mean no offense, Empress Mathilda!" the chancellor called out behind me.

"Ha! I have felt the offense, I assure you!" I shouted in their direction, then settled back into my seat just in time for the party to set off at a furious pace, pressing on to the north.

I looked across and saw the ladies sitting as they were before: braiding each other's hair and paying no heed to the clamor around them.

"Ah, to be ignorant and happy!" I thought to myself.

It was not until we reached Sutri that I learned the result. The Normans had fled upon seeing our forces. It appeared there was to be no battle after all. Best of all, Drogo had returned and pledged to me many times over that he would never place himself in such danger again unless it was of utmost necessity. With this promise, I was able to sleep as well as the Holy Father, which is to say that I woke up quite often and worried about the days ahead.

We dwelt for the remainder of that year in the territories to the north, Tuscany and Romagna. It was a pleasant time in which we visited several charming cities, among them Bologna, Volterra, and Pisa. Ah, Pisa! What a magnificent work was taking place there by the sea! We were able to view the new cathedral in all its glory, its rows of arches rising up from the ground, with marble walls both white and dark, and crowned by a magnificent dome. The men told us a craftsman named Rainaldo, though he was long since dead when we visited, began it. Even now the Pisans are building a baptistery that will be the envy of all Italy.

Throughout those months I was filled with concern for my husband. I wished to inquire after his condition, but I could not think of how to do so without giving offense. Still, I did witness a small improvement toward the end of the summer. At first I thought this was due to a lessening of his pain, but I soon learned that he had received news from the South: Pope Paschal was taken ill and now spent his days in bed, the sickness brought on by an excess of heat. It was said that his physicians believed he would not survive the autumn.

Yet survive he did, and as the weather grew cold once again, we had word that the pope was able to lift himself from his sickbed and say Mass. I harbored no ill will toward the old man, but I guessed the emperor's thinking: if Paschal were to die, it would present an opportunity for the situation to change swiftly. The work of a generation might be accomplished in the space of a week. It was just as Bruno had always told me: "At times, one must simply wait for a person to die."

Of course, no man could say whether a new pope, whoever he might be, would be more or less disposed to treat with the emperor. It would all depend on who was installed as Paschal's successor, and who was to install him. Doubtless Rome would command that its voice must be heard, as would the rest of the Gregorians, but the emperor would place upon them his own demands, along with all Christendom.

During the days of Advent, the pope was well enough to travel and perform his usual duties, accompanied by Peter Colonna and other nobles faithful to the papal court. The Pierleoni still held some territory within Rome itself, and soon we received a letter from Abbot Berald of Farfa that the pope had arrived in Trastevere with a new army.

"We are at a loss, for we can see no path forward that does not involve substantial peril for ourselves and our allies," he wrote. "All Rome seems to welcome them now with open arms. The prefect and consuls still hold Saint Peter's Church, but the rest of our possessions across the river have fallen. The engines of war are pointed toward Vatican Hill. The pope and his allies rest now in the fortress of Sant'Angelo. Be so good as to send us word of how you wish to proceed. The count and I are well-nigh desperate for some remedy."

"There is nothing that can be done at the moment," the emperor concluded, setting the parchment aside. "It would be unwise for us to return under the present circumstances, and even if I were to ride to their aid, it would take two or three days at the very least. We would not arrive in time to prevent them taking the basilica. Therefore, let us wait and see what comes of this. They may hold."

Then came the message that we both sought and feared. It was carried by one of the Frangipane men and arrived a few days later. I was not there when it was opened, but it did not take long for the news to spread throughout the camp.

The pope had died after all, never having made it out of the Castel Sant'Angelo. They were forced to bury him in the Lateran church rather than next to Saint Peter. That was surely a blow for some in the papal party, but any mourning for Paschal was of necessity quite brief. Within a few days, the cardinals would appoint a new leader, and my husband was intent that the imperial right should be respected. His forbears had often chosen those who were to sit upon the papal throne, and he was unwilling to surrender this privilege. The task would not be an easy one. With his dying breath, Paschal had charged his brethren to maintain their resistance against "the usurpation of the Germans." The hatred between the opposing sides was of such a nature that I doubted they could reach an agreement. Nevertheless, the emperor immediately rode south to influence the proceedings. It was January, and the air was very chill. I suspected that his reception there would be just as cold.

About a week after his departure, a messenger reached our position near Bologna. I had taken up many of the duties of the imperial court in my husband's absence, and on this day I was discussing a matter of local import with a jurist by the name of Iubaldus. As Philip of Ravenna and several of the others had joined Emperor Henry on his return to Rome, I relied heavily on Iubaldus and the remaining men of letters for instruction. We were sitting there in the *villa*—the name of which I cannot remember—and attempting to produce an accord between two landowners who were at odds. For myself, I cared not where either man placed his pigsty, but maintaining peace was fundamental. As we considered the matter, the rider from the South was brought into our presence and declared that he had news for us to hear.

"Is this news of the emperor?" I asked. "Has he made any progress?"

"Not as such, Your Grace," the messenger replied. "By the time he reached the city, the cardinals had already chosen Paschal's successor. I suppose we must now consider whether the emperor will abide by their decision or put forth a contender of his own."

"Who is it then? Who is the new pope?"

"Cardinal Giovanni da Gaeta, though he is called now by the title Gelasius II."

"The same Giovanni da Gaeta who was lately papal chancellor?"

"The very same."

Here was a great misfortune. You will remember, Daughter, that Cardinal Giovanni had employed frightful slanders against the emperor, and he was one of the leaders of the anti-imperial forces within the Church. It seemed that my husband had traded his adversary Paschal for an even sterner enemy. There was little hope of a peaceful solution now.

"What of the emperor then?" I asked Iubaldus. "He cannot approve of this choice."

"His Highness was not called to the synod, and thus played no role in the election process," he answered. "However, I believe he intends to challenge this decision by the cardinals. It is only right that the lord emperor, anointed of God, should play some part in all of this. I am sure that Bologna's own Irnerius will advise him well, as will the bishop of Braga."

"I hardly think the cardinals will listen to him," I countered. "You were not there the last time he attempted to deal with these people. I thought there might be blood shed right there upon the graves of the saints. It was a woeful thing to witness."

"Have faith, Your Highness," the messenger replied. "When last I saw the emperor, he was in good spirits."

"Is that so? Was there a goblet in his hand?"

Both men were clearly at a loss as to how they should respond, so I decided to cease all attempts at humor and bring an end to the discussion. My thoughts turned silently from one matter to another. "I must send word to Bruno and seek his counsel. I must check on the ladies to see if they have finished embroidering my new robes. I must find a way to make the pig farmers happy. I must write another letter to my husband, urging him to act with moderation."

As fate would have it, moderation was not the watchword of those in Rome. This incessant breaking apart would stop for no man. One of the Frangipane brothers had the gall to make the pope his prisoner, an act that would have left us all perplexed were it not already an established *strategema* of the imperial party. In any case, fortunate Gelasius escaped with the help of the Roman citizens, and he held out for a short time before

Henry's forces drove him out of the city toward the beginning of March.

Gelasius made for his native town of Gaeta in the South, while the emperor declared the papal election null and void. Now was the time for the bishop of Braga to be rewarded for his acts of fidelity: the emperor had him appointed as pope in place of Gelasius, and the former Maurice Bourdin was declared Pope Gregory VIII. It remained to be seen which of the two men could command public support, not only in Rome, but also in the lands from north to south and east to west.

Having accomplished what he set out to do, Emperor Henry left Gregory VIII on Saint Peter's throne and returned north once again. Despite all that had taken place, I was pleased to hear that he should be arriving in a few days, for life had become rather dull in his absence. With the larger part of the court following the emperor to Rome, I had been left in Romagna to endure the long days of waiting. It was some comfort to have both Drogo and Altmann there with me, but I found that by this point I had grown weary of our Italian adventure. Were it not for my concern regarding the uprisings in Germany, I might have requested to return long beforehand.

"You may look for my arrival by the beginning of May, and possibly sooner," the emperor wrote. "I must stop to make a grant unto the abbey of Farfa; the least I can do to reward Abbot Berald. Then I shall make the final turn north. I must thank you for your letters, which have been a blessing to me in this time of crisis."

I could not think what he meant by this last sentence, for my kind addresses had surely been joined with words of caution, for which I was certain he could not be very thankful. Even so, I hoped that what he said was true, and that he did look forward to being with me once again. I knew as well that the longer we remained apart, the longer we would remain without children, and having entered my seventeenth year, I felt I could no longer put off this duty without causing rumors to form. Then there was the issue of the emperor's health, which I feared he would not attend to without my continual exhortation.

But I have not yet mentioned the worst news of that spring! You see, Emperor Henry V had up to that point been able to escape the ban of excommunication on account of the agreement he made with Pope Paschal II. However, Gelasius II had made no such promise, and he took the first opportunity afforded him to once again proclaim the *anathema* against the former bishop of Braga, now known as Antipope Gregory VIII. In addition, he did what Paschal had not been able to accomplish, proclaiming the emperor himself to be an excommunicate, cast out of God's holy Church.

My husband was now in the same position as his father, even as Bruno had warned; and as for me, I was the wife of the most hated man in Europe. Under such circumstances, one is tempted to declare, in the words of the ancients, "*O tempora! O mores!*"

Word came to us that I was to receive my husband at the same *villa* near Bologna where I had resided for the past few months. This pleased me, as I had grown fond of my new home, having found that city to be a true jewel of Italy. Scholars travel from all the Christian kingdoms to attend the *studium*, the greatest school of law yet created. In every part of the city, one might find French, English, Portuguese, or German pupils. I met one man who had traveled from the land of the Poles and another from Constantinople. For the most part, they preferred to remain with those of their own tongue, but there was also intercourse between the nations.

Once or twice I found myself in Bologna in the morning hours and marveled at the sight of hundreds of scholars walking to and fro, some with bundles of parchment in their arms, others with a basket full of writing instruments, and all looking most intent on their purpose. Tutor and student alike took part in this daily dance. I wished to attend one of those lectures, though the discussion would likely have ventured into subjects far beyond my knowledge.

Certain of those lecturers achieved a degree of fame, none more so than Irnerius, the lawyer whom my husband had sought out upon our first arrival. There was no one more expert in the laws of ancient Rome and their application to the present day. The clerk who served me during that time, Iubaldus, was one of his students and a tribute to his master. It was he who shared with me a secret that I will now pass on to you: no work of literature can ever be accomplished on an empty stomach. Thus it was his established policy to conduct much of his work in houses with a good supply of wine and other morsels to satisfy the appetite.

Have I mentioned the towers that seemed to line every street? The canals that so skillfully allotted water to every home? Of such things I could speak for hours, but now is not the time. I will simply say that I wish even now that I could enter those gates once again.

One day before my husband arrived, I was brought down by the same familiar illness that I had experienced several times since traveling south. The affliction was of a feeble sort, though it did leave me with hindered breath, an unending cough, and above all, weariness. I was determined to set this aside and join the others on the day of Emperor Henry's arrival, but unhappily it took some effort to rise up from my pallet and walk, so to speak. Thus the feast was well under way by the time I was dressed and ready to attend. As I moved to take my seat on the dais, I noticed that though the members of the court seemed to revel in the dance and drinks, those at the head table were more subdued. They all rose to their feet as I walked by, even the emperor, who, rather than waiting for a servant, moved himself to help me to my seat. This small kindness was most welcome. Perhaps he had missed me after all. Indeed, he seemed to confirm this when he said, "I am pleased to see you, Lady Mathilda. I heard that you were taken to bed yesterday, but I am glad that you are up and about. Do you have a fever?"

"No, none at all," I replied honestly, for despite my discomfort, I felt neither the rising heat nor the harsh chill. "Let us speak rather of Your Grace. How was your journey from Rome?"

"It might have been better had not that fool, Gelasius, set his will against us. I declare he makes it his goal in life to vex me."

"Give it time, Your Highness. Soon the Church will unite behind Pope Gregory VIII, and there will be no more talk of excommunication," said Philip of Ravenna. "The reign of that usurper Gelasius will not last the summer. Already I have heard rumors that he is unwell. This is surely the Lord's judgment."

"I fully agree," Irnerius said. "He may have the support of the cardinals, but all men of the law see the justice of your cause. I will undertake to prove the righteousness of your actions, which are in line with imperial law from Constantine to the present."

I felt that both men failed to consider the array of forces lined up against the emperor, but I reasoned that it was better to say nothing about the matter. I had begun to eat the roasted hare that had been placed in front of me when my husband set his hand upon my shoulder.

"Mathilda?" he said in a hushed tone.

"Yes, my lord?"

He seemed to waver for a moment, as if searching for the proper words. Then he continued, "How have you been these last few days? How did you take the news?"

This was beyond his usual level of concern, and I was touched by it. "I assure you, there is no need to worry. I admit that the news of Gelasius's declaration did cause my spirit distress at first, but as we saw with your father, such things may be reversed. I have every confidence that this will work out for the best."

Now I was the one expressing more hope than was warranted, but I could not speak harshly to my husband, who in any case already had most of Christendom calling him to repentance.

"You misunderstand me," he replied. "I was not speaking of that."

"Oh? Well, if you want to know, I promise you I am in good health. I have committed no sin that merits great penance. I am a bit tired, and I will miss the liveliness of Bologna, but such things must pass in time."

Evidently I had still not guessed at the emperor's meaning, for he sighed and even appeared somewhat grieved by my answer. I began to fear that there was some calamity of which I was not yet aware.

"What is it?" I asked him. "What have you heard? Have the Saxons risen up again? Did something happen to one of my ladies? I know it cannot be Drogo, for I saw him not five minutes ago." I then lowered my voice further and asked, "This is not to do with your . . . problem, is it?"

"It is none of that."

"Then you must tell me, or else I shall go mad! Nothing could be worse than what I fear."

"Maybe it would be better if we stepped into another room."

"Very well," I answered, now certain that something terrible had befallen us all, or he would have spoken the words there and then.

He took me by the hand and had started to lead me from the banquet hall when the chancellor stopped us and bowed.

"Empress Mathilda!" he said. "I was most sorry to hear of the death of your mother, the queen of England. Her godliness and generosity were well known within the empire. I trust you will let us know if there is anything that you require."

The words he spoke washed over me. Dead? It could not be true! But yes, he had said, "the death of your mother." Was this some mistake? I had received no word from England. Surely such news would have been sent to me directly. No, he must have her confused with someone else. Could it really be? I looked to my husband to belie the chancellor's comments. He made no sign, but instead seemed to look on me as one would a wounded animal that cannot be saved. It was those eyes rather than the words themselves that struck me in the belly and robbed me of breath.

So it was true, then. The queen of England was dead. My own mother was dead. I could feel the heat rising now from my toes even to my head, and I sank to my knees there on the cold stone floor, the emperor and his chancellor both reaching to brace me. The waves of pain began to hit me, one after the other, in swift succession.

I heard a voice saying, "Did she not know? Oh dear! What have I done?" Another seemed to reply, "You idiot! Can you not see how she suffers?" I heeded them not. The pain seemed to fill my very eyes, or perhaps it was the tears longing to break free.

Then I spoke, or rather something inside me spoke on my behalf: "Away! Get me away! I cannot be here."

Without another word the emperor drew me up into his arms and brought me into a side room, shutting the door behind us. There were none but a few servants there. I started to cry with such a force as I have seldom felt before or since. No polite tears were these. My spirit split open and my entire body writhed with the weight of sorrow. From somewhere inside me, howls of pain were released, and I was ever so glad to be away from the feast at that moment.

He laid me down upon a low bench and said to those present, "All of you must leave. The empress is in distress!" I was scarcely aware of any of them, but I can only assume that they fled as ants at the sight of a falling stone. He then returned to me and slowly wrapped me in an embrace. Not a word was uttered between the two of us, except that I might have yelled, "Oh God! Oh God have mercy on me!" And there was nothing to be done except to remain there as I continued to empty myself of that despair. Later on I would come to understand the service he did me that day, but in the moment there was naught but the pain. My thoughts continued to spin wildly, and when I was finally able to bring myself to reflect upon what had happened, it was in a state of lamentation. In the silence of my own mind, I cried out to my mother in words that seemed to spring forth from the deep recesses of my spirit.

"You were the light of my life, the beacon calling me home. Now the dread hours grow cold, my soul as empty as the barren woman's arms. What am I without you? Lord Jesus have mercy on me! The one who loved me like no other is gone . . . like the blooms of spring, or the leaves of autumn. That bond, once severed at birth, now torn by death. My mother, my queen is gone."

CHAPTER EIGHTEEN

May 1165
Rouen, Normandy

I t has been many years since I glimpsed anything worthy of praise in a mirror. I can still remember the first time I caught sight of a gray hair. I was merely twenty-five years old and rather upset that the signs of age should have appeared so soon. It was not long before they began to multiply, much to my dismay, and by the time I reached five and forty years, the ashen strands prevailed. I have heard that age brings with it an increase in both wisdom and honor, but if I possess any such wisdom, it has been gained in a manner none would prefer: through the endurance of a thousand bitter hardships. Likewise, if I appear honorable, it is due in no small part to that general fear that youth has of the aged, seeing them as harbingers of their own assured demise.

No, I shall find no solace in the attainment of years. There is an ache in my bones that will not cease. At the mere thought of labor, I often find myself tired. I cannot read the words on the page as well as I ought, for an impenetrable darkness has slowly crept in, and no power of man can relieve it. More than all, I am daily tried by the memory of those now gone and the things I have allowed to slip from my grasp.

Thus, my daughter, I must advise you, heed well the words of the ancient king Solomon: "Remember now your Creator in the days of your youth, while the evil days come not, nor the years approach wherein you shall say, 'I have no pleasure in them': while the sun is not dark, nor the light, nor the moon, nor the stars, nor the clouds return after the rain; when the keepers of the house shall tremble, and the strong men shall bow themselves, and the grinders shall cease because they are few, and they wax dark that look out by the windows; and the doors shall be shut without by the base sound of the grinding, and he shall rise up at the voice of the bird, and all the daughters of singing shall be abased."

But enough of this fretting! Allow me to recount what took place the day before last, when Queen Eleanor paid us a visit. Ah, gracious Eleanor! The smallest measure of that grace might prove as strong as that of a hundred lesser maids and matrons. Her grace is of a peculiar kind that lends itself most readily to those who presume to flatter it. Then again, I suppose that is not so peculiar.

Perhaps you think me too harsh. After all, is not her beauty the stuff of dreams, the muse that inspired a thousand songs? She is most comely, most accomplished, and, dare I say, most fruitful. She cannot but enter a room without summoning the glances of men and women alike. Of her temper less has been written, but suffice it to say that it would be better for a man to stand in the light of her face than sink beneath her shadow. Yes, the bestowal of her grace is a prize for which the bravest knight might hazard life and limb.

I have yet to speak of her chief virtue: the fields and rivers of Aquitaine. That duchy, which many a king has coveted, is a dowry without compare in my lifetime. Whether it was for this that my son sought her for his bride, or the innumerable qualities that I have already expounded, or if he even had much choice in the matter—for these questions, I shall never have an answer. I know well my own suspicions, but the matter is accomplished, and there we find an end of it. When she favored us with her presence, it was a source of jubilation throughout the town. I could hear their calls in the streets. "God save you, Queen Eleanor! God bless you, Queen Eleanor!" They strained to catch a glimpse of her.

For myself, the queen was of less interest than those who traveled with her: my most beloved grandchildren. Here I cannot fault the good lady, for she has more than answered the calling placed upon her. You might say that she breeds like the rabbit in spring, and with as little trouble in childbirth as any I have ever seen. One by one, she placed them in my arms: William, Henry, Mathilda, Richard, and Geoffrey. The first one passed from this world before entering his fourth year, but all the rest are as hale as one could desire. Such joy they have brought me in old age!

Now the queen's belly is full again, and she makes her way south to the home of her ancestors to give birth to the newest prince or princess. Thus they came to me from across the Channel—my own flesh and blood—for a brief visit. I would have more such occasions, even if they must be tempered by the inconstant humors of gracious Eleanor.

On the morning before last, after the king had departed once again for England, I made my way with some difficulty to the palace on the other side of the river. As you know, I prefer to spend my days at my own abode nearer the abbey of Notre-Dame-du-Pré, or in the lodgings provided for me within the monastery itself. However, Queen Eleanor insisted that our meeting take place in the palace where both she and her husband held their own private rooms. I must say that the adornments were not to my liking, being as they were in the style of the queen's native land and a bit too pompous for my taste. Still, I would have endured far worse to see those children.

We stood there in the great hall; myself, the newly installed archbishop of Rouen, my trusted friend Abbot Roger de Bailleul of Bec Abbey, Archdeacon Lawrence, and the rest of the attendants, among them dear Adela. In came the long-awaited visitors: Queen Eleanor, so plainly with child that I wondered why she had delayed her lying-in, and the two children with her, their golden-red tresses calling to mind my own mother.

Here was little Mathilda, barely nine years of age, clinging to her mother with one hand and a toy with the other. There was Richard, grown bolder since the departure of his older brother. I smiled to see their faces, such blessings from God on high. I only prayed that they had not forgotten mine.

"Greetings, my queen," says Archbishop Rotrou, lord of the city. "We praise the Lord for your return to Rouen. It has been too long." He bows deeply, then glances upward to mark its effect.

The queen responds in her native tongue. "*Qui es-ce? Je n'ai jamais vu cet homme dans ma vie! Ne me dites pas qu'il est le nouvel archevêque!*"

Guessing her general meaning, I offer, "Your Highness, this is indeed the new archbishop of Rouen. He was elected one month ago."

"*Cet homme?*" she says with some disdain, then looks the man up and down as if to search out some hidden quality that she might have missed. "Hum. I suppose he shall do."

"*Merci, ma dame,*" he replies, apparently content with this smallest commendation.

"Here, let us go into the other room. I have presents for the children," I tell her.

"Presents? Presents!" Richard cries with delight. Before I have a chance to embrace the boy, he runs off in search of the rumored gifts, almost trampling a small cat that happens across their path. Feeble thing! It leaps out of the way of danger, its knotted fur attempting to rise to twice its normal height.

"Where did you come from?" I ask the poor creature. Its yellow eyes provide no answer as it cowers in the corner. As I have not seen it here before, I conclude that it must have made its way up from the kitchens.

Little Mathilda stoops down and extends a hand toward the animal, which first sniffs and then licks her fingers in turn. When she is sure she has gained its trust, she lifts the cat into her arms and strokes its fur until it seems perfectly contented. She then becomes aware of my presence once again.

"Grandmother, may I have a kiss?" little Mathilda asks.

"Why, of course you can, my sweet! You shall have all the kisses you desire."

Upon this declaration, she finally lets go of the animal and hops into my arms. I cannot bear her weight as I once did, but I hold her close and rock her back and forth.

"There is one who will always love you, I think," the queen states, walking slowly in the direction of Richard, who has now discovered the carved wood swords awaiting him and is mounting an attack upon a nearby table. "Richard! *Arrête ça à la fois!*"

"Can I tell you something?" asks the young one in my arms.

"Anything you wish."

"I lost another tooth!"

"Did you really? It fell out?"

"No, Geoffrey pulled it out."

"What? You let him do that?"

"Yes, because it was just hanging there," she explains. "And he asked me if I wanted him to pull it, and I said yes, because it hurt whenever I ate food. But mother was upset, for it bled on everything."

"Perhaps next time you should let it fall out on its own," I advise her. "Come now! We should join the others."

As we walk together, I cannot but see the humor in the over-large Eleanor's attempting to herd her son as one might a sheep. Little Mathilda alone is well behaved, standing at attention by her mother's side.

"Mothers and daughters!" I think to myself. "A few years from now, she might not be so pliant."

The door opens and it is Adela, come to fetch the children away. Gracious Eleanor seems pleased to have a moment of rest, and reclines on a small couch set out for her. I settle for an available chair.

"So," I begin, "I hope your days have been passing pleasantly."

"How could they when I am in such a state?" she complains, rubbing her enlarged belly. "I tell you, this summer has been far too hot, and my feet, they are so . . . so . . . *enflé*. You understand? *Enflé*."

As it so happens, I do not know the word, but her meaning is clear.

"They are swollen?"

"Yes, this. Ah, it is so hot in here! *Sainte mère!* I fear I shall faint."

"Allow me to help," I reply, moving to open the windows. A slight wind enters the room, displacing some parchment that lands next to the queen.

"Here is luck!" she responds, and starts using it to fan herself. "You know, they say when a mother is always warm, it means she will have a boy, but my doctor already read it in the stars. He will be a strong boy—I know it."

"Should I call for some water?" I ask her.

"Water? *Qu'est-ce que c'est?* No, tell them to bring me wine!"

"Of course."

I step into the passage and call for one of the servants. Together we wait in silence for his arrival. Well, mostly in silence.

"I do hope this is a good wine from France and not that terrible drink they make in England," she says. "Always they try to make me believe it is wine, but I know better."

"Well, thank God for that!" I mutter, but she does not hear me, so lost is she in her own thoughts.

Finally the cupbearer arrives and pours us each a measure of his wares, which, fortunately, the queen deems acceptable. He departs as quickly as he came, leaving us once again in solitude. Without warning she broaches the subject that I had long suspected was the true reason for her visit.

"The king is too terrible to me! Not that I fault your ladyship, for I know there is only so much you can do, but he does not treat me as a man ought." She seems to choke slightly on this last word, producing a sound more like *caught*. Her recovery, however, is swift. "Do you know he used to worship me? I was his beloved Eleanor! Now he has taken up with some new . . . *putain!*" Her brows rise as she pronounces the word, then she helpfully translates it for me. "Whore!"

"Ah . . . I had heard a rumor, but I hoped it was not true."

"Hum hum . . . And while I am carrying his child!"

"I understand your concern, but is it not common . . . ," I begin, then pause when she casts me a glance worthy of Beelzebub himself.

"Is what common?" she responds, stressing each word.

"Lady Eleanor, you must know that kings often behave in this manner. I make no claims as to the righteousness of such actions, but surely you cannot be surprised!"

"Of course! I am not a child! He will lay with whatever whore he likes. I know this."

"Then why do you come to me?"

"Because, Queen Mother, he does not love me anymore, you see? Do not feign confusion. We know when a man lays with us, and we know when he loves us. They are not one and the same. What upsets me is not that he should go between some other woman's legs. You understand me. My first marriage was without love, but I believed that . . . that the king . . ."

"That he loved you?"

"Yes." She says the word almost in a whisper, the tears now becoming evident. "Now I see it is not I that he desired. He only wants the Aquitaine!"

"I pray this is not true," I tell her, but as she begins to weep, I sense that there is little I can do. I place a hand upon her shoulder and gently rub until she raises her head to speak again.

"Tell me, Queen Mother, do you think that love can endure when two are bound together, as are kings and queens, or do you think it must be free like a bird?"

"I cannot think why you should ask me."

"I will make him love me again; you will see. When I give him a son, he will love me again."

There is a desperate note in what she says, and I find myself pitying this woman who has so often irked me. Slowly I draw her hands together and raise them to my lips, placing a kiss upon them.

"Lady Eleanor," I respond, "I bid you take care. It may not be possible to create love in a man who has set his mind against it. However, I pray that you will succeed in this your quest, for I should hate to see any child of mine so unhappy."

"*Abeille! Abeille!*" she suddenly cries out, making for the other end of the room. "A bee!"

"Where?"

"Over there! It comes through the window. Kill it!"

"Perhaps if we wait it will leave of its own . . ."

"Kill it!"

As luck would have it, the bee did leave of its own accord before I was able to make an attempt on its life. Then came the demands that the windows be closed, death by heat apparently being less frightful than death by bee.

Such was our conversation. The queen has now departed for her lying-in. She has arranged to rest at her castle in Poitiers, but I cautioned her not to travel so far in her current state. I think perhaps she will stop in Angers, which is much closer. Let it be said then: the toils of a mother never cease, even in old age.

I still possess the letter that arrived for me upon that dreadful day at Canossa, written by the hand of Roger of Salisbury. It was hardly the first time he served as my bearer of ill tidings, nor would it be the last. Even now, I cannot read it without shedding a tear.

To the most glorious Empress Mathilda, queen of the Romans, Roger of Salisbury imparts the following message.

It is with great torment of spirit that I must inform you of the passing of our most beloved Queen Mathilda, mother to Your Highness and to all her subjects, who departed this world upon the first of May. The people mourn her as one of their own, for here was a great lady and one who shall be continually remembered. I am aware that this news must be most unwelcome to you, my lady: you who were always in her thoughts and prayers. I have no words to pass on by way of comfort except those set down by one Henry of Huntingdon in the household of the bishop of Lincoln, who is now at court and in the king's favor.

"Successes did not make her happy, nor did troubles make her sad: troubles brought a smile to her, successes fear. Beauty did not produce weakness in her, nor power pride: she alone was both powerful and humble, both beautiful and chaste. The first day of May, at nighttime as we reckon it on earth, took her away, to enter into endless day."

Virgil himself could not have writ a more seemly epitaph. I pray you now, seek out some boon of comfort within the land in which you now reside. Rest assured, for the monks of Saint Albans shall say a thousand Masses for her soul, though some may doubt she needs them. Eternity is sweet for those who fear the Lord.

These words were all I was to receive in regard to my mother. I had for a short time hoped that she might have left me one final note, whether or not it was of any significance. Alas, it was not to be.

A strange feeling came over me in the days and weeks that followed. Here was my life made hollow and cold, but all around me continued as it always had. Every hour I passed a hundred faces, each of them indifferent to my grief. And why should they not have been? Who was Mathilda of Scotland to them? An eminent person, surely, but she was not their sovereign. They knew little of her and cared even less. It was as if they lived in a different world from me—one not visited by tragedy—and the sorrow I felt every hour forbade me to enter that sphere of hope. Even so, there were three persons who sought to share in my grief. The first, it can hardly surprise you to hear, was Drogo. The second was Archbishop Bruno, who wrote from Trier to profess his anguish upon hearing the news, for he was not ignorant of the depths of affection between me and those I had left behind.

Last was my own husband, the emperor, who sought to put me at ease in any way possible. He gave orders to the ladies to grant me both privacy and consolation as the situation required. He commanded those in the kitchen to produce an array of food and drink in the hope that something might tempt me. He sent his musicians to play for me, his scribes to read to me, and his chaplain, Hartmann, to pray with me. While most of these attempts failed to grant me any lasting relief, I was nevertheless glad to see how he provided for me.

Sadly, matters in Germany had taken an ill turn. Henry's nephew, the Duke of Swabia, wrote that the rebels were gaining ground as the absence of their rightful lord grew overlong. The duke had been appointed along with the count palatine to maintain order, but he now feared that he would not be able to do so much longer. The rebels of Saxony were on the attack once again, and the emperor had no choice but to return to the North with as many men as he could afford to bring.

While the lands of the late *contessa* had been pacified for the time being, unrest seemed to fill the very air, and the enmity of Pope Gelasius was beyond doubt. Therefore it was decided that I, the empress, must remain in the South according to the emperor's pleasure, the visible symbol of imperial authority. Though I was honored by the faith he placed in me, I could not help but be afeard at the prospect of such a task.

I remember well the morning he set out. There was a mist about the plain that morning, and the dew still clung to each blade of grass. The hem of my gown grew wet as I walked across the field to bid him farewell. It is strange that I should remember such a small thing, and yet I cannot relate on what I supped three days past, is it not? Yet that is the way of things.

The emperor's groom was making ready his horse, fixing the saddle upon its broad back and feeding the animal a few last morsels before its long journey was to begin. Through the mist I could just see the emperor pacing toward us, slipping his fingers into his riding gloves, and muttering something to no one in particular.

"God save the emperor!" I called out to him, and this caught his attention.

"My lady! I did not see you. You should still be in bed."

"You are to ride now?"

"Yes, we must, and without delay. Frederick says the rebels are likely to march on the Rhineland, and while I have great faith in his abilities, I fear that our foes may find more allies than we should wish there. Perhaps I have stayed away too long. The people grow restless without their king, you see. They start to forget to whom their fealty is owed. All too easily, any man who seizes the opportunity might take them in. But we must not let that happen."

"Of course. I understand. Yet I am sorry to see you go."

With a wave of his hand, the emperor dismissed his groom, taking the reins and leading the horse toward the rest of the assembly. I followed beside him, and for the moment he did not send me away, but we simply walked in silence.

"My lord," I finally said, "I am worried about your health. Now that you are leaving, there will be none with you except the physician who know of your malady."

"My 'malady,' as you call it, is no cause for concern," he interrupted, his voice taking on a much different tone. Having foreseen this response, I continued as before.

"You are in pain; I see it daily. Though you have gone to great lengths to conceal it, and I have never spoken a word to a living soul, I fear that without the proper care your condition may worsen. If you would but—"

"Stop this!" he commanded. "It is true, I have trusted you with a great deal. I leave you here as my regent. I have granted you all the honors that are your due. Indeed, I have made allowances for you on several occasions when others might have objected, but here I must draw the line! Lest you forget, you are a woman, and it is not fit for you to speak of such things. Now, if I tell you there is no cause for concern, then that is God's truth, or do you doubt your emperor?"

For a moment I made no reply, for what was there to say? If I said I doubted him, I would surely merit an even harsher rebuke. If I sought merely to still his anger, I would deny the truth.

"My lord," I finally said, "may I speak plainly?"

He gave out a forced laugh that seemed to mock rather than encourage. "Since when have you ever sought permission before speaking plainly? I have never known you to do anything else."

"A serious fault, I am sure. Please, stop a moment if you will."

Begrudgingly, he halted his progress and turned to face me. His eyes seemed to cast censure on my words before they had been spoken.

"It is true, sir, I am a woman; that I have always been, and I always shall be. But I am also your wife, bone of your bone and flesh of your flesh. To what end did we join hands before God? Am I to share your bed and not your confidence?"

I was becoming quite upset, yet he allowed me to continue.

"It has been several years now, and still I am not with child. It is a wonder that there has not been more gossip at court. I know what they say of me: 'That pitiful Mathilda! She cannot get the emperor a son. She has all the fertility of a gaunt old maid.' You see, it is not you alone that this question touches. Tell me, will we ever be able to have children, or do I hope in vain? That night when I ran to fetch the physician, I saw something in your eyes I had never seen there before, even when you faced down the full force of your adversaries: I saw fear. So as much as you might seek to deny it, tell me what is the matter! I am your wife!"

For a moment my breath continued to labor, so frantic had my speech been. I struggled to brace myself for the answer that was bound to come. My husband paused for a moment, casting his eyes down toward the ground while evidently deciding how to respond. Then came his reply, which was rather different than I had imagined.

"The truth is, I don't know," he said softly. "I cannot tell you, because I do not know. It is possible that the disease will go away, and just as possible that it will continue. There has been no change of late. The truth is, I fear . . . I fear . . ." His voice seemed to trail off into the distance along with his gaze.

"What do you fear?"

He met my eyes again. "I fear that I might have . . . No, I cannot say, but I have heard that such things are often the judgment of God, and there are some that would say I am owed only wrath."

"And do you set store by such comments?"

"No! That is to say, I am not certain. The will of God is a curious thing. Who am I to question his judgments? Yet, I truly believe . . . I must believe that he has placed me here for a purpose. Mathilda, you do not understand, because you are not of our race, but Germania! The idea of it, the promise of it—I see now that God has appointed my rule for this hour, to build up this kingdom to stand on its own, free from meddling foreigners. You will always have this in England, I think, for the sea grants you its protection. But for me to do that, here and now, for my own people—what greater legacy could I leave not only to our children, but to all the children who are yet to be?"

I sensed that we had long since passed the original subject of conversation, but I was not perturbed. Rather I stood in awe at the words I was hearing. I felt that for once I had been permitted to enter a world that was once closed to me, and to know my husband for who he truly was.

"I have not heard you speak in that way before," I responded. "So if you say that God has appointed you, then why should you fear his curse?"

He let out a sigh and admitted, "Because after all, I am still a man. I saw what became of my father. He wrestled with God and man, and the cost proved too high."

Around us the men were making their final preparations for departure. I sensed that the time for discussion was at an end.

"I shall pray for you, Husband, both day and night, that the Lord will grant you victory against the rebels."

"And I shall pray that he grants you peace," he concluded. He then mounted his horse with an ease I could hardly have matched and said, "Farewell, Lady Mathilda! May we meet again in a happier hour!"

"Wait!" I called out. I reached under my cloak for the purse attached to my girdle. Within its folds, my fingers retrieved that most prized of all my possessions: the amber stone.

"Here," I said to him. "Carry this with you. It will bring you good fortune."

"What is it?" he asked, turning it over in his hand and examining it. "Is that a dead fly?"

"A moth; a very special kind of moth that a friend gave me long ago. I wish for you to keep it until we meet again. It might grant me some solace."

"Well, as you wish then," he said, placing the curious object within his own pocket. "To the North!"

His horse galloped eagerly into the distance, its form soon veiled by the last of the morning mist.

"Until we meet again," I whispered.

Alas, poor Gelasius! Truly, I pitied him, though he was my husband's deadliest enemy. For no sooner had Gelasius ascended the throne of Saint Peter than he suffered one calamity after another. Few indeed are the bishops of Rome who have been vexed with such an ill-favored tenure.

I have told how Gelasius fled from Rome almost as soon as the staff was placed in his hand. In July of that year, the pope succeeded in entering the city once again under the protection of his Norman allies, but he failed to contain the Frangipane

menace. When he was at last bold enough to enter their territory
and celebrate the Lord's Mass at the Church of Saint Praxedes,
he was rewarded with an armed uprising. Forced once again
into exile, Gelasius elected this time to go north rather than
south. With the help of the friendly bishops of Lombardy and
Savoy, he was able to escape first to Marseille and then on to
Avignon, greeted all the while by throngs of people delighted to
welcome him. Most eager of all was the archbishop of Vienne,
Guy of Burgundy. He was chief among the sons of Gregory, and
through his influence the natural animosity of the French and
Burgundians toward the empire was given new life. It was this
same Guy who had first announced the order of excommunication against the emperor.

There in Vienne, Pope Gelasius made ready for a general
council that would attempt to settle the controversy over investiture once and for all. He made for Cluny in the depths of winter,
there to garner support for his cause, knowing full well that he
would find an immense supply of friends. It was to be his last
journey. On the fourth before the kalends of February, in the
year of our Lord 1119, Gelasius breathed his last, having been
pope for just over a year.

If anyone in the emperor's camp took comfort from this
news, it was not to last. Only nine cardinals were in Cluny at the
time of the pope's demise, yet they determined that it was best
to move forward with the selection of a successor without their
brothers in Rome, a choice that was bound to cause some vexation. There could have been no more favorable set of circumstances for the archbishop of Vienne, who was elected within the
week and rechristened Pope Calixtus II. It was a strange choice
of name, for after all, did not Hippolytus refer to the first pope
of that title as "a man crafty in evil, and versatile in deceit, as-
piring to the episcopal throne"? An obscure quote, to be sure,
but one that an army of imperial clerks was more than able to

uncover. Such pearls we must treasure, but I doubt Calixtus II would have been amused by the comparison.

By the following summer, I was back in the emperor's company, my Italian adventure having come to an end. Leaving Tuscany and Lombardy behind us, we took the Great Saint Bernard Pass through the mountains and arrived near that most familiar of sites: the River Rhine. My husband remained in those days within that region which had granted him the strongest support and contained many of the hereditary lands of his family. He could not venture up into Saxony without being attacked, and even in the South he was locked in a battle of wills with the archbishop of Mainz, Adalbert. Yes, the very same Adalbert who had been restored to the imperial bosom before our departure for Italy had now returned to his old ways, crafting infinite designs to enrich himself and the rest of the House of Saarbrücken by seizing imperial territories under some pretense of legality.

Of late Adalbert had allied himself with one Kuno, cardinal bishop of Praeneste and papal legate. They had convened a synod in Fritzlar the summer before, in which they proclaimed the emperor's excommunication—that which was announced by Pope Gelasius—within the Kingdom of Germany. Whatever love might have remained between the emperor and his former chancellor before this incident was now a thing of the past.

Despite this, not all the news was bad. Bruno of Trier had reclaimed his place as the emperor's chief counselor and came to visit us often. If poor health prevented this, he would send some message by the hand of his servant, Herman. When the emperor was forced to attend the Reichstag at Tibur, there to answer the charges of the German nobles, it was Bruno's counsel that allowed him to walk away strengthened.

Ever since Emperor Henry's return from the South, the archbishop of Trier had slowly endeavored to turn the royal mind toward peace. Both sides agreed that the conflicts—both between emperor and pope and between emperor and nobles—had gone on far too long. The lords in particular yearned for an end to bloodshed and a more stable future. Having failed to achieve a resolution on his own terms, Henry V now sensed that he would need to make peace with Pope Calixtus in order to bring his own vassals under control.

This would not be easy, for Calixtus had stood in firm opposition to the emperor even before he ascended the throne of Saint Peter, and it was clear that he did not intend to yield in regard to investiture. Nevertheless, the emperor had little choice; he had seen how the papal *anathema* had destroyed his father. Therefore, he sent word to the papal party that he would receive such persons as His Holiness wished to send to the town of Straßburg, there to settle an accord.

Straßburg sits upon an isle near the Rhine, in the region between the Alps, the Vogesen hills, and that land which the Germans call Schwarzwald, the "black forest." On account of its position, that city saw many a traveler come and go: ships carried wares up or down the river, while merchants' carts moved east and west in search of buyers. Bruno had lectured me about such places, which were often the subject of dispute between lords and kingdoms.

There we made our home for several days while awaiting the arrival of the pope's ambassadors. The summer had drawn to a close, and the storks had long since abandoned their high perches to make their winter travels. Where they flew, no man could say, but they always returned with the break of spring. With the birds no longer among us, a different kind of visitor, whose fidelity was far more in doubt, made its entrance through the city gates and arrived at our abode about midday.

His Holiness saw fit to send but two men: our old familiar Abbot Pontius of Cluny, and the bishop of Châlons, William of Champeaux. The bishop was a renowned scholar of both logic and rhetoric. He had made his reputation in the realm of theology and founded Saint Victor's Abbey before being called to the office of bishop. Having established their legacies with the Church, both men sought now to do it an even greater service by performing a miracle of arbitration that would free Christendom from the dispute over investiture and lay the foundation for a more peaceful era.

Thus I found myself sitting at the feast with the emperor on one side and the pope's ambassadors on the other. As always, the emperor's nephews enjoyed their prime position next to him, and with a hundred other magnates seeking their place at the high table, I was nowhere near the person with whom I most wished to speak: Bruno of Trier. Almost an hour passed before I was finally able to excuse myself and move in his direction. I found him already in conversation with a man whom I did not recognize, so I assumed he was one of the papal party. When the archbishop was finally made aware of my presence, he and his companion both stood and made their addresses.

"Most gracious empress!" Bruno said with a smile. "How may I be of service?"

"Peace, my lord! I have not come to harry you, but merely to talk."

"Well, then you had better take a seat," he replied, making room on the wood bench. "We did not think to be entertained by a queen tonight."

"Oh, I am afraid I don't have much to entertain. But who is your fellow here?"

"This is Karl of Worms. As you can see, he is a man of the cloth, but he also attracts many students. He is under Adalbert's jurisdiction, but given the current circumstances, I have been overseeing his labors and providing counsel as it is needed."

"You are of our party then, sir? You are for the emperor?" I asked.

"If you mean that I respect his right to rule and submit myself to his decrees insofar as they are in accordance with the Holy Scriptures, then yes, I am," he replied, "but I prefer to spend more time with my flock or my students."

"How very dull!" I said in jest. "I am surprised you and the archbishop can keep company with each other. He will preach to you about the merits of power. In fact, I believe he lives for it. He has never met a *strategema* that he did not like."

Again the priest spoke. "Perhaps you mistake me. I did not mean to imply that the workings of government are of no value, nor that they are beyond the interest of our Lord—I hope that I am the kind of man one would look to when courage is required—but I prefer a book in my hand rather than a sword."

"Yes, though I think that more than all, you prefer to hold a glass," Bruno declared.

"Ah, now you hit on our point of agreement! Tell me, Empress Mathilda, do you approve of the swill they pass off as beer in these parts, or do you obey the words of Christ and drink of the aqua vitae?"

"Aqua vitae? Do you mean *aquam vivam?*"

"For Karl, they are one and the same," said Bruno. "Show her that rubbish of yours."

The priest then produced a pewter drinking vessel of the type that the Germans call *Krug*, the like of which I had never seen before: it appeared large enough to satisfy any thirst, and upon it were carved figures I was unable to name, though I soon found that there was no need.

"They are from the life of Saint Augustine," he proclaimed cheerfully.

"I see. How nice." These were the fairest words I could utter honestly, for I did not share his love of what appeared to my eyes to be a rather ugly and needless object.

"Bruno," I said, attempting to change the subject, "what can you tell me about the bishop of Châlons?"

"William of Champeaux? You will find him a decent sort of fellow, though he is heart and soul for the papacy and the French king, which is to say that he is unlikely to encourage Calixtus to yield much, even were it for the clear benefit of Christendom." He then laughed as if amused by some memory. "He used to teach in Paris, you know. He was one of the tutors of Pierre Abélard, the young scholar of whom everyone now speaks."

"I have heard of him," I replied, hoping to impress them both a little with my knowledge of world affairs.

"Well, it seems that the scholar found a match and then some in his pupil. Rumor has it that they were often at odds, for Abélard was able to defeat him in their exchanges and carried himself with something less than humility."

"The poor man ended up surrendering and taking his leave," Karl added. "I pity him. It must be difficult to face a student more talented than oneself. Of course, I have never had that problem."

"Abélard is now the more famous teacher, though the ill repute brought on by his wanton behavior may well do him in," Bruno concluded. "I should not be surprised if he becomes the most renowned scholar of our age. There are not one in a thousand minds like his. However, the fellow cannot seem to contain his passions."

After a good deal more conversation like this, I found myself tiring of the festivities. The affairs of French scholars were of little interest to me. I offered my regards to each of the eminent guests and then made for my chamber without the aid of any of my ladies, as I believed I was quite able to walk the short distance without a train of followers. As usual, this prompted many complaints, but I would hear none of it and set off immediately.

There was a sort of cloister along my route, and I was a bit surprised to see that the night watch had abandoned their duties and made for the banquet hall.

"Some guardians they are," I muttered. "They did not even keep all the torches burning."

I took down one of the remaining flames from its perch on the wall and used it to light my way. The moon gave off no glow that evening, and even the fire seemed to struggle to break through the darkness. I was halfway down the passage when I sensed that I was not alone. There was someone standing in the shadows, just a few paces yonder.

"Who goes there?" I called. "Declare yourself!"

The figure stepped slowly into the light. It was a man whom I recognized but a little: a groom who had lately come into the emperor's service. He was of about middle age, with a long beard and the kind of powerful figure that would be helpful in his profession.

"Good evening, and God save you, Empress Mathilda," he said. "I am one of his lord's grooms. Conrad is my name."

"Yes, I think perhaps we met once before," I answered, now hoping to avoid any further discussion. "Good night to you, then."

I took a step or two in the direction of my chamber, but he moved ever so slightly to block my route.

"Forgive me, my lady, but may I ask you something?"

"I suppose." I could see now that there would be no way of avoiding this delay, so I attempted to make the best of it.

"Is the emperor to stay long at Straßburg?"

"Only as long as it takes to reach an accord, which is to say, it could be over tomorrow, or it could go on till Judgment Day."

"I see."

I was rather put off by his presumption, and thus I added, "I am sure you will be ready to perform your duty for the emperor come what may, or do you have some pressing appointment elsewhere?"

He laughed, a choice that I deemed rather unwise under the circumstances. "They said you had spirit, but I could not have guessed. Indeed, I have heard many tales of you and the emperor since arriving here."

"Ah. And what have you heard?" Though I wished to be gone from his presence, I reasoned that it might not hurt to know the inner thoughts of those around us, if he was so willing to betray them.

"Just the usual."

"The usual?"

"Well, there have been rumors, you know, as to why you have never been with child."

I was taken aback by his words. I suppose I should not have been. Public gossip is never kind. Still, I was incensed that he would broach the subject to my face.

"I do not know what you have heard, sir, but I assure you that there is nothing which requires your consideration."

Once again I moved to leave, but he was clearly unwilling to let me pass without satisfying his curiosity.

"The lads and I, we all have our own ideas," he said. "Some of them think he must be a sodomite."

"What? How dare you make such an accusation? Along with the clear offense against the emperor's person, your words are not fit for polite conversation with your lawful queen! I demand that you beg pardon at once!"

"I note that you did not deny it," was his only answer.

"Perverse man! I suppose that only one who is foul himself could devise such a slander. Tell me, are you a sodomite?"

I considered this reply to be rather clever, as it placed him on the defense, but he had an answer ready.

"Hardly! To hell with all the sodomites!"

"To hell with you!"

For the third time I attempted to get around him, but this time he pushed me against the wall with such a degree of force that I was robbed of breath. His hands pressed against my waist and my arms were pinned. I had dropped the torch, and it now lay upon the stone pavement. The light reflected in his eyes and made them appear even more menacing.

"You know what I think?" he continued, his voice betraying a kind of madness. "I think that the good emperor has never touched you, and that is why you are not with child. Everyone is saying it: he's left you a maid because he prefers the company of other men." Here he spit upon the ground in a show of utter loathing.

"Let go of me, slanderer!" I cried. "The emperor will have your head for this violence!"

He pressed one of his hands against my mouth to silence my pleas. I was in great distress and my mind seemed unable to devise a method of escape. His weight upon my body was such that I could not move, even as he groped at my breasts.

"I suppose there is something you should know about me," he said. "When I see something gone to waste, I hate to leave it that way. It is a pity you aren't more handsome, but I'll have my fill just the same."

An endless string of curses rushed through my mind, along with an anguished prayer for deliverance. I had lost all hope when something happened which neither of us had foreseen. Out of nowhere, my attacker cried out in pain as he received some blow from behind. I could not see his challenger, but caught a glimpse of the large object that was brought down upon his head, placing the groom in a stupor. His body fell to the ground in a heap, and there before me stood Karl of Worms, his hands holding what remained of his beloved *Krug*, which was now sadly dented.

"You!" I cried, unable to find any other words to express my relief.

"Yes, it is indeed I," he replied. "Are you harmed, my lady?"

"I don't believe so, save for a few scrapes." I feared the priest might have mistaken what he had seen, so I added, "This man sought to defile me. I struggled to get away, but could not. I swear that I did not encourage him in any way."

"I believe you. Loathsome creature! I shall report this immediately, if it has not already caught the attention of the guard."

Even as he said this, several men came running toward us, having apparently heard the clamor. Among them, to my great relief, was Drogo.

"What happened here?" the knight asked.

"This man, Conrad, tried to assault my womanhood! Indeed, he would have succeeded were it not for this priest, who was good enough to hit him over the head." A thought suddenly came to me. "What were you doing here, anyway?" I asked my rescuer.

"Oh, I was just hoping to take care of some necessary business. Aqua vitae does not stay in eternally . . ."

"We must inform the emperor," Drogo said, choosing not to press for any further information. "This crime shall be punished. Philip, return to the hall and fetch the lords immediately! I will accompany the empress back to her room. Father Karl, we are in your debt."

Drogo offered me his arm, and I clung to it with both of my own. I was in too much of a daze to venture any further words of thanks. When I was finally safe inside my chamber, I did ask if my guard could be doubled for the night, a request that was happily granted. Not one moment of sleep did I achieve in that long night, for my every fiber seemed to shake with the terror. The incident continued to play itself over in my mind, an endless nightmare that bound my waking thoughts.

I never saw the man Conrad again. My husband had him put to death before the break of day. There was a report that the emperor beat the criminal with his own hands until he begged for mercy, which was only granted in the form of execution. I have never spoken of this to a single soul—that is, until you, my daughter. Such a humiliation I have seldom felt. My only comfort is that he burns in the fires of hell.

CHAPTER NINETEEN

When a man thinks of himself, he cannot do so without considering the land to which he belongs. His mind turns to the village where he was born and raised, the lord he serves, and the king to whom he is ever faithful. He belongs to the land, and the land belongs to him. But what of those few who find themselves cleft, born in one land and living in another? They are as vagabonds upon the face of the earth—men and women without a constant home. To whom is their fealty due, and to what do their thoughts turn when men inquire as to their origin?

When I was young, I knew that land to which I belonged: England, most blessed kingdom on God's earth. To be sure, my father was as much the ruler of Normandy as he was over the English, but it would be many years until I visited that land, and to me it was only the stuff of tales. Owing in part to the influence of my mother, I always felt that England was my home.

However, by the year of our Lord 1119, I had dwelt longer within the empire than I had in the isles of Britain. I had so few occasions on which to speak my native tongue that I found myself forgetting certain words or patterns of speech. With the death of Queen Mathilda, I lost my chief source of news from England, and I felt as if I were farther from that kingdom than ever. I wondered, if I were to travel there, would they recognize me still as one of their own? Surely it was a matter of little consequence, for I did not suppose that I should ever set foot upon those shores again.

Nevertheless, I was able to gain some intelligence concerning the situation in the West. As was so often the case, battles against the king of France and his vassals continued. "France is the natural enemy of this kingdom," my father had told me, and he did everything in his power not only to defend his own lands, but also to make incursions into those territories faithful to Louis VI.

There was no greater dispute between them than the question of who held the dukedom of Normandy. It had once belonged to my uncle, Robert Curthose, but he took up arms unwisely against King Henry and was defeated at Tinchebrai. I was only a small girl when that fiercest of battles was waged and my father took the duke as his prisoner. From that time the Kingdom of England and the Duchy of Normandy were brought together under King Henry's rule.

Yet Uncle Robert had a son: my own cousin William, called Clito. He became the standard under which all the king's enemies could unite. They did not love him so much as the opportunity he provided to forsake their rightful lord. As you might remember, William Clito had been placed in the care of the Count of Arques, a relative through marriage; but in the year 1113, Clito was seized and brought to the French court, where he was able to form an alliance.

King Louis of France was first among those who declared William Clito to be the lawful Duke of Normandy. Surely this was for the benefit of the French king's own interests, and it forced my father into a drawn-out contest over who would control that land. King Louis demanded that any Duke of Normandy must perform homage to the French crown, but my father was loath to suffer such a humiliation. A king cannot bow to another king, for they are equals. Beyond that, he would not do homage for something that he already possessed entirely.

So the two kingdoms fought, until one day—the thirteenth before the kalends of September in the year 1119—Louis marched once again into Normandy with a force of four hundred knights arrayed for battle. The French king desired to meet my father in battle, yet he had been unable to do so. Now their paths met just west of Gisors, in a field named Brémule.

King Henry was not without defenders, for some five hundred of his own knights stood beside him, the flower of French nobility against that of England. Brother Robert was there to fight on behalf of his father, as was Richard, another of the king's offspring. Do you think it strange that I never met this brother of mine? Then I suppose your own father has not lent his seed to so many bastards as did my own, many of them rather obscure or set apart by many leagues from myself.

Those men of Normandy who remained true fought beneath the standard of Henry, while the treacherous barons sided against their natural lord. Chief among these traitors was William Crispin. Then there was William Clito, puppet of his French lord, who sought to avenge his father and free the former duke from his prison in Devises.

Now, King Louis VI was known to be no small man, to such a point that his own countrymen gave him the title *Louis le Gros*. Yet, as only his appetite for battle exceeded his appetite for food, he would fight beside his knights, though he did totter upon his horse. Two separate French charges were driven back by King Henry's men. So fierce was the fighting that more than one English knight reached out to take the reins of Louis's horse and proclaim with a loud voice, "The king is taken!" But what he lacked in grace, the French king made up for in strength, pushing back each one in turn and proclaiming, "The king is not taken—neither at war nor at checks!"

The angels were not on France's side that day. One by one, their captains were unhorsed and taken captive, until King Louis had no choice but to withdraw. In the chaos of that moment, even after his force of knights had been defeated, the traitor William Crispin found himself free to charge at King Henry. With malice in his heart, he raised his great sword and struck at the king's head. Oh, the cries of despair which must have been raised! An Englishman by the name of Roger brought the coward down from his horse and pinned him to the ground, sparing his life in an act of great mercy.

As I said, fortune was on the side of England, for the king's hauberk held firm against the blow, and he suffered no serious injury to his royal person. Despite this outrage, the English proved themselves to be gentlemen of the highest class; they returned King Louis's horse after the French ruler was forced to flee on foot. My own brother, William Ætheling, sent back William Clito's palfrey along with many gifts, none of which the traitor merited. The end result of this defeat was that Louis was forced to accept Prince William as the rightful Duke of Normandy and future king of England. He was granted the duchy the following year, though the French king continued to support William Clito whenever possible. My brother had finally reached that lofty height which was his right by birth.

Two months earlier, in June of that year, William Ætheling had wed the daughter of Fulk V, Count of Anjou, in order to build their alliance against France. He was now properly placed to succeed our father. Through all of this, I was absent—naught but a memory in the land of my birth. The letters grew ever fewer, to the point that I even treasured the ones from Roger of Salisbury.

When I did receive a parcel from England in early autumn, it brought me a joy that was mixed with grief. An ivory box was presented to me, carved with figures from the life of the Virgin. With great care I raised the lid, finding inside it an object as familiar to me as my own hands: the jasper rosary belonging to my mother and to her mother before her. I took it and shifted the beads with my fingers. How many times had I seen Queen Mathilda do this? There was a kind of magic about it, as if I inhabited her very space or she had reached to me from beyond. So I imagined it to be, but of course this was only a trick of the mind. Stones are naught but stones . . . But what of the stone from which Moses drew water? Here was a question to which I would never know the answer.

Having received my piece of amber back from the emperor—I fear he never assigned it the same value as did his wife—I placed both it and the jasper chain within the same purse that I had carried with me for years. Here was the last of England, my final link to the land beyond the sea. I was queen of the Germans now and empress of the Romans. The rest was memory.

Now return with me to matters within the empire. The forum in Straßburg was something better than defeat, and yet less than a triumph. The bishop of Châlons had put before the emperor the demand that, if he truly desired peace, he must give up the right to invest all bishops and abbots. Having heard this charge before, the emperor put to them the question of how he could do so without diminishing his own kingship. The pope's messengers replied with the usual assurances of fidelity and begged that he remember the donation made by his predecessor, Constantine the Great, many years earlier.

Emperor Henry had never been of a mind to surrender authority over such a large portion of his kingdom, for the princes of the church were princes indeed, possessing immense lands and estates, and they were endowed with all the marks of earthly glory. Yet, partially due to Bruno's urging, and in light of the substantial losses sustained over many years of warfare, he sought to pacify his nobles and have the sentence of *anathema* reversed, lest he end up as his father. He agreed to meet with the pope and made but two demands: that the Holy Father would act in good faith and with true justice, and that any agreement would bring with it the restoration of all lands which had been lost and the creation of a lasting peace. The papal ambassadors left in good spirits, and the Kingdom of Germany awaited their meeting in great suspense.

In mid-October the imperial household departed Straßburg and headed west toward Metz, where we crossed over the River Moselle. The pope had convened a synod in Reims, a city whose claim to the French monarchy was almost as strong as that of Paris itself. Having been placed under the ban of excommunication, it was impossible for my husband to enter the city. For his part, the emperor desired that any meeting with Calixtus should take place within his own borders, so as to ensure a fair hearing, for he knew too well how all the bishops and nobles of France were against him.

We were halfway between Metz and Verdun, with the full imperial army in our company, when a new band of papal ambassadors met us on the road. Among them were the bishop of Châlons, the bishop of Ostia, and Cardinal Gregory *ex latere*. The second man, Lamberto Scannabecchi, cardinal bishop of Ostia, was a counselor to both Pope Calixtus II and Pope Gelasius II before him, and we had already seen him once before: he was one of the three cardinals who challenged the emperor during his procession into Rome.

A tent was made ready in which the two parties could meet. With the emperor were Count Palatine Godfrey and Duke Welf of Bavaria, along with bishops, lords, and many servants. The clerks made ready their vellum and inkwells, ready to set down whatever words might be said. The pope's men proceeded likewise. I had been allowed to attend on the condition that I not disturb them.

Once we were all seated around the hastily laid table, my husband offered a few words of welcome to the visitors. It was a rather strange business, for as Emperor Henry had been placed under the ban, it was not strictly permitted for the men opposite to acknowledge his authority, but out of a desire to proceed amicably, they did make some show of respect.

"My lord," the bishop of Ostia began, "we have just come from Reims, where even now His Holiness is preparing to hold a council to address matters of doctrine and the issue which we have gathered here to discuss, namely that of investiture. He wishes you to know that he has heard your promises and is willing to remove the order of excommunication should you prove true. I believe his exact words were, 'I wish that it had been done already, if it could be done without fraud.' So you see, you and he are really of the same mind."

"I am glad to hear it," my husband replied.

"Excellent! Now, we have here the decree, which we hope you will sign. Please take a moment to study it."

The bishop handed over a roll of parchment that the emperor opened and read aloud.

"'I, Henry, august emperor of the Romans by the grace of God, out of my love for God, the blessed Peter, and the lord Pope Calixtus, give up all investiture of all churches and give true peace to all those who, from the time this strife began, have been or are at war for the Church's sake; furthermore, the possessions of the churches and of all those who have labored for the Church which I now hold, I return; what I do not hold, I shall help them faithfully to reacquire. And if a dispute should arise from this, let things ecclesiastical be settled by canonical judgment and things secular by secular judgment.'"

The emperor then paused for the space of a few minutes, his eyes looking over the page again and again, searching for any hidden meanings not apparent upon the first reading. He then whispered in German to Count Godfrey, who was seated just beside him. Each pointed to different portions of the text, until at length they seemed to reach an accord.

"Very well," the emperor said. "We have seen what you wish for me to sign. What of Calixtus? Do you have one for him as well?"

"Of course," said the bishop of Ostia, turning to look at the man on his left: William Champeaux, bishop of Châlons.

"The pope has indeed agreed to a signed decree," Champeaux answered, producing another page from within the folds of his cloak. "I shall read it to you now. 'I, Calixtus II, catholic bishop of the Roman Church by the grace of God, give true peace to Henry, august emperor of the Romans and to all who were or are with him against the Church . . .'"

"The emperor is not against the Church," Chancellor David argued. "He is against the abuses brought about by corrupt men within the Church. He is against the withholding of ancient rights due to the empire. But I assure you, he stands in opposition against neither the Church nor the Holy Father."

"Be that as it may," Champeaux continued, "here is the rest of the testimony: 'Their possessions, which they lost because of this war, I return those that I have; and those I do not have, I shall help them faithfully to reacquire. And if a dispute should arise from this, let things ecclesiastical be settled by canonical judgment, and things secular by secular judgment.'"

For a moment no one spoke. The only words I heard were within my own mind, where the sentiment "This is all so very dull" prevailed. Was this how all the fighting and shouting was to end, with ponderous legal language that seemed to avoid the real points of dispute? Even as I listened to those words, I could already sense that their meaning would be subject to personal opinion. Yes, the emperor was offering to give the right of investiture back to the Church, but the greatest scholars of the age disagreed as to the meaning of the word *investiture*. Some favored the view that a bishop receives his office from the Church, but his lands and possessions come from the king, and are thus subject to the king's laws. Others argued that secular rulers hold no power of any kind over the Church and its endless estates. Still others sought some form of compromise between king and pope, like those that were achieved in England and France. It seemed unlikely that the emperor would agree to the broad interpretation of Church powers favored by the Gregorians.

It was perhaps because of this uncertainty that Emperor Henry and his men were able to sign their names upon that document in good faith. My husband knew full well that given the power of the lords within his kingdom, he could not hope to grant such powers to the clergy without gaining their consent. That would be a matter for another day. For the moment the two parties agreed to a meeting at Mouzon in a few days' time. This would allow Henry to travel from Verdun up the river to Liége, stopping along the way for the meeting with the pope. It was also near the border between the Kingdom of France and the empire.

For no other reason was Mouzon chosen, for I assure you that it is a town of little significance, being neither the seat of a bishop, nor the residence of a great noble, nor a center of much business. There was no house fit to receive either an emperor or a pope, but given the size of the imperial army, one feature of this site was vital: it was surrounded by plentiful fields in which the horses could graze, and the fall harvest had left a good supply of food for their riders.

On Thursday, Calixtus finally arrived near the site at a very late hour, having been delayed since his departure the morning before. "Popes never travel quickly," Drogo observed, "except perhaps when they are chased by an angry mob."

The next day, the pope remained in the council of the bishops and other men of the Church. Messengers traveled back and forth bringing all the latest news. It was said that the bishops were considering the precise meaning of the decree that the emperor had signed. The Holy Father was now calling what had been plain enough to the ambassadors into question.

That afternoon, I happened to see Emperor Henry sitting alone in his tent, where he was attempting to read through a stack of letters. I approached the entrance with caution, only making my presence known after careful consideration.

"My lord?"

He looked up from the papers in front of him. "Yes. What is it?"

"May I enter?"

He let out a sigh and then answered, "I suppose, but there is no chair. You will have to stand."

You will note that my husband did not offer me the chair in which he was sitting, but I decided not to fault him too heavily for this. When I reached his side, he asked me, "Are you going to tell me what this is about, or must I draw it out?"

"I was wondering if you might know the cause of the pope's delay. He has spent the whole day debating with his men across the river. Will he never come to meet us?"

"Calixtus does not trust me. He does not trust any of us. He will be plotting some design that will force me to surrender even more than I have already offered, for he believes me to be weak."

"Are you weak?"

"Not in mind, not in spirit . . . perhaps in body, but that must not be known."

"It is true, then? The pain has grown worse?"

"It is more frequent, and the physician suspects some disease. The mass is larger than it used to be."

This no more than confirmed my suspicion, for my husband had not asked me to his bed for many weeks, and I knew it was because the pain was more than he could bear.

"Let us speak no more of it," I offered. "Tell me, why are you more willing to treat with the pope than you used to be? When we were in Italy, I saw no sign of surrender in you, but now I have my doubts. Have you simply grown weary?"

"Nothing of the sort! No, I assure you that everything is proceeding as it should be."

There was a game of checks laid out just to the side. Evidently the emperor had been using it to pass the time with some of his counselors. Now he reached over and picked up a piece of ivory meant to represent the king. He showed it to me, then laid his right palm out flat and balanced the piece upon his fingers.

"See how the king stays upright?" he asked.

"Yes."

"It stands because it is supported by all of my fingers. Now, heed what I say—I am the king, and each of my fingers is one of the five duchies: Franconia, Lotharingia, Swabia, Bavaria, and—"

"Saxony," I said, "mother of all rebellions."

"Not quite true, but I can see you have been listening to Bruno. The king must have support in order to stand."

He then pulled back his fingers one at a time, and with each one the carved piece became less stable, until finally it fell onto the table.

"That is what happens if you lose the support of the duchies," he continued, "even as the duchies have their purpose in holding up the king. It may be possible to stand from time to time without the support of one of those regions, but if too many are removed, then you no longer have an empire."

"And Saxony stirs with discontent, and Adalbert seeks to steal away Franconia as well. That leaves only three."

He nodded and replied, "A king may stand for a while under such conditions, but the weight of years might finally sever the thread by which his crown hangs. I hear reports daily of Adalbert's efforts to undermine our kingship. He would use this dispute with Calixtus to bring all the bishops under his sway. We must not let him."

There our conversation ceased, for the messengers had returned from the pope: the bishops of Ostia and Châlons, Abbot Pontius of Cluny, and all the rest. They alighted from their horses and once again entered the emperor's pavilion, bearing still more papers in their arms.

"Here is your signed decree," the abbot said, placing it on the table in front of the emperor, "and here is the one by His Holiness. These are the notes from our meeting, in regard to the exact meanings of different words. This one . . . yes, this one is a further note which we would like you to view . . ."

"Wait!" Chancellor David called. "You said this one is the decree by Calixtus?"

"The very same," he replied.

"Then where is his mark?"

"Ah, well, he was unable to sign without first going over a few points."

"What do you mean?" asked the emperor. "You presented these words to us, written by your own hands."

"Yes, but we now wish to confirm that your understanding of them is the same as ours," the bishop of Ostia said.

"Perhaps you should tell us what you think they mean," my husband offered. His voice was rather cold, and he did not seem in any way amused by this new delay.

"It is our understanding," the bishop continued, "that the right of investiture includes not only the act of ordination or the granting of the pallium, but also those territories and marks of authority which were bestowed upon the Church from the time of Charles the Great down to the present age. This is what you agreed to give up."

"I think you will find that I did not."

The bishops were confounded and looked at each other. The bishop of Ostia then replied, "We stood here and watched you put your name to this . . . here . . ." He reached for the piece of parchment that clearly bore Henry's mark. "See here: 'I renounce every investiture of all churches.' That is what you signed!"

"Maybe so, but I fear your definition goes much too far. How could any king agree to such a refusal of his rights? You would have our kingdom, nay, our empire ruled entirely by the bishops! They may have received grants from my predecessors, but they are duty bound to submit themselves to our righteous decrees, even as Saint Paul taught. Such is the way things are done in both England and France. Why should it not be the same within the empire?"

The bishop of Châlons then broke his silence. "I cannot believe what I am hearing! If, lord king, you wish to deny the text which we hold in our hands and the understanding of it that you have heard, with the religious men who have been between me and you as my witnesses, I am prepared to swear on the relics of the saints or on the Gospel of Christ that you confirmed all that I have in my hand and that I received it from you with this understanding!"

"Perhaps that was your understanding, and that I signed it I have no wish to deny—but you must know that such an agreement as you propose would certainly diminish our royal authority. That is something to which I cannot submit!"

The older man scoffed. "In what we have promised, lord king, you shall find us completely reliable. For the lord pope is not attempting in any way to diminish the status of the empire or the crown of the kingship, as some sowers of discord claim." Here he gave an evil glare to the emperor's companions. "To the contrary, he proclaims before all that in the provision of military service and in all the other things in which the churches customarily served you and your predecessors, they shall continue to serve you in every way. But if you judge the status of the empire to be diminished in the fact that you are no longer allowed to sell bishoprics, you ought rather to hope it will be to the increase and profit of your kingship if you cast off for the love of God what is contrary to him!"

"How dare you accuse me of simony!" the emperor responded. "I know just how much corruption there is within the ranks of the Gregorians themselves. I have seen the streets of Rome, sir, and they are crawling with whores and traders of ill repute, and that is only the clergy! Any man knows that he might purchase the regard of the Church for the right price. No, do not accuse me of simony, but rather take the plank out of your own eye!"

"My lord emperor!" a voice called. I looked and saw that it belonged to Duke Welf of Bavaria. Every head turned as he said, "Might I not speak, as a member of the German nobility?"

Now, the duke and the emperor were not what you might call the best of friends. My husband at first laughed at the suggestion, but he finally beckoned all those of the imperial party to speak in private. Uncertain as to how they should respond, the papal party finally decided to hold their own private discussion, until the emperor declared, "My lords, I have heard all that you have said, but I find that I cannot proceed without discussing this matter further with the princes of my realm. Therefore I must delay until morning."

I turned back to see the looks on the bishops' faces, which displayed a mixture of disdain, surprise, and annoyance at the new delay. Nevertheless they had no choice but to accept Henry's decision. Mounting their horses, they rode back to their master across the river without having achieved their goal.

"Churlish knaves," the emperor muttered. "I suppose they would have me hold the pot for Calixtus to piss in as well."

"No, I believe the bishop of Ostia has already perfected that task," the chancellor replied. "Though His Holiness might permit you to hold the towel for him."

There was to be no meeting between the emperor and the pope after all. The next morning, the pope's messengers returned and repeated the same protestations. When Henry stated once again that he must have time to call a general council of all the princes within his realm, the bishops left without so much as a word of farewell. Before the sun had set, the Holy Father made haste to return by that road on which he had come. Henry begged Calixtus to stay at least until the beginning of the following week, at which point he might be able to provide an answer, but the pope had his mind set. "I have not found the things of peace in him," he was said to have uttered.

In later days, some would claim that it was the sight of the imperial army that had caused Calixtus to flee, but I cannot imagine how he could have been ignorant of the movement of such a large company of troops. No, this was merely an excuse. In fact, it seemed that the Holy Father had grown so doubtful of the emperor's word that he would not remain even a few days to see the thing done.

The papal synod in Reims proceeded to hand down five decrees, three of which were plainly aimed at the emperor. The first forbade the practice of simony in all its forms and warned any man who sought to offend that "unless he repents, he shall, once pierced through with the sword of *anathema*, be cast utterly from the Church of God which he has harmed."

The second decree removed any doubt remaining as to where the pope stood on the question of investiture. "We absolutely forbid the investiture of episcopacies and abbacies to be carried out at the hands of laymen. Any layman, therefore, who presumes to invest from now on, shall be subject to the punishment of *anathema.*" So much for the emperor's efforts to reverse his excommunication!

The third was perhaps the harshest of all, for it proclaimed an end to imperial rights in terms not only of the sacred, but also of the profane. "We decree that all the churches' property which has been granted to them by the largesse of princes or offering of the faithful shall remain undisturbed and inviolate for ever. And if someone shall seize, usurp, or retain them with tyrannical power, he shall be wounded with perpetual *anathema.*" Therefore, the very privileges that had been granted to the Church by kings were now to be placed beyond the power of kings, come what may.

As their final action, the pope, cardinals, and bishops read out the names of all those persons who were placed under the ban of excommunication, chief among them the emperor and the antipope "Burdinus," that is, Gregory VIII. How pleased must Calixtus II have been to harm his two greatest enemies, for so he believed them to be. In truth, the emperor had forsaken his allegiance to the antipope as an act of good faith to aid the discussions, and even I sensed that he was well rid of the man. Emperor Henry did take some comfort in the news that the Reims council had determined that the ban on lay investiture applied only to the appointment of bishops, abbots, and other Church officials, but not to the actual *regalia*: the ring and crozier. Here he saw a small chance for future agreement. Still, there was no question as to who had produced the best result.

The lords of Germany remained at odds, even as the pope made a triumphal procession through Lombardy and Tuscany, arriving in Rome the following June to a glorious reception and the news that Burdinus had fled north to Sutri. It did not take long for the citizens of that town to surrender their fugitive, and Calixtus had the false pope humiliated and sent off to a monastery, where he lived out the rest of his days in solitude.

Having ensured his hold over Rome, Calixtus set his sights once again on the North. He boldly appointed Archbishop Adalbert of Mainz as the new papal legate within the empire. Such a boon must have sent the archbishop's spirits into a state of ecstasy, for here was another weapon with which to wage his war against the emperor. The city of Mainz lay within his power, for he held the support of the public.

It was now Henry's turn to act boldly. He took up arms against Mainz and forced the city to submit to his rule. Although it was all a rotten business, this action did allow the emperor to reclaim control of most of Franconia. He also sought to improve relations with Archbishop Frederick of Cologne, who for the first time in years seemed willing to listen. Enraged by all of this, Adalbert set out to rouse the Saxon nobles once again in defiance of their rightful king. But this rising was not to produce the same calamity as took place at Welfesholz. Henry moved to Goslar, and from there fought the rebels to a truce, even forcing Adalbert to come to terms.

All in all, it was a rather fortunate year, and as we returned to the Rhine Valley to savor the autumn, I found myself feeling happier than I had for many days past. Of course, the emperor's daily pain hung over us like a dark cloud, and he attempted to treat it with an increase in all forms of drink. Even so, his spirits seemed to be high, and as we arrived in Mainz for the season of feasting, I was pleased to reside once again in that city where I had first been crowned as queen of the Romans.

On the last Sunday of November, the emperor and I made our way as always to the cathedral, there to celebrate Mass in the

Gotthard Chapel. The newest of the cathedral chapels, it was the child of Adalbert's ambition, a construction designed for easy access to the episcopal palace. The final adornment was still taking place, but it seemed fitter for such a small gathering than the immense cathedral nave. The archbishop himself was not in town, for whatever truce he had reached with the emperor was not of a kind that made him wish to spend time in close quarters with his sometime enemy. Therefore it was Hartmann, Emperor Henry's principal chaplain, who performed the service.

I remember being tired that morning, so it was with great pleasure that I sat down for the Scripture reading. In the warmth of my winter cloak, and with the scent of incense and the light of the candles creating a most serene aura, I was in great danger of passing into the land of slumber. This was no place for a queen to venture in public, yet I could not help myself. I struggled to comprehend the words issuing from the chaplain's mouth. Although it was now the season of Advent, he was reading from the book of Jonah, an odd choice.

"'Then Jonah prayed unto the Lord his God out of the fish's belly, and said, "I cried in my affliction unto the Lord, and he heard me; out of the belly of hell cried I, and you heard my voice. For you had cast me into the bottom in the midst of the sea, and the floods compassed me about: all your surges and your waves passed over me. Then I said, I am cast out of your sight, yet I will look again toward your holy Temple. The waters compassed me about unto the soul. The depth closed me round about, and the weeds were wrapped around my head. I went down to the bottoms of the mountains; the earth with her bars was about me for ever, yet you have brought up my life from the pit, O Lord my God."'"

"I imagined we might hear some words of prophecy relating to the birth of Christ," my husband whispered into my ear.

"I know. All this talk of fish bellies makes me long for a decent meal," I replied.

"Perhaps he thinks we are the Ninevites and in need of repentance."

Even as Hartmann began to chant the litany of Eucharist, a loud sound seemed to break the spell of the service. Someone had entered the hall and allowed the great wood door to shut loudly. I looked up to see the source of this noise, even as Hartmann continued his prayer as if there had been no interruption. I could see that it was the clerk Burchard. To my great surprise, he marched down the aisle and straight to the emperor's side, placing a hand upon his shoulder.

"What is the meaning of this?" Emperor Henry half whispered, half shouted.

"I must speak to you and the empress," he replied. "It is a matter of utmost significance."

"Now?" I asked. "Can it not wait until the end of the Mass?"

"No, I am afraid it cannot. You must come with me immediately."

The look in Burchard's eyes was almost desperate. I could see that there would be no refusing him.

"Let us go," I said to the emperor. "I must know what he has to say, or I will go mad."

"Very well," my husband replied, and the three of us moved with all haste to depart the chapel.

Once we had entered the portal connecting the Gotthard Chapel with the cathedral, Burchard turned toward us and began to recite his tale.

"My emperor, Empress Mathilda, what I have to tell you is most grim. We just received word from a messenger who came across country to bring this news."

"So what is it?" the emperor asked, clearly impatient.

"My dearest lady," he continued, turning his eyes toward me, "I am afraid that what I have to say concerns your family."

He paused for a moment, evidently seeking the courage to continue. My heart was filled with dismay, and I suspected strongly that he was about to tell me that my father had suffered a terrible accident or had been claimed by the plague or some such misfortune. I was on the point of ordering him to tell me more when he proceeded.

"A few days ago, King Henry and his court set out from the port of Barfleur to make their return to England. The king and many of the leading nobles were in one ship, but there was another—a marvelous white creation made just for the occasion—and on this vessel the prince and his companions traveled. They set out in the evening. King Henry's ship arrived in Dover without any ill effects, but the other ship . . . the White Ship . . . it was never sighted."

"What do you mean?" I asked, hoping that there was some misunderstanding.

"My lady, the ship was swallowed up by the sea." With great difficulty he concluded, "There was but one survivor, and he of no name."

For a moment I simply stared at Burchard. His words seemed so strange—so foreign, as if he were speaking in another tongue. "Swallowed by the sea . . ." My mind strained to take it in, and then at once my lips uttered, "William! My dear brother! William!"

"Yes," the clerk replied, "he is passed from this world."

"This cannot be!" the emperor said. "He is the heir!"

I was in such distress over this loss that it was only when my husband spoke those words that I comprehended the full significance of what had happened. Prince William, the future king of England, was never to reign. My father had no other legitimate sons. Indeed, he had no other legitimate children of any kind, except . . . I turned to look at my husband, my eyes filled with tears, but my spirit filled with a strange determination.

"My brother is departed from this world. William Ætheling is no more," I said. "There is now only one person alive in whom the royal lines of England and Normandy are joined together. I, Mathilda, empress of the Romans: I am the heir."

REFERENCES

Anonymous, *Liber pontificalis*

Augustine, *Confessions*

Caedmon, *Hymn*

Cicero, *In Catilinam*

Einhard. *Life of Charlemagne.* Translated by Samuel Epes Turner. American Book Company, 1880.

Eusebius of Caesarea. *The History of the Church from Christ to Constantine.* Translated by G. A. Williamson. London: Penguin Books, 1989.

Meyer von Konau, Gerold. *Jarbücher des Deutschen reiches unter Heinrich IV und Heinrich V.* Leipzig: Verlag von Duncker & Humblot, 1907.

Gildas, *On the Ruin of Britain*

Henry of Huntingdon. *The History of the English People 1000–1054.* Translated by Diana Greenway. Oxford University Press, 2009.

W. L. North, "A brief description of how the case between the king and the Lord Pope began and proceeded," translating the account by Hesso of Reims, appearing in the edition of W. Wattenbach in MGH <u>Scriptores</u> XII (Hannover: 1856)

Officium stelle quotes are from Peter Dronke, *Nine Medieval Plays* (Cambridge: Cambridge University Press, 1994)

Tertullian, *On the Apparel of Women*

Titus Livius. *Ab urbe condita*

Wipo of Burgundy, *Gesta Chuonradi II imperatoris*

This is only a partial list of those sources that were specifically quoted. A more complete list can be found at www.chronicleofmaud.com.

Made in the USA
Middletown, DE
08 October 2018